ANIMA

Artorian's Archives Book Six

DENNIS VANDERKERKEN
DAKOTA KROUT

MOUNTAINDALE
PRESS

ACKNOWLEDGMENTS

From Dennis:

There are many people who have made this book possible. First is Dakota himself, for without whom this entire series would never have come about. In addition to letting me write in his universe, he has taken it upon himself to edit and keep straight all the madness for which I am responsible, with resulting hilarity therein.

A thank you to my late grandfather, after whom a significant chunk of Artorian's personality is indebted. He was a man of mighty strides, and is missed dearly.

A special thank you to my parents, for being ever supportive in my odd endeavors, Mountaindale Press for being a fantastic publisher, Jess for keeping us all on task, and all the fans of Artorian's Archives, Divine Dungeon, and Completionist Chronicles who are responsible for the popularity for this to come to pass. May your affinity channels be strong, and plentiful!

Last of all, thank you. Thank you for picking this up and giving it a read. Anima is the continuation of a multi-book series, and I dearly hope you will enjoy them as the story keeps progressing. Artorian's Archives may start before Divine Dungeon, but don't worry! It's going all the way past the end of Completionist Chronicles! So if you liked this, keep an eye out for more things from Mountaindale Press!

PROLOGUE

"Barry the Devourer?" Dawn tasted the words, rolling them around in her mouth while peering at the domed stained-glass ceiling. "Sounds like a narcissistic title. Who is this and why should I care? We have a handful of other S-rankers that we are solidly keeping under. Why point out *this one*?"

Tatum made the inner circle chair creak by leaning backwards. It threatened to break, but there were backups for if that happened… again. He bit his thumb, trying to think of how best to convey this cod of a conversation—as it was exceedingly fishy—without breaking down into a seven-hour sermon. Luckily for the hoarder of knowledge in all things occult and obscure, their dungeon overlord wasn't going to let anyone else complain about that slippery fish first.

"He tried to eat *me*! Abyss-near *succeeded* too!" A fuming Cale broke up through the floor in haste, an ethereal multi-tool in the form of a wrench held tight in his hand as his human form fully ejected from the cracked open crevice. He stamped over and slid into his inner circle chair right away. "That beast of an S-ranker had a personal statue devoted to him due to the misery he caused me, from before we all lived in the Soul Space. That hungry hippo ate my entire original third floor! Greedy High Elf glutton. I'm *still* offended."

Dawn felt a smirk crawl onto her lips. "Because he was a glutton, and that's *your* thing? Mr. Sipping on Planet-Sized Essence on the daily. Or because he caused that horrible thing we all hate, called 'setbacks'?"

Cale furiously dropped his heavy wrench onto the table. "Both! Plus he's an insufferable… is there a layer of expletives? I need *all of them* for this guy. Xenocide too, I guess, but *especially* this guy!"

Tatum thought about it, then just nodded. Cale's face snapped to him with disbelief. There *was* a layer of expletives? "You're joking."

The old Master copied Dawn's smirk, and nonchalantly shrugged. "Incarnate, get those chains off, and go look. It's a whole wide world, layered like a delicious, endless cream cake. I mean I'm sure there's edges and ends, but not that I've found while in the double-S ranks. Speaking of, so we *do* have other Incarnates in stasis? I was convinced Dawn and I were the only ones. Save for Barry."

Cale made an unpleasant sound, waving his hands. "Not all of the Incarnates I have a direct deal with are people I like. Or feel I can talk to. The methods with which they would help me might classify as… malicious compliance? They would help because of the deal. Though the results would cause those lovely *setbacks* we hate so much. So while they *are* here, I have… conveniently forgotten to give them a body to reside in, save for an orb in a box that provides no sensory data and doesn't allow for Essence or Mana movements. Why are we talking about this nail in my coffin?"

"Precautions." Tatum cut to the chase. "It was odd to me, since we made both our deals with what was essentially our dying breaths. I'm here. He's not. Your deal, unless ours are different, requires you to let people live in your Soul Space before letting them out when you're able. Not letting Barry 'live' for lack of better specification, is going to *stress* that oath."

Cale shrugged. "It'll be *fi~i~ine*! It's not like I can reasonably provide you a body yet that stays… stable. No need to rush. Heck, even as an S-ranker, I might not be able to properly support Barry, so it's on the backburner. He doesn't *need* to be around."

Tatum crossed his arms, his face a displeased scowl. "Maybe. Eventually, you will reach the double-S ranks, and then by your own admission you will *need* to let him live. Same for the others. I don't look forward to that day."

Cale adjusted uncomfortably. It was just too soon to talk about this. "It'll be fine! You'll all be much more powerful, we will probably have some systems in place or something. We'll have plenty of people. What's the worst that could happen? Now, I really do need to get back to pylon patching. Toodles!"

The dungeon's chair reformed in a snap and straightened, sending him sliding down into an evacuation tube that opened wide below him. He slid off with a liberated **wheeee**!

Dawn bit her thumb this time. "He's getting bored faster. Those spurts of mania are all that's keeping him focused at times. Since even the dungeon is up in arms about this 'Barry,' I'll see if I can't find the spare time for some kind of contingency plan, though I really can't say I understand what I'm dealing with. Variety among Incarnates is nothing to laugh at, and it's not like we have the convenient Ascendant scale to measure things by."

Tatum sank back into his chair like a sad potato. "Cal isn't going to take this seriously until it's far too late. As, unfortunately, he's right. It's too soon for this talk. Especially if he can keep the problematic S-rankers under wraps. Still, even I *only* know about Barry. There's others? When and how did these deals get made? I'm the master of all knowledge obscure and facts forgotten. This is *my* field!"

Dawn pointed at his arm, and upon inspection, Tatum groaned louder. The damaging cracks were forming already. "Abyss. Again? I swear I can't do anything without going up like a badly-tuned Gnomish contraption on overcharge."

She nodded with a barely noticeable sigh. "Are you keeping count of the craters you've made on Hel? Never mind. Why don't we just level? Tell me about Barry. I'll tell you about... the *other* problems. We have plenty of time before the moot starts, as we're here far too early. Because you're right: *Cal* didn't bring them in. Guess *who else* has a big Soul Space they can hide things in."

Tatum squeezed his hands together in agitation, his slump unmoved as he grumbled out the realization. "*Eternium.*"

CHAPTER ONE

"What do you mean, 'if we stay awake too long, we *die*'? That is not an amusing joke." Queen Marie, decked in her usual impenetrable full plate, crossed her arms in further defiance as muttering and unpleasant chatter went around the table. Her usual aura lay heavy, but the inner circle was one of the places where that just didn't matter. To anyone.

"I have a *Queendom* to run. I already shirk away from my normal needs for sleep, and my schedule is *full*. I don't even have time to work on my techniques. Now you want me to take *multi-year* breaks? I won't have a society to come back to! *No*! I will not stop mid-progress just to *start over* every time I wake up. That is *not* the path to a civilization of **Glory**."

Odin sniffed loud and gruff, clad in multiple layers of shiny, golden gladiator plate. His voice rumbled, and the usual tethers of lightning rolled off his skin as he spoke. "First our overlord creates hefty time penalties for death, and now there are hefty time penalties just for doing what we were put in place to? This is a ruse! Something else is at play, and I too refuse this calling. I don't even believe your proof. Those shard hunks on the table could be *any* gem. You can say it was the Prime's Core all you want, but this is too much. This demand goes too far. I too am unwilling to leave my mountain and role of overseer. My people cannot function without me! What would I return to if I left now? *Shambles*! Shambles, I say!"

His fist thundered as it hit the clock-table. Many were upset; most were silent. Especially those who had delivered the news. Even more so those that knew the truth, and were unwilling to accept it.

Brianna was one such ruler, and while she'd succeeded in spreading her supervisory tasks, she was no less impervious to hubris. The Dark Elven Queen remained quiet, because she *knew* this information. She knew that they were as gods, and yet that they could die. Her spies had lurked in the moon, drawn secrets from their locked confines, and brought them to bear.

She knew Bob was dying, but she just couldn't for the life of her *accept it*. The denial was mighty. It wasn't true. It couldn't be true. Brianna held firm to the convenient lie that this was a ruse, rather than accept this news could hold a nugget of revelation. She floated in the same boat as Odin. Brianna acted as the *pinnacle* of her society. The supreme Matriarch, and all information and tribute flowed as water to her whims and graces. She'd created a unified realm so tight-knit even her mother would have been jealous. They would not be fettered by concerns of backstabbing; there would be no loss of allegiance.

Brianna kept this to herself, though it was no secret that she was opposed to the long sleep. Ten years in stasis for every one year they spent waking? How long had they been here? Easily over a decade. Perhaps even two, if counted at ordinary speed. Two hundred years without oversight, influence, or knowledge of events that were happening in the regions they had meticulously worked on and invested in? The Administrator must be *mad* to think he could *enforce* it.

Aiden raised his massive paw. When motioned to, he cleared his throat with a half howl. "If my packs can gain some safety in my absence, I am not opposed. Provide my people a safe haven, and I'll sleep."

Chandra's vines twisted, making a hand tentacle motion at him. "Your packs are welcomed in my forests, unlike the children of man. You do not keep cutting mine down. I am *still* thorny about that fact, *Henry*."

The ruler of the human Kingdom, King Henry, exhaled harshly and said nothing. His Aura was laid out much like Marie's, frame donned in near identical seamless full plate. Henry's lack of either response or excuse only made the nature Mage feel further irritation, though this was nothing new.

Instead, Henry threw his hands in the air to end the awkward silence he'd created. "Honestly. I am with my friend, Aiden, on the topic. Unlike Marie, I have *not* been doing fantastic with my attempts at Kingdom management. The following is a terrible thought, but a true one. If I leave, or rather, *when* I leave, my Kingdom is *going* to collapse. The nobility present will rise, consolidate power, and make it a land of Dukedoms. A Viscount or Marquis might squeeze in, but it's going to collapse. If two hundred years pass… they will have *forgotten* all about King Henry, who founded the first castle and dug the first moat."

Henry removed his helmet, placing it upon the table. "When I wake, I will still be a Mage. One without great control over himself or his techniques, but a Mage regardless. Since Midgard is unlikely to be allowed to keep people of my caliber, I can play the role of the Hero. Since I expect things to have gone terribly awry, I can swoop in and conquer the lands back under my name. As the savior of the people, rather than some… *unknown founder* who doesn't have the time to leave his castle. I would then try to start some semblance of a family, so that when I go to sleep after ten years of ruling, a century later there is a resurgence with a golden child who brings the Kingdom back up to its silvered days from whatever state it has fallen to."

He kneaded his brow, Mana so poorly controlled that it sputtered and flecked from his skin. "Each time I rise again, I can make an improvement. Again, then again, then again… It's a miserable existence to play patchmaker, but I believe the Administrator when there is mention of an actual threat to our well-being. Personally, I am fine with ruling for ten years, and sleeping for a hundred. I am... I don't know if you all recall, but I am *not* an experienced Mage. I scarcely know what I'm doing with my own new form, and I only found out a few weeks ago that I no longer qualify as 'human,' because of what I'm *made* of. It's been a bother, and I'm still putting together an argument for just how much I disagree."

Artorian put his hand in the air, and Henry passed him the ball. "About that. When we had that very *passing* conversation, that comment was meant specifically in terms of what you are made of. Your meaty bits and normal cellular functions are very much gone, and without the human limitations and weaknesses, you physically qualify as something else. I meant nothing by it concerning the perspective, understandings, or social ways of being. If you see yourself as a human, and wish to continue carrying yourself as such, that's neither something incorrect, nor something that's wrong. So, if you were going to come and rebuke my mention because being in a different body, whether more or less able, doesn't make you human, you can call it a win. Being more or less able has zero impact on one's worth as a person. *None.* You're solid, my boy."

The mention turned Henry's concern, and his argument, into a fine pile of sawdust that sprinkled to the winds. Henry felt better, and continued. "I think we should talk more, another time. As it stands, if nobody is opposed to me trying to save and repair my Kingdom in the way I've mentioned, I think that's how I would like to try to do it. There's better ways... I hope. If I go to sleep, I don't have the threat of having *that* happen to my Core. Right?"

His finger accused the shards rather pointedly. "So I have all the time in the world to find a better method? Because eventually, when we leave Cal, even if I fail *here*, I don't want to fail *out there*, when I've only got *one shot.*"

That message rang home to a few people, and looks of

consideration settled in. Tatum turned his head, making a motion to Henry in request for the ball, who just handed it over. "I think it would have helped if either Bob or Minya were here to help corroborate this story. Currently all we have is some odd tension, a somber Great Spirit, a surprisingly nervous Administrator, and pieces of a shattered crystal that happen to look like a Seed Core. Where are they?"

Cale slowly drew a physical breath as he listened to the arguments. A self-soothing measure. "Minya entered stasis. She will be asleep for easily the next thousand years. There were some complications, and that number might double. As for Bob… the Bobs have left us. Those who knew him best had a private get-together as we saw the last one off. Bob Prime hung on as best as he could, and he left us with some warm words."

Cale trailed off at a visual memory, which he shared before picking the topic back up. "A grateful smile lingering on his face, he said his tribe has the best home it could ever have hoped for, and he never expected to live forever. He went out surrounded by loved ones with bright futures. For a Goblin that survived from the earliest days of my dungeon, when their race was still all the worst parts it could be… that was one Cal of an accomplishment. He said he was ready to go."

Silence hung heavy over the inner circle. The second circle remained empty today. This wasn't news for their ears. Nobody complained. Deverash flopped back in his small, raised seat. "Can I avoid it by swapping into a geometric body?"

The silent *no* he got back via a solemn shake of the head made him grit his teeth. He'd had… problems on Vanaheim. Turbulent discoveries he didn't want to tell anyone about. Even if a few people likely knew. He expected Cal to remain quiet so he could solve it himself, but Brianna could be a danger if she brought it up. She hadn't, and his philosophic friend hadn't either. He figured they just trusted him to see it through, and didn't need to draw a fuss.

Tatum continued, since he technically still had the ball in his court. "I don't mind entering stasis, but I'm not feeling any of this strain that was talked about. Life on Hel is *incredibly* dull. Sleeping will be no different. If I'm stuck there long-term for my own, and everyone else's safety... it's just a lonely existence. The visits to Midgard help."

Chandra squeezed a vine bracelet around his wrist in support, without ever needing to move her hand over to touch him. "If you go into stasis, I'm going in for an equal amount. I doubt we have to be kept in stasis for the exact time period. Only that we have to catch up on it."

Cale pressed his lips into a thin line, looking hopefully over to Artorian. The Administrator kept his hands folded, not needing to meet the dungeon's stare for him to get the message. "About that... as Incarnates, Tatum and Dawn don't seem to have the mortality problem the rest of us do. They can *choose* to enter stasis if they want, but it's not life-critical, like it is for you and I."

Dawn raised an eyebrow, her chin tilting. "You're *silly* if you think I'm staying awake to hang around while you're dozing. I've had enough of that as is. I've handled things in my realm so I can hand over anytime. My worry is that my named ones will not live to see my return. If I go into stasis and come out to find I missed all of Caliph's life, I'm going to be very upset."

Cale felt the need to swiftly protect himself. "That won't be a problem. There's several ways around that, and it all comes down to creatures being bound to Nodes or not. Most creatures on Muspelheim are Mage-ranked, but that *doesn't* mean they have Node connections. Only those with connections will need to join you in sleep, but those who have them are effectively immortal."

He motioned to the moon. "Those who don't can literally just be saved in a memory stone, and decanted when you're back without it seeming like a day has passed. You *can* leave them out in the world, but their lives will continue. It doesn't prevent me from making a memory copy at a later time, but it doesn't seem that's what you want. So choose either between saving your most precious few in memory stones, or whether you want to take a few decades and have them go through the cultivation process to Node-connect them. I expect it will be easier when they are premade of Mana. Still, your call."

Dawn sat back, her pose a copy of the Gnome's as she had much to think about. Her leg extended, and her high heels nudged into Artorian's shin. "What are you doing?"

The table's eyes meandered to the Administrator, who had never sat so rigid and stern at the table for this long. His nerves were tense. He was even in some outfit that made him look important. Some uniform, rather than the usual grandfatherly comfort-is-king robes.

"Well... I will be finishing my current set of tasks. I've crossed the majority of works from my to-do list. Then, I am going into stasis until there's no seed strain left. I've asked to be decanted when I'm at tip-top one-hundred percent. When I go back to sleep after... I will decide from there."

He glanced at the clock table. "I have chosen to hang my robes up soon. A few more years of activity at most. When I am back out, there are *several* projects I need to begin at that time. Including speaking to anyone who has *refused* to go to sleep."

Brianna smiled with coy venom. "You will do *what* at such a time? Come to *forcibly* dethrone us and make us slumber?"

The reason Artorian sat stern came to bear. This was the exact question he'd been dreading. One of three. His gaze, wisened and stoic, turned to lock eyes with the Queen of Assassins. Artorian's answer arrived with resolute resignation. "If I *must*, Brianna. Only if I *must*."

CHAPTER TWO

After that particularly haunting inner circle moot had taken its toll, Artorian hid in his warehouse of whizbangs and fiddlesticks for a month. On the plus side, broken items were being sealed and documented at a prodigious pace. On the downside, he wasn't being particularly social. Unlike the usual routes where he sought escape from the confined space, this time he'd sought out the self-imposed exile like a mountain hermit.

When he again ventured out to sit on the porch of the pagoda to meet the sky, it felt like it had been a very long time indeed. To his surprise, the front door was gone. One of Zelia's children informed her of his activity, and as was usual for matters with her Dreamer, she went *personally*.

This was a nice day for Jotunheim. Pleasant even. The general air was cool, with steady warm waves brushing through fluttering robes. The opposite of a summer day, but just as enjoyable to bask in as the wind whistled across the Jotunheim mountains. This passing breeze sounded newly added wind-chimes. Some easily the size of buildings. Artorian relaxed, indulging in their calming notes, and pleasantly humming melody.

Zelia daintily held her spidersilk paper umbrella as she approached, gracefully seating her violet kimono-clad self next to her Dreamer. She had a full wardrobe of such fine quality now. Clothes and attire were a passion, even if she didn't fully grasp all the sympathies involved that led to her having such a drive. Her voice mimicked the pleasant local chimes. "The door appears to be missing, my Dreamer."

Artorian, clad in simple and dull, dirty white robes, nodded wordlessly. He provided a response after a few more lengthy chime chinks, realizing he was part of why. "All intelligent items are scrapped. Recanted as people in memory or Seed Cores. There's no need for further possible complications at this stage. Not when we can pack the project in and test intelligent items again when things are stable. A reintroduction is planned for Alpha Two, now that Cal has scheduled a date. Again, not without its own set of complications."

His Arachnid chosen wasn't following what he was on about. That mattered little. Zelia was ever supportive, but not any less concerned for the strange news after her Dreamer's long month of isolation. She attempted to lace her words with calm tones, as Halcyon naturally did. "You speak as if the world is ending."

"It is." His terse reply was not what she'd expected. The statement even made her head jerk away a few inches because she couldn't believe it had been said.

After a thoughtful moment, Zelia moved forwards again to resume graceful seating. Her hand wavered as it formed back into a carapace claw. A result from the rough time she suddenly experienced with self-control. Her two eyes became six, but she did her best to control the stress and managed to stabilize there. "That did not sound like one of your amusing jokes, my Dreamer. Nor a playful scheme you have enacted, and we know you have enacted many."

Artorian held his own hands, thumbs rolling over one another as he hunched forwards. "It's not a joke. Nor is it amusing. It's quite the cause for trouble. When I finish that big to-do list down in the basement... the one taking up an entire wall? I will be going to sleep for a while. A very long, long while. When I wake again, the world will be different."

The breeze kicked up, fluttering his robes. "Then, depending on what the other supervisors have chosen, I have to go do some difficult things to save their lives. When all supervisors who remained have been recanted, what you said will occur. The world will end."

Artorian's tone stayed soft, borderline somber. "Cal is going to reset it back to how it was at the start, with minor alterations that have shown to offer a consistent improvement. People and creatures will be kept in pause, let free to roam once again without ever being aware of the subtle differences. They won't even question that whole rivers will have moved, or that herds prefer an entirely different diet."

Zelia's kimono threatened to rip as her form wavered further. While her upper half successfully held onto its human guise, her mass below the waist reverted to being entirely spider-like, multiple legs and all. "So you're telling me that not only will you be leaving us for a very long time, but that when you return, we will forget the life we knew as we start all this work back over?"

He shook his head no, and that set her, ever so slightly, back at ease. "The first part, yes. The second part... no. I have options for you, and I don't want to choose them for you. I trust my three named ones, but the choices are difficult. Except perhaps for you, my dear. *Yours* is the easiest."

Zelia rolled her wrist, the sharp claw making a 'go on' motion. Her Dreamer spoke at her request. "*Either* we store the few important souls into memory Cores. Safely taking them back out without them being aware they lost a day of time. Their personal growth remains unaffected, and if they ever wish the satisfaction of a natural lifespan... They will have it. Not *all* wish to live forever, so I have learned from Bob."

Artorian drew a fresh breath. "*Or*, we take the time to increase their personal growth, until they can Ascend and be tied to a Seed Core. Then, *even if* their body dies, their mind will not. They will live eternal, but be forced to adhere to the same sleeping patterns I am subject to. Ten years of slumber, for every one of waking."

He tried to be supportive about the next part. "Your choice is easy, Zelia, because you are already tied to the **Teleportation** Node. Even if you didn't fully know it. You didn't begin with a Beast Core, as Halcyon did. Nor a cultivation center, like Yuki. You're on super secret track three, having started life as a dungeon Core."

Artorian wasn't certain how to categorize the look he was getting. "I'm going to assume several things I just said didn't make sense to you. I'll simplify. The choice is for a natural end to one's life, or to deny that. Living until all you know is a burden; for no reason other than seeing whatever you hold on to, to fruition, until the very end."

Zelia calmed, and the light flickering behind her eyes spoke volumes of the energy she was investing into thinking this over. "Will you end *naturally*, Dreamer? Or is it too late for you, as I think is the case?"

Feeling like an old man, he eased his grasp over and squeezed her claws. "Too late for me, I'm afraid. I'm here for the full duration. That includes living on well past the time where we are stuck in this Soul Space. All the supervisors are in this position, everyone in charge of a realm. It's part of what got us the position, you see."

He rubbed his thumb over her smooth carapace. "We made a deal with Cal for it, the Great Spirit. It includes an unbreakable vow of loyalty, so he can trust us. While we all have different methods, it's in his interest to let us roam free and see to our tasks. No, my dear. I will *not* end naturally. My end will be chosen, or forced."

Artorian needed a moment to breathe. "I... I have a *third* option, but it is currently well outside my grasp, and even then I am simply not certain it is a path I wish to tread."

Zelia decisively squared her shoulders. "Then my choice is

easy. I choose the latter, and choose to stay. I don't know what the dungeon Core track is, but if it did come with a natural end, I choose to throw that away. I refuse to leave my Dreamer, and you will have to deal with me through famine and feast. Tell me how I am already tied to whatever this Node is. I have always felt strangely about my comparison to the other chosen. All my growth is… horizontal. Never vertical. I do not grow stronger, I grow more skilled. Meanwhile Halcyon and Yuki *do* develop vertically, and their power wells."

Artorian released her claw, but she did not pull it away. Choosing to resettle it on his shoulder instead for a firmer grip. He didn't mind. The touch was a kindness. "Yuki's method of growth is similar to my own, before I became 'The Administrator.' In our old world, it worked like this: One gathers energy to build oneself up, and at a certain point—after much toil—one is able to Ascend and connect to a Node. A **Law**."

He focused some energy above his palm, forming a glowing pink orb. "A kernel of truth in and of the universe to which they seek to further dedicate themselves. A deep point of focus and purpose. When one Ascends to such a point, cultivation must continue for vertical growth to continue. As you have no such method, I'm not surprised by your words. I believe keeping you at the B-rank you are, with that body malleable as it may be, was intentional. Yet if you wish to change that, I will sink my considerable efforts into your well. So you may see it fill."

Zelia approved of this. "What of Halcyon?"

His mouth opened to speak, but closed for a pensive moment as he released the orb. "Halcyon started on the Beast Core track. She began as a beast, and has gained intelligence and power from that point. All she has to do for growth is to keep doing what she's doing, and eat plenty. She will never have the utility or plethora of skill you or Yuki will, but her raw affinity for the few things she can do will be extreme. I figure that's how she got a hold of flight so quickly. It's just more swimming, except through the sky."

That mention made them share a soft smile. "Yuki had

memories of cultivation before she arrived, and while she does not have all the clues, knows enough to fuel her growth. I expect when she hits a bottleneck, I will receive a visit. I planned to tackle it then. There are some additional difficulties when mixing D-ranked cultivation skills with a body in the mid B-ranks."

The Arachnid next to him was taking her time molding back into a humanoid shape. It was slow going, but he let her take all the time she wanted without a single snappy comment. She calmed when she managed to sit properly on her butt once again, her kimono untarnished as she picked the paper umbrella back up. "You will ask them the same question?"

The Administrator nodded. "I will. I honestly expect them to choose the former. Yuki and Cy are supportive, but they have their own lives. I do not wish to strip those from them. Cal and I had a behind the scenes talk about that. He was fiddling around with something he's calling 'Titles,' and they're supposed to provide innate traits when 'applied.'"

He wibble-wobbled his hand. "Not sure what he means yet, but he mentioned that if a named one chose to remain natural, the Named Aspect could become a Title. That Title could then resurface later in the family line, with someone who would be fitting of it. They would *seek* me at that point, I am told. Informed by some kind of prompt. It's in the works, so who knows."

Zelia's parasol twirled. "I will tell them. This news will be easier for them if it comes from me. Yuki is warming, but her frost is strong. She doesn't know what to think of you, still. I, on the other hand, am considered a friendly face. As I meet with her often, concerning documents, stories, and the like."

She verbally mulled things through. "Halcyon may take your request well, but her heart will break when you must tell her that you are leaving. I don't know what our normal lifespans are, but her worries will grow deep when she dwells on it. Especially of possibly expiring before you return. She requires more of your time, and attention. Perhaps do not be free from us too soon? What you have prepared will cause others to have a taxing time."

The soft nod she received set her at ease once more. Artorian spoke while mired in thought. "I'm sure some last-minute scribbles will mysteriously appear on my to-do list. Anchoring me longer."

He paused, squinting at something in the distance as his vision went on the fritz again. "On an unrelated note, is that a *Dark* Elf in that mountain over there, setting up an observation post? Since when is Brianna trying to keep an eye on me?"

The thought of why struck him immediately after. "Ah… well. After the last meeting… Why am I not surprised? I'll take that offer, my dear. Thank you for helping me with the burden. Let us speak of your power growth again in the future. In the meanwhile… Would be a *shame* if that observer went *missing*."

Zelia enthusiastically clicked. Her children were already on their way, massing in large swarms as she playfully twirled her umbrella. In the far distance of the mountains, the border wind chimes rang, covering up any fearful screams that may have occurred.

"Indeed, my Dreamer. A true *shame*."

CHAPTER THREE

<Administrator, do you have a moment?> Henry's voice called from the senate, accompanying a pulsing ping for a private forum request. Artorian had been seven screens deep in figuring out why a staff of coruscating fireballs always inflicted 'maximum damage,' as Cal was calling it. He dismissed the screens, and replied in kind as he accepted the forum request for a private conversation.

<Of course, my boy. What's the trouble?> Artorian's mental tone hung somewhere between wistful, and surprisingly pleasant. Odd for Henry, as he had expected a more stern, or possibly grumbly attitude. He was happy to be mistaken.

<You seem chipper! That's pleasant. I have a small problem I'm not sure how to solve. It would be easier to show you in person, but I can talk if not.>

Artorian closed his eyes, fully lapsing into the forum. His mote popped up with a puffed glimmer of celestine light. The smooth answer was a comfort to the Midgard King. <All's well, Henry. You're actually the *fourth* to contact me with this method in recent times. I knew the senate and forum had an update, but nobody was using it. So I am quite happy to find it trending

back into popularity! That's what has me so chipper. We're *actually* conversing, after being somewhat akin to distant relatives who give each other the side eye over the fence for a few years. I'll just pop over. Mind setting me a location?>

When a marker appeared, Artorian just stood and folded space around him. He appeared in the designated location with a fuff and fluffy accompaniment of the usual down feathers. To not fall, in case the height was once again wrong, he stood on bricks of hard light. Not that they were visible today. Once present, he had a look around to get his bearings.

"Edge of the world? Looks like the edge of the world. Forest as far as the eye can see, then suddenly: cliff. Oh, oh dear." Good thing he'd prepared those bricks, he was a little close to the edge for comfort. "Well, if you dropped something, I think we're in a pickle."

Henry stood nearby, present in his usual seamless full plate. Looking over the same cliff edge, his hand kept pressed to the bottom of the visor. "Oh... I... well, that ends that right away then."

The Administrator broke into a flimsy laugh. "Ha! What did you drop?"

Henry was clearly trying to play it off, weaving and bobbing from side to side as his Aura flattened the nearby foliage from sheer pressure as he moved. "Ma~a~aybe my *sword*. I was practicing after having snuck away. A difficult task by itself, mind you. I'm trying to get a hold of my own power, but nothing is working. It's tiring to walk around and press everyone down to a knee without really meaning to, but I just can't get a grip on fielding. Something is different about my Aura. It's like parts have fused, and become *all* of me. My Aura no longer acts and responds like I expect, and while I can change my shielding, I don't have the control that I did as a C-ranker. Anytime I move my Aura, it's like I am moving *all of myself*, and my body just follows suit."

Artorian nodded. Sounded about right. "Yes, we're par for the course. I'm afraid you'll have to resort to quiet meditation and carefully practicing self-control over your Aura to make progress there. Swinging a stick around isn't going to help. This Aura control requires a reflective growth, not an activity growth. You didn't *actually* call me for the sword... did you?"

Henry scratched the back of his head. Helmet or no. "Heh. You saw right through me. I just don't know what else to do. I also wanted to ask if there was an alternative to... *forcibly* dethroning Marie? She's not taking it well. Not as poorly as Brianna is obviously taking it; I know she's got spies here now. They're no longer subtle."

The old man folded his hands behind his back. "I'm aware. I'm keeping a running tally. As for Marie, if you can convince her to just go into stasis with you, I don't have to do anything. Honestly, I'm not sure why she was against it, resting means time with you when you both first decant again."

Henry grumbled. "Marie's mind is on her Queendom non-stop, all the time. We've barely had time for one another. I don't think it even entered her thoughts. I should... *ask*. It would be nice to get away. Just the two of us. Maybe even delay a short while before picking the mantle back up. Maybe... skip a world version. *Just the two of us...* doesn't have to stay just *two*. I... Artorian, I know I pulled you over on a whim. I apologize, but I think I need to run off right away."

Ideas were clearly striking Henry, and he was not the sort for slow plans of action.

Artorian nodded. Pleased he was holding onto positives. "Go, my boy. Though... where *are* we? I've never been to Midgard much, and I don't rightly know where we are on the continent. This area looks new. Like it was added in later."

Henry hurried to pack up his things. Mostly just two large bags with practice material useful for a C-ranker. Not so much where he was now. "It was! Cal is evening out realm imbalances and that resulted in added landmass. Because this place is not on the map yet, nobody knows and I can slip away. I call it the fringe of Midgard. Have a pleasant day, Administrator!"

The old man rubbed his chin as the youth ran off, flattening forest as he went. Granted, he didn't know Henry's actual age, being a cultivator and all. Still, the behavior was that of a young'un, and he was fond of the lad for it. *Good on you. You chase those dreams.*

Artorian remained in place, looking down to see particles of land further add on to the existing edges. "The Fringe, you say? Well… *Excuse me* for not passing up an opportunity like that when it falls into my lap."

Rubbing his hands together, Artorian pulled up a screen only he had, thanks to Administrator privileges. Everyone could edit items and creatures so long as they were broken, but he could edit *anything*. So long as it was in some way part of the system.

With a wry smile, he tapped into the landscape and began altering the place. This was a great location for a lake. A *salt* lake. Some hills here and there. Places trees would not populate via allotted zoning, a nice river, and tentative plans for structures. Structures cost him *actual points,* so he ignored those for now.

His additions weren't much, but it was a start. He had to decant his personal friends and family *somewhere* on Midgard to get started, after all. He'd thought of whisking them straight to Jotunheim's interior, but they would either have Decorum's problem, or go *squish*. Neither were acceptable. What *was* acceptable was offering them all the Ascension path.

Those who took it, he would train and guide personally, along with Zelia or Yuki. A warm-up for the Academy he wanted to put up. A proper one, this time. Perhaps he could do that nearby? The Midgard fringe region would need some kind of export. "Salted foods? Something salt. *Definitely* something with food."

He mused and planned it out over the course of a few months while tinkering in his warehouse. When he thought of something, it was added to the fringe build list. He had a running tally of who he was going to decant, and where, once the time came. Artorian was feeling impatient about it, but knew the time was not right. At minimum, *not* in world iteration Alpha One. There would be angry Dwarven cursing if he tried.

Still, a place very conveniently *not on a map* and out of the way, in Midgard? Tantalizing! He had a beacon set and already placed. He'd told Henry it was to 'help him sneak away with Marie,' and that he would 'put some things up for them later.' Just to obscure the true value of the place.

In the meanwhile it was their little getaway spot, and Marie decompressed in a very healthy fashion from all the time *away* from royal operations. The message that Marie wasn't going to cause a stir—no longer resistant to being canted—even came in the format of a hand-written letter.

He'd forgotten they could do that!

Marie's named one had brought it to a beacon, and Zelia played post-woman after chatting up the humanized version of Manny the Manticore. Marie's theme exemplified **Glory**, and Manny's aesthetics certainly counted. Even humanized, he walked tall. Carrying powerful pride while clad in armor of his own, inferior, discarded forms. He even purred when he spoke.

Henry's named one, Sleipnir, had initially offered to go. He was a powerful horned and four-armed centaur who relished in clearing fields with a seven-foot cleaver in each hand. However, Manny was peculiar when it came to certain tasks he otherwise considered *beneath* him. A conversation with the delicate Jotunheim spiderling—that was *anything but harmless*—brought him great satisfaction. The camaraderie found in being around a creature possessing venomous hidden power *sang* to his aesthetics.

So without fail, Manny saw to the mail.

The letter was folded and added to the temporary archive. Speaking of archives, the Sun project was done! This time it would get plunked into the sky, and preferably reach operational capacity *without* exploding into chunks. Thinking of it, he should get to that. If he left now, he would be early, but another distraction or two and he might be late. "Best pop to it then." *Fuff*.

On arrival, Artorian lost count of all the Gnomes he saw. They were *Gnomes*, right? Some of them had already opted for the geometric body replacements. The messy spectacle involved watching a smattering of random math-dice float about and manipulate details on a giant gyroscopic orb. Was it still a gyro? The solar construct had the look of one, but the details were all artfully different.

"Artorian! There you are!" The Administrator looked around, but failed to discern the real source of the voice. His eyes stopped on an eight-sided die multiple times. Yet he looked elsewhere just to be sure. "Haha! No, you got it right the first time. The prismatic eight-sided die. That's me. Dev! I know it's only socially acceptable to Gnome around in the proper body, but it works! A~a~and I didn't feel like adhering to agreed-upon Vanaheim customs today, or really anytime when I'm *not* on Vanaheim."

Artorian stared at the eight-sided, multi-colored die. He didn't gape his mouth, and he didn't frown. Instead, he was boring his sight through the object, inspecting any details about it that he could. To his annoyance, that turned out to be cracker-crumbs *little*. Artorian felt stumped. "Alright. You're going to have to explain that later. How do you even... *do anything?*"

The die spun in place, twinkled, and gleamed as a face of some kind appeared in dot format upon one of the surfaces. Dev added what could be considered a smiling face in some kind of circle. The die had Deverash's voice, but no mouth to... how, even? *What?*

Deverash did not contain his glee. "Cal calls it 'telekinesis.' It's an Auric function. The means that let us move, control, and manipulate real things with the shaping of our Aura? That, except with more kinetic force. Us Gnomes can move our Auras better than hands, without any of the restrictions, at distances otherwise impossible for us. Slotted into a Pylon, this becomes [Telekinesis], since we're essentially moving things with our minds. Just... easier, even if in some manner more complicated in function. The Pylon makes it so simple for us that this trick beats out any normal ways of handling just about anything. Give it a try sometime; it's easily my favorite Pylon."

The rings on the large solar construct warbled and thrummed with sound, causing a hefty distraction. Both Artorian and the Deverash Die turned to face it as Cale winked into existence, throwing his arms out like some grand conductor in an orchestra. "I declare these archives *open*. Let there be light! Nobody look straight at it now!"

The solar construct warbled louder, like someone playing the bongos with drumsticks of thunder. As all the spell Runes and formations were simultaneously fed and activated, it squealed discordantly; synthesizing a monstrous cacophony.

Artorian covered his ears. "Holy Cal, suns are *loud*!"

The light from the very center blazed into being in a massive burst. Heat now pouring out of the construct in oppressive waves. To compensate, the construct moved farther and farther outwards from its berth. Shooting skywards at a steady speed where it would slot into a well-calculated orbit.

Cal opened a senate channel, explaining what the sudden change in Soul-Space-wide lighting was about. "The sun is up! I'm going to keep it dim and weak, but this will be more than enough for a natural day and night cycle. I'm done. I'm finally *done* with this one! *Woo*! Great success!"

Everyone felt a pull on their stomachs, the world dilation speed upgrading as Cal went up another rank. Where was he now? A-rank seven? Eight? They didn't actually know, but it was somewhere up there. Looking away, the old man watched the rising geometric shapes as the Gnomes cheered and hooted. Interesting how one could *bob* with so much emotion. Artorian slid on his sunglasses and calmly applauded, joining the merriment. "*Shiny*!"

CHAPTER FOUR

After the celebrations—and since he could—a curious Artorian fuffed into the star's center to have a look at the decorated interior. Cale was waiting for him, one of those self-satisfied smirks plastered on his face. Like he'd known the Administrator would not be able to hold back his curiosity. "*Ta-da*! One sun, working as intended, complete with bonus residence hidden away on the inside. I even got all the details right this time. Plus, that library wing is done, spacious too with just how much ridiculously larger this construct is. What do you think?"

The old man barked a short laugh, pulling out a chair to sit. "Like I said. Shiny. I'm pleasantly surprised to find it's *cool* in here. Not burny or toasty in the slightest. There's even a fireplace. How thoughtful. I was under the impression that I was going to provide help. Turns out you just lit her up like a candle, and she was good to go."

Cale stretched, putting his boots up on the table. His arms settled behind his head, and he leaned his chair back precariously. "I had the entire pattern this time. With the core structure from Vanaheim, the rest was just a matter of energy. The accumulators are all drained, but the Essence mechanism is working as planned up here now. It's not *quite* a fire elemental source, but it's cycling previously stagnant energy. That's good enough for me."

The dungeon thought of something else, and smiled. "A little bird came and told me Marie is no longer going to make it difficult for us. Nice to hear. I don't want to *boot* any of my current supervisors from the circle. That divine business really needs to stop, though."

Cale ran his fingers through his hair. "Next run. We'll sort it *next run*."

The Administrator nodded, and extended his hand to a cup on the counter. Dev's words momentarily came to his attention, and now was as good of a time as any. His hand remained outstretched to the object a good twelve feet away from him, then he spoke the word Dev taught him. "[Telekinesis]."

The feeling was astounding. Artorian felt like a whole new arm manifested. One that he could control and manipulate to the finest detail. The limb had invisibly sprung from his side, and instinctively Artorian felt some kind of timer. To his amazement, this reaching grasp wasn't physically present, until he desired that it *was*. The kinetic hand squeezed around the cup, and he brought it towards him with *less* difficulty than moving his actual limbs. When the cup *thunked* onto the table, he could do naught but stare at it until the effect ended. The feeling of the invisible extra arm fading once the timer ran dry.

Cale just sat there. *Smirking*. "Nice, huh? Try it on liquids too. You can form the potential shape of a bowl and it will carry water."

Not hesitating at such a suggestion, Artorian acted. Using the spell again, he pulled all of the water out from a different container without a fuss. He did so by shaping the telekinesis container within an existing, physical container. Creating a smaller copy of the exact shape. The telekinetic feeling bent and reformed on exit through the funnel, but the amphora-shaped mass of water hovered in front of him regardless.

Artorian could not contain his excitement. "I'm not even

using my water affinity channel to do this. It's all external. Even then, I'm not sure *just* water channels could make the container shape float in mid-air like this. It's not even Mana-costly. I love it!"

The vesseled water was poured into the cups only to be gawked at a moment. He returned excess liquid to the amphora before the telekinetic effect expired, changing the shape of the vessel a few times before letting go. Artorian had to then sip on the water in his cup, just to make sure it was real. *"Fascinating."*

He leaned back in the chair, full of bright ideas. They wavered when he realized Cale was still here. Normally the dungeon ran off swiftly, so the old man addressed it in his usual grandfatherly style. "Something on your mind, my friend?"

Cale thoughtfully considered how to broach the subject. To make it easy on himself, he brought up several three-dimensional maps of his Soul Space. Each Continent had its own map, and dots of celestine blue illuminated all across their reaches. Artorian choked on his water, coughing when he realized those dots were his teleportation beacons.

Cale suddenly sounded tired when he spoke, as if there was a weight pressing to his chest. "With Bob at permanent rest, I took over many of the tasks so I could discern who to best hand them back out to. In doing my audit, I came across some faulty Pylon code. I notice you're sitting at a very cozy A-rank zero right now, but I barely found any records of you having time to cultivate. None of the supervisors have."

Artorian gently placed his cup back down. Rats! He'd been discovered. So much for his convenient Mana recoupment method. Alright, he should call it what it was. *Cheating.* It was cheating. Cal pulled the Jotunheim maps close, and snickered on seeing the waving line that appeared on the legend as the Long Mark Two. He was just going to let it hang there as a flag, a reminder to his Administrator that he wasn't good at *everything*.

Cale spoke more kindly than Artorian expected. "I've removed the teleportation feature from the shop, and all buildings relating to it. Until I can repair the jumble of Pylons responsible. Now, because the platforms are conveniently all in place, rather than giving my supervisors personal teleportation access, I'm giving them a keygem that will let them use those beacons like my old dungeon portal system. The same method some of the chosen are currently using."

Artorian patiently listened, waiting for the other shoe to drop. When Cale dismissed the diagrams, the old man was starting to feel unsettled. So he just asked. "Cale? No mention of costs, or debt, or 'oh, this is going to be bad for you'? I expected *some* backlash for doing this to your system."

Cale took his boots from the table, and pulled his chair closer so he could fold his hands together. "It's too minor of an issue. I have a bigger problem that I can only talk to a handful of people about. Out of curiosity, what rank do you think I am?"

The Administrator softly rubbed the top of his head while thinking it over. "Oh, I'd wager… somewhere in the middling A-eight ranks? It's very difficult to discern the details with you, without your actual Core to look at. Even I can barely tell at all. I'd lob my ball at 'high tier' and see if it goes through the net."

Cale rubbed one of his thumbs around the other, and didn't seem pleased to be speaking about the topic. Like it was bad news. "As of… a few moments ago? A-rank nine, Zenith."

Artorian pushed up from his chair and hooted, fists punching to the air with an elated expression. He performed a swift side to side shimmy while miniature fireworks bounced and exploded off from his aura. "You're at the zeeeenith, you're at the zeeeenith! Cal, this is *fantastic*!"

His wide smile slowly turned drab, and his butt found a seat on the chair. "So… why are you anything *but* happy?"

Cale's digits pressed into his temples, his head dipping low. So low that his forehead just about touched the table. When Cale sat back up, he seemed lost. "I watched the same memories you did. I lived through Dawn and Tatum's experiences of the event. Even with that, I'm not ready, because of what the *side effects* might be."

Artorian thought about it, and certain puzzle pieces fit into place in locations he *really didn't* want them to be. "I… Ah. I can see a particularly nasty event. Since the soul version inverts, all 'stuff' in your Soul Space will likely be turned inside out as well, and that doesn't bode well for everyone living inside of you. I have no idea if that's an event we can survive. *At all.*"

Cale nodded at one of the possible major issues, and a very deflated Artorian squeezed both his hands over his mouth and chin. Sliding down in his chair until he was at full slump. "Oh, abyss…"

Cale held the side of his head as he leaned. "That's *one.* There's a few more, nastier events that might occur. As an example, the oath I made to let everyone back out when it was safe might smite me if I can't uphold my part of the deal. Did Dawn ever tell you about the timer she was on, when she was going through her Incarnation?"

Artorian nodded. That had been a very hefty conversation during what had otherwise been a very pleasant coconut-sipping day. "She did. I'm her go-to when she's got bothersome things on her mind. What else is eating you, my friend? There appears to be more."

The dungeon just talked, rather than really think on how it wanted to phrase things. The topic was difficult enough just to talk about at all. "I won't have one. A timer, I mean. There's no existing S-rankers for Acme, and as soon as I reach the requisite Essence density. *Pop.* Since outside in the real world, my ley lines are still chugging on and sending me all the world's Essence, it's not an event I can stop or slow down."

He wavered. "I have started looking into measures for *how* to slow it down. Once the chains are off. Otherwise, people who I let out will just die from Essence deprivation out in *the real.* Because I really *am* taking *everything.*"

The old man squeezed both sides of his chin. "How are you on the self-identity front? Dawn really struggled, but made it with help. I'm confident you have all those memories, even if the whole 'Liminal Energy' concept is a tough nut. I didn't know about that until recently."

Cale just shrugged that off. "The thoughts-turned-reality? You've all been handling the broken items and creatures. Those were *my* Liminal problems, and it was *specifically important* that I could not affect, notice, or solve them myself. I apologize about the throw pillow. I really didn't know it was down in the insect nest, nor that it was *that one*. I never found it in your recovered bag of holding goods, and chose never to mention it unless it specifically came up. My good news on that front is that I have enough of the Liminal recouped and held safely in my center to perform my overhaul, that's not a bottleneck."

Artorian felt a little jealous, and it showed in his expression. He didn't chide the dungeon for his good fortune. Each Liminal issue seemed to have oddities and peculiarities required for resolution. "How long do you have?"

Cale frowned, a touch pensive. "Before the sun? I thought I had somewhere between centuries to millennia. After the sun? Weeks to months. Maybe less. Maybe I'm wrong entirely and it's exactly one hundred and two years, three months, and four days. I am currently in the process of canting all Beasts and animals into relevant memory stones. So expect them to vanish seemingly overnight, now that we *have* a night. I'm glad Deverash went overboard with his memory Core creation endeavor. Turns out I am in desperate need of them."

Pulling his chair out, Artorian stood up and paced around the living room for a short while. He didn't know what to say just yet. "So, in effect, you have no idea. It will happen randomly, and there will be no warning."

Cale buried his face into his hands, mumbling between his fingers. "In essence, yes."

The old man held the middle of his beard as he faced the fireplace. "Does anyone *else* know?"

The reply was about as half-hearted as he'd expected it. "No. Not yet. I need to pull in Dawn and Tatum later to talk over what might make it easier, but honestly, I already have all their memories and can imagine the responses they might have. I wanted to try and broach it to you first for the exact same reasons Dawn does. You're a good go-to, Artorian. You don't judge, you don't have massive negative or judgmental reactions. Usually, you also pull magical answers out of nowhere. Those I *can't get* out of memory Cores. So… do you have anything?"

Artorian pressed his forehead to the stone above the fireplace. He sighed, closed his eyes, and spoke his mind. "*Yes*… but you're *not* going to like it."

CHAPTER FIVE

Halcyon rushed to the administrator's residence upon being called, shortly after a flash of light struck the walking path in front of the Jotunheim pagoda. Her orca form glimmered and broke sound barriers as she flew, descending in a full nosedive from the clouds above. Her Dreamer was waiting for her on the steps below, inspecting a set of statues out in the front courtyard that detailed his several spectacular failures and most embarrassing moments from his Administrator's tenure here so far. "Did the Demon's Maw incident really need such a big one?"

Artorian smiled tiredly at her when she landed, humanizing fully in the span of a few seconds. She hustled over as Zelia's bright clothing flowed around her tall dark form, naturally unfurling during the change. "You summoned, Dreamer?"

Artorian was momentarily elsewhere, but he beamed at her when his attention reoccupied the moment. His voice was one of exhaustion. "Cy! Apologies for the short notice. I wanted to know if you'd be interested in spending some time with me while I do the next set of realm checks. I wanted someone along and felt we haven't been having enough time together. I also believe I can't currently do it alone, and well… you're so terribly good at taking care of me. Would you please?"

Halcyon *eeeeed* in delight with excited tip-toe bounces. "I would love to! Can we get something to eat on the way? I would like to try the regional seafood."

Her Dreamer snorted, amused and delighted. He felt some energy restore itself to his spirit right away. He'd asked the right soul for company. "A grand thought! Let us go explore the culinary spectacle of the many realms. We should perhaps do the difficult ones first then, as Tatum's place doesn't exactly offer… edible goods. Build up an appetite as we go places that actually have menu items. Saving Midgard for last has an added bonus. Oh, if you'd been around when Madame Chandra ran the *Pleasure House*."

He kissed his fingers and closed his eyes at the decadent memories, then sent them out to the winds. "Delicious."

Halcyon upgraded to tiny jumps, overjoyed at the surprise field trip. "What must I pack? Am I dressed well? Do I need an extra bag?"

Her sudden childlike tenderness had Artorian enjoy a warm, grandfatherly moment. His hand waved gently, indicating that wasn't necessary. "You look fine, as always. My only current worry is the realm pressure. Even I had significant difficulties with the upper A's, and I only managed Asgard through some hefty Mana use. Let me ask Tatum to see if anything can be done about that since we're starting on the soot-ball. One moment, dear. Pack whatever you'd like."

Cy jumped with joy! "Okay!"

She twisted into her black and metallic gold orca form, seamlessly swimming through the air toward her pagoda level to gather a few things. Artorian smiled, ever so proud as he watched her go. He stepped into the Senate, and knocked on the forum door for a conversation. <Tatum, do you have a moment? I'd like to come by with a chosen.>

Occultatum opened the door to his forum space, and Artorian eased in for a private chat. In the corner of his vision, he noticed a previously pleased Zelia hiding in the open windowsill form a minor scowl. She was doing secretarial work from her hammock, now unable to sneakily hijack conversation connections once her Dreamer went to a forum. *Stay in the senate where you can be spied on, old man!*

Artorian would of course do no such thing. Tatum's mote popped in from the void. <Sorry about the delay. I'm trying to stabilize a very moody set of interlocking spell arrays. What is the matter, Administrator?>

The wait for an answer unsettled Tatum. That usually spelled bad news. When the Administrator did get to speaking about recent events, the Incarnate didn't like what he heard.

Tatum replied with frowned weight. <I understand Cale entering the S-ranks is cause for... concern. I would need to go speak to him personally, but this current task is sensitive. I really cannot keep my eyes off it, or the identities will waver. Like I said. It's moody. Come by. I shall make a space where gravity isn't murderous. Adding the marker shortly. If you can keep the array in line, I will visit Cal's sanctum. This is not something to be spoken of at a distance... as odd as it is to consider 'distance' in a Soul Space.>

Halcyon was back and ready while her Dreamer was still concentrating, his eyes kept closed as his cloud-patterned spidersilk robes moved with the breeze. Zelia had changed him while her Dreamer had been distracted. As if she would abide him wearing anything that wasn't her latest and greatest clothing line. A folded, matching bundle was waiting for Halcyon as well, and she donned them with glee like the exciting presents they were. She matched!

Artorian came back to his body slowly after the lengthy forum conversation. Tatum had spoken of the task with ease, but seeing to it was a different matter. Artorian could not fold them to the location too early, as he needed to wait for the area to be safe. Accidental squishing was a terrible way to go, and that's not what he wanted for his adored chosen.

After sitting to meditate a good twenty minutes, Tatum's

voice reached him once more with welcome. <All set, come on over. Good job actually telling me before your trip. Look at you, improving.>

Artorian cut the connection to confirm the message and opened his eyes. That had been a 'friendly' nudge in his ribs. He looked up only to brightly smile at Halcyon. "Why, look at you! Oh, we match!"

He let himself enjoy a good laugh and dancing flourish with Halcyon, as she tried to copy his dance steps. Just a little fun between the two of them. When he stopped, he pressed his hands to his new robes and looked up at her. "Cy, we're all set. Hand?"

Halcyon nodded and took his hand like she was being led into the next stage of the performance, allowing her Dreamer to fold space around them. Zelia watched them fade into the slipstream as they went. Tracking them as they teleported from the pagoda's path to a prepared spot on Hel's surface. She secretly wrote the location down in her personal notes, in the event it was ever useful to know where a safe zone existed on Hel.

On Hel, the Jotunheim duo was trying to process what they saw on arrival. A vast, moving, three-dimensional set of Runes hovered before them. Spells? Probably spells given the arrays were stable while they clicked and moved into one another as a vast and intricate house-sized puzzle. "Tatum, what in Cal am I looking at?"

Dressed in healer's attire, the man pulled a plague doctor mask off his face. He hooked the mask at his side, and cleaned off his hands in a nearby bucket of water. What kind of array work got one's hands dirty? "Do I even want to know why your hands are covered in…? No. Never mind. I didn't ask."

Tatum just broke into a pleased smirk. "I'm just working on my chosen one. He's a real honk of a good time. Also, hello. I don't believe I've met you before."

The Incarnate offered his clean hand to an unsettled Halcyon, who had taken to hiding behind her Dreamer with a tense, sudden movement. She was hungry, but her appetite currently felt stifled. Something about the dark lands where creatures of bone roamed shattered her footing. The lack of water bodies also definitely had something to do with it. That and the terrifying feeling in front of her that she didn't have the words to describe. Tatum just felt insurmountably massive, and it made her shrink away before him.

Cautiously, she shook Tatum's wrist. Never once moving an inch out from behind her Dreamer, who stood still purely for her comfort. Like he was her own massive thing she could hide behind. Artorian thought the display was somewhat adorable, though he'd expected her to be confident. This meekness was unexpected, and that worry showed on his easily read wrinkles.

Tatum saw the interplay and filled him in, not exactly surprised at the behavior. This was something normal to see as an Incarnate of his rank, and he'd simply not explained that before. "Your concerns are not as severe as they seem, Administrator. As an entity based on a Beast Core, your chosen one has an innate threat sense. A bestial feeling of the creatures around her, if you will. Just like an animal can easily discern a predator from prey, or a threat from a harmless blade of grass. We are seen... or rather, felt, as incredibly imposing threats."

He thought of an example, and moved his hand to mold some Mana into small animals which chased one another. "Think of being a rabbit. When surrounded by other rabbits, and one wolf. It is the wolf one is wary of. If, behind that wolf, the mountain suddenly moves and seems to be hungry, that is an entirely different category of inherent fear response."

He dismissed the Mana animals, and moved his hands behind his back. "We are those mountains, my friend."

Artorian glanced over his shoulder to Halcyon, who was holding onto his back for dear life. He supposed Tatum was right, and the old man shifted his Auric signature into the starlight configuration to soothe her. It helped well enough. Her grip eased, and her breaths evened out as both men heard Cy's heartbeat stabilize since they were paying close attention to her wellbeing.

Halcyon centered herself when she was able to think, kept safe in her Dreamer's pleasant, tingling starfield. She wasn't alone, and had her own mountain. He beamed warmly when she glanced down. Halcyon took her time reclaiming intelligent sense from her primal and bestial responses, but she succeeded.

Artorian was glad he'd taken her. It was good for Cy to have these experiences to strengthen her self-control. Patting her clamped grip, she gently eased and let go. Artorian spoke with fondness. "I'm very proud of her, she's making leaps and strides. Did you know she can swim through the air in Jotunheim? It's a joy to see her fly. So natural, a shooting star all on her own."

Tatum couldn't help but make the quip. "In comparison to a certain Long-flag hanging in a tree?"

Artorian cough-grumbled, crossing his arms and looking away. "Yeah… well. It's. Mmm. I just got roasted."

Halcyon and Tatum shared a snicker, which helped craft the start of a budding friendship now that the initial tension was fading. Artorian cut in before they could keep poking at his… less than positive test results. "So, what's this spell-form thing I need to keep in line? How does one even do that? It sounds as mysterious and confusing as the Dwarves 'convincing' stone into shape."

Tatum nodded, agreeing with the comparison. "That's exactly what this is. That profession is far more difficult than it seems, and it makes me gain a great grain of respect for them. This array is made of Mana, and the complexity of it is providing borderline sentience to the pattern being created within. Rock doesn't have sentience, but still those rough-hewn Dwarves manage to turn that rock into a wall. Because they convinced some pebbles that they should be a wall. A rock, Artorian. An abyss-blasted boulder. They can convince a boulder, while I am struggling with something far more malleable."

Artorian just waited as Tatum walked in circles, his hands waving wildly.

Tatum was venting, and he didn't want to interrupt the good feeling that came with getting something bothersome off your chest. Artorian supposed he was the resident vent-holder, but that was fine. The Incarnate pointed to the darkened section of the moving puzzle-form, which got his attention. "All you need to do is keep an eye on that chunk, and when it tries to do… anything. It doesn't matter what. Anything. You just tell it no. I'm all set to visit Cal. Think you can handle this for a while?"

The old man gave a thumbs up. "Tatum, that sounds so easy, Halcyon here could do it in her sleep."

The giantess flushed pink, and hid her face behind both her hands as she turned, trying to make herself look small. It didn't work, but gosh was it adorable. "We'll be fine, Tatum. Go help Cal. We'll stick around until you get back, even though we likely can't be of much help."

The Incarnate gave an appropriate nod, and void stepped out. Leaving the Jotunheim duo alone with Hel in all its dreary splendor. Artorian pressed his hands to his hips, and tried not to let his fatigue get to him. It was just… Abyss, this place was boring. If it wasn't for the array to keep attention to, there was no real movement here. He could spot bone-creatures in the distance, but they didn't really move.

When for a moment they did, the thoughts that they should continue… stopped. Their steps halted along with the cessation of their purpose. Artorian considered that it must be difficult to be a creature without needs, lacking higher thought. What does a creature like that even do, aside from remain at rest?

He then considered prodding them, but that might be exactly the kind of dangerous stimuli that would set A-rank nine creatures loose on his tail. A whirring sound came to his attention and… the array! With his attention resuming function, he took a step forward only to feel his momentary sense of panic melt away.

Without Tatum around, Halcyon had quickly recovered all her self-confidence. The arms-crossed chosen was also directly applying her regained moxy to the problem, having taken her Dreamer's words as a suggestion rather than merely praise.

She was staring down the inconsistency in the array with an impassioned solidity. In doing so, her golden lines pulsed with metallic energy. Cy's active Aura stifled the waves that emanated from the array as it tried to... Artorian could only describe the sight as the array attempting to spontaneously evolve. Her general Auric pressure felt like one of pulsing certainty, and Artorian had to admit even he felt more secure and stable from the sonic pattern of the pod call she repeated.

Halcyon put the array in its place just like any other member of her pod that was being a brat. Artorian had been on the copper with his earlier statement. She did have this in the bag, and by Cal, she was a natural! He would have needed to study what was going on in that messy spellform before he stopped anything, to make sure he didn't cause accidental harm.

Halcyon experienced no such thought process. She saw a newborn act out of line, and snapped it to attention. Getting the newborn right back under the protective fin of the pod. With her calls strong and confident, the entire array shifted, folding into itself as the spell format rearranged itself under the orca's natural guidance.

Like Essence seeking a purpose, the array was trying to figure itself out, lashing out where it was uncertain. Instead of bouncing against Tatum's chalkboard methodology, it instead found the guiding fin of a mom. Halcyon's heavy, repeated pulsing became louder as she sent pod calls across the rippling surface of the puzzle array. Artorian just crossed his arms, watching the display as the array slowed.

What was he looking at? A pattern? Was this a... creature, or a spell effect? He supposed he could try Invoking the pattern, and see what happened. Wouldn't that be incredibly dumb? Surely only a fool would try that.

He flicked his arm and did it anyway. "Oops?"

Halcyon glared over her shoulder as she heard a sucking

fwop of space collapsing together. Her Dreamer flashed a big, toothy smile. Keeping both his hands behind his back, hidden from view. After a long minute, there was no… visible change to their surroundings. His arms dropped, face squeezing into Tibbin's expression as, to his partial sadness, nothing further happened.

Under the orca's judging glare, the old man sauntered off. She had it all well in fin anyway, and he was just going to keep finding distractions. About an hour later, Artorian stood on the precipice of Tatum's boring little corner in Hel. The Incarnate's chosen home-base structure reminded him of a butcher's shop. Surely, just overseeing the place for a little while could not be that bad? Everything may be several ranks higher than him, but—

Honk.

What was that? That was a strange noise.

Artorian leaned forwards to peer around the bend, and saw a skeletal creature with a large bill peering back at him. Just the head poked out from behind the large spotted rock. As if to affirm he was real, it honked at him again.

"Must be one of Tatu—"

Honk Honk Honk!

"Oh sweet crackers and toast!" He remembered now! This was one of those goose monstrosities! Bolting for safety, Artorian glanced over his shoulder mid-stride to see the bill about to bite him in the butt! What? How was this thing so fast! This wasn't f—

Ow!

"Shoo, shoo! Get!"

CHAPTER SIX

Days later, Artorian was *so very happy* to be out of Hel. Abyss-blasted *death-honker*. His posterior hurt from all the bites! Rubbing it dejectedly while pouting with a thick and stuck out lower lip, he sighed while Halcyon shot him side-eye. He got what he deserved as far as she was concerned. She was happy to be spending time around her Dreamer, but he was as rambunctious as a fledgling. "No need to give me that scowl, Cy. I probably learned my lesson."

His grumbles didn't go unheard.

Yuki cleared her icy throat as she waited for their attention. Her graceful form stood on the rainbow path leading away from the teleportation platform, while the freshly arrived duo remained turned the wrong way. The path Cy and Artorian looked at led down the mountainside, to the realm of mortals. The administrative business was on the mountaintop. Still, it sounded like there was a *story* here. She'd get the details out of Cy when they had a moment. "What *lesson* might that be?"

The Administrator jumped and turned on a copper, hand swiftly pressed over his heart from the startle. "Crackers! What is it with people scaring poor old Artorian today? Did I not do enough of that earlier?"

Only after turning did he notice Yuki had a companion. The rocky critter sat stoic on her shoulder, tiny arms crossed. "Oh, Yuki, it appears you have a friend. Who's the strong lad?"

The lady of ice moved her hand at the mention, rubbing across the Rock Squirrel's head with a single digit. She seemed proud of him. "This is Hulk. We see eye to eye on how to handle people that try to live by the swagger, to be the bigger bragger. He makes them stagger, and I do so enjoy writing the tale."

Halcyon gently applauded the lovely rhyme, which visually made Yuki happy. Even if her expression didn't change one iota. The squirrel shot Artorian the stink eye, and the old man didn't want to step so much as a *toe* into that puddle of trouble. "Right. Well. I sent a heads up, but I don't see Odin around?"

Hulk turned his tiny head, glaring down below the cloud layer at the mention of the number-one ranked unpleasantry. Pulling a nut from a tiny, personalized satchel, Hulk tore a chunk from it, gnawing on the bite while his accusatory gaze deepened. Yuki moved her shoulder a fraction of a millimeter, and they shared a look.

Hulk nodded, unceremoniously shoved the food into his maw, and bounced off the bridge to fall towards the depths below. Off to go check if Odin was *actually* doing his work, instead of having a good time in a mortal mead hall somewhere.

Yuki smiled, in a good mood thanks to the squirrel. "He's no-nonsense. I adopted him shortly after discovering Odin's particular *history* with the species. The results are... noteworthy. Come. There is much to do and I no longer wish to see you *gawk*. You may be my Dreamer, but you are worlds away from good standing. Not you, Halcyon dear. You're a sweet snowdrop and I'm thrilled to see you."

The giantess turned pink in the face. Covering her eyes with her hands, she again turned away while making a high-pitched peep. Cy, please stop being so adorable. On second thought. You be as adorable as you want. Artorian managed to not say the thoughts out loud, but his wrinkles spoke volumes to betray his feelings. An icy atmosphere clamped around his ankles, and it spurred him into motion behind Yuki. "Yes, *yes*. Coming, *coming*!"

The trio passed several ostentatious structures on the way to the main drinking hall, and Artorian was surprised that Yuki was taking them there. He'd expected somewhere quieter.

At their approach, the massive Valkyries gave the visitors a respectful bow, their weapons raised to form an arch over the trio. The story of the Administrator was decently known, but they all visibly showed immense respect to the snow lady. Anyone who could keep an Odin-sized pest in line was deserving of the highest seat at the table. It was easier to die gloriously in battle than it was to accomplish *that* feat.

When the mead hall's horn sounded, the occupants loudly barked with pomp and furor. Whatever warrior had fallen in the realms below would be heralded as a champ... Oh, mountains above, it was the *Jotun*. A call rang out from the occupants inside. "Quick! Hide your mead, straighten your helmet. Wipe the stains off your shirt and stand in line at attention!"

A flabbergasted Artorian couldn't believe the sight of several dozen A-ranked powerhouses *scrambling*. Falling over each other to cease their quibbling and boasting just to stand at attention in a neat row. Their helmets were pressed to their chests as they stood, forming a clear path for Yuki.

Artorian looked at her with incredulity. "What did you *do* here?"

Yuki's response was flat. "It is *impolite* to boast, Dreamer. I did nothing worth mention."

Several of the mead hall's common flock paled at the *reminder*, a shade of panic crossing their half-drunken cheeks. The Administrator wondered if he'd accidentally unleashed some kind of end-boss on this poor, unsuspecting realm. Surely Yuki couldn't have frightened them *all*? Sure, she was a little cold around the edges, but this response was extreme. Were those A-rankers *shivering*? They were holding their tongues tight, and drunken mirth in check. Just what 'mention' was she on about, and why did he want to know so *terribly much*?

A collective sigh of relief rolled through the hall when they passed under an exiting archway, leaving the space behind. The occupants were out of sight, but the strength of their exhale made a gust of wind roll against their backs and shoulders. The merriment resumed shortly after, tankards refilled from massive vats.

Artorian addressed it. "I take it you're just not going to tell me why an entire realm is shivering in their panic boots at the sight of you."

Yuki didn't pause her stride. "Nothing harmful. They're… *expressive*. I merely wrote down some of their antics, and distributed it amongst the populace below. It is a surprisingly effective deterrent when a newcomer attends the hall, knowing stories of their most *humiliating and embarrassing* moments. If they want to be seen as mighty, proud warriors. *Well*. They better *act like it*."

Halcyon and Artorian shared a look. Yuki was one *scary* lady. "Right. Well… This was supposed to be a realm check-up, and I needed to talk to Odin about willingly being canted when the time came. Where are we headed?"

The snow lady pushed open a gate made entirely of heavy mercury bars. Artorian instantly recognized the open space as a cultivation hotspot. Frost and cold swirled here, as the location was positioned just right for the wind to chill this spot perpetually below freezing.

Yuki motioned to the small alcove of ice. "Here. I wanted… well. I say want, but the correct word is *needed*. I am entirely stuck on my cultivation progress, and don't know where to turn."

Artorian understood now why she'd pulled them away. "You didn't want anyone to know you needed a hand. Well, I can't say I didn't expect this. Cy, dear. You're likely not going to follow the next few hours of explanation, but you are by no means rebuked from the lessons I'm about to give. Even if they're not that useful for you."

"This… does give me an important opportunity to ask you a question, Yuki. If, say, I don't know. *The world were to end.* Would you want to call it a good life, and pass with old age? Or would you…?""

A cold finger pressed to his lips, shutting him up. Yuki's voice was usually fairly frosty, but currently it was arctic. "Stop. How heartless can you be? Cy is here."

The snow lady glanced at the giantess, but the visual response from Halcyon had her hesitantly pull the cold finger away. "Cy? Tell me this crass fool did not…"

Halcyon slowly shook her head. "Zelia told me, and already gave me the entire rundown in a private mental conversation. I know the details, as I'm sure you do as well. Given your snappy response to our Dreamer. I appreciate you wishing to protect me from painful information, but I already know. It's merely our Dreamer that doesn't have our answers."

Artorian felt confusion. Just how much gossip went on behind his back? From the sound of it, seamstress-levels worth. He didn't get a chance to ask, as his chosen cut in with a need to speak.

Halcyon placed her large hands on his shoulders. "There's a reason I asked to… *eat a lot.* On this trip. I need to grow stronger to endure, yes? Especially when I plan to stick around. I know I am not constantly sharp, like Yuki. Or have things as well in claw as Zelia does. Still, it is our decision to make. You keep your realm as such. The choice you give us is *rare*, compared to most of the other realms. They do not adhere to that idea. I have also been told that being a chosen instilled in us an innate sense of loyalty. I don't know if this loyalty is forced, or whether we gravitate to it naturally. I have had long, difficult talks with Yuki already. *I* believe it is natural…"

Yuki finished Halcyon's dwindling words. "While I believed it is *forced*. Though, the tethers have not attempted to latch onto me. They merely *wait* for my will. I had expected you to attempt to encroach, and demand greater control of me. You have not so far, and that gives credence to my own decision."

The snow whirled around the cold lady, stilling when she finally settled on her choice. "Like Cy, I choose that I will… stick around. As sleet you can't get off. Though our reasons differ vastly. I initially considered asking for a cultivation technique, in trade to stay. It isn't my… as the residents here would call it. *Style*. I do not barter. I do not trade. I do not beg. I do not bend. I make my choices, and listen to a memory I know is not mine. Yet it speaks loud, and I keep it close."

Artorian remained silent. It hadn't been right to speak, or interrupt. So he did not. In the temporary lull, he asked a question of his own. "What memory might that be, dear?"

Yuki cocked her head to the side, closing her eyes as it played in her mind. "The only choice worth making is the choice I will not regret."

When her eyes opened, light flickered behind her irises. "It speaks to me, as some of your memories speak strongly to the other chosen. I know I haven't been kind to you, Dreamer. I know I have been harsh, and especially *cold*. It took me months of doubt to even consider if I wanted to ask for your help or not. Because *if* I asked, it would mean that an important part of me had decided to actually trust you. My cultivation was my life, once. Though those memories are blurry, the feeling remains."

The Administrator took a moment to do what he was good at, and organized the information. "I understand. So before I had a chance to ask, Zelia slid in with the hard news. You've clearly had time to think and talk it over, and you've decided that even though it's going to be a rough journey, you'd rather stick it out, and see it through with me? Can I be honest and say I expected both of you to choose a gentle, normal end?"

Halcyon squeezed his shoulders. "And leave your fledgling self to haplessly flop around like a beached fish? Someone needs to keep an eye on you. You're no good on your own. You were your *best self* when surrounded by a great number of souls. Do you remember our original pod, in the beneath? I know you didn't speak whale, but the great majority of the pod adored you. I bet you don't even understand why. Just know they did."

Artorian felt touched. Both in the emotional sense, but also because to his surprise, Yuki's hand wasn't cold when it took his, taking over the conversation thread. "I choose to carry on, because a story should be told in full. Not awkwardly ended midway. I can't say I like you, because you have some personality traits that *truly* rub me the wrong way…"

Yuki hesitated, experiencing a strong recollection from a set of memories she kept reliving. "However… There was a moment, when a light pulsed from a mountaintop. There was a journey you went through? Know it or not, your chosen experience such travels as well. Or at least, *I* did when the memories welcomed me, and I welcomed them in turn."

She turned to face him fully, her hands atop one another. "I thought of you as a *heartless* thing of cold. A hapless Ancient that does as he pleases without regard for the rest of life. Yet, you wrote experiences and stories that you had carved on your heart. In those moments, I felt both your joy, and the *pain*. I understood why you don't want a civilization on Jotunheim, and why you try not to involve yourself deeply with those on the ground. Why you silently watch as you stand in the sky, and sit on your mountain. It *hurts*."

The old man felt his jaw clench. Oh… how *insightful* his chosen were. With their sympathetic access to some of his core values and memories. He managed a sad smile, and moved his hand so hers laid between. "I'm sorry, my dear. I know there is much that I… should have done. I couldn't, as you said, make the choices one will not regret. Sometimes, there are *no good choices*, and you are guaranteed to regret the outcome of whichever path you did not take. I'm afraid I don't have a response, aside from a gentle thank you. Thank you, both, for choosing to stick around with an old fool that's nothing but trouble."

His chosen hugged him.

Again, something he hadn't expected from Yuki. His arms quickly swung around her when she made an unexpected gasp of pain. Artorian hurriedly held her up as she accepted a previously denied sympathy, having received an answer to a question that had bothered her. She chose to commit. The sun sigil formed in platinum on the back of her hand, and her Mana strengthened several steps as she accepted her role as a chosen.

Now that he had her so close, Artorian could *see* her cultivation progress. It was *abysmal*. What was that awful triskelion spiral in her center? He hadn't seen a technique that weak since Maccreus Tarrean flaunted it during the Fringe days.

Artorian reflected on what he'd just thought. Oh, how far he'd come. He was *impressed* by it back then. When Yuki managed to steady herself, her irises shifted coloration, adopting a solid platinum hue as the connections stabilized. "You're alright, my dear. You're alright. Why don't we sit for a while? I think we can definitely do something about that cultivation technique of yours."

With Halcyon's steady help, Yuki elegantly sat on the ground in her private cultivation spot. It was too cold for the normal residents. Even if they could handle the chill, it was folly to *barge in*. Who knew, it might cause another awful tale. The snow lady nodded as she moved, and Artorian kept her palms firmly in hand. "That was a deep sign of trust you just slapped me with, Yuki. Do you mind if I reply with my own in turn?"

She slowly shook her head no. She didn't mind, though her building frown spoke volumes that she wanted an explanation first. A thought raced to her mind, and she verbalized it. "Don't... Don't be concerned with Odin. He will willingly be canted when the time comes. I will... *convince him*. Now, what are you doing? My hands, they feel warm?"

Artorian smiled, musing out his plan. "You have latent memories, I believe? Tell me, my dear, what do you know about *Echoing* a cultivation technique?"

CHAPTER SEVEN

Nearly a full year after Halcyon and Artorian had first stepped foot on Asgard, the Jotun trio appeared on a very tall pillar in what *used to be* the middle of the barren Muspelheim desert. That's how long it had taken for Artorian to work through the additional difficulties of Echoing. Copying over a technique from an A-ranked Mage to a B-ranked Mage, *without* it affecting that standing, turned out to be far more difficult than when he'd done it for Jiivra. His own control had needed *several months* of attention, and Yuki had never *once* held back on the snappy remarks and cutting cold to keep him focused.

Unlike a resplendent sun, Yuki's cultivation technique warped with the overbearing chill of an icy comet hurtling through space. Her very walk now carried an air of misty atmosphere, leaving behind a crystalline coma. Those frosty vapor trails that comets tended to have as they moved. The design of the cultivation technique wasn't any different, but the affinities at play changed the method of its function. When Yuki eventually had both it and her Mana under proper control again, her platinum sun would be *polar*, rather than warm.

Yuki had moved with grace before, but after practicing with

a gathering method worth her salt, she moved through the landscape as if she were a natural part of it. Unlike common cultivators that loved to laud their Presence, Yuki wasn't noticeable even if she was standing right in front of your nose. Her signature vanished below the ambient mess of existence. A Mage paying attention was more likely to see a blade of grass move than shift perception to her steps. Only mundane sight caught one's awareness, as the chill and the vapor trail were all that distinguished her from the surroundings.

She was left incredibly vulnerable from keeping her Auric flow in that configuration, but when Yuki could slide up next to someone without their notice, their panicked, fearful reactions usually made A-ranked Asgard Mages scramble away from her. She could be anywhere, and they'd never know. It kept the mead hall residents on their toes. Frightened, chilly toes.

Due to Yuki's temporary absence over many months of secluded Echoing—an event that couldn't be interrupted without great detriment to both parties—Halcyon picked up the snow lady's mantle. Cy's methods of overseeing were different from Yuki's, especially when she properly came into her own in this new realm. Where Yuki had everyone tiptoe, Halcyon was cause for joy and merriment!

Rather than chide the residents for actions, Halcyon instead smirked and taunted them. Saying 'they couldn't do it.' When some *inconvenient* task was mentioned, such as cleaning the mead hall, if they sputtered excuses, Halcyon off-handedly mentioned she'd tell Yuki later, since they 'clearly could not do something even a mortal could.' That lit fires in their hearts, and they made a boisterous show of getting to task. Unable to do something? Pah! A mead hall member of Asgard would *not* be known for such.

This happened frequently, as Halcyon quickly figured out just *how much* the mead hall boys *loved* to show off. She made events into little competitions. Setting arbitrary rules and strange rewards. Such as the honor to tap a new vat of ale, and have the first mug if 'victorious' over something. Her popularity among the Valkyries went equally unmatched, as her flight outpaced theirs in sheer aerial dexterity. That the winged women were larger than her also brought Cy sheer delight. She didn't need to hold back against those larger than her, like she was used to on Jotunheim.

Standing on the desert platform with her friend and Dreamer, a smiling Halcyon sported a full set of Valkyrie armor, customized to her 'smaller' form. She twirled an earned trident in her grip, still smirking as she stood behind Artorian to take in the sights. The environment had after all, drastically changed.

Artorian said nothing at first, just puzzling out what in Cal he was looking at. According to his last memory, he had plunked this pole-shaped teleportation pad in the middle of an empty desert. Not the *middle* of an abyss-blasted *city*. He pushed some tassels away from the tent structure that had been erected at the top of the cylinder. Just to be able to see better over the *sprawling mess* that was a thriving populace. How did a *desert* support this many people?

He squinted to inspect one, and saw cat ears twitch on a merchant's head. Fish? The lad was selling *fish*. In the *desert*? Artorian didn't speak, so his accompanying chosen kept quiet for the moment. Instead, they watched the goings on for a few minutes. Just to get a grasp on this different realm.

For starters, it was *hot* here. Oppressively so. If it wasn't for Yuki's passive aura emanations, this would have been a very unpleasant place to keep overwatch.

Artorian observed cat-people in various stages of humanization. One or two stood out that could go from Cat to full person, but keeping certain vestigial features. What else was there? Goblins, lizard people, anubites… C'towl-people? Was that a humanized *scorpion* over there? The city here was vast, sporting many open spaces. Were those little squares and patches of greenery sprinkled about for color? It was! Every building seemed to have hanging gardens. Self-sufficiency perhaps? Where was all the *water* coming from?

He nosed around with his sight until he found a well. It was quite the contraption. Was that some sort of rope-pulley system carrying buckets of water up all the way from the below? It must have been. The buckets were full of crystal-clear liquid, and it looked sparkling fresh. Some thick-muscled man with horns was turning a wheel to make it work, and a small line of more of them turned a second, perpendicular to the ground wheel to facilitate. Complicated, but it worked.

Yuki's chill brushed over his shoulder, and Artorian returned to task. "*Hmm?* Oh, yes, yes. I'll go and ask. This doesn't appear to be the correct platform. I was sure Surtur meant *this one* during the chat. Let me get a confirmation."

Artorian knocked on a mental space, and Surtur jumped. At least, he felt her do so. Even if she was nowhere near. Mental connections were funny. <Surty, are we in the wrong place? I took Yuki along like she wanted, but I appear to be in some busy city. I was expecting to find you waiting on us.>

Surtur didn't reply right away, and her thoughts were else-where. Artorian could tell she had her hands full with some-thing. Like she was handling a child before she could reply. <Dreamer. My apologies. Caliph is being… *Ack*. Not my face!>

Artorian smiled silently, and slapped his palm over his eyes. His chosen shot him a look, but counted it as progress. Even if it was silly progress since they could not overhear the conversa-tion. That was a Zelia trick. <Never mind, Surty, I found your geo-location. I'll come over the hard way.>

Exhaling with satisfaction, he offered a palm to each of his chosen. "There was a hold up. We will just go directly. I've got the location marked now."

When they took his palms, Artorian folded space, tele-porting them without the use of the beacon-system. When they appeared on significantly less populated sands next to a desert-trade caravan, Artorian let go of his chosen because he buckled over with weak laughter. The sight was just too much.

Surtur was on the ground, trying to coil around a *very unco-operative toddler* that was slipperier than a ball of grease. His hand was in her face, and he squeezed free from her coils without difficulty. Not wanting to be held or constrained in any way, that he needed to behave so they could get a move on was unimportant to the Djinn.

"Can you—*Ack*. Can you *please* take him?" Surtur was kicked in the face by a smoky, half-materialized leg. It was enough of a distraction for Halcyon to slide close and pick Caliph up under his arms when he was free. Rather than try to detain him, she just tossed him into the air. There, have some freedom. He made a sharp noise to signify that this too wasn't wanted. Cy caught him, and he clung to her chest with wide-eyed confusion, looking around with an expression that clearly stated he didn't understand what had just happened.

Artorian was still belly-down on the sands from laughter. Something Surtur didn't appreciate while a foot-shaped mist mark stuck to her face like a dirty sticker.

Tapping his claws on his upper arm, Karakum said nothing. He just sat at the head of the caravan with his arms and legs crossed, enjoying a solid smirk. Cy gently bobbed the toddler in her grip, and kept him close. The movements assuaged the child, and that small token placated Caliph. Surtur wiped her face off, visibly agitated as she got up. "That is not fair. Why does that work for *you*?"

Cy just looked the other way with a *hmph*. "Is it difficult? He's tired, but still has energy and doesn't know what to do with it. He didn't want to play, just get away. Look at his droopy little eyes now that he's being carried instead of held back. He'll be a snoozy little bundle soon."

Yuki stabbed their Dreamer in his thigh with an icicle, but didn't move one inch from her position to do so. Artorian just jumped up with a yowl, and rubbed his thigh while he got a hold of himself. He cleared his throat, but Karakum spoke before he could ask the question. "Get on the carts. Since we've picked you up, we can veer off and change direction to the Palace."

With some confusion, and a desire for questions, the Jotun group boarded the caravan. Only after did Artorian notice there was nothing drawing or pulling them. "How exactly do these stationary little carts *go anywhere*? Mana?"

Karakum winked snootily, and with a minor tug of the reins caused a massive millipede resting below the sands to spring into action. The sections were mounted on its back, and Artorian felt his further questions stifle at the sight of this giant, harmless insect carrying them over great distances with surprising speed. Was a millipede even an insect? He didn't know for sure, and distracted himself with a quick-fire question. Since his head remained poked out of the window to see if he could see the tail-end of the critter. "Dawn has a palace? Since when?"

The man-scorpion's mouth clicked in agitation. "She does not. There is a palace, and a place was made for her in it. Our Dreamer was invited, and the accommodations were *very nice*. I have never met a more *charismatic Goblin* in my life. I think he used to be an Elven bard in a previous life or something. That little pest is *sickeningly likable*, and dangerous with a lute."

Artorian held his further questions, watching the sands go by. Peering into the distance, he noted they approached some... he was going to call it an interlocking set of structures. Except that they moved. The thing appeared to be a massive sundial, where the main building continually shifted. Remaining under the most optimally available solar conditions. Interesting invention, now that they had a functional day and night cycle.

It also told the time, he supposed.

A small army was waiting for them. Thousands of Goblin soldiers lined up and formed so the incoming millipede caravan had a straight-shot walkway to alabaster stairs. Leading up to a structure that appeared to be coated entirely in tin. Strange choice, but who was he to consider something strange.

Taking in the sights of the army, he wondered why one was necessary. Surtur filled him in based on the questioning bend of his wrinkles. "Sand worms. They're a pain, but their bowels naturally cultivate very expensive and rich spices. The economy must flow, and thus, so must the spice. Bags of measured spice are Muspelheim's established currency method. The more refined, or stronger the blend, the more value it has. It changes colors depending on said quality, so it's easy to tell. We can either consume it to give our otherwise bland food some truly spectacular flavor, or it is, as I said, currency for goods and services."

Understanding nods made the rounds, and Artorian got out to help Halcyon and Yuki down from the caravan, even if they didn't really need it. As Yuki elegantly descended the steps, a well-dressed Goblin wearing a huge smile bolted madly down the parted line towards them. He was chased by several rowdy advisors and counselors. Some waved papers at him, yelling in the Goblinoid language.

Artorian again lamented the loss of the Bobs, and especially Translation Bob. He was going to have to learn all these languages the hard way, or find a memory stone somewhere.

After a very swift bow that turned into a spiraling skid, the pleased-as-punch Goblin spoke to Yuki directly. She raised an eyebrow and turned to her Dreamer, who shrugged his shoulders to convey he didn't know what was going on either.

Karakum was dying from laughter at the head of the caravan, and fell back into his cart. They figured some misunderstanding was at play, so Surtur planted her hand onto her face, and slithered over to translate. With a sigh, she explained the situation to the confused Jotun group. "Emperor P'dink says he is *delighted* to meet the Dreamer of another realm."

Halcyon pointed at Yuki with confusion. Their group frowned, trying to make heads or tails of this. Artorian bent away a little, speaking to Surtur behind Yuki's back. "Wait. He thinks *Yuki* is the Dreamer?"

The Lamia just slowly nodded to the positive, and Artorian flashed a toothy grin. He turned to Yuki, and winked. "Know what? Sure. Play with it. Have some fun."

The snow lady didn't physically respond, nor did her face move. But the lack of amusement was palpable. He couldn't be *serious*. No... No, this was *their Dreamer* they were talking about.

The playful fool was *serious*. A cold exhale of frost left her, and she extended a cold hand to the strange, pint-sized Goblin emperor who was being practically dragged away by his administrative staff. He screeched in joy at the quick shake, and yelled things back while being literally carried off above the heads of his staff.

There was paperwork to do!

The Goblin advisors slammed the palace doors on the way in, but aides quickly worked to get them back open. Those doors were open to receive the guests! Surtur's face remained buried in her hands. Karakum was still laughing, and the Jotun group didn't know what to make of the Goblin emperor. Artorian just spoke his mind. "This did not go as expected. This is going to be *so much fun*."

CHAPTER EIGHT

Emperor P'dink was not a Goblin that enjoyed work. He was a Goblin that enjoyed serenading with his lute in the middle of the night to proclaim his love for Yuki. Her responses were as chilly as expected. During a fancy dinner a few evenings later, Halcyon got into a row with the cooks since she ate her food faster than they could make it. Yuki had side-stepped the Emperor entirely without a second glance to his schmoozy advances.

P'dink was nearly eating his own crown after a week of the coldest shoulder he'd ever attempted to sweet talk. Goblin-crushed Dreamers! The rest of the chosen were in tears from continued laughter each time he tried another tactic, with *equally* dreadful results.

He was the great P'dink! Bringer of the smiling word. Everyone was elated in his presence, and good cheer surely followed. But this *one. Single. Impossible.* Frozen Dreamer just *wasn't thawing*. Was she immune to bluster? Why? Her old attendant had the worst of it, needing to excuse himself several times before breaking down with laughter around a corner somewhere. What was *so funny*?

Karakum quietly sipped spiced fruit juice from a flute, shooting side-eyes to the entire affair. Surtur had left to do 'actual work,' or so she'd said. The scorpion man knew she just didn't want to deal with this anymore, and wanted to wait until their Dreamer showed up.

Karakum thought *he* at least was holding up well! So long as nobody paid attention that this was his thirteenth fruit juice in the last hour. He did *not* have a strawberry problem! They were just the best fruit, that's *all* there was to it. If that Oni down on the trireme said *raspberry* was better *one more time…* He put the flute down and walked away, passing an old man heaving for breath, who leaned against Halcyon's side. Meanwhile Cy held a well-fed Caliph with the other arm. She had become the Djinn's designated nap spot.

When Dawn *vwumphed* into the palace center, she needed a moment to blink and take in the scene. Karakum was sitting down with some lizard folk, having decided to actually talk about his juice problem. The sugar was just so good! Surtur was nowhere to be found.

Dawn located her in the trireme, lying face down, depressed, in a bundle of pillows. Sunny was here, but he was in pain from laughing. Her sweet baby Caliph was doing well, nestled in the arms of one of Sunny's chosen. Then there was P'dink, nearly in tears and on his knees to try to make a very frosty lady do so much as *smile*. He was getting nowhere, and his advisory crew was trying their best to haul the embarrassment away. Her other chosen lingered across the continent, seeming to be doing actual tasks.

When Artorian staggered over, Dawn caught him by the shoulders as he tried his best to stop giggling and tell her what was going on. When she understood Yuki had been pretending to be the 'Dreamer' and P'dink was talking her up to try to gain good favor, Dawn couldn't help but smile. The chilly, silent smackdown to the otherwise charisma-oozing Goblin that always got his way was a delight.

Dawn purred out her response. "I arrived later than

expected. Not even a single trumpet? What discord have you sown."

Artorian knocked himself on the chest. "Ah… Yes. A little. I'm not fond of the way the Goblin is acting, but Yuki is just making the entire affair solid gold. Or glittering spice? Interesting economy in Muspy. Where'd you go? It's unlike you not to be punctual."

Dawn wrapped an arm around his shoulders, leaning. "Tatum came to get me for Cal. We've been talking it over and slating solutions onto the drawing boards."

The old man nodded. "I hope it's helping. Let me know if that horrible idea of mine needs an addendum."

The Fire Soul wobbled her head from left to right, not too keen on the topic. "Well… you *did* tell him he wasn't going to like it. I wouldn't like it if in that position, but it sounds… safe? I'd rather not get into that right away. First things first: I want my boy."

Artorian played confused, motioning to himself. "I'm already here."

She flicked the back of his ear, knowing he was joking, and stepped to take Caliph from Halcyon, who pleasantly handed him over with a big smile. Cy provided Dawn a rundown on events, Djinn behaviors, and his general health while in her care. The Muspelheim chosen had attempted to take Caliph away from Cy, of course. With results about as effective as Surtur trying to coil around him in the first place.

Caliph was half asleep when back in his mother's arms, but he conked out right away from the familiar comfort, snoozing with gentle little breaths. The gasp that erupted from P'dink captured their conglomerate attention. The Emperor had seen the Dreamer of the realm, and grasped his chest upon realizing she hadn't been welcomed. He, of course, tried to rush towards her and perform a litany of greetings, but his advisory crew again carried him off above their heads while Goblin compliments fell endlessly from his face.

He was *not* doing this again!

As P'dink forcibly left the premises, Yuki actually exhaled in relief. A frosty veneer covered the space her breath touched, letting it shine and glimmer a moment before evaporating into a fine mist. "He is exasperating. I thought *Odin* was bad. That prickly icicle is the worst parts of two Dreamers rolled into *one.*"

Dawn smirked, supremely amused. "He isssss, isn't he?"

Yuki elegantly held her hands before her waist sash, and respectfully bowed while addressing the source that spoke. Her eyes momentarily flickered to the tiny child in Dawn's arms, but she froze her heart, and said nothing of it. "Flame Dreamer."

Unfortunately for Yuki, Dawn was *far* too perceptive. Her ability to read a battle was natural, except that it was Yuki who was fighting with herself. When the snow lady rose, Dawn was already in front of her, the very Presence of the Fire Soul cancelling out the frosty space around the chosen.

Dawn's words were soft, whispered, and supportive. "Would you like to hold him?"

The statuesque expression on Yuki's face shattered. A moment of pain struck, too great to bear. Her jaw moved, but the words didn't make themselves heard. Dawn understood the message anyway. Yuki's expression said: "I don't... *I shouldn't.*"

Yuki's arms acted on their own when the Dreamer of fire slowly and gently moved. She eased her bundled Djinn into Yuki's arms, who held the boy with natural instinct. Yuki slid him into the proper carrying position without a single thought. Conflict roiled in her center as she held Caliph. Yuki didn't know if her heart was going to shatter, or if she would break down.

Her strained gaze turned to her Dreamer. Eyes full of pleading uncertainty. Artorian heard 'I'm not ready,' even though it was again said without words. His hands were on her shoulders a moment later, the reply one of truth, and support. "Life does not wait for people to be ready. It merely comes, and it is up to you to decide what to do when it does. What do you want to happen, my dear? Will you let the pain take you? You can. It's allowed. It's alright. We will be here for you if it does, whether you choose that path or not."

Caliph's eyes were open when a conflicted Yuki looked down. Their gazes met, and the Djinn knew her wishes before she ever did herself. His tiny hand rose, and curled miniscule digits around one of hers. Caliph squeezed, and the snow lady's frosty Aura shuddered away into a loose steam. That small gesture melted entire layers of deathly chill from the walls around her heart. Her tears froze against her cheeks, turning to tender fog after a few seconds. Yuki stood there helplessly, trapped in her own world as her emotions surged wildly.

No matter the internal chaos, there was a steadiness to her shoulders. Different hands held tight on either side, as two Dreamers felt the turbulence within her. She had lost her own child, and that pain haunted her. It froze her very soul, and the loss had become a cornerstone of her being. She hadn't wanted to hold Caliph. Her every thought shrieked that it would only remind her of the agony.

There was no pain.

Her hand felt warm from the grip on her digit, which was trying its best not to freeze the little sweetling or do harm. Yuki slowly realized it was never rejection she'd been afraid of. It was acceptance that threatened to melt her pillar. To change her from who she was, into someone else entirely.

She had sought escape, or a handhold. Yet found herself both in good hands, and surrounded by warming hearts. She swallowed, and fleshy skin tone seeped into her skin from where Caliph held her digits. The unbroken sleet sheen on her icy white-blue body gave way to pinks and reds that mixed and settled, making her indistinguishable from any other normal human being. Her mind was still catching up to decide, but by the time she could reasonably come to a decision, she found her heart had already made it for her.

She was simply late to the party.

Yuki frowned, and for the first time her face didn't shatter from doing so. Dawn smiled pleasantly at her. Her own Dreamer carried an expression of greater concern, but not one without support for her well-being. She again felt the squeeze, and looked down again to see Caliph had closed his eyes. The toddler had fallen asleep as warmth radiated from Yuki's being. Her words fell from her lips without thought. "I... I love him."

Dawn was proud as a peacock, nodding like it was the truest statement in the world. Artorian, on the other hand, felt punched in the gut. Releasing Yuki with a noisy *ooof*! as some of his cultivation got nicked. Sympathetic tethers formed to Yuki as she stopped rebuking several connective concepts.

Yuki bobbed Caliph, just a bit. She'd seen Cy do it, and the little one liked it. The sleepy complaint that left the toddler— along with a slight whining noise—made her melt from how adorable that was. "It... it doesn't hurt. I expected my heart to shatter, and my world to crack."

She looked at Dawn, clearly grasping at straws for why the expected response didn't trigger. "Why doesn't it hurt? My heart is warm, and I adore him so."

The Fire Soul jabbed her nose over at the old man, who was picking himself back up after pressing hands to his knees. He cleared his throat, rolling an arm to make the tingling vanish. "Love isn't a pie. There is not less simply because it was shared. The truth, my dear, is that I have *no idea* why you're not in pain. Why your heart didn't squeeze, or why your chest didn't clench."

He walked close, and laid his hand on the back of her shoulder blade once more. "In my eyes, I saw a sweet girl, who has never stopped being a very good mother. Do her *absolute best* to hold a little one, and treat it with the deepest of care. You seemed stuck in your own head, yet your Aura doesn't lie, my dear. You held Caliph in your arms, and your Auric signature ran full tilt away from what it was. No matter how uncomfortable, or how uncertain you may have felt."

He gently patted her. "A core part of you deemed that

Caliph's well-being was to be placed before yours. Your face and mind were conflicted, but not *your soul*, my dear. Your soul races ahead, and speaks your true feelings. Unfettered and unbiased, without strings or bad memories. You held a sweetling that needed you, and you would have given everything you had to keep it safe, and well cared for."

He softly motioned to her hand, still being held. "You fear for your heart, but your inner cold unfetters. Your frost abates. Your entire composition changed in front of our eyes for the sheer reason that what you are, and what you have subconsciously chosen to be, is a person that never wants to see a sweetling come to harm."

Artorian beamed at her. "Somewhere deep, you knew your icy veneer might hurt Caliph. So you *threw it away* in an instant. You knew the rampant cold field you carry might not be good for him. That too, you *threw away* in an instant. You knew that keeping your signature buried in the ambient would mean you were invisible, and he would not know you were there for him. So you *threw it away* in an instant. Can you see it, my dear? The colors and identity of your Aura? Do you see the single, shining, overbearing love it desperately radiates?"

Yuki's Dreamer squeezed her shoulder, and she was silently glad for it. "Whatever you are afraid of, my dear, you are *not* alone. No matter how painful you might think it could be, or the danger you think you'll find yourself in. You're not alone, and we will support the person you *want* to become. Loss is ever present, but one does not have to face that burden on their own. I am sorry for what happened to you. Yet, my dear, look at who you are holding. Then attempt to tell me, in earnest, that you do not care for his well-being."

Yuki frowned, bordering flat-out upset. "What are you talking about? *Of course I care.* I…"

Her words faltered, and both the Dreamers were proud of her. Artorian let go of her shoulder, no longer needed as support. "You realize, my dear, this is the first time you have ever told me that you cared about anything other than *stories*? How does it feel, then?"

Yuki swallowed, her footing unsteady without the added support. To her relief, Dawn remained firmly at her side. Not judging the chosen while she experienced a trying time. Dawn had been informed about Yuki's particular past, and thought this an excellent time to embody the world that did not wait. For she was fire, and would burn freely.

Yuki leaned into the Fire Soul, and they both smiled as Caliph yawned. "Good. It feels… good. Yet my strength wanes swiftly. Please, take him. I cannot steady my footing while my heart beats so loudly."

Dawn accepted, and eased the bundle back into her own arms. Caliph buried his face into her warm chest, and loudly snored a single time. Yuki's entire form sleeted over when she no longer held Caliph. Her skin tones vanished, returning back to the standard icy white-blue. However, when she turned to look at Caliph, her smile formed naturally, and didn't crack her face.

Artorian beamed, privately speaking to Dawn in a forum. <How nice it is to see her smile. Thank you, dearest. That was a dangerous little gamble you just pulled. I did not think it would go well, or that Yuki would bounce towards a positive aspect. That could have *easily* gone to Asgard.>

Dawn just mentally punched him in the shoulder, her reply not remotely as uncertain. <She is *strong*, Sunny. As was the case with me, something Yuki needed was a solid example that others except her Dreamer are willing to put *trust* in her. I heard she essentially rules Asgard with a frozen fist. Caliph is smarter than he lets on. He saw her conflict, and decided that he too, would be there for her. Clever little *brat*. He has a nose for good souls. You should have seen what he did for some of the wishes of those who didn't have good intentions. My little boy royally abyssed them over with a smile on his face. Like I said. Clever *brat*.>

Artorian sighed mentally, physically remaining supportive as

Yuki got her bearings. <We'll see how it goes. How's things in Muspy anyway? I'm here for another check up, but you're not exactly someone I need to ask concerning willing canting. If even necessary.>

Dawn made it easy on him, her tone supportive. <Muspy essentially runs itself. I don't have to be here, and neither do my chosen. My realm is all set and ready for Cal's cycling process so we can find optimal improvements and starting points. Tatum and I are going to let our realms do their own thing and just stick with Cal for a while. His realm is fairly dull, as I've heard.>

Dawn gave her bestie a warming mental squeeze. <When Cal successfully Incarnates—and yes, it *will* be a success—Hel is going to instantly become S-ranked as well, and all those creatures are going from A-ranked threats to S-ranked threats. Trust me, it's quiet now, but it's going to get... *Mmmm*. I don't think you've ever seen S-ranked creatures? They're... They're a lot to handle. You'll see. Anyway, I just came to pick up Caliph. He seems to like Cy; I'll remember that. Good luck in the next realm. Brianna is...>

Artorian didn't need her to finish that sentence. <*Being Brianna*. Yes, I have an awareness of it. The power completely went to her head. I expect it to be a slog, and at least a few fights. Don't suppose I could borrow a few of your chosen as backup? I'm taking this duo, but you heard the Niflheim rumors.>

Dawn mentally assented, and broke the connection. She walked to the Love Mage that had been strangely stationary a little too long, and softly punched him in the shoulder. "You'll do great, Sunny. Take Karakum and Surtur. Good luck."

They shared a hug, and said their temporary goodbyes. Artorian and the assembled four chosen were on the teleportation beacon an hour later. He was doing final checks when they all saw P'dink running up to them in haste. The chosen groaned, and Yuki closed her eyes sharply, her comments *scathing*. "I would rather deal with endless caverns filled with murderous Dark Elves than this one. *Single. Goblin.* Can we *please* go?"

By the time P'dink made it to the stairs, celestine light flashed. The group of five had winked out. The Emperor fell to his knees, lamenting loudly as one of his advisors finally saw fit to fill him in that Yuki was, in fact, *not* the Dreamer.

CHAPTER NINE

Arriving in Niflheim, the very air felt… wrong. Artorian didn't like this feeling, nor what he saw, his hands pressing to his hips right away. "This is *not* where I told the platform to go."

The well-armed Surtur, Karakum, Yuki, and Halcyon surrounded an arms-crossed, grumbly old man. Artorian complained loudly. "I set the port to go straight to the Palace. Why are we at the bottom of the entire continent? I can nearly see my house from here!"

Cy leaned over, looking off the edge of the beacon. Which existed at the bottom-most section of Niflheim. To be specific, this platform represented the lowest possible point on the continent. While they could see a continent below them, it wasn't easy to tell which one it actually was. "Can you actually?"

Artorian sighed, hanging his head to shake it in the negative. "No… No, I can't. I'm just venting because my teleportation access is blocked. This is the *only* pad I can reasonably get to without punching through a barrier that would cost me a frankly horrid amount of Mana. I mean… I *could*, but I wouldn't be in a great place after. Please tell me I don't have to make a continental climb manually."

A self-satisfied laugh broke out in the corner. Gomei removed his invisibility, tossing and catching a knife with the biggest grin plastered on his face. "That's exactly what you'll have to do, Administrator. The Queen *does not* bid you welcome, as we expect your next conversation to be one that is less than kind. Did we not treat you kindly when last you came? Yet as of late, some of our scouts have been going missing. Surely you wouldn't know anything about that, *right*, human?"

Artorian kneaded his temples, the chosen around him raising their weapons. Something that amused the General to no end. His knife vanished, and the cadre took the equivalent of a step back, their backs pressing to Artorian as they didn't know where the knife had gone. Karakum drew a sharp breath when it appeared next to his ear, the object trapped between the Administrator's fingers before it could cut a killing blow.

Artorian's words were terse. "I understand, *messenger*. Do tell Brianna I'll be back? It appears that even with some help, I've come poorly prepared."

Gomei flashed a toothy smile as a full contingent of occluded assassins all threw Mana-imbued daggers at the platform in response. They had been well-hidden. Well enough to fool the chosen.

Unfortunately for Gomei, Artorian had felt his Auric signature before. He'd known the Dark Elf was there when they ported in. When the Elf undid his Aura effect to *gloat* pridefully, Artorian had seen the rest of the Nobles as well. It was one of these hidden warriors that had thrown the real dagger, while Gomei had merely played with some textbook sleight of hand to make his own knife vanish.

The group of five on the platform winked out in a *vwop* of celestine light. Mana daggers chinked, stabbed, and peppered the beacon in enough sharp things that the platform could be mistaken as a person-sized cheese grater. Gomei clicked his tongue. His prey was gone, and *for now* they could not follow. "Next time, *brat*. Next time."

The Tibbins expression was plastered on Artorian's face

when the cadre arrived in Midgard, his expression flat with lips squeezed down to a thin line. The chosen were defensively positioned against nothing as the air of the fringe region struck them with pleasant freshness. They hadn't noticed before now that the Niflheim air had some… strange-scented effects to it. The clarity of the air here made the difference clear, and only now did the chosen realize that they felt *sluggish*. Karakum threw his envenomed rapier into the grass, stabbing the blade a foot deep. "They *poisoned* us with a misty gas? Those backstabbing two-copper spice sack thieves!"

The newly humanized scorpion was understandably agitated, and he stomped to a nearby tree just to claw at it. Surtur's flared hood made her own anger clear as day, but she just silently seethed while slithering from the platform. Sitting down in the grass on a coiled up pile of her own tail, Surtur wanted to wait for the debilitating effect to wear off so the world stopped feeling like it moved a third as slow.

Yuki remained entirely unaffected, and was holding a very much *not okay* Halcyon tight. Cy had taken very poorly to whatever the poison mixture of the gas had been. She seemed sick, dark purple color clouding her cheeks.

Artorian stepped from the platform and let his starlight Aura chug into activity. *Ugh*, his Mana was *slow*. Slower than normal. It reminded him of Oak's custom blend, except that it also affected Auric transfer speeds. How awful. He was glad they hadn't stayed for long. That was a death trap if ever he saw one. Still, he'd succeeded in a sly-worded ruse, and had to hope the detail would survive the years.

He flopped to his butt on the grass, sighing heavily at the incredibly quick failure. "Well, Niflheim is scrapped. I'll cover it after my century-long nap. I might be alright with some additional preparations, but my plan to take you four as backup is only going to lead to terrible ends. I didn't even notice the gas. I was too busy looking for their Aura signatures to see where the assassins were hiding. They snuck that poison right by me. I forget how devious those Niflheim Elves are."

Halcyon visibly began looking much better as the waves of starlight rolled across her being. The violet discoloration faded as her breathing eased. Artorian recalled he should probably tell them where they were. "We're on Midgard. I forgot until just now you can't automatically tell. I'm not sure you've been here before, but it's the lowest-pressure realm. I didn't really choose it so much as I just picked the closest one. Oh well, at least I suppose we know what continent was below Niflheim when we looked. Sadly, that won't remain constant."

The four chosen didn't respond to him, all agitated or considering other things. He sighed and thought over what to do next. This hadn't gone... *well*. Best fill people in. He knocked on a forum door. <Dawn. Less than stellar news. Nif rebuked us entirely. Complete death trap on arrival. That checkup isn't happening at my current power level. They'll floor me unless I cheat. I got our chosen out of there, I'll send them back shortly.>

Dawn's response was calm, like she expected this outcome. <*Hmmm?* Oh, let them return when they want. I expect the fire in their hearts is lit now, and they'll have a drive to improve. Surtur and Karakum have both been straying. I think this setback might prod them to start improving again. Do you have a place in Jotunheim for them to train? I expect they'll ask you shortly. I doubt they want to come home with that quick and complete defeat hanging from their shoulders. I'm needed elsewhere, Sunny, talk later?>

Artorian nodded through the mental connection. <Talk later, dear. I'll see to the current state of affairs.>

Ending the connection, the old man buried his face into his hands. He had not expected such a brutal, swift kick in the pants. They hadn't even gotten off the teleportation beacon. "Well. I feel like an embarrassment. I did terribly. I'm sorry for dragging you all into that. That wasn't how I expected it to go."

Done clawing up a tree, Karakum stomped to Artorian. With a nasty scowl, the scorpion controlled himself as he spoke. "Teach me."

The Administrator knew Dawn had just said it might happen, but hadn't actually believed her. "Pardon, my boy? I think I misheard you."

Karakum squeezed his hands together, trying his best not to waver and lose the humanization form. His tail was already back, and he didn't want any more of his pride chafed today. "I spoke true. Teach me. You caught the knife I did not see. I don't even know how it got so close to my head without being noticeable. It vexes me. I have strength, but am lacking in other areas."

Artorian extended a hand for help getting up, and Karakum got the old man to his feet. The old academic fell right into a lecturing step. "I'm not surprised. You would have had to know what to look for. It's called an S.E.P. field. Short for 'someone else's problem.' Nasty effect. Why am I not surprised *they* figured it out? The field obscures anything you're not *directly* looking for, and even then, the object or person of your search feels elsewhere. That particular Mana signature was coated around the knife that got thrown at you. I've felt it before, so I knew what to look for. Which is the only thing that allowed for a save back there. Otherwise I would be applying some serious healing to your head right now. That was no fault of yours, my boy."

Karakum didn't take the deflection. "You succeeded where I failed, and this sounds like a skill. Not some unattainable ability."

Artorian could not deny that fact, but he hadn't exactly the time for such things at the moment. There was work to do! Work that... was important... in some way. What was he supposed to be doing again? He couldn't recall his exact tasks. The thoughts had left him, and his checklist was hazy. Being attacked had severely distracted him from the goal, and he needed a moment.

When he looked up from his deep frown, the four chosen surrounded him. Giving him the same expectant look. He looked from one to the other, but the four chosen all had the distinct impression that they were not happy, not knowing how to deal with what just happened. That encounter would have killed them all, and there was nothing they could have done about it. They hated it, with a passion. "All four of you?"

Artorian sighed again when their silent expressions replied loud and unified. "Well… I sort of brought this on myself, I think. I doubt Jotunheim needs a further check, Alfheim and Svartalfheim are going to be the expected mess. Midgard… well, Midgard has four supervisors and I expected to be here for a small decade. I have broken items to un-puzzle, but… aside from that, I now *cannot* remember what I was supposed to do."

Surtur snapped to the point. "So you have time to teach, then."

The old man looked like he wanted to deflect, but Halcyon squeezed him by the shoulder. He regarded her when she spoke. "Are you okay with letting people you care about be vulnerable to something you know can kill them, that they are *very likely* to have to deal with again in the future?"

"No. I. Am. *Not.*" His jaw clenched, and Artorian put his foot down. That decided it, and he pushed his sleeves up, looking around as he changed mindsets. "Cy. You're right. Though… Not here. We'll make no progress here. I always wanted to add the academy to the Beneath in Jotunheim. I may as well defer previous plans, put it up, and teach for a year before entering the long slumber. Brianna can… be a pain. I will see what's come of things, after the rest. If Nif remains active for a century, I will likely be severely outmatched when I go to… *administrate*. I'll have to put some schemes together."

Artorian turned with a flourish of his Asgard robe, and marched back to the teleportation beacon. He extended his hands, expression turning stern. He'd decided on a course of action. Knocking on a forum connection, Zelia answered with some confusion. Why hadn't he used the *direct* connection? <My Dreamer? This is unprecedented. Are you well?>

Artorian chose not to waste time. <Zelia. Clear my schedule. I am returning to Jotun with familiar faces, and I'm estab-

lishing a training space in our Beneath. Something came up. I'm sure Cy and Yuki will be more than happy to vent to you, and rope you into the reason for why we're all *miffed*.>

Zelia's response remained professional, but there was a hurry to her thoughts. An urgency and directness pressed forth as her Dreamer spoke, and she had learned that while there were many times where he was being a playful fool. *This*? Was not one of them. <Understood, Dreamer. I shall learn of events, and we shall make preparations. Come home.>

CHAPTER TEN

Zelia burned with silent rage when word of 'teleportation blockers' came to light. Those cavern-loving knife-ears had *lied* to her, and used her grievance-limiting tools for personal gain. After being fully filled in, she offhandedly mentioned she would go off and collect some things for the group to use. Unbeknownst to them all, she folded herself to Niflheim.

She was *anything* but happy.

Gomei was delighted to see their insider informant and secret ally appear on the beacon platform. "*Zelia.* Favorite of our Queen. My heart leaps at your Presence, and deeply welcomes you to the realm of death and mist. How did your Dreamer enjoy our greetings? We have running bets on just how far his tail has dipped between the legs."

Zelia's face was flat, and her human veneer broke as six arachnid eyes opened up. Her bestial form bled through regardless of her sizable self-control. "I do not enjoy being lied to, *knife boy.*"

Gomei laughed, and twirled the knives in question. Several dozen danced like coins between his fingers, the sharp weapons swirling around his arms. "Oh, *which ones*? I have such a *collec-*

tion. Do we speak of one of my favorites? Or perhaps the tools of my trade? Or just the ones I keep for the aesthetics?"

The Arachnae pulsed her Aura, and the surrounding air gained a sticky quality, webbing all movement in her immediate vicinity. The knives stopped twirling around Gomei's arms. In a fake and demeaning tone, the Moon Elf spoke dejectedly. "Aww."

The alteration revealed that it was merely four daggers which had been moving, while the rest had been illusions. "Come now, Favorite of the Queen. We are *assassins.* Surely you did not expect we would have a concept such as honor? At least, not one that applies *outside* of our race."

Zelia squinted her livid silvered eyes at him, but her seething rage formed into a thin-lipped smile. "I understand. In that case... you won't mind if I *collect* some of my things that I've *carelessly* left lying about."

Gomei's amusement dropped when Zelia just vanished from the place she was standing. He had no understanding of tele-portation, save for that it was something that existed. He defi-nitely lacked the nuances of control that came with it. That Zelia's method of moving through slipspace was one of the most optimal methods it could be was equally something that eluded the assassin. What did not elude him was that the favored lady had just poofed in a manner that would make any professed assassin grievously jealous. "Abyss. Raise the alarm! We have an intruder!"

Mushrooms all over Niflheim released a scent that signified danger, trouble, and caution. The occupants of the whole realm knew something was amiss, even if they did not know exactly what. Replies ran through the discordant communications network as something was disrupting their—Alright, what *wasn't* suddenly going wrong? It was like they were dealing with a threat that could be anywhere it wanted to be, at any time. While said threat had a deep working knowledge of where they kept important... Abyss!

Rampant reports struck the chamber of judges as hand-delivered missives were brought in and shouted one after the other. So dire had the situation become in but a matter of moments. "The vaults are breached! All our blueprints and designs for arrays and teleportation blockers are gone! The vault wasn't even cracked open, the contents are just *gone*."

Another messenger tumbled in, staggering as he fell over the still-speaking man before him. "The Phosgen have gone wild! Our control rods have vanished! They are rampaging and taking over entire sections of Niflheim as their own, claiming local fauna as theirs and establishing territory! We are experiencing a full-cascade shutdown of regional controls!"

A third courier of lower status fell over the first two, but that didn't stop her from delivering the message. "My Judg—*Hurk*! My Judges! The mushroom mimics are free! Some caverns are infected by puffballs, and we've got rogue mycelium spores going rampant. It's being distributed all over the continent; we do not know how."

A fourth courier looked frightened as could be, and equally fell over the existing courier pile. Though, his message was a little different. "*Cheese! Dire cheese*! It's everywhere, it's seeking revenge and eating us! Our healing cheese *hungers*!"

The Judges in the room worked to pull the messengers off one another; this was not acceptable behavior for what should be a well-oiled and neatly tailored organization. The Niflheim Elves got to the matters at hand as swiftly as they could. Unfortunately for them, problems just kept pouring in as a single, very pissed spider withdrew all her parts of joint projects, stealing away all their prized progress.

As far as Zelia was concerned, if they were going to abuse it, then they could not have it. She was going to reverse engineer all their work, find the weaknesses in all the Niflheim defenses, and then just hand the results over to her Dreamer. In the meanwhile, on top of all the other regional problems the Dark Elves had to deal with, Zelia decided it was time for an *invasion*.

Brianna teleported mistily into the relevant chamber,

speaking before Zelia had a chance to slipspace out. "Zelia! What is the meaning of this! You were *favored*! How *dare* you betray me like this?"

The arachnid clicked, mightily annoyed. "I betrayed *you*? No, knife ear. Inspect *well* the betrayals of your Judges! For they have orchestrated this rebellion within your ranks, that I have fallen victim to. Your reputation with me has withered entirely as a result."

A silvered spark flashed in Zelia's gaze, and a devious thought struck after she made up false information purely to sow discord. "Though, I know how fond you always were of my children. You always lamented never having any in your realm, if I recall? Know what, realm Queen? I have been a scrooge. You want my children? Worry not your perfect pretty face. They *will* come. They will come in *waves*."

Brianna tried to get another word in, but it was too late. With all the reclaimed goods in tow, Zelia vanished as the teleportation beacon she stood on powered down and *died*. The rest of the beacons on Niflheim followed suit, leaving behind a nearly impossible to control realm that rapidly divided. Internally collapsing in response to being locked off from leadership as a whole.

Several Judges and Dukes had to take matters into their own hands as brutally powerful Phosgen blocked vital paths, trade routes, and more. Fracturing Brianna's seamless, unified kingdom into a conglomerate of smaller rulerships that swiftly sprung into place for sheer survival.

Over the coming months, progress would have been made if it was *merely* the man-eating cheese, deadly fungi, or surprisingly intelligent monarchy-creating Phosgen the Niflheim Elves had to contend with. Access to proper food, fresh water, and other necessary goods that even Mages needed was a tough acquisition with the beacon system down, leaving only the natural twisting paths inside Niflheim for the shattered people to seek a safe haven.

Given the sheer scale and size of the continent, that was

more problematic than initially assumed. Yet none of it, *none of it* would have been so difficult if it wasn't for the sudden appearance of *grievously* angered waves of teleporting spiders. Each child of Zelia's carried her hatred. Her burning need and desire for vengeance and retribution against the assault and insult carried out upon her Dreamer went mirrored by her war host.

Brianna remembered swiftly that chosen were fiercely loyal, and while her own worked to protect her, there was something ominous about knowing that an enemy could teleport directly onto your face at any given moment. Doubly unfortunate was just how *many* children Zelia had. They weren't optimized for combat in caverns and caves, but they were right at home if left alive for too long.

With the arachnid's methods geared towards dispatching Jotunheim threats, the Dark Elves had entirely unexpected issues to contend with. The attack patterns of Zelia's children were just not listed in the assassin's playbook, as they were pushed back into small communities over the course of a decade. Losing far more ground than they gained as they were forced to establish themselves in areas the Niflheim Elves could survive and actually defend.

This left the great majority of Niflheim free for monsters to roam, and rule. Woe to your being, and may the Queen help if you encountered a random block of *cheese*. The design of the place having lent itself to be as one single, massive, endless dungeon now worked against the residents' favor, as the Elves could no longer control the intricate network that prevented layers and layers of traps from being set off at their passing.

A particularly nasty pink Phosgen occupied that control room; to the pained chagrin of the entire race. It was a bloody insane one to boot. That Phosgen gained control over the whole system in less than a few months, expanding its personal realm control from that one space. It even made a friend in the form of a deviously smart Shroomish who called itself Sett. The special thing about Sett was that it knew everything there was to know about fungi and bacteria. Having been a Fungus Mage in a prior life, Sett was not particularly well-disposed towards leg-walkers. The knife-ears fearfully referred to them as 'Plinky and the Brain.'

Together, they made the dungeon their playground, excelling at playing the role of evil overlords as they took over the world. The misty realm of Niflheim entered a new dark age. A dark age of spores, assimilator tentacles, and *cheese*.

Immediately after Zelia had left Brianna in the cold, she stowed her goodies in her personal room on the pagoda. After safely nestling it all away, she popped down to the Beneath, where her Dreamer was having some difficulties. The Jotun-heim Beneath held a vast, bright, underground lake. Now with reflective moss steadily growing on the walls and ceiling. The moss mirrored the clear blue color of the water, causing rather beautiful lines of light to bounce up and down between them as the refractions formed.

Zelia approached the hovering hard-light platform where four chosen with attitude waited impatiently, watching the Dreamer kick at the water below as he stood upon its surface. Something clearly wasn't working as intended. Zelia calmly queried her chosen sister when close enough, doing her best not to betray the deep anger she still felt from mere moments ago. "What's the problem?"

Halcyon sighed, her golden hue regaining some luminance. "From what we can hear from up here, something about it being 'too expensive' and how he 'doesn't have enough Mana or points' for some kind of 'purchase.' Whoever he is arguing with isn't giving him an inch of leeway, and it's making our Dreamer very frustrated. My nose says it's the great spirit."

Zelia pressed her claws to her face, which gave away to her friend that she'd gone through something turbulent recently. Otherwise that would have been a seamless hand. Halcyon gently leaned her shoulder against the arachnid, opening a private mental conversation. <Are you hurt?>

The spider physically clenched her claws, doing her best to respond with gentleness. <A little. I went to get payback, and

the very air in Nif did a number on me. It's painfully difficult for me to move. *At all.* Like my joints are filled with spikes and glue. I have to rest soon, and purge this out of me over time. I have something I can do while lying down, but the damage I took is going to completely take me out of the events that our Dreamer is planning. What are they, anyway?>

Halcyon pulled Zelia close, her arm sliding under both of Zelia's as the orca mom picked her up, princess-carrying her for the moment. Zelia didn't say a word of complaint, as with her still-impeccable kimono on, she looked like a little royal when carried. It made her smile, just a touch.

Artorian yelled something up at them, but the Jotun duo needed it repeated to understand since they'd been distracted. Cy turned her head and queried. "What did he say?"

Yuki turned and reiterated the message while thinking over a possible answer. Karakum and Surtur were stumped. They just didn't have the regional knowledge. "He asked, 'Where are the largest mountain-sized wind chimes?' We will be training on top of those instead."

Zelia smiled, and winked back in response. Her lay of the land knowledge was both immense and impeccable. Playing the secretary was definitely a role she could fulfill. "Oh, I know *just* the ones."

CHAPTER ELEVEN

In the Jotunheim cold, where colossal wind-chimes formed a line between the mountains, Artorian *thunked* the tips of his toes against metal. They rang against the newly added surface of a now not-remotely-as-loud wind chime. Shame to tune them down like that, but what good was a cylinder with an open hole at the top when it came to a place to stand on?

He peered over to the next one, and saw that Surtur and Karakum had just turned their wind chime cylinder sideways, having attached the other end to a pole equally as high as the one their chime was originally chained to. It made for a nice platform that gently swung in the breeze.

Artorian slapped his forehead, and closed the administrative menu that let him change objects. Their method was smarter, and far less costly. They'd nicked the chain from another chime to do it, and that chime was being pried apart to form a flattened platform by Cy and Yuki.

"Know what? I'll just leave it." He clearly didn't know best here, to the great pleasure of the four chosen. They were all smirking when just out of sight. The quick win over a Dreamer meant something to them, and that good cheer was a necessity.

Artorian hopped off the rim and onto the side of the large support pole, latching onto it with a hand as he slowly slid down to the next chime down. He found his foot made an excellent speedbreak during the downward slide.

Descending to get a second look at the contraption Cy and Yuki were putting together, he scratched his head at what they were doing. They'd made their platform, and were now folding the edges in beneath it. Creating a cavity under that flattened floor as they installed the dome in the mountainside. He didn't follow why they were doing this until Cy began to draw. Ah! It was a combat ring! "I really should have seen that coming."

Now that he thought about it… why was he slipping up so often lately? That was unnatural. Artorian rubbed at his eyes, and felt tired. Not physically tired, but like he needed a severe, extended nap.

Was he feeling the effects of being awake too long already? Surely not. It hadn't been that long. Granted, he had entirely lost count. His current tally was likely counted in years. A handful of those caused a transfer interruption that was this noticeable? He felt terrible for Minya. The awful *abyss* she must have gone through.

Considering this taxing malady helped him better understand the breakdown of Bob. If this disconnect was noticeable at a handful of years, then the mental discordancy must have become truly unbearable as the eons dragged on.

Artorian mentally tallied his remaining time. A few more months to a year. That's what he had before his nap. He needed to snap out of it. "No more reminiscing, old boy. Pay attention to the now."

Since the chosen were doing so much better than him at arena-crafting, he checked in to the senate to attend to other matters for a moment. Artorian knocked on Chandra's forum door, and it swung open in a hurry. <Administrator! I'm glad you had a moment. I have a few needs before canting. Could I come over?>

The old man smiled at the fresh breath of positivity in her

voice. Whatever Chandra's needs were, they would come with some kind of good news based on the tune alone. His reply was thus fruitfully chipper. <Of course, my dear. Would it be alright to request something to snack on? I have a hungry chosen that has been hoping to taste your cooked crafts, ever since I foolishly gushed that nothing in the world has ever been better.>

Chandra laughed pridefully, her amusement rising with her good mood and pleasant cheer. <I will put something together; I see a beacon just linked itself to the one in my personal grove. I take it that's your doing?>

Artorian *mhm'd* mentally. <We're setting up a training area, if you want to brush up on a topic. My chosen are going to be rolling through lessons for at minimum a few months.>

Chandra's responses slowed at his mention, turning pensive. <*Could*… could I just attend those myself? In fact, I think all the supervisors here would be very happy with a reprieve. Things are tense on Midgard right now.>

That was a surprising tidbit of news, but the academic saw no reason not to increase pleasant company. <I don't see why not! Let me transfer the topic to the senate and bring it up. Might as well invite everyone willing at the same time. I expect a few… less than positive responses.>

Chandra laughed out loud, but the words sounded as if spoken through the hollow of a tree. She caught herself and stuck to human vocal chords. <Yes, my plants have been sending me steady updates from the sheer abyss your chosen caused on Niflheim. Though in my opinion Brianna had it coming, and I am grinning from ear to ear that this will knock her down a peg. I will pack and be over, my apologies if I don't respond in the senate.>

The private connection closed, since Artorian had no further response.

He felt bewilderment. What did Chandra mean with 'your chosen wiped the floor with Brianna?' He had gotten *trounced*, with *four* chosen as backup. How had Zelia, *by herself*, raised the abyss in Niflheim? Who else could it have been? The card pile was empty and there were no draws left to make. It *had* to have been Zelia. He'd bring it up if he had an opportunity.

"First things first." He cleared his throat, and winked his celestine mote into the senate.

To his surprise, Tatum, Dawn, and Cal were present and conversing. Strange. He hadn't heard them? Actually, even though he was in the shared space and could feel and see their motes blink as if they were speaking, he was completely unable to overhear them at all. Was this something new? He shrugged it off, and spoke to the senate as normal. <Are the Midgard people around? Or anyone, really. I'm having a little training get-together on Jotun, and am making it open invitation to supervisors and their chosen.>

Brianna's mote, to Artorian's continued surprise, misted in for just a moment. She yelled at him before winking out. "Abyss *eat* you!"

The celestine mote quietly bobbed as the senate populated with the other motes, who had overheard that particular angry snap. Cal, Dawn, and Tatum turned to see the commotion, but chose to wink out and go elsewhere as they were dealing with Incarnate-only problems. Henry wobbled close, and well-meaningly bumped into the celestine orb. <*Hey.* You alright there? That sounded very personal, and just a little… *mad.*>

Marie's mote drop-kicked Henry out of the way with a **smash** from above. The human King's orb went bouncing around the senate space, and Marie's mote pressed her coruscating glory against that of the celestine. Like she was pressing her face against Artorian's without any regard for personal space. <*Explain.* We don't hear from you for far too long, and then suddenly, *that.*>

Artorian did the equivalent of shooting his arms up into the air. <I'm innocent, I swear!>

The glare didn't abate, but Marie did return his personal space as she backed off an inch to catch a mid-flight Henry when his bounces whizzed him by. The poor lad was very out of sorts once caught, dizzy and wobbling with unnatural sway. <Was… that… I didn't deserve that.>

Marie pulled him in by the lapels. <You *absolutely* deserved that for showing up *late* to our date yesterday.>

Henry tried to weakly deflect. <You said it was fine! We had a lovely time rowing a boat across the lake.>

She glared holes into his mote. <You think that made me forget? You need to be on time. You know how horrendous it is to sneak out of one's own kingdom. Don't make a lady wait, Henry. If you say sundown… you be there at *sundown*, and not after.>

Henry copied Artorian's pose, mental arms shooting into the air so it appeared they were both surrendering to a bandit's hold-up. Artorian gently leaned his mote to the side. If whispering existed here, he would have done it. <Don't anger the missus, my boy. Soon you'll be chased with pans and rolling pins.>

Marie pulsed hot red. <I can hear you!>

Artorian's mote ran away to the other side of the senate, and Marie's burning glow chased him all about the three-dimensional space while he quickly rambled through the message he wanted to deliver. <I'm holding training sessions on Jotun, for chosen and supervisors that want to take a bit to practice their skills without the use of Cal's system. Improving the old way before we all have to take a long nap. Relevant beacons have been *li~i~i~inked*—oh, *sweet Cal,* that was too close for comfort.>

Marie had shaped her mote so it carried a toothpick-sized sword, and she'd swung it at the Administrator's rear. Scraping him *ever so barely*. It was enough for him to feel the threat of the sharp stabby thing was very much *real*, and he winked out of the senate before she had a chance to skewer him. He didn't care if she was just venting, or joking. Not taking that risk! "Good luck Henry!"

Fuff!

Artorian opened his eyes, body still standing on the rim of

the oversized wind chime. He drew a deep, chilly breath from the crisp mountain air. Then coughed it out when a very angry 'Artoriaa~a~a~n!' rang through the mountains in a distinctively Marie tone from the direction of his teleportation beacon. Oh *come on*! He couldn't have possibly made her that mad from such a tiny comment. "Uh… girls? I think I need to… go. Back in a pop."

The old man vanished, and Karakum threw his hands up in defiance. "Girls? Do I look like a lady? Get back here, you codger! I am first on the training block. I am going to skewer you with my rapier until… *ow!*"

Yuki *splatched* the back of Karakum's head with a frozen ball. Half made of sleet, and half of snow. She tossed a second one into the air just to catch it, her expression cold and pointed. "Pincers off our Dreamer."

Karakum turned, shooting her a venomous look as he drew his rapier, zipping it through the air in a cutting form to sign the letter 'K'. Then he pointed the tip straight at the snow lady. "En garde! You molten icicle!"

Another sleet ball *splatched* him in the face. He steamed hot, wildly slashing his sword up in the air. Turned out he couldn't fly, thus becoming subject to endless pelting from the unamused snow lady who could. Enraged, he took to cutting the projectiles, but then developed a clever idea. Striking with the side of the blade, he coated the projectile in venomous fire Mana and batted it right back at her. "*Ha!*"

Cy and Surtur watched them go at it as streaks of light cut through the sky. They didn't know why their Dreamer was being chased by another, *angrier Dreamer*. Though it didn't seem like he was fighting back as the attacks of scintillating **Glory** kept streaking towards him. So they didn't respond to it. Instead, they just had a chat as Cy verbalized a thought. "Technically, this… counts? As *practice*, I mean."

Surtur sighed, and had to agree. "It does. Karakum couldn't do that projectile returning trick before today. I suppose we should just… join the combative festivities? I was expecting a classroom setting. Not a super smash *melee* free-for-all."

Halcyon shrugged, pulling her trident from her back to give it a twirl. "I mean, I would not mind learning how to use this thing better. The Valkyries have a very strict, single style in which they use it. Which honestly doesn't work for me since I don't have arms in my Orca form, and dive bombs are... *eh*."

Surtur pulled her own spear free, the tip ever-burning. "I know a thing or two. Want to just spar for a bit and share pointers? I haven't fought anything that counted as an actual threat in so long that I'm not certain if I am any good with stabby here. All the enemies I used to fight are now allies."

They shared a grin, and joined the festivities as their weapons struck one another. Sparks flew as Surtur's fire met the trident's inherent electricity. Such was the scene that Chandra walked into when she appeared on the beacon. Several chosen from the other realms were all aimlessly standing around, completely uncertain of what to do while watching the free-for-all.

Henry was chasing Marie. Marie was chasing the Administrator. Aiden just gawked, but turned and walked back to the beacon, winking out. "Forget it. I'm not doing this."

Chandra blinked, and nearly dropped her cake when Odin appeared in the beacon space behind her. "What is the commotion ab—*A fight*! Oh great mountains above! Now that is my kind of get-together! Come, my chosen! Haul the mead and open the casks! Revelry awaits us today. To battle! *To battle!*"

The Asgardian war cries made the cringing nature Mage close her eyes, inhale deep, and belt out a truly inhuman sound that forced the entire gathering to cover their ears. "You will all come and share this meal, and you can play as children after you have eaten. Provide me a table *this instant*! Or I will make *the mountain* get up to detain you."

Odin stumbled mid-air, tripped over nothing, and pouted. His hands motioning to the fight. "Awww... but... *Fun!*"

Yuki cleared her throat at him, and when he noticed who it

was from at a glance, he flew full tilt back down to prepare the feast table. "At least make that abyss-blasted rock squirrel *not be here!*"

Laughter and good cheer broke the awkward pause. With Chandra's motherly outburst to pull them all back down to reality, the impromptu get-together turned into a feast! One of *Pleasure House*-quality food, and the best of Asgardian mead.

Halcyon shed tears when she ate, actively weeping through consuming entire mouthfuls of the scrumptious, edible works of art. Chandra considered it a great honor, keeping their plates burdened and full. Only after the feast, that accidentally lasted a week, did the true classes begin. They couldn't help it. Chandra's cooking was *magic*.

CHAPTER TWELVE

When festivities came to a close, a full month of active cultivation needed to happen just so they would have some reserves to work with, proving that they were all horribly behind. They managed this while they all meditated in a mini ley line array. Something Odin designed to keep fresh energy flooding their direction, and didn't at all steal from Cal's records. Or so he claimed.

While those who needed to gather Mana worked, those who didn't operated in the background. Zelia, as example, decided a brand-new clothing line for the whole gathering was now a necessity. Which, at the end of the month, she was proud to have ready.

"There. Matching outfits for everyone." Zelia clapped her hands together, wiping them off on a cloth rag. Or what counted for one in the spider's line up of exquisite crafts. Even that supposed rag was fit to be a queen's handkerchief.

Odin made a sour face as he pulled at the yellow ginkgo-leaf attire. "Do we *have to*?"

His prime Valkyrie glared at him, so he conceded swiftly as

his chosen quipped in an adopted icy tone. "Look at that, growth!"

Valhalla, the Valkyrie chosen, was a kind soul. She didn't match the fury of her sisters, but in recompense possessed a truly uncanny ability to adapt and learn. Yuki had provided Valhalla many great lessons which had bolstered and influenced her early growth. Following her first teacher's example, she fluttered her wings, and made Odin get back to concentrating.

Together, the large group brushed up on a plethora of cultivation needs. Though not without a new set of difficulties that needed to be addressed.

Passive cultivation didn't work so well in Cal's Soul Space. Even with tweaking, it was the space itself that drew Essence and Mana out of *them*. The Mana bodies Cal had cobbled together for supervisors were decently efficient, but not without loss. Only Odin, who had an elemental air channel, Artorian, who had been a dirty cheater, and their S-rankers who were not in attendance had Mana stores that could be measured in a state other than 'laughable.'

Their cultivation situation didn't look stellar.

The reliance on Cal's forms was making them oblivious to the self-control necessary to uphold their own, original forms. Had these been their own Mana bodies, some of them would have suffered burnout just from being here.

Cal had given them a boon and a malus all in one. Due to the inherent rigidity of these forms, the gathered supervisors couldn't try to control them better. They didn't even know where to start where their physical beings were concerned. With the entire matter out of their hands, all they could do was work on techniques, or Aura control.

As an A-ranker, Chandra had it the best of them. Yet lecture without being able to put progress into practice was only getting them so far. Artorian quickly learned that this rowdy bunch was not the theorizing sort. How he forgot that being academically inclined was the... uncommon, path. Better to have power that could be applied, according to the others.

Once they were all at minimum B-rank one in terms of available Mana, they could start practicing methods of control. Starting with D- to C-ranked techniques with a focus on minimizing loss, rather than maximizing output. The latter was easy for a Mage, just throw more *oomph* at it! So the former became the main focus.

Artorian struggled with good explanations, but encountered an epiphany. He snapped his fingers. "Why don't we use the Pylon forms? The bracket speech. Since the system is sort of busted, one of us could get a hyper-efficient version we could all try to copy. Then get a feel for what a good, cost-effective method *feels like*."

"My system functions *very well*. Thank you." Deverash's eight-sided die menacingly hovered behind him. Though the ex-Gnome slowly changed his tune. "*I* will show the spells, and explain them. I don't want half of Vanaheim's Beneath shattered because a few zealous Mages wanted to try something."

Shut down on the spot, Artorian shoved his arms in the air and defeatedly trotted away. "*Crackers*. Now Deverash knows to go look. Hopefully he'll be too busy to dig... *particularly* deep."

A smattering of giggles broke out as Artorian walked off. They all knew about the Demon's Maw incident, and it was still funny. When Deverash the Die brought them some spellforms, the supervisors began with comparisons; practical people did well when they had an example to compare their results with.

Spellforms unfortunately didn't help the automatic fielding issues Marie and Henry were consistently experiencing. That was a matter of inner focus, but sitting around introspectively wasn't their idea of a good time. Not when actual progress could be made with the rest of the group. Particularly in this rare setting where they could get immediate feedback.

The S-rankers didn't attend, but Chandra had the experience to talk those present through most Mana problems. If a person stalled, Artorian could give on-the-spot feedback of exactly what they were doing. Plus actually show them!

Deverash caused the largest commotion. Not because his

lessons were... *odd*. Rather because it was strange to take instruction from a geometric shape. Would it have killed him to show up as a Gnome? His chosen also came, and the gathered had a good laugh.

They were *also* geometrically shaped. A full dice set worth of them, which is exactly what they looked like. Dev's insight was helpful, but sweet Cal did his explanations get technical. At least nothing blew up in the background more than once during his enthusiastic attempts to show off what Pylons could do. Even if that was counted *per* attempt. This kerfuffle allowed for a hushed gamble on just how many dice-shaped holes were to be added to the landscape that day.

After a week of hashing things out, those present determined that supervisors and chosen needed different lessons. Chandra told days' worth of stories on what Artorian's odd concepts were supposed to feel like, while Deverash explained the more mechanical concepts the Pylons applied. Spellforms assisted with diminishing the harsh costs of their abilities.

A strange development arose when it was Artorian who had the most difficult time improving. That had not been the expected progression path for the old man. Though, it made the others secretly smirk; it was possible he was visibly struggling in front of them on purpose... but that seemed unlikely.

Once they had a real chance to sit down and talk, Henry, Marie, Artorian, Deverash, Odin, and Chandra each made strides with personal cultivation difficulties. Brushing up left their realms in the cold, but with the reset coming, and their hearts bleak at what that meant... they all just took some time for themselves.

Personal progress took more time than they'd care to admit, but good results did get produced. Henry got his flight under control. Marie and Chandra actually got to talking about Midgard problems instead of shooting one another sword-edged side-eye over the fence. They even quibbled at length on the future, and how to improve things the second time around.

Odin proudly managed to get his passive electric emanations under control. While Artorian finally managed to get a *single* technique under his belt. Unfortunately, and to the great laughter of his peers, the ability that had managed to succeed on that front was his sleeping field. In retribution, he made them all enjoy a pleasant nap before they poked fun at the fact that the old man wasn't immune to his own shenanigans. He'd pelted them with pillows the remainder of the day, but it had at worst caused them to collapse in giggle fits.

Artorian thought he'd been doing alright with his tricks and attacks! Back in those early days when he was climbing up the Skyspear, to take it over from Cataphron, his little schemes had been such boons! It was rough to be a fool. Those skills were smears on the floor when he compared them to what the others could do.

They practiced basic shaping for months. Lines, cones, blades, orbs, radii, orbitals, and area-of-effect forms. Some techniques and shapes came with more difficulty than others, as visualization didn't come easy for some. Given the same information and patterns to work with, Henry's first air blade mimicry cut clean through a Jotunheim mountain. 'Oops,' he'd said. Artorian had thrown his proverbial hat to the ground. "'Oops' my foot, young man!"

Chandra rocked a vastly different method of going about techniques, to the great wonder of those in study. She could shape, move, and alter anything living. Turning tree roots into deadly weapons at the flick of a branch. She turned leaves into shields and blades of grass into honest-to-Cal murdersticks. To see that mess of death swirl around her like they were nothing but petals in a summer breeze was impressive.

Like a nail in Artorian's coffin, that was *without* her using Aura to make it easier. Chandra gleefully showed him up with raw technique, adding another notch to her stick. "Another win for me! You're all making this easy since we're excluding Aura manipulation practice."

The lack of Aura manipulation practice was for a good reason.

Their group had to stick to Mana-refining skills, as both the human royals simply didn't have the repertoire to engage with the concept. They may have been potent C-rankers, but as Mages they were beached whales. So long as their Aura fielded itself, they were going to see no progress until they no longer experienced difficulty tugging it back in. They'd work on it as they had time, but it was low on the list of abilities they wanted to shore up on.

Fielding was a nuisance, avoiding burnout a requirement.

On the plus side, their weighty Auras were helpful for scaring off the local Jotun that liked to *peep*. Due to constant fielding, the signature they both gave off made Henry and Marie come across as massive beings. Giant creatures of significant size and girth, as their Auras determined how untrained others evaluated their size. The feeling they both exuded wasn't believed, and didn't correlate when the Jotuns saw them. These observations were grounds for skepticism, and many a glory-seeker strode out to overthrow this odd gathering of people.

Fielding forced a fierce demerit on one's fighting capacity, limiting Henry and Marie's ability to properly defend themselves from an aggressor's Auric attacks. If they ever got struck with a high-density effect, or got trapped in a wide-scale explosion of some kind, they'd be burnt toast.

Henry was essentially defenseless against Mana-based explosions. Marie was better, but it was a hair's difference. They would have to rely on impeccable physical combat prowess until they managed to get their fielding under control, but building those skills would take up precious time all on its own.

Time they didn't have.

CHAPTER THIRTEEN

Where the supervisors could be considered to be 'stuck in their ways,' their chosen were visionaries of adaptation. Unfettered by thought patterns instilled across decades of life in a troubled world they didn't know, the chosen flourished. They possessed flashes of memories gained from their Dreamers, sure. But they didn't suffer from deeply ingrained social patterns, nor learned ways of thinking.

Chandra had summarized the situation excellently. "The chosen compare to young adventurers in their prime, while us supers are old fogies."

For Artorian and company, them checking in was akin to watching the talented grow and come by their tavern with ever growing tales of amazing acts and daring bravado. The Dreamers silently lamented as they watched their chosen show them up like gifted children.

Artorian sighed. "Abyss, what a *difference*. Yet Celestials above am I proud."

The Dreamers played it safe with their growth. Testing basic, simple forms. Practicing them. Getting a grip for what was efficient, practical, and easier to control. They were focused on how to advance to the A- and S-ranks, and the requirements for such journeys. The latter being an unattainable aspect at the moment, since their resident S-rankers were occupied with Cal.

The news behind why they were unavailable had inevitably done the rounds, and that had led to a week of eating, drinking, and napping. Nobody had been able to find the energy to improve for a while when the secret got out. The prospect of being turned inside out when Cal did was… stomach twisting. So they watched their chosen make impossible strides in power and ability after having provided what the supervisors considered basic instruction. There was a warmth to be found there. Those smiling young faces, eagerly discovering new goodies day after day.

Surtur and Valhalla needed a while to get their cultivation techniques up to snuff, but once present, they took off. Karakum and Zelia took to cultivation so naturally that the supers tried their best to chew away the jealousy with heavy plate helpings of Chandra's finest.

Those with Beast Cores couldn't acquire a cultivation technique, but that mattered little since they were ravenous hungry monsters in their own right. All Manny, Sleipnir, and Halcyon had to do to gain power was eat the fallen, and those *with* the techniques caused *plenty* of those.

Jotunheim's natural predators and fauna wouldn't need any additional mopping up, because the chosen going around made quick work of them. If they had a few more years to go *hard* on hunting, they would have undoubtedly cleared out the whole continent.

Artorian flopped onto the grass in his pink rose petal robes. He thumbed them over, wondering why they looked so incredibly familiar. Why not just ask? <Say, Zelia, where did you get this pattern? I'm confident I've seen this before.>

Zelia rested in a nearby hammock, a wispy cloud of purple gathering above her as she further purged the accrued Niflheim poison. Purging was a slow process, even with assistance. Her voice cracked when she tried to speak, so she silenced and did it mentally instead. <Your memories, my Dreamer, or… the memories of a person named Rosewood. Persons? They are difficult to parse. I know the events as if I watched them through several pairs of eyes, who see through the prior pair. Details are blurred, but I have years if not decades of passionate knowledge from the one with that name.>

A fondness filled her mental tone. <She wished to cover the world in her clothes, and have everyone wear them. This was her dream. Her wish. I carry that wish within me, and walk that path as well. The memories may not be mine, but the *passion*? The passion is. These designs are hers, as were the original methods. I have made changes of my own, but I do call what you are wearing the Rose collection. When we wake on the next iteration of the realm, my children and I are going to try to mass produce them. I am no Djinn, but I will fulfill her wish.>

The old man understood, nodded, and didn't judge. That was touching. He closed his eyes and dropped into his Soul Space. Extending a hand, a person-sized pillow *fuffed* into his grasp. His A-ranked Soul Item. He'd been building on it little by little during the time where he could not help the others, nor be helped by them.

In his opinion, gaining Essence and Mana in Cal should not be the focus. They would get the energy; that wasn't going to be the problem. The issue was establishing the pillars of advancement. He didn't have a proper support crew this time to help him through the ranks. So, progress would be slow. Like it was for everyone else!

How he *missed* being ballsy. Scheming under the watchful eyes of a full crew of healers, while he opened meridians just to make them yelp and jump to it.

Floating freely in his personal Soul Space, he grumbled that the darn thing now had borders. Cal's soul was pushing in on him from all sides after the dungeon Core connection was put in place. He expected his space allotment might open up once he returned to the real, but there was just no feasible timeline for when that might be. So he would work with what he had.

As planned, the stuffing for his pillows were just smaller pillows. Once he had a few together, he formed a new cover over them, then compressed their size down to something manageable. All it took was Mana and time. "Rinse, weave, repeat."

Still, he'd found that making his pillow wasn't the real advancement bottleneck. The actual limiter was that since achieving A-rank zero, he hadn't budged a solitary inch from that position. Artorian held supreme suspicion that he wasn't supposed to be at this rank at all, and his **Law** had just helped him get there to make a point to Cal. He felt like he needed to play catch-up on *something*, but couldn't figure out what. Chandra didn't have any answers for him. Was it the Soul Item? So far there was no change to his rank even though he'd been building on it.

How did Cal improve? He built his Soul Space, sure. Though that by itself didn't seem to count as thresholds for when he made progress. Only when he had applied his concepts and knowledge. Then, when putting it into practice, did Cal appear to cross barriers and make strides. So what was he supposed to do? Exemplify methods of **Love**? Wasn't he already doing that *daily*? He grumbled and released the latest pillow improvement, pulling himself back up to his body.

His eyes opened to greet the night sky. At least it was a *familiar* sky. Always a bonus. He turned his head, having a gander at the party his chosen were having around a campfire. Was Yuki in armor? No, that Zelia-made kimono was just reinforced and imbued with some spectacular power. Oh, there was material from Vanaheim woven in. No wonder. Defensively, Zelia had them covered. Offensively, they'd all gone with some interesting choices.

Zelia had chosen the parasol as her *public* weapon. Yuki went with a fan, and Cy had stuck to her trident. Though she was eagerly eying up other options, such as tonfas. Their adopted fighting styles matched the idea of what their own realms taught.

Where Vanaheim was meant to instill the idea of preparing for the unexpected, Jotunheim didn't care for any of that, and sought to instill methods of how to face overwhelming odds, power, and might.

Neither Dev nor Artorian's realms were big on civilization for people to embed themselves in. Their realms were meant as specific challenges that travelers would need to overcome to continue forward. If one attempted to tackle Niflheim, given the current rumors, without mastering oneself on Vanaheim first, they'd *just die*.

Equally, based on the bridge layout plans, travelers would be able to head into Muspelheim and pass by Jotun entirely. Doing so without some mastery of Jotunheim would make the attempt a laughable experience. Good luck tackling a unified empire that lived in gravity conditions which crushed you on principle.

Artorian considered that thought a second time. It wasn't pleasant thinking travelers would just be able to skip realms. They should institute some kind of gate that required unlocking first. Didn't Cal mention something about this in a meeting? World bosses? Yes, he believed so. Before a traveler could open a bridge to the next realm, they would need to tackle the world boss. Then, they would be able to realm-skip.

A fair challenge, he supposed. Unless the challenge was *Crabby*. Not a single Jotun had managed that. Well, the hard-shelled pain had been *A-ranked*, so that was unfair. Maybe world bosses were a bad idea. Cal should change it to something tied to personal progress.

Did he have a high B-ranked threat that could currently count as a world boss? He turned his head to look off into the distance, and spotted the Long-flag. Oh, Abyss… could he *not*? That form was a pain to control! Still, he didn't have anything else that would currently count. Might as well. Plus… it was one of Bob's last, proper, finalized creations.

"Do the Gobbo *proud*."

Sitting up, he watched a momentary interaction between Manny and Zelia. The manticore had taken a greater shine to the spider at the prospect of more time together. The miniature escapades enjoyed during moments of postal service just didn't offer the same quality time experience.

Sleipnir wasn't amused at Manny's dawdling since he wanted to return to the newly minted sport of Jotun-hunting. Those frost giants were weeds that needed tending, and his cleavers were perfect to cut the problem down to size. Still, the lad was rebuked by mutual spider and manticore glares. Instead he went off with Valhalla. At least she was a *proper* huntress.

Artorian tried not to smirk too hard, but said nothing of it. Their chosen had their own lives and favored activities. Who was he to get in between that? If they came to him with questions, as they often did, that was one thing. Sticking his nose into budding romances that would be injured by his doing so? He spoke to himself without realizing. "*Mmmno.* Let them be happy, the canting will come any day now."

Cal mentally nudged him. <Did you realize you said that out loud? Also, not any day. *Today.* Are you all set? I know about Brianna; what are you doing about that?>

Artorian stepped into the forum space Cal had opened with a dejected spirit. He hadn't wanted this day to come. Instead, he got straight to answering questions. <Brianna is going to… *enjoy* what it's like to be active over the century, while we're all taking a nap. When we decant, I'm going to brush up a little more, get settled, and then go knock on some doors to… Well. If she won't willingly be canted *then*, I'll have to shatter her. I told her as much, and she's taken it poorly. So, we'll see. As for the rest, everyone here has been dreading it, but we're ready. Got all your monsters Cored and stored?>

The dungeon nodded. <I've got some *special plans* for Niflheim. I'm doing long-term wake tests on those mobs, while the Dark Elves are active. Shame what happened to the Dusk Elves, they were sweet. Every other realm save for Jotun is cleaned and vacant, as planned. I'll be wiping the slate here once you're all asleep. Then I begin rolling into resets after collating what patterns stay from Alpha-one. Dawn and Tatum are going to

keep me company, along with my many Wisps. Who are, thankfully, immune to a great many of the upcoming problems. Alright, enough dallying, tell them.>

Artorian opened his eyes as he left the forum. Again, what a lovely night's sky. He pushed to his feet, sighed, and clapped his hands together so loud that the *wub* it formed shuddered across the full reach of the realm. It cracked his own Manabody something fierce, and *mercy*, that hurt. Not that it mattered, he was about to lose it to canting anyway.

Still, it got everyone's attention. Waking or no.

<*It's time.*>

CHAPTER FOURTEEN

Canting was a strange experience.

Particularly, because there was *nothing* to experience. The mind moved into the Core, and felt like floating through a long, dreamless slumber. It merely woke when it was time.

The last thing Artorian remembered was closing his eyes in Jotunheim as his body shattered. His view snapped to darkness, his mind moved to the Seed Core in the Silverwood Tree. Once there, it felt akin to snacking on a nightcap and falling face first into a mountain of pillows and blankets. He was asleep right away.

The first thing he saw when he woke back up was the inside of a hungry mouth. It was a rather *big* mouth. Lots of saliva, big sharp teeth. The maw was trying its sincere best to bite or chew his head off. Hard to tell. He blinked, taking a moment to re-establish himself in this A-ranked Mana body. Still Mana? Cal hadn't Incarnated yet then. Good, he supposed.

The maw again clenched down on him with a loud, snarling chomp. Seriously, *what* was trying to eat him? "Excuse me. What in *Cal* do you think you're doing?"

A very hungry and confused carnosaur jumped back when

the supposed meal started to speak. The primal beast paced about, looking its prey up and down to try to understand why it wasn't successfully eating this food. Artorian returned the look, studying the feather-coated bipedal critter. "Just *what* are you supposed to be? I've never seen something like you before. Are you from the moon?"

The dinosaur didn't 'do' speech. It hissed at him in a pattern the old man didn't understand. Now that he considered it, where was he? He didn't recognize the surroundings. He'd check in a moment; one problem at a time. First was checking in. Being dumped on a continent after decanting was not something he considered natural. <Cal. I'm up. What just tried to eat my face?>

Cal didn't respond. Instead, a screen popped into being in front of him. Artorian fussed at it before even reading the message, from the gesture alone. "Is our *great spirit* avoiding speaking to people again? Did I not slap him hard enough last time? I swear if I have to hit the S-ranks just to do that again, I *will*."

Grumbling to himself like an old codger, he read the screen while the monster kept trying to—very unsuccessfully—bite chunks out of him.

"Welcome back, decanted individual!
Dani, remind me to update this screen so it shows the person's name instead?
This doesn't feel like personalized writing. This is how you leave a comment on a document, right?"

Artorian already had to knead his brow. "We're off to a *great* start."

He skipped to the next paragraph, as the prior involved Dani and Cal having a full-on conversation.

"We are currently in version fourteen of realm resets.
Now, before you ask! We've had to do a reset at least once every

decade, so far. Not having supervisors accelerated certain developments. Good news!
You'll have plenty to do when you're back!"

Artorian held the side of his head with trepidation. "*Fantastic.*"

"You'll notice many things have changed, and realms aren't the way you left them.
If you're a supervisor, please have a look around before imposing your will. Access to old features have been temporarily revoked. Please focus on sealing the rest of the borked items. We should be *out* of the creature variants. If you're a chosen, please feel free to go wild!
Dani, what else was I supposed to put here?"

The academic felt old as he suffered through this mess of an explanation. Rather than read the rest, he took the edge of the screen and hurled it at the critter that just wouldn't stop biting at him. He didn't feel the chomps, because the carnosaur was C-ranked, but it was annoying! *P'thunk*!

The screen dinged the dinosaur's skull, and the creature fell over in a twitchy daze. Wait. *Really*? Those screens were *kinetic* now? The rectangle flickered and flashed while embedded in a tree. Entirely unharmed. Wanting it back, he stretched his arm out towards it. "[Telekinesis]."

When nothing happened, he shoved his hand to the scene again, but there wasn't a difference. Had Pylon access been revoked? How annoying. He tried to pull up the shop and the edit screen, but neither succeeded. How was he supposed to work on items if he didn't have the tools? "Dangit, Cal! He must have made the messages out of order, and revoked the access after telling the supers what to work on. Then completely forgot they needed one to do the other. Sounds like a *Cal* thing to do."

Moseying over, he physically tugged the screen out of the

tree. The edges must be sharp, because it sliced deep. On inspection, the screen didn't even appear to *have* edges. How did the darn thing work? He fiddled with it, but ended up having to scroll to the bottom before it winked out.

{*Ding*!
You have gained a title!
Title gained: Administrator
Please slot this title to gain access to features relevant to the title!}

"Why is nothing *standardized*?" Artorian stared at the text that hovered in front of him before it dissipated. He felt exasperated. "Explain things, Cal! Add the what to the *where*? *How*?"

Sound behind him made it clear that the carnosaur stirred. The massive beast was getting back to its feet, and it was clearly unhappy with the snack that had slapped it. Artorian had long lost the mood to be patient. "You *behave*!"

Fielding his Aura, A-ranked pressure fell on the carnosaur with all the impact of it suddenly being *smushed* at the bottom of an ocean. The beast gasped for breath, heaving as it was unable to do that otherwise very easy and basic thing. What was a C-rank beastie even doing in Jo… was he in Jotunheim? It didn't actually feel like it. Pulling his Aura back around himself, he rolled his shoulders as the panicked dinosaur finally managed a breath. It twitched on the ground, shivering and fearful as it was unable to cope with what just happened. The carnosaur simply didn't have the mind for it.

Well darn. Now he felt *bad* for the face chewer. "Alright… alright. Let's have a look at you and see if you're hurt."

The carnosaur was too afraid to move a muscle, doing its best to play dead as the not-prey picked it up without a shred of difficulty. Its head was moved, maw opened, eyes checked, and claws measured. The carnosaur didn't know what feeling violated was, but it wasn't dead, being eaten, or really being harmed. So it didn't think about it twice until the not-prey pressed its oddly soft non-claw to its forehead.

The dinosaur didn't do language, until the not-prey spoke a word of power. Then, the carnosaur understood what language was. Pain shuddered through the dinosaur's body as a new Beast Core formed as a crest right on the front of his skull. It hurt! Yet new power pulsed through his form, bulking the frame and tightening the muscles as the C-rank two creature shot straight to the zenith rank. It's prior, minor Beast Core was consumed by the new one.

It had been named.

Artorian pulled his palm off the forming crystal crest. "Not a sun this time? *Odd*. It had always been a sun before. Still, Cal had mentioned on his screen that things were different."

Best to just assume that meant nothing was the same, and he needed to learn the ways of the world all over again. Including the 'title' thing. He could swear that had come up before… something about his chosen having a lineage?

He snapped his fingers as the information came easily when he called upon it. The nap had clear and distinct results, and his memories were clear as day. "Titles!"

He remembered now. Still, that didn't tell him how to apply them. He crossed his arms, and glanced over to the writhing dinosaur that was going through adaptive changes. He nodded at the positive alterations. "Looks like that went smoothly. Can you understand me now, *Voltekka*?"

Vol got to his feet, head shaking as clarity filled his eyes. Sapience had kicked his door down as the dinosaur grew entirely new brain matter. In addition to increased intellect, the new raw size and power increase streamlined his form. Teslaic force rolled from his legs, and crackling energy emanations similar to Odin's freely blitzed across his feathers and skin. The effect formed lines of bright teal energy between individual feathers when he had a shake.

Vol blinked at Artorian.

He had been addressed, but wasn't up to speed with what he

had been asked. He needed to be *faster*. The desire roiled through his connection, and the adaptive energy still coursing through Vol followed suit and streamlined him further. The electricity internalized, vastly improving the carnosaur's reaction speed, ability to notice and process, and physical mobility.

The Administrator gave the dino plenty of time getting his bearings as Vol siphoned some power from him. Artorian was working through his own problems. Mainly, how to slot this blasted title. "Slot Title. No? Open Menu. Also no. Title list! Nothing… *uhhh*."

He tried to enter the senate, heard static, and found he could not. "Oh *come. On.* Let *something* work."

Vol fell over several times during his improvement phase of the chosen connection. His building muscle adjusted, and readjusted as he suffered through the transfer progress of Mana trading down to Essence, while that Essence smothered him in cascading power.

He felt like a fresh-hatched, learning how to walk again. Except that his basic trudge now was now as fast as his previous, wildest, outright run. Vol broke trees as he rolled, thrashing around and flattening a broad section of the local thick jungle.

Artorian said nothing as it reminded him of his own Long problems. Oh. *Right*. He needed to work on that as well. "Titles. List. Options. Cal toys. *Status*. Bl—oh, *that worked*!"

With the correct keyword, Artorian's personal status popped up as a screen before him. He jumped for joy and punched the sky. His exuberance cleared the cloud layer above, a literal hole opening from the exertion of his Mana. He should be careful with that. He was at maybe a B-ranked… nothing? Why could he not feel his own rank, or how much Mana he had stored?

This felt *awful*.

Relief rolled over him when he saw the information listed on the screen he had just pulled up. Finally, something to work with!

Player: Artorian.

Body: A-rank zero.
Reserves: A-rank zero.
Last used ability: Naming a Chosen.

Artorian scratched his head, crossing his arms after as he could only see a little of the screen at a time. "'Player'? What is that about?"

Was Cal considering them as pawns in a game? He wouldn't put it past the dungeon. Scrolling down, he found there was much more information on the screen, but he couldn't make heads or tails on what half of it meant. "This is organized incredibly poorly. Oh, there it is. Titles!"

Moving a digit to try and press something, the relevant section lit up. Another one of those message screens popped into view nearby as well. Joined by Cal's voice playing a recorded clip.

}Please slot the desired title from the list!
Titles can be combined for special effects, when I get it to work.}

"That one even has a backward *bracket*! Fix your notifications!" Given he had no other options available in the list he was shown, Artorian pressed down on 'Administrator.' A screen asking if he was sure appeared when he did so. The prompt asked a simple yes or no confirmation, so he went ahead and pressed yes. Then, he felt 'normal' again. "*Ahhhh*, there we go."

He could feel his Mana, his rank, the senate access, the editing ability, and all his tools return to his fingertips as if he'd just remembered how to do all of those things properly. "*Oooof.* What a *feeling*. That's dangerous. Revelations like that could be downright addicting."

He rolled his arms and shoulders, getting a feel for the A-rank zero body. It felt natural, moved as he remembered it, and could do the things he wanted it to. He hovered up and made a stairway of light platforms in a circular pattern. Drafting a stairway to heaven so he could stand on his homemade lookout tower to find where he was. "Midgard. *Definitely* Midgard."

He looked down, and saw Vol still having a rough time. Poor baby, he'd naturalize eventually. "Kiddo! You take your time, alright? Just let me know when you're feeling better. You're going to feel like *aces* when you can be out and ab—"

Vol bashed his face into a tree and roared in pain. Artorian backtracked his plan and hopped down, grabbing the panicked creature. He effortlessly pulled the carnosaur's head into his lap, sitting down cross-legged with the reborn baby. Artorian tenderly brushed his hand over the heavily breathing boy's feathered head. "Never mind. There's not a chance in Cal I'm letting you do this alone. This is far more difficult on you than I thought it was going to be, so I'm going to be here until you're okay."

The size difference between them felt awkward. Artorian thought of a solution, and molded his Mana like he did in order to form the owl wings. Save that he formed a full-body copy of himself, merely in a far larger size of his current shape. The idea was similar to the construct form he'd made for Cy. When he formed the larger body, Artorian diminished the golden luminance of the light construct so as not to blind his boy.

After the size increase, Vol's head lay in a lap that could easily hold it snug. The dinosaur had been afraid. Afraid and in pain. He still thrashed, but caring hands kept him close. The harm stopped as soothing warmth rolled off the bright creature currently holding him. The heat felt nice, reminding him of lying in the clutch when he was young.

Vol stopped thrashing, feeling sleepy only a moment before conking out. Artorian proudly kept him tight. "It might be the *only* technique I got right, but heavens is it useful. You have a good nap, my boy. I promise, you will feel better when you wake up."

Something else roared nearby.

Artorian glanced over to see a Tyrannotitan charging him. To the massive predator's sight, the glowing object didn't seem scary, and a sleeping snack was laying in its lap! The charging predator didn't get very far, as a luminous hand squeezed its approaching trap shut. Turning that roar into a half-hearted *flurp*.

Creatures in the vicinity learned it was a great idea to give that particularly bright spot some space, as a Tyrannotitan took speedy space flight lessons *away* from that location. The carnivore was hurled all the way to another realm, screaming before it broke out of the Midgardian orbit. Artorian vented his frustrations, yelling after it while shaking his fist, though it was long out of earshot. "*Jaws off my baby!*"

CHAPTER FIFTEEN

A few days later, Artorian perched on a light platform high in the air, watching Vol hunt. The newly renamed 'Teslasaur' had figured out how to dim his bioluminescence today, and was successfully pulling off a stalking. Grand!

Vol hunched down, cautiously lurked, and *lunged*! Artorian made tiny squeaking jumps, clapping his hands together as his boy successfully landed himself his own meal! "Wonderful! So proud of you."

Fleshy chunks were torn out of a dinosaur Artorian didn't know the name for. He winced, deciding he didn't need to see the whole event of Vol eating. The Beast Core creature had needed but a scant few days to get a grasp on what he now was. Vol didn't quite have the mind of his other chosen, but his instincts were *sharp*. Perhaps it would come over time.

Artorian didn't have a solid grasp on how long it had taken Halcyon, he hadn't been around for that. He'd hopefully have better luck with Tekka here.

Still, Vol was all set to be on his own now. He could defend himself, hunt, and roam free. Granted, he was roaming free at *Mach one*. From *zero to zoom* if Vol wasn't careful, since he caused thunderclaps by taking off into hunting sprints. On the upside, that electric bite of his paralyzed prey, but that effect barely had time to register. Between the speed and power of the bite, he swiftly killed what he chomped.

Artorian turned, wondering what to do first now that nurse-maiding had concluded. Vol wasn't even paying attention to him anymore. The hungry boy was a creature of independence, and the wild. This Teslasaur was not one to linger in the nest.

Artorian tried to enter the senate, and *tsk'd*. *Static*. Still *static*. He had access, but the senate wasn't functional, and neither were the forums. He wasn't able to initiate private connections, and his personal methods equally just fuzzed over. No dice on communication. Next plan. Where to next… *aha*!

A beacon!

Artorian ran through the sky, veering straight down to an overgrown, dirt-covered teleportation pad. It was unpowered, and seemed to be dead. Still, progress! Continents were so dang spacious, so he was elated to have found something he recognized. Kneeling onto the beacon, he hurriedly brushed it off with his hands. Clearing dirt off so the entire platform became uncovered. He could have used Mana for it, but only thought about it after he was already done.

Though, the *last time* he'd shifted his Aura to a starlight configuration, the plants in his surroundings had eaten it up. Flora had begun to spontaneously mutate, and that section had to be burned down for… *safety reasons*. A large toothy lizard with lightning in its blood? Sure! Plant life that could *eat* said toothy lizard and reproduced faster than he committed stupidities? *Nyope*!

So, how to power a dead beacon? Don't suppose he could just… *shove* some Mana into it? He stepped a foot down, and spiked some of his power in.

Fuff.

Artorian blinked. Floating in space. "*What*? How did I end up in the middle of nowhere?"

He checked his surroundings like he had done when stuck in

The Between. Oh! This is where the moon used to be! The orbit path seemed right, it was just the *actual moon* that had been placed elsewhere. Yup, it was over yonder now. Still, he didn't land on a beacon. Had the network just saved the space coordinate of where it *would* have been? Why not bring him to another active beacon?

He slapped his forehead. Of course. There *was no* other active beacon. A hundred years without some love? That beacon system was dead in the water. He needed to let it power itself somehow. *Mmmm*.

Maybe it could be public use, and those using it could pay some kind of upkeep cost to keep the whole thing up and running? He'd have to remember that idea. He steadied himself to sit on a light platform. Now he was *stuck* in space, without a paddle.

He attempted a personal teleport. *Static.* "Cal, what is the *point* of giving me my toys if I can't play with them? Did all the supers go through this problem? Probably not."

Was there anyone else that would figure out the title thing? He hoped so. He wobbled from side to side and dismissed the platform. He shifted into flight for a second, but the drain was *brutal*. No-go on flight. With his fist pressed to his cheek, he mulled it over. This wasn't his first time being stuck in space. What had he done last time?

"*Essence thrusters!*" Spiraling the Mana along his shoulders, back, and spine, Artorian tested minimal input. He remembered how it went last time, but forgot to take into account that he was using Essence then. A-rank Mana was a *touch* more potent. Applying just a drop, he sent himself hurtling through the Soul Space like a streaking comet. It was the pyrite-blasted magnetic rock problem all over again!

Crashing through the rock-wall of a continent, he groaned dispassionately once stationary. Not because it hurt, but because that just wasn't something *pleasant*. There was ground, and gravity. Chalk it up as a w—*Aww. Noo.* Not *here*. Why did he need to crash *here*? The gravity was all wrong, and he pulled a face of disgust while stepping away and throwing his arms up, whining to himself.

Why, of all places, did he have to crash into *Niflheim?* "No~o."

His Aura shifted into starlight to start scrubbing his surroundings right away. That misty poison was no joke, and he wasn't chancing a *thing.* He set the force of his indiscriminate Auric signature to full-blast, and altered the identity to scrub and destroy rather than heal. Right away, fungi, plants, and unpleasant smoky vapors in his vicinity caught aflame in bursts of popping celestine light. The threats self-conflagrated in a hurry. A creature or two hiding camouflaged as snakes in the walls followed suit, causing a strange notification to blur on the edge of his vision.

Checking his status, he noticed he had been awarded Mana for his kills. Including something tallied as 'experience,' whatever that was supposed to be. He focused on the Mana gain instead, as there was a math formula present. Followed by a numerical representation of the exact amount he had been granted for a kill. Hey! He could also see the drain his Aura took from his reserves while it upheld his desired effects. He smiled when he noticed what modified the costs. Now *that* was handy! *"Information!"*

He moved the status to his side, but didn't dismiss it. No reason to drop it since he could try things and see what the system told him about it. Let's see, he'd just killed two 'Mimics.' Okay? That didn't help much. What also didn't help is that he had no idea where he was going in this ant's nest. Didn't he have something for that? Clapping his hands together in a directional wave, the **wub** sound mixed with echolocation. The caster threw it out into the world, and watched with bleak realization as the Essence numbers representing his reserves plummeted.

Awch! He had *invoked* that effect. Oops! Then again, his status was populating faster than he could read the kills. A map icon was also blinking angrily at him. He tapped it, and

saw the map evolve and update in real time as his sound revealed further and further sections of the continent. Including strange dots that represented creatures his sound blast hadn't killed. His reserves bubbled with energy, the growing kill counter replenishing the bar's representation. Neat!

He tried tapping one, and a prompt appeared. That was unexpected.

{{Alpha test feature: Apply perception attributes?}}

"Who is doing the *editing* on these screens! Fire them, Cal!" That was a lovely jumble of words, that Artorian maybe understood half of. He stared at the message for a minute, then got irritated and pushed the button that correlated to the positive. Nameplates populated via thin lines to the dots that hadn't died, and the Administrator's eyebrows went up. "Well, would you look at that. Found the knife ears."

Whatever Zelia had done to them must have had some rippling effects, because they weren't doing so great. Along with names and basic information, he could see the representation of their health and Essence.

They were really not doing so hot, busy holding off a different colored dot called a 'Phosgen.' He'd heard about those. Big-eyed orbs with Assimilator abilities. How was he able to see this? Surely there was a list somewhere. Leaving the Dark Elves to their fun, he pulled the status back in front of him and went on a scrolling adventure. He breezed along until he found something that roughly correlated to perception attributes. "Names subject to change."

He shrugged. Of course names would change. In the meanwhile, what was he working with? He opened a sub-menu, and found a listing of how his skills were calculated. Some calculations were outright missing, and many entries had personalized notes. He opened the perception one, and laughed as he read Cal's note. "Artorian seems to notice abyss-near everything. So this is just being set to the maximum value at all times. So I don't have to deal with it."

Wiping a tear away as he smirked, he sat down on a rock and just read through the list. Might as well consume the rest and see what was available to him according to the system. He wasn't in a rush.

Deep in Niflheim, in a room confounded by contraptions and controls, Plinky and the Brain were deeply invested in discovering why they had just lost dominance over an *entire hub*. Plinky couldn't even get reliable information, except from a rival Phosgen in the vicinity sassily mentioning that 'it was bright.' That Phosgen was dealing with some of the original locals, and Plinky needed more to work with. Not that he was going to get it from rival Phosgen, and he knew better than to make bets. That's how his name had become 'Plinky.'

Sett, a fungaloid that had been nicknamed Brain, couldn't get a single spore remotely close to the hub. He just lost contact with his spore's information as they came into contact with the mystery luminance. The fungaloid *bristled*, and diverted a small army of plant and fungal-based monstrosities to swarm the hub so they could reclaim it. That would sort the issue. They would just throw numbers at it.

Artorian peacefully hummed, leaning back against a reshaped part of the wall so he had somewhere cozy to put his Soul Item. He rested snug on the pillow. That was optimal as he read through menu after menu. Cal had littered the thing with notes, and it was clearly nowhere close to finished. Still, it was workable, and clearly showed Cal was heading in a clear direction that would lead to a spectacular end-product. This was worth working on.

"Abyss. This might even be *fun*."

A rumbling pulled him away from enjoying the numbers. Curious, Artorian leaned forward in his seat. As he bent to sneak a peek behind the corner of the wall, his long beard hung to touch the floor. The fungaloid he saw was just as lost as the old man, and neither had any idea what the other was looking at. Artorian observed a blue-green creature that was shaped like a mushroom, sporting two arms and four legs. Except that it wore a *spiffing hat* made of blue cheese.

Fugum, The Inspector General of floor three hundred and sixty-nine, pressed a monocle over a space that didn't have eyes. It reasonably should have, but that's not how the fungaloid saw the world.

Plinky and the Brain observed through Fugum's visual spectrum. Sett did his best to puppeteer the inspector, adjusting both the cheesy monocle and fermented hat so they could get a better look at what they were dealing with. Was that a *human*? Those things actually existed? The dungeon overlords shared a look of 'this can't be right.'

Their attention was stolen away when the outcry *'Sacre bleu!'* was blurted through the connection, a moment before Fugum burned away in celestine fire. A high pitched **eeeee** played through the control room from auditory feedback, and Plinky shook his massive Phosgen head from discomfort. He tentacle-slammed a lever to turn that awful amplification effect off. This was not a creature to be engaged with directly. Brain stuck his agitated arm into the air, declaring his order before dropping it towards the invader. *"Prepare the traps!"*

Artorian leaned over the small pile of ash, arms crossed. He inspected the remains, and couldn't for the life of him grasp why the status bar had tagged it as an 'Inspector General.' Nor why 'Cheese Overmind' was listed right below that entry. Stranger still, the Cheese Overmind had provided him *ten times* the reward that the fungaloid had. Zelia couldn't have been responsible for this. This must have been… something else.

"Still. *Cheese?*"

Pulling the revealed map close, he sifted pensive fingers through his beard and made the area representation smaller. He could see more continental areas all at once this way. *"Cal, this place is just too big."*

Some pathways outright made no sense. No, there was a marker that showed the direction of gravity changed. How *convoluted*. Even *with* the map, he felt lost. No messing around. He was inconveniently in Niflheim, so, what was he here for?

"Brianna? Brianna."

Charging a second **wub**, he condensed the advanced effect into a bouncy-ball and hurled it into the tunnel system somewhere around Mach six. Each time it struck a surface and bounced, a litany of sound exploded. Pulverizing solid matter into deharmonized particles. He'd been prepared this time, and watched several million Essence units drink away from his pool. He saw it on the status screen, watching as the formula displayed. He'd never known his Invocations were *that* expensive. Granted, he was hovering around the billion mark as an A-ranker, but that was a lot of Essence *oomph*.

The map showed him where the bouncy ball went rabid. As swiftly as his Mana bar had drained, it refilled just as smoothly. The log of things he killed for that to happen? *Less than smooth.* More of an ugly blur of text that was likely about to burn out a Pylon somewhere. It was scrolling so fast, Artorian couldn't read a single line. "*Eh*. Oh well."

Plopping back down on his Soul Item, he watched the map as the bouncy ball did its best to follow advanced instructions. 'Bounce towards the highest non-caster Mana signature.' Simple enough. The bouncing orb of discordant doom shot up, up, and up into the twisted continent's paths. Would it be so rough of a guess to think Bri-bri might be in her palace? Probably.

He toyed with the end of his beard. Wondering how to traverse skywards the swiftest way. He could exit the continent via the way he came in. Walk along the outside and bust back in near the top. That likely wouldn't get him any Mana expenditure back. He was going to rely on thrusters and good ol' climbing if he went that route. He grumbled, and watched the Mana bar refill as creatures perished in droves. A Nixie Tube popped bright and luminous above his head, and a huge beaming smile crossed his face.

Stowing his Soul Item, Artorian the foolish moved to

perform some basic stretches. Why go the long way around, when there was the direct way? He mused to himself, thinking it over in terms for the game. "I think this will one day be called... *Power leveling.*"

Thrusters burgeoned to life at the bottom of his feet. Slapping his hands together above him, Mana swirled in excess. The energy formed a drill that would pierce the heavens as the spiraling green luminance around Artorian's hands rotated ever faster. "If there is no path, make your own!"

Artorian the drill launched upwards. Breaking through packed stone like it was hot, molten butter. With a heroic **yeaaaaah**! the old man took the speedy-route in the topside direction. His celestine Aura acted as a giant broom that swept things under the rug. His creature kills almost balanced out the constant Mana loss. Old habits died hard, and he'd been doing things the mundane way again. "Must remember you're a Mage! Not human!"

Plinky and the Brain panicked. The invader had vanished.

In his place, a twelve-by-twelve, perfectly cylindrical tunnel had appeared. Going straight up. Artorian's disappearance dropped the threat level, as the dungeon duo had long been passed. On second thought, that likely wasn't a human. It also didn't seem to have been here for them. Chalk that up as a relief.

As a sudden convenience, this through-the-world hypha highway was exactly what they needed to reach some otherwise unbreachable emplacements. Sett's army was on the way regardless... no reason they couldn't go ahead and spore it up.

Artorian haphazardly broke through the floor of the misty-mists-smoke-place palace. Or whatever Brianna had called it. Who cares! A few more floors, and his long-deactivated thrusters finally fizzled out entirely. Note of importance. Drilling through corrupted rock? Painless. Falling skywards through corrupted rock and using your face to slow down? Not recommended. Also not painless. "Ow."

Artorian slammed into the onyx ceiling of the council

chamber with an *ooof*! then fell right back down into the hole he'd made to get here. He grabbed at the edge so he wouldn't fall *all the way* back down. He grumbled and rolled onto his back, pulling himself out. The old man coughed as the Judges present at the triangular table stared in disbelief. That was Rune-*reinforced* flooring.

When Artorian wobbled to his feet and brushed his robe off, he flashed the group a smile. "Hello there! I'm looking for Brianna. Is she *still* mad at me?"

Given the Judges attacked him immediately after, he unfortunately had to take that as a 'yes.' "*Crackers and toast.*"

CHAPTER SIXTEEN

The council jumped from their seats, managed perhaps a few steps, then flopped to the ground in a meaty pile of limbs. Instead of sudden violent action, now they all sawed heavy-logged snores through the room. Artorian was doing his best not to laugh as he held his ribs and snickered. "That worked? Oh, sweet Cal. That worked. No way!"

He nudged a snoozing Judge with his foot, his Aura radiating the sleeping effect. They were so adorable when sleeping. "Right. No reason to really perform a snappening here. Let's just try to find…"

He snapped his fingers, and pointed at a chunk of wall that was doing its very best not to appear like the door it was. "There she is! Hello, Brianna! How have you been? Are you alright? Should I have brought tea? I can likely get some tea. *Mmmm… Tea.*"

The not-door blew open while Brianna seethed behind it, Artorian kicking the barrier away to expose the entrance to one of her private getaway chambers. He wasn't going to say it, but she looked awful. Had she ever slept? She appeared frazzled. Borderline disheveled. Twitchy, and unsteady. That was never a state he expected to see a Mage in. Much less pride-Queen Bri-Bri.

She screamed at him without words, then blurred from existence.

Prediction lines winked into being before Artorian's vision. *Oho*! Actual threats! Look at that! The golden lines swiftly altered colors, designating that the assassin's attacks were anything but sluggish or uncoordinated. She was definitely trying to murder him dead.

Playing the dodging game, the old man ducked from side to side and hopped over a few low-swept strikes. "Bri-Bri, come now. We can *talk* about this!"

Her attacks stopped only for a moment, violet eyes leering at him as invisible cogs turned in her head. He was acrobat-dodging her rampage *far* too smoothly. She changed something, and Artorian's prediction lines winked out.

Then a Mana blade suddenly sliced open his robe. "*Whoa, Cal!*"

Her next set of attacks he didn't see coming at all. Infernal energy laced her being, and her blade furled in thick gray winds that… disintegrated? *Oh no.* Not *more* geese features. He'd had enough of those! His butt ached with phantom pains from recollection alone. Do not go the way of the goose! Brianna now easily took additional chunks out of his robes, his dodging not remotely as effective given he couldn't determine her strikes.

Artorian decided to just run away. He wanted to talk first, not get *minced* by an angry whirlwind of knives! "Brianna! Be reasonable! We can t—ow!"

He jumped as she successfully stabbed him in the butt. He canceled out the side effects with celestial Essence configurations to guide the Mana. But she'd still gotten him. Oh, best nix that venom too. Why always the butt! Granted, he was running around the room and bouncing away, maybe he should… y'know. *Do something.* The sleep field clearly wasn't working on her.

He skidded to a halt and threw an arm up, remembering to

actually use the Pylon system. He really, *really hoped* he had access now.

This was as good a time as any to test it. "[Sticky Grid]!"

The light-frame grid sprang to life from his position. Self-replicating light lines adapted the sticky feature as they siphoned Mana out of the air. Including whatever they connected to. Currently, that was an enraged assassin lady, and a few conked Judges on the floor that he'd been doing his best to avoid. Free Mana! "Bri-bri! Talk to me. It *doesn't* have to go this way."

Brianna was raving, and she snarled at him as she reverted to a language she hadn't used in nearly a decade. "You lie! You come back after ninety years instead of the expected hundred! Before anyone else is decanted. You came to get rid of me before anyone else could know, or find out. You came straight here. Straight to *me*. You think I didn't feel that ridiculous Essence signature boring up through my old empire? I am frayed at the abyss-burned edges. I can't keep a thought straight. Cal woke you up to get me. I know it. I just know it! Now stand there and die! Come back in another ninety years! I won't be toppled. I won't! *I won't!*"

She faltered to dry heave. An unexpected action for an A-ranker. Brianna was also successfully breaking his light grid, and the entire structure rippled, soon to shatter outright from the counter-strain she was putting on the emplaced effect. It had a second, maybe two, before she returned to being a bladewind. Artorian used it to plead one last time. "I'm *not* here to kill you! I told you a century ago. Only if I *must*. There is another way."

The grid shattered, but the bladewind didn't lunge for his throat. He hadn't truly attacked her this entire time. Not really. Her Judges were asleep on the floor. Not dead. Hopefully that helped? The space between him and Brianna opened up into a fang-filled maw and collapsed down in the spot where Artorian had stood. His eyes flickered with Mana in response, and finally he managed to pull up her stat card. Sheet? Screen? The thing with the *numbers*!

He slid his back foot into position, and placed his fists against his sides. Drawing a steadying breath, the space in their vicinity burned as celestine might purged the poison mist from the air. The change in his demeanor made the blurred Brianna falter, her shattered frame of mind unable to anticipate patterns she didn't already have memories of. Her dagger sliced down with a black flash, but was bumped away at the wrist via a slide of the old man's palm.

Brianna's Soul Item flickered and vanished, her hip bending to send a cutting leg straight through his midriff as her own Aura molded to become the dagger she'd just lost.

Artorian had to keep her closely inspected. Because *eeesh*! Forget Sword Aura, the entity Bri-Bri hung on her sleeve and embedded into her Auric signature was one far more dangerous than mere 'cutting' or embodying the idea of a sword. Her limbs moved through space, and that space became a lingering embodiment of 'cutting.'

The assassin Queen had not been idle in the near-century of isolation, suffering defeat after defeat as she attempted to re-establish control of Niflheim. She could defeat Phosgen, Greater Phosgen, and Dire Phosgen. Yet therein lay the problem. *Only* she could defeat certain variants, and she was unable to be everywhere at once without the beacon system functional.

The Dark Elves had tried to jury rig it, but hijacking a system made by a tier seven-twenty **Law** had proven to be an unattainable feat. They could have just overpowered it by shoving enough Mana in to compensate for the tier difference, but they just didn't have the remaining organized manpower. Not without kneecapping the remains of their local defenses.

The brawl between Administrator and supervisor was a rough one. Artorian was a great Mana manipulator, but merely an okay melee combatant. He got beaten to the ground several times as Brianna, who was a top-notch melee combatant, floored him. Given her discord, her Mana control left much to be desired.

The balancing measure in this fight came down to the details. The actually dooming effects of her strikes were nullified as the academic applied his patented 'No' style. Sure, it wasn't great to get kicked in the stomach, but it wasn't deadly so long as it was 'just' being kicked in the stomach. It wasn't so bad after he crashed through a few palace walls and projections, finding he could handle it. Oh hey, those were still functional? Great craftsmansh— "*Abyss!*"

Dancing into her follow up attack, Brianna shrieked out the word: "Kingsbane!"

Artorian rolled out of the way when her soul dagger reformed, cutting through the floor and ceiling with a range it should not have reasonably had. The deft physical dagger Brianna held was by itself perhaps... a foot in length? Add an '*ish*'? The range of the blasted Kingsbane, on the other hand, was actually an invisible line that extended from said dagger. One that proved it to be much, much longer. She could cut people in twain without them ever being the wiser!

Chink.

Artorian didn't follow for a second. Chink? Why did he hear the sound of a blade piercing armor? Oh. He'd been stabbed in his Mana body. *Ow?* A fake Brianna was behind him. Was that a very realistic copy? No, that was her! How was she in two places at once? Had she *split* her Presence? What kind of *suicidal nonsense* was... ow! "Oh. *Right.* Dagger in the kidney. Ruminate later."

He pulsed his Aura, rebuking her with kinetic force that omnidirectionally repulsed matter. It did a number on the stately room they were in, crumpling furniture and stone alike as matter compressed outwards against the newly reshaped wall. Their room remodeled into the shape of a cracked ball.

Something really hurt, but Artorian found out why with a glance. He was leaking Mana from the new wound, and fairly egregiously at that. Crackers, now he was on a timer.

Brianna reformed with her other self, twitchy as could be. Her form clearly threatened to split again as the reformed

Brianna wavered with discordant static. That wasn't good. Arto-rian guessed that there was a Seed Core disconnect at play.

"Well… so much for trying it the loving way."

Abyss, that dagger really hurt. With another quick check, he realized the wound was spreading, and that injury was getting worse by the second. That Kingsbane dagger was *nasty*! "Come on! I don't get to see Halcyon grow up, and now I have to skip Vol too? What *is it* with people and not wanting me to see my kids? *Fine*, Brianna. You've made it clear. *I must*."

With his health bar plummeting at a steady rate, Artorian didn't give an abyss about his Mana expenditure. It was all going to *poof* momentarily anyway. Directed attacks she was just going to dodge. Melee was out of the question, and he'd been a dum-dum to try it in the first place. She was a *professed assassin*, you academic nut! Actually, what hadn't she dodged this entire fight? The realization jolted him. Oh my word, he hadn't gotten a single hit in on her. This was early Irene all over again. So, he needed… *something special*.

Rail Palm wasn't going to fly here. That was an empowering attack to go at zippy speeds. She'd bat him out of the air like a bothersome fly. Mass driver? No time to charge it. Orbital suns? No time. Fix by fireball? *Tch*. She'd *dodge*. The only thing he'd seen her specifically dart away from was his kinetic pulse just now.

The Nixie Tube illuminated above his head as genius struck him. Well he was going to die anyway. Blaze of glory? He shot her a Mana-leaking smile. Blaze of abyss-burned glory! Let's make Marie's **Law** proud. He coughed, and managed a wry smile. "Hey Bri-Bri. *Dodge this*."

The confidence melted from her face as his Auric signature inverted, sucking energy towards him instead of repelling it. She was having none of his second wind madness. Breaking the ground by throwing herself forwards, the ever-blurred assassin sliced the room in a multi-line star pattern. How she was cutting easily twenty-plus paths with a single strike, Artorian didn't know. Also, it didn't matter. He got the words that popped into his head out in time, even if he flubbed the first one. "[Majin Repulsor, Spiral Drill]."

Brianna didn't understand the words, and didn't believe they would do anything.

Artorian, on the other hand—he *did* believe. An orb-shaped pulse rippled from his form before her criss-crossing cuts reached him. The spirals forming on Artorian's Auric surface blocked all the impacts, and plinked them away. Forcing her attack to veer, and cut several layers deep through the palace as entire walls collapsed from whole columns being Kingsbane-cleaved.

Green and white spirals twisted into being on Artorian's Aura, twisting faster, then faster still. That same spiral design was forming in the old man's eyes when Brianna glanced at him. She didn't know this pattern and was instantly unsettled. She needed to backpedal. To back off and veer away as her attacks had. Brianna did move backwards, but not by choice, as the orb shaped Aura around Artorian expanded with a spherical pulse.

The surface evolved! The spirals were now going at such speeds that they covered him in omnidirectional drills. Each of which ground Brianna's Magenta Palace into little more than broken hunks of dust and gravel.

The resulting sound was terrible, but neither of the combatants heard it. Brianna screeched in defiance. A cloak of Mana-daggers formed to clink and chink against the expanding dome of green, spiraling drills that limited her mobility and pressed her ever more outwards. The surrounding Judges that woke from no longer being trapped in a sleeping field took it the worst, unable to dodge the destruction as they were already plastered to the walls.

Brianna fumed. She would have effortlessly beaten such an indiscriminate effect back, had the Administrator not poured a full tier of Mana into it. After all, he wasn't about to need it.

Artorian's health representation flashed dangerously red, and went ignored.

In response to being cornered, Brianna summoned every dagger she had and attacked. Save for her Soul Item, her weapons shattered against the spiraling field. With a shout of finality at being pushed back once more, her actual form touched the wall of drills, trapped against the wall as her back was flattened to a section of ground-reinforcing Runes.

Brianna may have been stuck, but the green wall didn't stop expanding. With the sound of grinding metal and shattering glass, it was over. Artorian managed another cough as he watched Brianna's A-ranked form fragment into... triangles and confetti? He unwillingly dropped to a knee, hand no longer over the wound as he noticed that the entire left section of his chest and midriff was completely missing. "*Welp.*"

<Congratulations!>

Artorian winced as he could *swear* he just heard Cal's voice. He unfortunately couldn't reply; his Mana allotment was too low, and the sensation of pain overbearing. Why did that dungeon snoot see a need to add pain receptors?

Cal sounded delighted when he spoke again, and dropped a left boot near Artorian as reward. A joke from his old dungeon days. <Looks like I didn't need to do it myself after all. Perfect, that's the better outcome. Nice going with that body! It wouldn't have held up for more than a week anyway, so don't be too worried that it's about to blow up. Mana bodies just can't compensate where my system is involved. Anywho. I'm about to Incarnate, so you go ahead and finish that nap! Catch you on the other side!>

Artorian swallowed, his form slowly disintegrating as he verbally complained. Brianna had been *right*. He'd been played like a pawn. "Cal, I'm gonna..."

Artorian's mind was back in the Seed Core before he was able to finish his sentence.

Within the private meeting space for S-rankers in the solar archives, Cale spun in his chair. He jumped out of it to hoot wildly and punch both his arms to the sky. He was in a great mood! Sadly for him, his company did not share his good cheer.

Tatum and Dawn looked at him with murderous displeasure. Dani's expression wasn't much different. Cale just shrugged. "What? He said he would take the task and the responsibility. *So what* if I brought him back a little early?"

The living bonfire seated next to Tatum exhaled flame. "You used my favorite person as a pawn. Cut off his communication with us. Didn't tell him an abyss-blasted thing, and left him to flounder. He had no idea that he was alone down there. You populated places purely for test results, and nearly lost the thread a few times. He made a chosen, and you messed up the sigil. Do you know how badly that would have backfired had he puzzled it out there? Even then, you showed up at the end. He's going to be furious with you when you bring him back. You *should* have just told him."

Cale mumbled and flopped back into his seat, feeling disgruntled with his own situation. "Well... I couldn't. It was important that I didn't interfere, because events could have played out differently if I *did* tell him. Now I have a set of events from when he knows nothing, and look! Success on both fronts. Made it to Niflheim, and canted Brianna. A month before my expected Incarnation date no less."

The glares weren't letting up, so Cale conceded. "I'll... find a way to apologize and make it up to him. *Alright?* We've got all the supervisors, and I can now go ahead to box, gem, and memory stone the remaining people and creatures. *Aaaand, done!* That's it. That's everything. Every mind is stored, and every realm save for our little spot is completely bare and barren. Save for the plants, but I have the samples."

Dawn stopped burning up, though her arms remained crossed in displeasure. "Fine. Shall we get started then? *You have enough.*"

Tatum nodded in rigid agreement. "She's right. I'll go ahead and knock on the Tower."

Cale frowned, not feeling ready. "Wait. *Wow.* Hold on. *Just wait a moment!*"

Dawn vanished with Dani in tow, leaving a definitely-not-prepared Cale to momentarily panic as Tatum did exactly as he said he would. The man was *acquiring attention*. Cale's hands shot out towards Tatum to stop him, but it was too late. "Hey, no. Not yet! I have a month! *I have a month*! Cease this instant! I will shove you into *obscurity* for this!"

Vwop.

CHAPTER SEVENTEEN

"*Finally!*" Dawn stretched with utter relief.

Tatum was right there with her, breaking into entirely unnecessary elaborate yoga poses. "*Oooh, yeah.* Preach to the choir, sister. This is *so* much better. Not *quite* there for me, but *definitely* better. No more replacing bodies every few days, this'll do me!"

Dani copied Dawn's stretches, testing her new human-shaped body. Her voice was its usual level of matronly, which pleased her. "It's my first time in one of these, but wow. These are *special*. It doesn't even feel like I'm in a body, it's just so malleable and utterly *natural*."

The Fire Soul tapped her own hip, showcasing a stretch properly performed before responding. "Mhm! Incarnate bodies aren't so much bodies as they are thoughts shaped into being. Using an energy that's… Well. You feel it now. Isn't it great? Just try to hold onto the wavelength you currently feel. Take it from us, falling into a different layer by accident is *anything* but fun. As a bonus, we can come get you if you do. So just *yell*, and we'll hear you. Don't worry if the space you're in is made from kaleidoscopes, or seems as if you're stuck in nothing. It's a place, and we can get there."

Dani nodded, looking over her shoulder as she put her hands to her waist to flourish her new chartreuse romper. "Wonderful! *Soo...* does that mean you're about to go fetch Cal from whatever layer he just plunged into? I didn't expect Incarnating to... uh. Break so much."

Both the Incarnates shrugged, miming the same uncertain: "*Eeeeh.*"

Tatum wavered his hands up and down, truly lacking in certainty about that action as his hips swayed for effect. "Maybe in a bit. He's not going anywhere, given where he's stuck."

Dawn nodded and jumped in place, testing her reconnection to a form of Incarnate energy. It was incredibly liberating, and she loved it. "*Mm.* What layer is he on? I didn't track it. I don't notice him on *bordering* wavelengths."

Occultatum formed, then reformed the robes he was wearing. He just wasn't pleased with them. It didn't take more than mere thought at this stage, so he was cycling for fashion. "He tumbled and ended up in the Pi layer."

Dani turned on her heel, the ground beneath her foot moving so quickly that she caused an honest-to-Cal earthquake in Niflheim. *Eh.* What were a few more displaced pathways? "A layer of pie? As in the confection? An entire universe filled with *pastry*? I wanna go!"

The Incarnates shared a good laugh, and their grayscale burst into being around them. Dawn punched the air in success. "There it is! Took a bit of traded Mana, but looks like the safety field works. I moved our laughs into a higher layer. So it should..."

The grayscale around them faded, and Dani opened and closed her palms. She felt perplexed. "No pressure? I expected to be locked down."

Tatum filled her in on both fronts. "Pi, as in a realm dedicated entirely to this weird, *one number*. A full layer is needed to store the full sequence string. It's a strange place. No confections, sadly. As for the lockdown effect, you're counted as a true Incarnate, so given we don't have the energy to really throw our weight around, you're just not affected. We should be picky about who we bring back first. An Incarnate body in this Soul Space is going to sap the free Mana right away."

Dani waved it off. "Let's not bring anyone out just yet. Please go fetch our village totem pole from the number realm. I'd rather he institute his system specifically so that doesn't happen. I'm just glad we didn't lose the stored minds. I expect that when it comes to things we did lose, we lost more than we can see. I want my inventory audited."

Tatum didn't argue and ceased existing where he was. A moment later, he was standing back in the spot he'd occupied a moment ago. Holding a very pale Cale by the shoulder. Cale stammered. "*I never want to do that again.* I'm… just… going to sit down. *I'm not okay.*"

"Shh… he's been traumatized by pi." Tatum's voice was a whisper. The slightest movement from Cale's human body grayscaled the entire Soul Space, and outright locked every occupant down. Cale could move freely, even if at a wobble. He couldn't walk right for some reason, and collapsed to the grass like a fresh-born fawn. When he stilled, the global gray field faded, allowing the others a breath they didn't need. They took it regardless, just for comfort.

Dani shot Tatum a demanding look. "*You said we'd be unaffected!*"

Tatum bent over, hands pressed to his knees. He raised an arm without straightening his body, gaze firmly on the ground as he reiterated an earlier point. "Given we don't have the energy to throw our weight around! Mr. Seven-twenty-plus over there has gobs of it. He is unwittingly trading all his Mana into Incarnate energy. Compared to us, he is energetically loaded. It doesn't even matter that I'm technically a double S-rank, the difference is just too large."

When Tatum finally straightened, it was with both hands to his back as it popped, mimicking mortal features. He felt better, and finally remembered a question now that he had a half-decent body again. "Dawn. Is there by chance a convenient ancient word for S-ranked energy? Calling it something-energy all the time isn't remotely as convenient as the term we have for Mana. Though I'm aware that's an acronym."

Dawn cleared her throat. "*Spirit* is the common term. No bells or whistles."

Dani liked the sound of that. "Stick with that. Back to brass tacks. Cale. Take a look at the *quackening* that occurred. I think we need your system in place in a hurry. You can take two guesses which creations self-manifested when you Incarnated."

Cale discorporated his body, returning to being a disembodied voice. That didn't cause the grayscaling effect, so it was better for now. <I don't need two guesses, I can see the Incarnate goose roaming on Hel. I am having some difficulties affecting it. That's strange? It's in my Soul Space. That shouldn't happ... *ooohh*. It's higher rank than me, and has gone *rogue*. If it was out in the real, that would be a dungeon-breakout monster. It's the blasted *abyss cat* all over again. Awww, *me*. It spotted me. Welp, I'm not looking at Hel for a while. Good luck, Tatum!>

Tatum raised his arms to just let them fall to his sides with a **fumph**. "Why *me*?"

He knew why, but was deflecting. "*Fine*. Just don't make it rain tar while I'm getting chased by that bundle of Incarnate feathers. Have you ever needed to fight an S-ranked critter before? It's horrible. *They're horrible.*"

Tatum threw his head back with a groan and void-stepped to Hel. Wanting to deal with *the honker* right away. Territorial pain in his—*Ow*. He should have never let Artorian oversee his patch of soot! *Now* the cobra chicken liked to bite people in the ass. *Great.*

He had once been one of the most powerful people on the planet, feared and respected across all the lands as The Master! *Now* look at him. Ah well. The goose had a body now, rather than merely appearing as a skeletal rack. "Guess it's time to brush up on those butcher skills."

Honk!

"*C'mere you!*"

Back on the Niflheim topside, Dani wobbled as she tried to walk. Luckily, she had a free-floating Dawn to hold onto as a support platform. "How are you *doing that*? I took this form because as a Wisp I'm just plastered to the ground. Same with Gracie and the others."

Exhilarated to exist, the in-the-proper-body-again Fire Soul just smiled. Her supernova irises swirled while her long hair drifted behind her as a twinkling nebula. Dawn freely let waves of power roll from her S-ranked skin, just to enjoy it.

Her consciousness realized late that she had been addressed, but the question filtered in, and she answered. "It becomes natural when you've gone through the progression path yourself. I imagine that, for you, it feels like you are suddenly in the shape of a body that does what you want, sooner than you want it. Incarnate forms are responsive like that. There is no delay between thought and action, for your form is your thoughts, and your thoughts and soul are one. Or it should be, if it wasn't for the disconnect that you are a mind occupying that form *without* the natural progression."

Dawn paused, recounting a piece of information her own teachers had once told her. It made more sense now that she repeated it. "My every action is an effigy to a personal truth."

"Since when are you *wordy*?" Dani narrowed her eyes at the woman waxing poetic. "That's the *other one's* job. Just tell me how you're flying. Or however. I'm not sure what you're doing."

Dawn gently shrugged without blowing up a chunk of the Niflheim topside. "My explanation won't be useful. Let me use someone else's words. Think of a Mage as… one of Cal's spells. It is contained before going off. You've got something to say 'not yet.' Since, as a Mage, keeping your power reined in is one of the big breaking points of staying alive. So for people living as Mages, that gets serious practice."

Dawn differentiated. "As an Incarnate, the first difference is that you no longer have the 'not yet.' You are a spell, continually exploding and going off in the world. You cannot stop, there is no container. That's why for unskilled Incarnates, that grayscale field is so rampant. It's a safety net to keep the rest of the world safe, even if it causes side effects such as lockdown. When it comes to flight, or what you currently see as flight…"

She mulled it over. It would be easier if she had Sunny to explain, but he wasn't at this stage yet. She'd fill him in eventually. "Our favorite long-beard would say, 'That's a misconception.' Complete with a waggle of the finger and pacing about with an arm across his lumbar."

They snickered, and Dawn continued. "The second big leap is that you don't actually have a body. Or I don't. What you see is the effect of that spell never stopping. My power has to do something, and it has to do it all the time, because my soul cannot suddenly stop existing. So my *effects* can't either. The more power you have, the more you need to invest it somewhere. So usually, Incarnates spend the first chunk on a body, which they then inhabit. As we are so, so very used to having an ambulatory form. Almost *nobody* is a Deverash, able to live as an object for long periods of time."

Dani rolled her wrist, wanting her to get on with it. She just wanted to know how to fly in this thing. Dawn just smirked. "The thing about this body being just a thought is that it moves with the same function. Just a thought. You walk because you think you walk. You breathe because you think you breathe. You fly, *because*…"

Dani's feet ceased touching the ground when it clicked. She hovered about free as could be, and rolled around with all the agility and flawless aerial grace one would expect of a Wisp. She beamed, and then flailed as she lost the thought-thread of just flying, and instead held the thought not to fall. That kept her in the air, but removed all the fine movement control. "I had it for a second there!"

Dawn said nothing. Dani recovered just by thinking of flight again, her thoughts placing her body where it needed to be. The Incarnate form just followed. Thought, to action. The Wisp mom snapped at the oversensitive controls. "This thing has no filter!"

Dawn nodded, as that was correct. "On average? Takes a century for a true S-rank zero to manage existing without feeling like a floundering fish. Less if your mind is more deep-thought inclined. So, all those prodigies and geniuses that fly through the lower ranks without a second thought? Usually much longer for them."

A realization struck her. "Oh, I should also clear up *that* misunderstanding. It's just S-rank. There is no S-rank zero. I misspoke because of how the rest of your system works. There are nuances in the soul ranks that make the oddities in the A-ranks look like playground arguments. Unless someone takes the second step, it is outright impossible to tell an Incarnate's specific level, or create any sort of measurable differences."

Dani practiced hovering, then just walking but without touching the ground. To her surprise, that functioned without flaw. "I am walking on nothing, but am still moving. Like I am... *This is so strange.*"

Dawn slunk over and poked the human-form Wisp in the hip. Rather than send her tumbling and hurtling away, it was akin to booping a soap bubble and gently pushing it off course. Dani kept walking, influenced by the new direction. "Uh... well. I can go forwards, but I don't know how to undo the tunnel effect you just caused."

The Fire Soul decided to make it easy on her, stabbing a straight line of fire through the air. "Walk on that. Just think about it. Honestly, that's it and that's all."

With the straight line in place, Dani's mind meandered to it. Her form hovered to the starting point. As she did, her body once again aligned as normal with the ground. "How...? Did my body just align because *I thought* I should be right side up?"

Dawn shot her a simple thumbs up. "You have a unique case, as you both are and are not a natural Incarnate due to being a bonded Wisp. Your mind is in the spirit body. So while you don't have the full benefits of Incarnate power, how to *operate the thing* functions much the same. Your Wisp body is plastered to the ground because it is an A-rank form existing in a realm of S-rank pressure. It needs to be Incarnated properly."

That earned Dawn a sharp look of confusion, so the Fire Soul did her best to clarify. "You have a *separate* soul. You might share one of the most solid connections there are, but that doesn't include you in Cal's Ascension club. He likely forgot that, and thought you'd have an Incarnate form by default. That's not how it works. You need a facsimile of the Wisp form. Cal Incarnated. You… *did not*."

Dawn made placating hand motions. "I know, *I know*. Connected. Still a *no*. On second thought, that also means Tatum was wrong before. You can't fall through layers unless you're a true Incarnate. Having a toe over the line doesn't count. That's why Cal fell, and you didn't."

Dani burned a hole into her friend, her sad words causing the air around them to fracture as the ground pulverized. A field of gray stopped the worst of it before fading away. "Why *nooooot?*"

Dawn thought that was obvious. "Is your idea of **Acme** the same as Cal's? *Exactly* the same? Even then, there can only be *one* S-ranker per Node. So when Cal hits double S, your soul will likely First-Step, taking his current position. Until then, welcome to the *wonderful world of Incarnate confusion*. You're in for a few millennia of '*why did that happen*' and '*I had no idea this worked that way.*' *Trust me*, it is going to happen *constantly*. Some of them outright will not make sense. So don't panic. Just call out. We *will* hear you. Some Incarnates keep an item around for grounding if needed. Traditionally, it's a towel. Tatum and I know how to keep our ear to the layers for Cal. There are only a *few* places we outright ignore and don't go. If he ends up in one of *those*, we will *definitely* know."

Dani's form collapsed, and a luminous Wisp frame uncertainly bobbed through the Soul Space. "Whoa… That… *What?*"

Her friend slapped her knee with a laugh. "I *just* told you, that you're in for a few millennia of 'I had no idea.' Let me guess, you thought of being a Wisp. Believed it with an utter certainty, and then were confused when your form shifted?"

The Wisp didn't think Dawn was a mind reader… so that guess must have just been experience. "That's right, but I didn't expect my human body to be able to just change like that. I thought Incarnate bodies were stuck forever once they were that way?"

Dawn waggled her hand. "It's complicated. For most people it's a hard yes due to some… events. That happens when you're an Incarnate. There are moments where holding onto your personality is of the utmost importance. Cal's Soul Space helps prevent those moments, which lets true Incarnates be more malleable. I suppose there's three types."

She counted on her fingers. "A true Incarnate, whatever you are, and a facsimile Incarnate."

Dani thought she had this one in the bag. "Let me give this a go. A fake Incarnate is a person in a body of Spirit, but doesn't have the natural powers or drawbacks a true one has. So a C- or B-ranker could have one and be fine, but advancing further will be difficult. You are a true Incarnate, so in a Spirit body you have full access to all your toys. I am in the middle due to my connection with Cal, but I am essentially no different from a fake one, since my soul didn't do the thing. Spirit bodies are *weird*."

The Fire Soul repressed her giggle, but smirked regardless. "What *is* a body? I don't know how Sunny does it, repeating lessons to students all the time."

Dani, much happier with her Wisp form, settled on Dawn's head to be done with this uncertainty nonsense for the moment. "He doesn't. I have rarely seen him explain things twice. It's *the students*. They're either gifted, or he makes them gifted. He gives them information that goes over their heads, but is never out of their reach. I remember the eyes of the young, twinkling and full of hope and wonder. What was the thing he used to say? During that thought game he let students play?"

Dawn smirked. Parroting the words with the same old-man tone and elderly smile before calling it a day. "You can *certainly* try."

The Wisp matron laughed, setting in place. "Ha! Well, at least he'll be able to rest for a while. With his tier what it is, I don't think we're waking him up anytime soon."

The Fire Soul snickered. "Artorian's favorite! *Lazily resting.* I wonder where he got that trait."

CHAPTER EIGHTEEN

"*Run, boy, run!*"

The old authoritative voice *boomed* when it found out he'd done it *again*. Encouraging a young boy to bolt. It was *so* loud, that the words reverberated through the halls of the branch family home. The child heaved as he ran, running at full sprint away from his previously silent father. Who chased him. Fast. How was his father *always faster*?

Branch family members clapped their hands, cheering and laughing as the boy shouldered through an already partially opened door. *They* were who had told him to run. Water carriers entered the house as he did, and their clay pots fell and shattered as the kid fell on his rear to slide between the porter's legs. That's what his father got for ordering the floor to stay so shiny all the time. They were slippery and smooth!

Bright sun slapped his face as he tumbled onto the court-yard path. The youth's previously immaculate robes dirt-stained immediately. *Just another thing* he was going to get chastised over. As he did with everything, apparently. All those dumb tasks, he loathed them! On his feet and back on the run, he was face-deep in bluegrass before the doors behind him nearly blew from their hinges.

Crackers! There was *Father*. Holding those dreaded, awful-tasting pills in hand. He didn't want to take more of the medicine! He wasn't sick. It was the pills making him sick! He knew for sure now! He'd stopped taking them for a few weeks, hiding them away under a floorboard after sneaking them into the hem of his child's robe when he was supposed to take them. The most minor act in sleight of hand. Always useful to know how to *palm*. The scroll had said so!

How he loved scrolls.

How his family hated finding him tucked away in a corner with yet another memoir or ledger. So what if he didn't understand the numbers! He liked seeing the squiggles. He enjoyed tracing his fingers over the material, wondering how such pretty scratches were made.

Still bolting, he was breathing heavy when passing another porter that was filling pots from a piece of redirected river. That porter snickered, and smiled with deep wrinkles. The branch family member knew the drill, shouting as the lad passed without having a moment to stop.

"*Run, boy, run!*"

What did they think he was *doing*? Bluegrass slapped him in the face, and his father was *once again* gaining ground. Pushing foliage out of the way, he hated how blind he was in this tall field of bluegrass. He was too slow! He needed to be faster. *Faster*. So much faster.

He drew a breath, and forced another foot in front of the other at speed. The porter at the river laughed. The boy *knew* the man pointed in his direction. Nobody challenged Father. It was folly. So why did he *keep* doing it? Right. Father had a *plan* for him. A way he wanted his son's world to work.

"*Merli*, you come to your patriarch *this instant* and take your medicine!"

The boy grit his teeth, wincing as he tried not to let the pain of his heart get to him. Would it kill Father to actually call himself *Father,* instead of *patriarch?* He didn't need some high-title family leader in his life. He needed something far more personal, and it didn't exist in the main family hall, nor the branch family hall. It didn't matter where he was taken. Father was there with his imperious will, telling him '*no*' at every turn.

Stand in the corner and don't speak, Merli. Sit behind this bench and don't move, Merli. Take this awful set of pills that makes you sick, Merli. Do what you're told. Do what you're told. *Do what you're told.*

His eyes were full of tears, jaw grit as the sun dipped below the horizon. A painting of colors presented itself, forming the lengthy evening aurora. A corona of lovely oranges, reds, and violets that painted the sky under which he ran. Now that. *That* was worth running to.

Forget the stark, organized halls. The rules and the dumb customs. The pills, and being sick. There was *color* ahead. Color splashed onto the canvas of the sky, unbridled and *wild*. *Free. Liberated.* A canvas filled with nothing but choice.

How he *wished* he had a choice.

His feet took him, and took him. Hands pushed away the tall grass to keep moving, but his heavy breathing betrayed his location. He knew his father had found him. When Merli dared glance behind him, there was only the reaching grasp of a demanding, open hand. How he feared this hand. This *ever-reaching* hand.

No! Without thought, he shrieked, then jumped! The reaching hand did not find purchase, and Merli gasped his next breath twelve feet up in the air.

The patriarch's voice was panicked. "Merli, *no*! You *must* take your medicine. Your vital energy is unstable! You are not well!"

The boy didn't hear his father. He was on the canvas. He was *in* the canvas. He was one with color, and sound, and the *wild* of the pattern. His heart pounded, his eyes were wet, his cheeks stained. His mind knew fear, but his *spirit*?

His spirit was *free*.

Merli's vision went dark before he ever collapsed onto the ground. The vital energy surging, spiking, and forcing the young body —which was unprepared for such a high-tension use— to pass out. Merli never hit the dirt. His father caught his unconscious form.

The patriarch slapped his cheek a few times, but Merli's eyes were gray and glazed over. Reflecting the quiet tapestry of colors above, rather than the spirit that lived within. The medicine was forced into his mouth as his father fussed. "You hellion. You broke both your legs, again. Your vital energy is as wild as your spirit, but if we don't get it under control, it will kill you, *my son.*"

Silence followed.

It made Artorian's bonfire world all the more *dark.*

Dark, but full of falling petals of simple silver. They reflected light that didn't have a source, but provided enough illumination for Artorian to see when he opened his eyes in his bonfire space. His gaze dropped, watching his own open hands listlessly lying on his knees as he sat. Discomfort had him. Now that he was mentally awake, he sighed and assessed his situation.

He didn't like this space so much anymore. The sanctum was currently more of a prison, as the looming pair of pink eyes watched him from above. Artorian knew they were there without glancing. He sighed, and slunk back against the Silverwood Tree in his bonfire space. His voice sounded despondent. "I never knew. He actually called me *his son.* Oh… *Father.* What a *hellion* you indeed have."

He wiped his tear-stained face with his sleeve when the 'rain' came. After a few minutes of just letting himself feel, he looked up at the pink irises staring back down. The old man felt ancient, cracked like a mirror. His heart wasn't ready for this. Yet here he was.

Artorian's mind hopped to it, gluing the pieces together once he was okay. When he'd died by Brianna's blade, his mind had been canted in the Seed Core. Unlike last time, he did not fall into a pleasant, long, dreamless slumber.

This time, someone was waiting for him. For Scilla had been right. He had to sleep, and when he did, she'd be there. With his regrets that he said he would face, and then hadn't. His voice remained despondent, but he was no longer talking to himself. "Why, Scilla... why? Why show me a memory that wasn't mine?"

Scilla's blighted form slunk from the ceiling, settling in the shape of the innocent Chasuble girl as she sat next to him. Donned in his favorite pink-petal robe, no less. Everything was *pink* with this one. Surely adding the robe was going overboard? She didn't indulge his musings, her young voice answering. "Everything has a beginning. Some meddling old stranger I know started at the end, and worked backwards."

Artorian mockingly mumbled, and pulled his Soul Item into this space. He wasn't surprised when it worked. Just thankful. "I'll work on this instead, thank you very much."

Scilla didn't bat an eye. "Go ahead. It won't help you. Not even a little bit. Get it as big and puffy as you want, until it has gravity all by itself and pulls whole moons into its orbit. It won't let you reach A-rank *one*."

The old man grumbled louder, biting into the edge of the pillow just to muffle his own outcry. When sated, he vanished the item back to where it had come from, and regarded Scilla with a very downcast expression. "Fine. What *will*, then?"

Scilla didn't smile. Her response was just flat, and to the point. "Me. It's *me*. I decide now. The **Law** has a *soft spot* for you. She would let you *cheat*. Cheat all the way to the Third-Step soul ranks. Just so you can run right towards her and take the baton. She wants you to. She's ready to go. However, she also knows that she's only given you the kind lessons. The gentle gains. **Love** isn't all sunshine and rainbows. There is pain. There is so, so *much* pain. She's a tender soul at heart, and I? *I'm not*. I will beat you with that baton until you advance. Only when you tackle the ten big regrets I choose from your life, and work through them, will I hand over your Liminal energy so you can Incarnate."

Artorian raised a brow. "Why ten?"

Scilla wiggled her finger, ten blighted orbs forming around the digit to hover. "A-rank zero to A-rank zenith. A *rank* for a *regret*. You may no longer lock them away, but that doesn't mean you resolved them. The **Law** let it be my choice, and this is my choice. You will never make an increase again without me. Because I don't care how wonderful you make that pillow. I don't care for your excuses. I don't care for what you're trying to *do*. Both the **Law** and I know that you will exemplify the concept just by existing. You don't bind to a **Law** that high without being *suitable*. It seems that people either like to forget, or are oblivious, to the *costs* the higher **Laws** incur. To know **Love**, you must know and feel all facets, and you must feel them without filter. Without defenses. In full, and with all the joy and agony that comes with it. You must let it flow over you, through you, and past you. Like a fear usurped."

Artorian swallowed. The horror gripping his heart was apt, and he didn't know of a challenge he'd faced worse than this. He would have to experience a few unpleasant things all over again. Well… nobody got anywhere by sitting still. "I take it… we start the day of the shovel, and the rain?"

Scilla wagged her finger to the negative. "Earlier. We start the day you ran away. The day you led yourself astray. We start with the first choice that began the path nobody expected. The path that twists through fields of blue, heralded by a voice of stone, to bring you where you are today."

Artorian clenched his teeth and his hands. "So… what do I do?"

Scilla's head turned, addressing him with a directness that stabbed straight to his soul. His vision twisted as he was wrenched from the bonfire room in more ways than one, his form breaking to become something—and someone—else as Scilla spoke.

"*Run, boy, run!*"

CHAPTER NINETEEN

Bright sun slapped Merli's face as he tumbled onto the courtyard path. His previously immaculate robes immediately dirt-stained. As they frequently were any time he did this, and he'd sure built up a reputation for it over his youth. He was freshly twelve, and had been so big a thorn in his family's side that his free-spirited nature was legendary.

Unfortunately, a mere single foot out the door, and Father had him by the scruff of his neck. Robe in this case, but neck all the same. Merli opened his mouth to protest, but a hand with pills was slapped onto it, forcing him to swallow the incredibly bitter-tasting medicine. The pills made his face scrunch as if he'd just bitten into the sourest of lemons.

His father snapped, tone stern. "Stop trying to run away! You have studies to do and calligraphy to finish. I know your brother went out into the world a few years ago, and you are aching to chase him. You cannot, your constitution is weak. Return to your chambers and rest, drink the herbal tea. I know it's bitter."

Merli struggled, face contorted like an unhappy trapped animal. "No! I'm twelve! You can't keep me! *You can't!*"

His father looked as stern as he sounded. Draped in flawless violet and gold-hem robes, the patriarch wasn't having any of his youngest's pish. "I can, and *I will*. You will live in this household, and you will die in this household. It's for your own good. You're fragile, and you keep hurting yourself. You think I like seeing you get hurt? Get back inside! I have more important things to do as Patriarch than to play overseer all day, every day."

Artorian's perspective in Merli snapped his hand to his heart from how painful that statement was, and Merli's actual body followed suit. That had not been something he'd done the first time. The original time that this had happened. He could *influence* the memory? Originally, he had just broken down and cried. Merli still did, but with his hand clamped to his heart.

Able to somewhat dissociate himself from Merli's perspective, he looked his young self over. Crackers… he was so small back then. Shouldn't the boy have gone through a growth spurt already? He was so puny, and awfully thin. No wonder he was held back. Nobody would believe the moxie that spouted from such a pint-sized bean sprout. No matter how you sliced it, Merli at twelve looked like a completely defenseless child. One that appeared sick. Abyss, was that gray on his throat and cheeks?

Merli was ushered back into the main family hall, and sat down next to one of the displeased branch family elders, who shot Merli a side-eye before ignoring him altogether. The youngest son of the patriarch was a disgrace to the family, and the elder mumbled under his breath in disdain. "Twelve already, and took so poorly to the pills that at best it's keeping his vital energy in check. What a *mistake* the heavens must have made in creating this child."

Merli heard him, and snapped back. "I'm not a *mistake*."

The hall elder just flashed him a rotten smile. "Doesn't make you *wanted*, whelp!"

Merli couldn't handle more negativity today. Not today. Not after overhearing that he might be forced to take the worst pill

DENNIS VANDERKERKEN & DAKOTA KROUT

his family had in its possession. That entombed evil-looking thing was named a 'sealing pill.' It was supposedly kept in reserve for the heinous, treacherous, and murderous. Instead, upon waking in the morning, his father had ordered him to take it. That didn't mean he wanted to take it, as he knew the pills were still making him sick. They'd been making him sick all his life, and he lost weeks of playtime to bedrest.

He shot up from the chair, saw nobody was looking—or perhaps cared—and ran back to the door he'd come from. His satchels were still on his back, and they jingled as he went. The elder grimaced with pleasure, indulging an evil, awful expression. Merli was back at the door in no time, bolting out through the courtyard and rushing into the blue field. He was not going to take that pill! He wasn't!

In the hall, the patriarch returned to the congregation of elders with a terrible display. He shocked the gathering to their hearts on seeing that his majestic long beard was cut off, and instead placed in a box. "My family elders... it is time. They come. We must declare."

The patriarch saw an empty seat and frowned. "Where is my son?"

His cultivator-powered eyes saw the trail of footsteps lead back to a very much open main hall door. "*Toast.*"

Artorian held his heart. *Right.* Crackers, *and toast.* Toast was his father's saying for when something went awry, while crackers had been his. When had he... adopted it? He didn't know. He could not call upon a connecting memory. Scilla just slapped him back to task, not letting him wiggle away for even a moment as Merli's perspective once again took the forefront.

Through endless fields of tall blue grass. Morovian grass. Merli ran, and ran. His feet took him faster than they should. Then they took him faster than they could. Yet as he ran, he was as the wind, and would be *free.* Unbeknownst to Merli, but very much visible to Artorian, Merli's stunted and shuttered center roiled. The sound of glass shattering was heard, and a lesser wind-based affinity channel opened in full within the youth.

A terrible thing to happen, as Artorian saw the corruption in his young body. How... so much. *How*? That was easily twelve times the amount he'd seen at fifty in the Fringe, when he had taken those initial observation notes. What happened? Had... had his family given him pills, *cultivation pills*, to try to make him stronger, when he hadn't had even a *single active affinity channel* before this point? No wonder it made him sick, so how was he still kicking?

Taking a second, deeper glance, he could now see resplendent light shine within the roiling mass of blackened filth. Not his sunlight, nor refined Essence as he knew it. Rather this was his vital energy, and sweet mercy, there was so much of it. His corruption couldn't tether to it? The vital energy rebuked it rather than letting the corruption adhere, take, and consume it like it normally would. Or should?

It didn't. That was the end result. The vital energy and the corruption didn't mix. Oh. No. *There*, the new Essence he was taking in through the weak air-affinity channel. That stuff was being converted and eaten by the corruption.

Then what the heck was *vital Essence*? Since apparently it was different. It... Artorian's mind leapt. "*Quintessence*?"

Merli spoke the word even though Artorian said it. Merli didn't register it. It hadn't happened in the original memory, so Merli acted no differently as he ran away through the fields of Morovia. His legs hurt. They were definitely taking him faster than they could handle. He knew he'd broken his legs before, just never *why*.

Merli wanted to see the path, and in response air Essence swirled behind his eyes. He needed to find the way, and that thought consumed him. Corruption lost its hold on the raw Essence, which instead flocked to the beacon of need. Then like the sudden appearance of a summer breeze, Merli saw, and the wind was his guide. Sound ceased around the boy, and grass parted before he passed to form the wake. The environment bent via the playful revolution of wind in response to the single, defined desire. A desire that wind, of all things, embodied best. *Run free*.

Artorian pressed his hands over his mouth. No, *nononono*. With that much corruption, using any Essence in the body would allow that corruption to enter the meridian pathways, and run rampant outside of the center.

Merli's skin was deathly gray before he reached the river. He had run free, and wild. He'd been the wind and it felt wonderful. Collapsing, he didn't notice that he'd broken his legs again. Only that he had when his eyes opened to see the reflection of the sky moving in the river, it wasn't pretty. Not this time. It was all just gray. Fairly drab, actually. The view lacked all color. Just as Merli's dull, glazed gray eyes did.

He didn't notice when his father picked him up in a panic, and hurriedly carried him back to the cauldron chamber. "The sealing pill! Untomb it! I need it. I need it now! We need everything in his power space out. It is killing my boy. It has to get out!"

The grimacing elder from before already had the keys and solvents ready. The seals were undone, chains broken, and the dreaded 'sealing pill' was properly unearthed. It had been the hope Merli would take it willingly. There were horrible side effects to those who took it *unwillingly*.

A pharmacist counselor was swiftly at the concerned patriarch's side. "It is ready, my lord. Here is the pill. I… I am sorry. It will strip him of everything. The supporting effects of every pill he has ever taken. Any advancement. Everything. The sealing pill will consume it, expending itself until the solvents reach its central component. The Immaculate Core at its center from the beast you killed in your youth. Then… then it's up to the heavens themselves."

Artorian jolted as he felt a sudden touch. Scilla held his shoulder. Just to tell him something. "Nothing you do—*nothing*—will have *any impact* on what's to come."

Artorian looked back at Scilla with desperation, falling into the memory when she instead pushed him back in.

Merli was slumped in someone's arms. While the boy was not unconscious, he was certainly not present. The sealing pill was administered, and Artorian felt unbridled terror as he watched. The pill's outer layers immediately sucked in corruption like a desert-dry sponge. Which cracked when heavily suffused to feed the core within.

Artorian had trouble believing it even as he saw it. He'd dismissed the pharmacist's words, but… an Immaculate Core? That must have meant something else in those days. Surely his father wouldn't have gotten an… he mumbled to himself in realization. "I'll be *abyssed*. That's an actual *Immaculate* Beast Core."

That would consume him. He was food to that wretched thing. Merli could in no way, shape, or form survive an encounter with a Core of that quality. Forget his corruption. He'd be dead in less than a minute. Artorian shot up from his seated position in the bonfire space, bursting with power as he just could not stand to sit there and do nothing. "No! *No!*"

The last shell around the Core crackled away, swallowed via consumption as the center of little Merli was laid bare. The Immaculate Core was freed. It woke, hungered, and saw bounty and riches. Paltry treasure, on second glance. It would consume all the same. It reached out with a mere desire, and further heaps of corruption vanished faster than a Dwarf could evaporate brandy in a drinking contest.

Still the Core hungered, and pulled further until it touched the delicious vital Essence. Now it would judge, and measure. A tether of it was pulled, but it gained none. A voice spoke to the Core, but it was not the one being addressed. Just the sound of an old man yelling at someone that didn't seem to be in the same room. "Impact or no, I will not sit by and do nothing!"

The Core pulled again, but there was interference that didn't belong in the memory. A hand espousing a single, defining, core characteristic rebuked it. The Core looked at what worthless fool was denying it a scrumptious meal should it find this heart to be filled with the dark, and it found only celestine vision. The concept of 'the unyielding' held it firm, and the Core didn't know if that aspect was something already present in the meal it was eating, or if the attribute was being added now. That wasn't right. Even the Core knew something was wrong. Just not what. Or how. Instead, the Core proposed an offer. An offer even the unyielding could not refuse.

In the twisted memory that was quickly degrading from his meddling, Artorian heard it say, "Grant me a future, and I shall grant this one theirs."

The Core ceased trying to pull at the well of vital energy, though freely consumed every last scrap of corruption. That wasn't protected as it posed the more important follow up question. "Do you *rebuke* me?"

The Core knew well of the side-effects it could cause to a body that was unwilling. The grip on it felt loosened. Rather than prevent its hunger, and detain it further, the idea of an open hand was offered. A strange gesture, but the Core was certainly old enough to understand the meaning. They shook on it, and Merli woke, choking as he coughed up the Immaculate Core. It harmlessly plinked onto the gleaming, reflective floor. That was too much for the memory to handle, tearing at the seams before shattering entirely.

Artorian was rebuked back to the bonfire space, his hand felt like it was on fire. He'd been thrown out when the memory had been changed too much. He was so confused. Especially given Scilla's note that nothing he did here would matter. "What… what happened?"

Scilla shrugged. "Nothing. That was just a memory. Nothing could have possibly happened. Time only goes forwards. Even if concepts and ideas can exist in a different layer altogether. I don't suppose you've ever had them? Thoughts of words never heard, but knew and understood? What do I know? I'm just a dreamt one, and you're not *done*."

Scilla reformed the memory—without the effects of his

tampering—letting it play from a later point before hurling her charge into it. Artorian fell. He tripped over his robes that were several sizes too big for his current form. "No. Wait. Scilla! *I have questions!*"

His pleas didn't matter to Scilla, he'd learn by doing.

Merli drew breath, and woke with a killer headache on his mother's lap. On the upside, he didn't feel sick. Just slow. Horribly slow as wall-shattering shouts and arguments occurred in a building he wasn't even in. So loud was this yelling that he heard it anyway, even if he didn't understand a word of it.

He was mentioned, though! He could tell that much in his woozy state. Elders bickered with his father, but his father wasn't having any of it and howled over their voices. "He must leave. We are sending him to the academy! He has no hope to survive what's coming. He must leave the homeland. I will not have your arguments. No, no, and again *no*! He is still my son. I will *not* let you put him in the cauldron to make pills out of him! You dare even suggest something like that to me? *You* will be made pills out of for such accusations! He is going to the academy and that. Is. Final. I do not care about the expected side-effects. Listen to the pharmacist!"

Artorian held his mouth when he understood what was meant by 'what was coming.' *The Guild.* It was the Guild that was coming. Per the money? Of course it was about the money. Yet it didn't make sense. That Core had no reason not to eat him whole. None. None at all.

The pharmacist unfortunately, was stumped as well, even as he appreciated the patriarch's support for his camp. "My... my lord Patriarch. I have no idea why the pill ejected itself, nor why it didn't harm your son even a little. Unconscious, he couldn't have accepted or rebuked the will of the pill. The heavens themselves have relayed this message to us. I agree with the Patriarch, Grand Elder Mang-du. The boy must live. He must go to the academy. You do not have my vote on this. I stand with the Patriarch."

The pharmacist was correct. Merli, at that point in time,

would have been utterly unable to accept or rebuke the will of that Core. It had been him? Yet it couldn't have been him. It simply couldn't have been. Time did not work that way. The heavens were not so kind.

Momentarily pulling himself back to the bonfire space, Artorian was trembling. Shaking. Something else was wrong. He moved his robes away to expose his hands. They were so puny. So small. So young. "Wh... what. *Why*."

Scilla's response was deadpan. "I told you last time, I believe, that your soul and self-image hovers strongly between *two points*. The one that comes next, and one far into Merli's memory future. Get back to it, I'm still repairing the original memory. I was expecting it to play five, perhaps six times before you chose to act and intervene. Though now you'll have to do the opposite."

Artorian, in the body of his twelve-year-old puny self, frowned. It looked as silly as it was adorable. "What could possibly have been the point of that? What lesson could I learn? What pain could I grasp? That makes no sense! That is not what is eating me. What was that Core? Why do I feel responsible? Why do I think it was me that saved... me? That's not... That's not how the universe works. It couldn't have been me."

Scilla cocked her head. "You're right. It couldn't have been Artorian, and yet Merli spat out that Core before it ate any of his vital Essence. That's a fact. That's truth. That's history. That is exactly what happened. Reason or no. Action or no. *That Core* didn't eat you."

She extended a hand for the physically twelve-year-old to take. "I told you. Nothing will have any impact on what's to come. You can shout at your memories. You can twist them. Manipulate them. Bend them. Break them. Doesn't matter. Not until you *face* the regret. For that I will run you through them again, and again, and again. Do you remember what you ran from back then? What you're still trying to deny? Even in that body?"

Artorian, stuck in Merli's body, gritted his teeth in the

bonfire room. It was difficult to tell who was who in this instance. It was like both of his selves were present in this moment. His jaw quivered, and he closed his eyes as he sunk back into the memory and did the part he failed again.

Merli was slumped, but *not* as unconscious as Artorian had convinced himself he was. Lost in thought for a moment, Artorian had the start of an epiphany. It was there. Right there. The beginning of the regret.

The sealing pill was administered, and he again felt the unbridled terror as the thing in him *ate* him. The Core reached his vital Essence, and this time... he squeezed his hands closed, and did nothing. Then he saw it. What he was food for. It had no color, but nothing had color anymore in this temporary world of gray. The Core seemed to ask him something, but used feelings to convey the words: 'Do you *rebuke* me?'

Merli didn't have words of his own to use. His throat didn't work, and his voice certainly didn't either. There was terror, but also a strange comfort. The solemn steadiness of knowing the end. The first thoughts he had were answer enough. "I have nothing left worth taking. I rebuke nothing. Eat me."

Artorian waited with bated breath for what he was convinced was the inevitable. Except that it didn't come. The Core didn't eat him. Instead it spoke, just not with the words Artorian heard the first time. Those prior words were twisted because he'd attempted to shape the memory and intervene.

As it was not rebuked, the Core gained full access to Merli. It studied him, measured him, and spoke in his mind. The tone was slow, methodical, and steady. <My name... is *Grant*. I... refuse, and I grant this one their future. I eat only those with hearts of granite, and those whose minds are dark. Live, child of luminous air. The color that belongs on the canvas is yours. Paint the sky with your spirit.>

Ending the connection, Grant severed their link. Merli spit out the Core while devoid of corruption, but without any loss to his vital Essence. The boy passed out completely.

Artorian held his heart, then collapsed to his knees in the

bonfire space, feeling overwhelmed. His head pressed to the ground as he tried to process what Scilla had shown him. "A Core? *A Core* took *pity* on me?"

Scilla pulled him back up, squeezing her arms around him. How strangely caring for someone who had proclaimed to be heartless. "Not pity. Never pity. An Immaculate Core of an intelligent creature saw you, and touched your heart. Then, when it realized what you had become, what did it give you? You tiny, childish old man. What did it truly give *you?*"

Artorian wasn't sure, but looked when the memory played on.

Merli remembered waking up, snug on his mother's lap. Held close in her loving arms. It was the next true and proper thing he remembered when the experiences with the Core became... fuzzy. Like Merli considered it little more than a strange dream. An event that didn't actually happen, and was thus swiftly forgotten. After that, all that was left was the warmth, and the sight of his father rushing to him. He looked at his dearest with deepest concern, but she just smiled as he asked the question that ached him. "My son. Is he well?"

His beauty of a mother nodded tenderly. "Our son is well, and still with us. I could not ask for a greater blessing. He is our world, dearest."

His father nodded, exhaling a deeply relieved sigh. "He is indeed. Our favorite little hellion. I only hope the academy will see to him better than we have. I should have known he was different. No other child of mine steals scrolls just to read them. Nor sneaks out nearly so often. Where did I go wrong, dearest?"

Merli's mother just shook her head no. "We wished to protect our little wombat against the world. So tight did we hold him that we did not see the span of his wings. What can we do, but give him a home, and let him fly free?"

The patriarch sighed deep, but assented with a nod as he pressed a hand to his youngest son's cheek. "He takes after you so strongly. Very well. I desire him safe in my heart. Always. Yet

I shall let him fly free. I shall argue with the elders, and make the arrangements. Keep him close?"

Merli's mother beamed. "For as long as he will let me. Before we find him dirty and in the grass again."

Artorian understood then, the reality of a moment long rebuked. "It… it gave me. It gave me… *Belonging*. They were always… *always my parents*, and they loved me. *Completely*. The one who was wrong. It was… it was *me*."

Scilla squeezed him tight, so very proud as he made the leap. A core memory set of his was shifting to be seen in a new light, and those were the cogs in the clock that Scilla wanted to see turn. Her words were softly spoken, though she firmly meant them.

"First regret. *Resolved*."

CHAPTER TWENTY

In an opulent Asgard training ring, Dawn cackled as Marie slammed face-first to the ground. Her aggrieved shrieks were muffled by the dirt as she simply couldn't get a handle on the basics of walking. She had *just* made such progress with her Magehood before the canting, and that progress had been undercut. Now Marie was in a Spirit body, and the whole set of rules was thrown out of the window and turned on its head. *Again*.

As an amusing bonus, the interplay of Asgard gravity and Marie's new form was an exercise in comedy. Marie's prideful demeanor didn't hold up so well when she went from 'being just fine,' to 'puddle.' The sight just tickled the Incarnate in the ribs.

Dawn's laughter died at the drop of a copper when she finally felt Cal decant her Artorian. A poor feeling accompanied it, prickling her skin. This decanting was wrong. *Very wrong*. Marie yelled some complaints, but Dawn didn't hear her. The Fire Soul had already shot right off Asgard's surface. Turning into a Mach ten projectile as soon as she was in the air, Dawn left a burning trail while hurriedly en route to Midgard. As far as she was concerned, Sunny's decanting had gone awry. <Cal! Stop! That's a *child*!>

Cal was painfully aware. His reply came swift and grim, clearly in the progress of working on it. <I know! This Spirit body is overriding my will to change into the elder form. It's the same frustrating experience as when you and Tatum formed your bodies. The 'thing that it is' is *corrupted* with a prior influence. I didn't know Soul energy could *have* corruption. I have no idea what else to call this. Come take over.>

"Artorian!" Dawn grabbed the air to slow down quickly enough, grayscaling the area with ferocity rather than tearing her surroundings asunder. Her feet hit Midgard ground hard, digging deep divots on impact that carved into full trenches when her gray dropped away. Worried sick to her stomach, she hustled over to the form of a very meager boy. "Sunny! Are you well? You have always been very particular about your—"

She stopped in her tracks. "Appearance."

The twelve-year-old sitting alone on the edge of a gazebo wore the telltale expression of one who had been crying, but was now all spent and out of tears. The boy looked tired, but the gleam in his blue eyes shone stalwart. Artorian was spent, but not broken. The youth weakly smiled up at the tall-in-comparison Ancient Elf. When he spoke, his childish voice matched his stature. "I'm fine, Dawny. Just went through a few things. How long has it been, this time? The Soul Space feels overhauled."

Dawn took a knee, concern plastered heavy on her face. "Cal is nearly at the double S-ranks long. Canting people into Incarnate bodies has been a challenge. Dani has been our guiding stone, but we ran into many problems and delays. There's also a goose on the loose, and it has consistently remained one rank above Cal just to spite him. Well, perhaps to bite him in the keister because it's trapped? Can we address the *obvious* here? Why are you a child?"

Artorian didn't reply, busy inspecting his hands, but she didn't need him to. The information available to Incarnates, true Incarnates, was impressive. She sucked breath between her teeth, her blazing eyes calming their investigative spin. "Oh, you poor thing. You're on the tribulations track of A-rank advancement. Instead of the power gathering or exemplar tracks. That is my least favorite of the three."

The young boy frowned, but it didn't carry the wrinkly impact his elder form did. "You... you can see what I went through?"

Dawn offered comfort by swinging her open arms, then collapsing them back around him. Sunny hugged her tightly in response. He hadn't expected to be picked up after, but it was fine. "Not quite. I recognize the *kind* of improvement you just made. You're at A-rank one, but you canted as an A-rank zero. I know for a fact you had no chance to advance on the other tracks to do that, and there's no way in Cal he'd give you the freebie. So. Tribulations track. Why didn't you tell me? That is easily the *worst* track to be on. Is your trial for A-rank two to be in the child form? They can be weird like that. They are always something off-the-wall odd. Remember how I told you I was a candle for a while?"

He shook his head to the negative, mind elsewhere. "I haven't wanted to speak of it, but I suppose it's too late now. Here comes the C'towl and the bag. Caliph, your dreamt one? I have one too. Her name is Scilla and, for lack of a better term, she lives in my mind. She got together with my **Law**, and now I'm on what you named the tribulations track, I suppose."

He needed to squeeze his grip, but Dawn didn't mind being his support one bit. "Throughout my life I have done a lot of things, and made many choices I'm not proud of. Scilla is making me face those. Until they are all done, she holds hostage my ability to Incarnate. By keeping *all* my Liminal energy. She also just established that I have to face a regret in order to gain a rank. So. One down. Nine to go. This first one was *not* gentle."

Dawn understood, and carried him like she carried Caliph. Artorian said nothing in response to the act. Honestly? As awkward and embarrassing as it was, it helped. He wouldn't say a word against things that helped. Not now. "Can I get a primer on events? Cal at double-S seems strange. He was A-zenith last I knew. I also recall I should be mad at him, but I honestly don't have the heart for it."

It was odd to see an eloquent child speak with such large words, while being held daintily. Dawn shrugged it off. "We both have much on our plate. Know I'm here for you, Sunny. I don't much care what form you're in."

She then considered his query. "What you missed? I don't know where to start. Tatum and I now both have Seed Cores. We got it to work with Cal being an Incarnate, which allows me to keep climbing. The Soul Space was vacant for a very long time, and then when we got people going, had to rebuild. Several realms got destroyed from people going rampant in poorly balanced Incarnate bodies. Cal has, in response, instituted his 'system' fully. He hasn't yet found a good way to lock off our old methods of cultivation, but they are essentially a *'please don't.'* I'll explain to Cal that's not an option for you."

Artorian was thankful, and nodded. "I don't appear to be breaking the world by existing?"

That was an easy answer for Dawn. "Do you by chance remember that cobbled together status screen during your last decanting? We all have them now, and we start as *'level one.'* Our big discovery was that the Mana bodies didn't have the malleability to handle the Pylon number system. Incarnate bodies rely on thought, and the constant stream of referenceable facts are very much adored. So making the bodies function based entirely on the system Cal has been harping about for all of forever? That works now. Unpleasant as this may sound, you are now based on numbers. Even if somewhere deep in the background you have personal cultivation progress. Expect to hear a kind of *static* when you try something that doesn't work."

Artorian twisted his palm over his ear. So *that* was the strange noise going off now and again. He'd tune it out eventually. "Sounds like progress. Is there more?"

Dawn squeezed his hand for support this time. "There is *always* more, Sunny. We're building and running a world here. Or we *were*. Beta stages are starting. Instead of supervising, we're now going to be play-testing. Oh, I suppose something worthy of note. Remember how you were decanted *first* before? That didn't happen this time. This time, you were *last*. Everyone else has been around for a while. Henry has *easily* gone through forty reincarnations to make his kingdom better. Marie had to step back because of unexpected Incarnation issues. Aiden is a recluse. Tatum and Chandra are likely doing very well as they spend time together. Odin hasn't changed a hair."

She paused a moment as she considered Vanaheim. "Dev-erash is no longer around. He is *one* with the system. Loved being a *dev* more than a Dev. Said he finally found something he was good at making. Oh, *developer*, instead of Deverash. He's a Cal subsystem and has never been happier, or so he says. He tidies things up. Keeps them *dapper*. Minya is back, and she's the big boss in charge now. *Brianna* is back too. I'll let you meet her rather than *spoil* anything."

Artorian nudged her. "What about you? How are *you*?"

Dawn merely winked at him with a smirk. "When Cal takes the second S-rank step, I'll be right behind him. I'm Cal-near kicking him in the rear about it. Though I let the goose do the hard work for me. I've been alright. Caliph grew up a long time ago. It was... *Good*. It was exactly what I needed. He's not around anymore, but I treasure his memory. One can't forever pretend not to know when a person is made from the Liminal, and that doesn't stick around. I always wondered why I never had an A-ranked Liminal event. I suppose it was just waiting *on me*. Caliph said that I had someone else to rely on for my Incarnation. Someone much better than anything he could have done for me."

Artorian just smiled, not saying anything in return. He just appreciated the mention.

Dawn sat under a large mahogany, her favorite person still in her arms. "I'm going to kiss you now. Okay?"

A little confused, he kept silent as his forehead got a peck. Ah... *so innocent*. He smiled, and held his commentary. He wouldn't sour her moment. She was clearly elated to have him close, and him being bundle-sized was a convenience for her. It was for him too, he supposed. He couldn't walk. Not that he was going to mention it just yet.

The sun pulled around Asgard, and they winced as the soft light turned into direct luminance. Dawn threw up a field, returning the grove to a reasonable brightness standard. One that *didn't* stab their eyes. She cocked her head as the twelve-year-old shook his balled fist at the sun. "We win *this time*, shiny sky orb. We win this time."

He burst into a fit of laughter afterwards, but Dawn didn't get the joke. "Ah... ahhh. It *got me*. It's... old joke. I don't even know how old now. What is time? What is *age?* I'm... I don't know how old. Stuck in the body of myself at twelve, because that's where my trial has me. I think I'll grow up as I face Scilla? Though that's conjecture. Why are you looking at me funny?"

Dawn raised an eyebrow. "I know and understand all of that. It just doesn't make it any weirder to hear such smart talk come out of a *twelve-year-old*. Also, you are a complete shrimp. I swore up and down you were sick when I first saw you, because you seem much smaller than you reasonably should be for your body's age."

He shrugged. "Corruption drawbacks. It'll mend. Are you level *one* as well? What of our chosen?"

Dawn shook her head no to the first question. "I am maxed out on everything the system offers, save for titles due to the limited slots. I test the highest-level content to set a baseline for what the 'maximum' is. If an effect we craft goes over that baseline, we know it needs to be scaled down, or tagged as a different category. Or fixed in any of a dozen ways. Do you remember sealing broken items? It's all like that now. Speaking of, I finished your warehouses for you. *You're welcome*."

The youngster mumbled out a thank you. Dawn continued after a firm '*mhm.*' "Our chosen are around. They function as end bosses for all the current continents. For the moment anyway. A few are very much out of place. Manny, for example, really doesn't want to be in Midgard, but what do you expect after a multi-millennia crush on Zelia? The flirting is *awful*. It's *so sappy*, but veiled in threats and venomous rhetoric. If you heard them talk, you would swear they were political adversaries out to murder one another. That's just how they show the other *affection*."

Rubbing her forehead, she tried to tally the account. "Let's see… you likely want to know about yours. We met Vol. Cute kid, complete monster. Joined all the other dinosaurs when they were moved en masse to Jotunheim. We also finally got the dumb realm pressure problem somewhat under control. We can put anything anywhere now, Incarnate bodies rock. Oh, except Hel. *The goose* rules Hel, with an *iron honk*. Do not challenge the goose."

Clearing her throat and dropping the finger she had up from that last statement, she returned to the topic. "Vol will always be a *beast* beast. He doesn't care for the idea of honor like the others do, and he just grows differently. Not a shred of interest in humanization. He's *all* dino-brain. Yuki's Incarnate form is a thing to behold. She's a Jotunheim end boss option, but she hangs out in Asgard because Odin never really stopped being Odin. Halcyon is the combination of everyone's mother, and resident caretaker. She *can* be an end boss option? It's not her thing. She prefers making sure everything works as intended on a *social* front. Then… there is *Zelia*."

From the deep breath the Fire Soul needed to take as she pressed both her hands to her chest, Artorian knew this was going to be a doozy. "Zelia is *special*. She already had the ability to be anywhere she wanted, but in an Incarnate form? *Sweet Cal*. I thought *I* could get mad at someone. She *roasted* Cal. He had *nowhere* left to hide. She is the current active end boss on Jotunheim, but she runs a massive secretarial substructure that keeps a great amount of hidden functions working as intended. If you thought the Fellhammer Inquisition was thorough back in Skyspear. *Fwhoooo*. They were banging rocks and making smoke signals in comparison. Zelia is *thorough*. After that spat with Brianna, Zelia has been the picture of *zeal*."

Artorian enjoyed a good laugh. It sounded like his dears were all doing well. He pulled up his status just to check it. Two things of note. One, Dawn had not noticed him do so, and didn't appear to see it. Two. A particular title was still slotted, and *active*. "Pleasant to hear. Well, teach me how to walk. Let's work on this level one business after. One can *Cal*or me interested!"

Dawn groaned at the terrible pun, happy to have something else to work on.

CHAPTER TWENTY-ONE

Two years later, Artorian had a late epiphany about just how right Dawn had been on his decanting day. There was always something else. Not that this was a great time for reminiscing, as matters were rather chaotic, and he was once again the only voice of reason. "Tom! Slow down. I will not go at your *ridiculous* pace. Either form up and be a good tank, or *die* with Henry as you both go *gallivanting off* into the hordes of poppies."

The charging duo of Berserker and Folk Hero both chose to ignore the twelve-year-old designated as party healer. Mr. No-Longer-Wrinkles just didn't carry the authority he'd had as an old man. The things that appearances could do were *astounding*.

The healer slapped his forehead, turning around to do his best to walk away. It was more of a loose stumble, as travel was still difficult. He barely understood the new system, but his current difficulties had to do with his stat line showing as 0.3s and 0.4s of the normal base average. Artorian stifled grumbles about the treatment even days after puzzling the meanings of this lineup. He could technically tap into his old cultivation and actual mana, but doing so was frowned upon, so he abstained.

These numbers did not represent basic cultivator attributes.

They represented basic *human* attributes. Complete with all the demerits for being a child. Cal could have at least set him at 1.0 to start, whatever *that* meant, and not make him needlessly suffer. He bet Cal had done it *just* so he would need to hold Rose or Marie's hand for long-distance trekking.

Sure enough, he stumbled over harmless grass and a minor difference in elevation. Rose caught him by the scruff of his everwhite robe, and Artorian pulled a dissatisfied scowl when he hung in her grasp like a cheap handbag. She was easily able to lift him like a bundle of arrows, sans quiver. He grumbled. "This is *embarrassing*."

Rose laughed at his mumbles, tossing him a few feet into the air so she could draw an arrow; nock it, mow down a line of killer poppies, and catch him on the way down in a single set of fluid motions. Rose and her darn 3.0 modifiers on all her darn stats... She looked over her shoulder, then spoke to him with amusement. "Sunny, looks like you're up again."

Artorian just buried his face in both his hands as Rose carried him over to a downed, poppy and posy-covered Tom and Henry. His sass flowed like water. "Let me guess. Tom swung his warhammer, and either missed or forgot that a smashy-strike doesn't do much against a *swarm*. Henry was just glad to be out of the capital and decided to *forego* tactics in favor of fun, because the supposed challenge of the poppies is laughable. They're now both lying on the ground with their status bars in the red."

Marie cackled behind them. The kid hadn't even looked and he'd guessed it in one. Well, not much of a guess when it kept happening. She smiled, but kicked Henry in the foot to get his attention. It didn't do another point of damage as expected, but the healer was here so it would be fine. "You really need to stop being so haphazard just because you have a title slotted that lets you be resurrected by a relevant ability, regardless of its level or supposed limitations. *Lion-phoenix*-boy. Or is it gryphon now? You're relying on that thing far too much, and look at what you're doing to our poor Artorian."

Hans appeared with his face next to the boy in question. His voice low, and whisper deep. "I could just assassinate them for you. *Poof.* No more headache for a *full day*. We'd all get to go home. Doesn't that sound lovely. You c—*ow!*"

Rose bopped him on the top of his head. "You hush! You just want to spend more time with me at home. I see that *twinkle* in your eye, mister. We are here to practice and test the basics of this temporary zone. It's not going to exist for much longer and I want my report to be complete, or did you *forget* how we make money now? Get out there and pick them up!"

Hans pressed his hand to his chest, seemingly offended with a dramatic pout. "I care only for everyone's *greatest* well-being. Including that of our poor, poor healer. Yet, *as you wish*, my love."

The pirouetting rogue danced into the flowery field, performed a dagger flourish, proudly smiled, and fell over dead. Marie and Rose saw it happen, but didn't believe it even when Hans' health bar blinked red. It momentarily cracked to gray as it emptied, Hans remaining flopped on the ground. Rose blinked. "Was that *supposed* to happen?"

Artorian, being turned the wrong way and unable to see, ventured a guess. "Is he lying down with them to be all dramatic? I bet with one of the posies bardically held to his chest so he can play dead. I heard the flop."

Marie waved her hand to the poppy field, and activated an ability. "Inspect."

She remained quiet for a moment, then turned and took off running. Leaving a very confused Rose to turn around and frown as she watched her teammate bolt. "We *just* reminded Hans that…"

Marie didn't have time. "*Rose*, run!"

With the archer turned, Artorian swung his own Inspect at the poppy field. The statuses of the very much dead troublesome trio appeared, along with some disturbing status effects. It wasn't three allied blue screens that worried Artorian as much as the roughly three hundred forty-something *red* ones did.

Those poppies weren't a swarm at all! Each was a fully individual monster. Only now that he was within nose-touching distance did he see the relevant information links, as his pathetic Novice level 'Inspect' worked for a change. Another ploy by Cal no doubt, to force someone's nose so close to a threat that it could jump them.

Artorian instantly agreed with Marie. "Run!"

Rose bolted. Unfortunately, in her haste she also dropped her spare quiver. Having forgotten that said spare quiver was Artorian. He *thunked* against the grassy knoll with an *ooof*. *Welp*, he couldn't get back up. He knew this was a party wipe as he read the red screens. These poppies had several 'fun' little abilities. Among them:

'Act as One': *Any number of poppies may share sensory data and active memory, allowing them to share information and act as a unit.*

While an individual poppy was as harmless as one might expect, the conjoined abilities made for one *evil* Cal-quality trap.

'Strike as One': *Any number of poppies may share their attack feature, combining the resulting damage into that one single strike. As a balancer, the cooldown for the strike also stacks.*

Fabulous. Even if a single poppy did at most a single damage, none of them save for their front liners currently had more than a few hundred health. Yet the poppies wouldn't be so bad if it wasn't for the third ability. Finally, there was:

'Poppy Possum': *This creature can make it seem that a downed foe is merely 'dying,' and their health measurement will show as 'in the red' rather than remain shattered to gray.*

Artorian had a quick glance at the three blue screens, and saw they were all afflicted by the 'possum' status. While he'd initially seen Hans' health as gray, it now flickered in the final stages of red. Source being the poppies. Yup, that was a personal Cal touch if he ever saw one. People would come attempting to heal the fallen, and they'd only join the pile instead.

"Ah well… so much for this test." Moving as a unit, the poppies rushed over his prone position to chase after the escaping duo of archer and caster. Given that his perspective blacked out, exited the Eternium dungeon Core, gathered in his Silverwood Core, and reformed in his resting twelve-year-old Incarnate form stationed in Midgard… Artorian figured it was best to call it a day.

"That wasn't fair, Cal!" Sunny's ear twitched as Henry yelled at a disembodied entity after getting his Spirit body out of the reclining chair. Which was specifically meant to hold them while they went to go test. "Those were first level enemies and they downed us like chumps!"

Cal was on the nose about the matter. <Well then stop approaching the problem like chumps. Maybe, I don't know, listen to your *healer*? You had ample opportunities to inspect the opponents. You were the one who charged in thinking the poppies functioned as a swarm-based creature. Not my fault you were absorbed in other matters.>

Henry fell on his butt attempting a rebuttal, nowhere near used to his Incarnate form enough to use it properly. He scowled, and shot the empty air a nasty look. Though, Cal wasn't there anymore. "This is awful! I figure out how to waddle here, and then get moved to testing where I lose it again. I get the hang of it in Eternium, and then I die and have to re-learn it again once I'm back in *this thing*."

Henry's Aura fielded itself in response to his rant, laying itself heavy on the surroundings. It served only to further detail how defeated he felt. "Then there's *this* pain in my Cal! I am never going to get my Aura under control at this rate! *Argh*!"

Artorian quietly snickered, and controlled his own Aura to give the man an example of how it worked. Given that Henry was paying attention… Artorian didn't get a shred of respect in his child form, so offering lessons had proved fruitless. They just didn't want to listen to him. *Fine.*

Tom offered the semi-snickering youth a hand. "A well-fought battle! Youngblood. My thanks for chasing us through the fields. It was a glorious time, and I do not count your support as negligible. I am sorry for my behavior. The exhilaration of new experiences is intoxicating, and I indulge freely when I know there is no true harm that can come of it."

Cal popped in without warning, his voice concerned as he heard something he didn't like. <Tom, could you *repeat* that?>

Tom pulled 'Thud' off the ground, resting the massive warhammer across both his shoulders. "Of course! Being in the other dungeon Core? It puts us in what I think of as a... *a spare* body. It's me, but it's not me. It's expendable, and even if I die, I will wake up here. There is no downside to just going wild and having fun, because I will just come back and be free to try again. I have no reason to try to remain serious, and Henry caught onto that fact. I know the rest of our practice team is trying to be all serious, but I simply cannot find the threat to be realistic. No matter the harm I take, and no matter the threat of death. It simply does not matter, and I see the journey only as an opportunity to have fun."

Cal grabbed his own body and pulled it into the present space. Cale then rolled his shoulders, and strolled up to the bulky Northman. "Tom? Just so I understand you right. You find *no challenge* to the game? Even if the enemies are tricky, or special, or clever?"

Tom laid his heavy hand on Cale's shoulder like he was welcoming a brother back into the hall. "Cale! Indeed. Having faced true threats, and having risked my life for far more dire consequences, this facsimile of danger you present at most makes me chuckle. I do not believe it will matter what type of foe you make me face, because when I am in Eternium, I cannot see those fake things as challenges. Whether I live or die does not matter. There is no cost to failure, and there is no enjoyment to the success. There is only my exhilaration for trying out yet another body. Like my friends, I have gone through many now. I see the game you have made only as a challenge in terms of practice for when I am back here. In a place where my *true* progress matters."

Cale clearly didn't like this mindset, but found it hard to rail against it in the current moment. "Well. That's not what I want. Do you have any suggestions for how it could be more engaging? I understand your mindset, but this feedback is horrible for me since I want to keep people engaged of their own free will. If you go in and start from a place of apathy, I am quite stuck."

A very frazzled Marie woke up with a gasp from her chair nearby. She was frozen in the moment, but eased when she realized where she was. Stumbling off, she picked up a nearby rock just to angrily throw it onto the ground. "They *got* me! Those flowery *vagrants*! I will burn every single poppy I come across, for the rest of always!"

She calmed when she saw the other supervisors looking at her. "I won't *actually*... I'm just... *venting*. I ran out of stamina and the flowers caught up to me. I don't know how Rose got away."

Rose woke with her own gasp, and performed the exact same rock smash move Marie had. She would have whined, but Marie addressed her. "Poppies get you too?"

Rose shot her a sharp look. "No! I fell through the *floor*!"

"*Uh oh*." Cale swallowed, choosing this moment to be the perfect time to puff out and not be here. He had some flooring to look at.

While Rose and Marie fired up girl gossip on their grievances, the boys had a huddle. Even Artorian got to be included. Tom started first, a little concerned. "Did I upset Cal?"

Henry shook his head and patted Tom's back. "No, the way we want to tromp around in Cal's Eternium just isn't what he envisioned. My friend, the problem is that you're correct. It doesn't work great for us. Hans, do you by chance have a good explanation? I feel like I'm going to fall over my own words."

Hans smiled like a child handed candy. "Oh yes. It's like

this, Tom-boy. We have been in real, life-threatening situations. The simulated ones don't register for us as a result. How can something that can't possibly hurt you be a threat? Especially a place where we have to start over from scratch as a normal, boring nobody. We have spent years, decades, centuries on our cultivation progress to *not be* where that game starts us. That process is ingrained in us, and when I appear in the fake world, I too feel like being snide for no other reason than: I feel *slighted*."

Hans tilted his face, squeezed his lips, and gave a playful mock glare. "It's not fun. It's not a challenge. It's just being put back in a place we left long ago and have no real interest in. It's not like it was in Cal's Soul Space. When we were tromping around in Midgard and making actual friends, progress, and abyss, our own Guilds, I *loved* that. I *love* being a Guild leader. Even if I had to merge the bards into my assassin cabal. This? Abyss *this*."

Tom nodded in agreement, and Henry couldn't find a rebuttal. He looked down to see a very pensive healer holding his tiny chin. "What's on your mind, kiddo?"

Artorian decided it was fruitless to tackle the way he was being titled, so he just got on task. "In my deal with Cal, I essentially promised that I would help him with everything needed if he helped me with my growth. He has helped me with my growth. The A-ranks isn't *nothing*, and the early Incarnate form, while an abyss of a pain to get used to, isn't a demerit either. So when Cale mentioned he wanted us to test this, I was gung-ho and on board from the get-go. Even if I neither understand the way things work in Eternium, nor have a grasp on the math. I really do want to uphold my end of the deal, but if I am being honest, it's *you lot* that are giving me the worst of it."

The trio frowned, and Tom wanted answers. "What do you mean? You are an excellent healer!"

Artorian needed to squeeze his eyes shut for a moment before he could reply. "My friend. There hasn't been an opponent in Eternium that should have made you *need* any healing, much less *resurrections*. I have been killed by horned rabbits, flowers, and the backlash of Henry's Lion-Phoenix martial arts. Out of those, I needed to resurrect the entire party twice while facing three *standard* rabbits. I was entirely unable to do anything with the posies, and Henry, that air backlash on your snap kick is so *wild* that I wonder if you even noticed I was there. I'm not struggling with Eternium because I don't understand what's going on, or don't see the point. That's not my box of toys. I'm struggling because you're all being bigger children than the body I'm currently stuck in."

The trio looked just a touch guilty. Hans squeezed the bridge of his nose. "I think we are the wrong group to use as test subjects. Personally, I want to go back to my Guild, except that I have learned it does not exist in *this* version of the world. It's disheartening to think of all the work it will take to put it back up, and I have no idea how the inner circle managed it. Henry, you have tried improving your kingdom *how many times* now?"

Henry shrugged. "I'm somewhere between forty and fifty, and honestly I've lost count. I don't even know what I'm doing wrong, as many of the same problems keep cropping up. A few people in charge get the genius idea to oppress the rest to stay in power. Sometimes there is a gimmick. Mostly the behavior doesn't go away regardless of how I change the rules, amend the law, change the city layout, or really do much of anything else. It's very frustrating. It's… I don't know."

Henry called it quits and just sat down cross-legged. "I feel like unless I actively lead, and try to keep my fingers in as many pies as possible, my human kingdom just runs itself into the ground. Even then, I miss so many things. There is always some plot, or organization, that does something within the rules that isn't right. They get away with it in some way, and I have to just do my best to deal with it from that point. Every iteration, something has happened that Marie and I just didn't catch until it was way too late."

Tom held his shoulder in support, and Henry calmed as he kept talking. "Every time Cal adds something, there's *another* thing they can exploit. No matter how many loops I do, there is *always* something else, or someone else to throw a wrench in the plan. I just can't catch them all. I just can't."

Tom decided more was needed, and sat with his friend to keep a hand on his back, like Henry had earlier. Tom spoke. "You have been doing very well. When I made my adventurer's hall, it was one of my greatest accomplishments. The friends and revelry I created there were matched only by the camaraderie from my original homeland. I miss it dearly. I, too, wish to return to that."

The four sat, and continued their chat as a disembodied Cal popped in, having secretly listened in to the whole talk. <Hey guys. I have some ideas I'd like to run by you. To make things *better*. Do you mind?>

The unexpected line Cal ended up throwing them made for a pleasant surprise, and was certainly appreciated. They were glad for the suggested changes, and heard Cal out the whole way. The longer the dungeon spoke, the more those smiles on their faces grew.

Good tidings were afoot.

CHAPTER TWENTY-TWO

A month after the latest playtest fiasco, and more people falling through the floor, Cal called for a gathering in Nifl-heim. Though he was late for his own circle moot. People kept quiet. Not because the tension was awkward, but because a pint-sized Artorian stood on the inner circle table with his hands on his hips. Glaring daggers into the eyes of a completely stoic Brianna. They badly wanted to get a word in, but they had the distinct feeling a soul dagger would find their way into a kidney if they had a say before the assassin Queen did.

Cal grabbed his body and popped in as Cale, then prepared for a boisterous greeting. He saw the scene, turned on his heel, and popped back out. Nobody commented on how jealous they were of his ability to just escape like that. They wanted that option!

Dani wasn't so spineless, and the glowing Wisp cleared her throat. "Children, please tell the other what you have to say instead of pretending to be two snide cats."

Artorian nudged his chin over at Brianna. "I'm waiting on our dear Dark Elf Queen. Unless Madame Won't-Cant-a-Lot doesn't feel like talking about the hundred years she spent being a snoot because she didn't want to give up her power."

Dani turned her attention to the still silent one. "Brianna, do you have anything to say?"

Brianna squeezed her own hands, her eyes locked on the optical daggers still being aimed her way. "I am sorry. You were right."

The moot participants blinked in disbelief, and Cale popped back into existence with a slack jaw. Just to relay very confused commentary. He just had to comment. "*What*? Did *Brianna* just apologize?"

Brianna pushed some of her curled locks behind her ear. "I can grow. I was just a cranky baby and needed to eat something and take a rest. I feel much better now. I wasn't myself for a while. Consider the lesson drilled in."

Artorian waited a moment further, but snappily turned to walk across the table. He dropped into his seat, laced his fingers, and cleared his throat. He squared up the documents before him by hitting the bottom of the stack on the table a few times. "I'd say we're sorted."

In truth, the gathering had expected a far more violent resolution to that old spat. Cale clapped his hands, having appeared in his seat with a smile. "Well, since things seem to be alright, on with the show! I have great news, that *so far* has made some of you happy. To begin, no more testing!"

Cheers and applause erupted from around the table. Even Brianna performed a soft clap, but the largest cheers easily came from Dawn and Tatum. They seemed relieved and elated about the entire mess being over.

Cale pressed his hands together, and smiled. "Instead, we're going to have memory-wiped decanted start flooding the world in Eternium and do all that work instead. En masse. We're going to do this after we have adjusted the soul world here to the exact configuration we want to import into Eternium. This includes the kingdoms, Guilds, and groups you've made. So if you want something in place before the big transfer, now is the time. If you want to remain in charge in Eternium after the fact, you are welcome to."

Tatum's hand rose. He had a concern. "We still have the goose problem."

Cale tried his best not to scrunch up his face; revealing how he actually felt about that topic. The effort put into the cover-up gave his displeasure away anyway. "It... it'll be *fine*. I have finally finished the formulas on how to *properly* transfer people's current power into Eternium. Using the same system you have all begrudgingly tested.

"Because Eternium is technically triple S-ranked, it *should* be fine. Transferring the goose should be as hard as making a portal for it to go through. It hates being stuck. A sudden portal will be too enticing to pass up. Even if it's not a true improvement. As a bonus, if someone does defeat it in Eternium, it also counts as killed for my purposes. Plus, it will be stuck in Hel. Win win."

Tatum slunk deep into his seat with great relief.

He mentally checked out of the meeting, needing a minute to take that revelation into himself. That blasted goose had been the bane of his existence. It was immune to any Essence or Mana-based abilities. Even when Spirit was used, it wasn't affected by elemental facsimile effects. The original abyssed beastie had also evolved into a hydra-goose, with *nine* heads. Each of which was as *friendly* as the original. He had already figured out that they were all identical, but *only* damage to the original head would count for anything. Telling the heads apart was a headache, and he'd taken to burying the blasted thing under the ground with a graveyard ritual.

Cale continued with the main topic. "Once you have all given your thumbs up on being done with the aspects you want to implement, I need to talk to each of you individually. Since I *do* want you in Eternium to help, even if not all the time. Rather than being bottom-level testers, I want you all to do what you would have wanted to do here. The only difference being that you're dealing with more numbers. Some of you have expressed that you really liked being in charge of an organization, but some of you I need for the more above-board mechanics that have to be looked at."

To illustrate his point, Cale pulled up some holograms as examples. "Basically, this job is what I would need the 'deities' of Eternium to do. You'll have an entirely different progress track on how to improve your deity level. It's essentially the same as being a supervisor here, except that your authority reaches into Eternium. I know that if the shop had been easier or cheaper, you'd have enjoyed it more. So that's being implemented."

Tom raised his hand, and Cale motioned for him. "Is this the position you told me about, that you wanted me to take? In truth, I would rather be a hall leader. Being a divine sounds detached from personal relations, and it is the joy of the people I relish."

Cale considered this while rolling his thumbs across one another. He *really* did want Tom to go the deity route. "Tom. How would you feel about doing both? I need someone to test that out, now that I think about it, and I honestly don't want to take you away from the part of the task you *actually* want to do. Would that be alright?"

Tom mulled it over, but that didn't sound too bad at all. "I would be delighted."

Hans playfully punched Tom in the shoulder to congratulate him. "Look at you! A divine adventurer. Now you have to make sure you perform deeds worthy of such a lofty title. I can't wait for the *stories*."

Tom's smile fell. He didn't know how to feel about *stories*. Not after he'd heard some of the things that had happened to Odin and the mead hall residents of Asgard. "I'll... No. I *will* do wonderfully. My stories shall ring through the realms as tales of wonder, to be cherished and chased by all who feel the call of adventure! They shall be known as the *Tales of Thud*!"

The youth next to Tatum was scribbling furiously, busy penning the start of Tom's tale since he didn't have much else to do at the moment. Artorian knew where this was headed, and had already puzzled out the list of tasks he needed to attend. He did have a question first and stuck his quill into the air. "This world we're copying to Eternium. Will it be *stable*, or is it going to change every ten years?"

Cale shook his head. "The landscape is essentially all done. Only things built on it are likely to change, and even then, we have refined the zoning over several hundred rounds and recursions of testing. I've got a solid grasp on where starting towns need to be, and where people are likely to branch out from there. While the world around these expansions still poses a consistent challenge. The world we are putting in Eternium is unlikely to be altered. Only if there are big problems, or a truly revolutionary improvement in my Soul Space, will we be dropping a new version to replace the old. Even if that happens, the people won't be aware of it. Whole buildings and street outlines could change in the blink of an eye, and I can make sure nobody will notice."

He waggled his hand with some uncertainty. "Now if you meant the *nuances* of the numbers, effects of titles, names of creatures, or balancing of effects, that's different. Those will be updating fast, and often. Usually as soon as I notice something or find what I consider not quite right. Then I will be implementing a change. That change won't be felt or noticed unless you're actively using that part of the Pylon system. Though it *will* happen. The version of the world, as it currently is, is not the best way it could be. I need people roaming free to get the rest right. I want to send snarky messages!"

The gathering stifled their giggles at his outburst. He just wanted to have fun, like the rest of them. What a relief. Artorian finished his scribbles, and slid them over to Tom. Whose smile swiftly became toothy with excitement. While it didn't have the impact of his older form, the youth cheekily tapped the side of his nose with a knowing smirk.

Cale asked for a tally. "Can I have a show of hands for the deity system?"

Artorian, Tatum, Dawn, and Brianna were up for it. Tom half-raised his hand, but was clearly still uncertain, regardless of his proud statement earlier. His hand joined the pile in the end. Chandra decided to join as well, albeit only after she saw that Tatum was in. If Cale was surprised at anyone, it was at Minya. Who wasn't moving her hands at all. "That's a surprise, I was certain you wanted to try it."

Minya just shook her head. "No. I have done enough high-level mechanics. If anything, I want to start an odds-and-ends shop. A step above peddling. I know I'm going to get called in for moon-related problems, so I want something normal. Something grounding and mundane. I want to feel like a part of a community after so many eons on my own. I'm spent. I can't anymore."

There was no pushback; Cale just accepted her decision. "We will find you a nice spot in Midgard, where most of the people will be. Snug in the thick of it."

Minya smiled, and appreciated that.

Marie leaned forward. "Cale. Are you alright? You're being both very lenient, and rather accepting. I don't know about the others, but I am very used to you just throwing your will around and expecting us to rush and fall in line. Are you well? You've been... dare I say, *gentle*, this entire meeting."

Nods of agreement did the rounds. Cale just shrugged. "My **Law** is... It requires a lot, and the part I have the most problems with is how to properly exemplify it. When it comes to the best way things can work, they often work best *without* some overdeity poking his nose in all the time. I'm a control freak. I like my fingers in every level, and in control of every button. To *grow*, that's not an option. I am working on myself, and my **Law**, by addressing how I handle those situations. So rather than place the burden on you all, I should do what works best. That's simply letting you do the things you would rather be doing anyway. Only Deverash really loves the Pylons, and lives in the numbers with me, so we are going to do that part, because that's what we want to do."

Dani leaned on his shoulder, very proud. Cale smiled up at her, and just nodded. "Listen. I'm going to wrap this moot up, and start individual meetings. I would do it as a group, but individual attention is just better. You appreciate it more. I appreciate it more. It doesn't feel like I'm just some overlord yelling commands at you. Like Marie said, that's just not how I want things to go, and I'm the only one that can really change it. As *I* am the one that's been a major part of the problem. So this is me, trying my best. Artorian, would you mind having a chat with me first? There's some other issues I'd like to run by you."

The youth smiled, and provided a thumbs up. "Sure thing, buddy. The usual table?"

Cale liked the thought of that. "The usual table. See you there!"

Cale and Dani vanished, leaving only the inner and outer circle present in the congregation. Hans still had his hand up for the deity option. "What, do I *not* get a mention? Was my hand not high enough? I'm being picked on, Cale is going to make me cry."

Rose pinched his side, and he jumped with a yelp. "You behave! Look me in the eye and tell me you wouldn't much rather be the master of the rogue's hall."

"*Fii~i~i~ine*. It *does* have a nice ring to it. I understand why Tatum was so enamored by it." Hans pouted dramatically, but knew his sweetheart wasn't wrong. He sent a playful wink in the man's direction, and Artorian thought that was a great moment to call it. He reached over to give Dawn's hand a shared squeeze, and **fuffed**.

CHAPTER TWENTY-THREE

Artorian teleported into his mostly unused abode within the sun, wondering why it all looked so much larger. No. He recalled his current stature. This was normal. Facing the wall of memory Cores, he slid his hands into his robe pockets. "It's time. I've been so looking forward to this. It's finally time. Gotta admit, it's going to be very awkward while I look like this."

Cale snickered at the table, freely downing strawberry beer from an oversized stein. "I figured you would want to decant them right away. I unfortunately have to disagree; they're going to be very confused to see you like that. Do you think they'll take well to Eternium?"

Artorian paused, raising an eyebrow as his lips adopted a tiny smirk. "Eternium? Oh, you sweet dungeon. You think I'm decanting them in *Eternium*?"

Cale cautiously put his stein on the table. "*Yes*? Where else would you decant them? My Soul Space is going to be pretty dang empty."

Artorian nodded. "Perfect."

Cale wasn't sure what was going on here, but he didn't think he liked this plan. "Why would you want to decant your closest relatives, adopted family, and favorite people, in a set of realms that are going to stay *empty*?"

The youth was all smiles, his voice awash with elation. "It's everything I needed! No natural threats, no silly numbers for them to get tangled up in. They all get to live their lives and explore the lands at leisure, with minimal risk and maximum freedom. Their own little paradise. It will be… enough. Enough for me to ask them the hard questions."

The dungeon considered raising some objections, but more problems than met the eye were at play here. "I'm not following, Artorian, walk me through this."

The Administrator nodded slowly, very interested in his feet for a few seconds. He made his way to the table and pulled out a chair with both hands before climbing into it. "Do you remember pulling one of my Dwarven family members out long ago? You used him to relay a message. He asked me to hold off on decanting them, because all the changes in the world would not go over well. I held to that tighter than I admit I should have."

He used telekinesis to bring some water and a cup over, and Artorian enjoyed a fresh drink. "When you mentioned the land would go through no further major changes, I considered that a big checkmark. I don't want to subject them to the game, because I want to give them what they never had. A normal life. One not marred by raiders, or scheming Choir members, or the like. Then, as they live that normal life, I want to ask them the same question I asked my chosen."

Cale rolled his wrist. "That being?"

Artorian wondered how to explain. "As an Incarnate, one is effectively immortal. There is a big problem with that supposed boon. The *reality* behind immortality is everybody else dying. I'm not sure if you remember, my friend. I never joined up with you for my sake. I was never interested in power for power's gain. All of this cultivation, all of this janitorial mess, all of this handling your soul world. It's all for the single purpose of making sure my family had a place to be. To grow, and be happy. I know this sounds odd coming from a twelve-year-old, but as you can surely understand, that's just the body. How old am I even, Cal? Do you know? I don't. I have no idea. I am completely unable to tally the decades, centuries, or more that I've been around. Even if your world wasn't clocking in at hypervelocity through the **Law** of **Time**. I'm clueless."

Cale bit his thumb. Right. There was some importance to all those Cores on the wall. Just not particularly to him. He didn't speak as the youth continued. Wise beyond his appearance. "My chosen decided that they would brave the frontier of eternity, and stick around. I haven't spoken to them yet, but even without doing so I can close my eyes and see the threads of connection. They are all well. They wait for me, for when I have time. Yet, my original family, the one I brought in here with me. They deserve *more* than a long, dreamless slumber on my wall."

Artorian drained his cup, and made his point. "Some of my adopted children from the Fringe were cultivators. I want them to have the option to continue, or delay. I want to ask them if they want to just... call their life a good life. *After* they have gotten to actually live it. Or, if like my chosen, they want to throw a natural end to the curb. To come along to see the end of it all. They are my links to the past. My tethers to promises ancient. Eventually, I am *going* to outlive them. Then what do I do, Cal? What does one do when they have lost the last pillars of their original self? I have you all, and Dawn, and my chosen."

He motioned his small hand to the wall. "Yet *they* are a special pillar. They are my impetus for *all* of cultivation. It was for them. It was *all* for them. Now here they are. Safe and stored. All these people who make up a part of my heart. I expect a piece of me to *die* when they do. I made a place for them in Midgard. I'm sure you've found it. Let's not pretend that got past you when you found all my beacons. They are pieces of our past, complete with cultures and social values that are nothing like whatever the people in your world have become. Cultures I grew to love, and want to experience again. Can you honestly tell me that can happen in your Eternium? Are there any other people you *haven't* recycled to Hel and back?"

Cale just shook his head and sighed. "Artorian... I... Look. No. I don't have available souls that I haven't used and reused to the point where I can guess their actions regardless of what situation I put them in. That's why I intend to slate them as natural inhabitants of the world in Eternium, because of some unpleasant side-effects that I actually wanted to talk to you about today."

Artorian sat back in his chair, and ceded the floor. Cale nodded appreciatively. "I don't have a good explanation. So I'm just going to talk, and you let me know when it starts sounding familiar to what you just told me. In short, the souls of the people stored in the moon Cores are spent. Not that they have lessened, or are any less strong. The repeated recycling *does in fact* take a toll, and I don't have a single person left, save for the ones kept safe on walls, that will truly be something we used to consider 'an adventurer.' It doesn't matter if the recycled souls were Mages, less, or more. They just stopped trying after a certain point."

Cale pulled up a diagram, showing something akin to 'enthusiasm' measurements. "They choose mundane lives and are happy with mundane actions. They no longer strive for change. They're not dead. That's why I said *spent*. Minya has it too. You saw it during the meeting. She's *done*. She's done too much, and seen too much. Eternity has gotten to her. Seed Core or not, it didn't matter in the end. She reached a point of experiences where anything more is 'too much.' She can still do the jobs I give her, but it's no longer with that fire she once had. I think you remember, from those early days, where she lived to make a cult for me? Those days are over, that fire has simmered. She's tired, and I don't mean physically."

Artorian was clearly concerned. "Why... why *just* Minya? What about the rest of us?"

Cale altered the diagram to show a list of supervisors. "As usual, Dawn and Tatum are immune. There's something… *unique*, that happens when you become an Incarnate. You live to strive for the ideal of your **Law** with a far deeper directness. Nothing else is needed to sustain you on this odd front I'm talking about, save for that concept. So long as you can further your bit of truth in the universe, you can keep going indefinitely. I know for sure. I feel it with certainty. A-rankers and below? Not so lucky."

Artorian sighed. He couldn't say he didn't understand. "No, no I get it, Cal. Even with a perfect memory, having your heart broken too many times makes you very jaded to similar events in the future. The act of living is no different. Eventually, it will be too much. For some people that point can come very early. For others it may seem to never come at all. When I think of what Minya has been through, that alone is obtrusive and a burden. When I consider that the last person *she* truly was latched to is essentially unavailable… I can't say I don't under-stand why she would sit down and feel unable to get back up. Even as a very potent Mage. Dawn was like that too, in the early Ember days. Unlike Ember, I can't be there for Minya the same way. She would need Dale."

Cale raised his hands in defeat. "Well, I don't think that's possible. It's not like I can make more b…"

His hands dropped, and his vision was elsewhere. Artorian reached over, prodding the dungeon in his human arm. "Buddy?"

Cale returned as the light blinked on behind his eyes. "I'm very stupid. Incarnates can have as many bodies as they abyss well like, and parsing the thought pattern of Dale into a spare Core for that body to use isn't even difficult. I'm… I need some advice on love."

Artorian calmly smiled. "My friend, as odd as this is to say, you have come to the right person. Take us to Minya. I think I have an idea how this is going to go. We can talk about the deity shop after."

They both vanished from the sun, appearing in thick bushes at the edge of Marie's kingdom. Or this oddball version of it anyway. Awfully much thatched straw. Cale nudged him in the ribs. "There's Minya."

Artorian followed Cale's pointing motion, and nodded when he saw. She was sitting on a slightly raised hill, facing the farms. Cale was nudged in the ribs back. "Let me help. You want to plunk him *ri~i~ight* there."

Minya watched the field being tilled in Eternium's version of Midgard. Her eyes felt heavy, and she should get up and consider finding what goods she wanted to peddle when eventually there was a store. It was a pleasant day, but every day was a pleasant day. It would be until the weather systems stopped being a cycle of utterly predictable patterns. A strange scream caught her attention. Something fell from the sky and splattered face-first into the nearby mud.

The figure extricated himself from the mess, and groaned at his continued misfortune. Dale whined loudly. "Oh, come on. Now what? How did I...? *Where* even...? Cal! *Cal*! What happened? I remember merging temporarily and needing to break into our own dungeon, and then it all gets horribly fuzzy. Cal! Are you there?"

Dale was booming his B-ranked voice at the sky. Or his Eternium equivalent of it. The actions may have felt the same, but life here was all numbers now. Dale looked around, and spotted the down-in-the-dumps person he recognized. He threw his arms up, celestially elated. "*Minya!*"

Minya's senses took some time to catch up. That voice was just a loud memory. It wasn't real. At least, it wasn't real until Dale dropped to a knee in front of her, arms outstretched in joy. He was hoping for a hug, but even Dale could tell she wasn't feeling like fresh peaches. Her voice was weak. "Cal? That *isn't* funny."

"Cal isn't here. Unless you can get that self-serving Core's attention somehow?" Dale frowned, his hands pushing to his knees. He shook his fist at the sky. "No matter how loudly I call for him! Honestly, all this *static* is terrible. Where is it even coming from?"

Minya looked Dale over, her eyes slowly gaining luminance. "Wait. Dale? *Dale*, Dale?"

The man in question rolled his eyes. "No, *Mountain*-Dale. Of course, it's me! Who *else* would it be? Do you have any idea what's going on? What happened to Mountaindale? Why are we in a random field? Wh… why are you crying? Minya? *Hey*. Come on, now. Can I hold you? Is that okay?"

Artorian pulled on Cale's shoulder as Minya's weeping became loud enough for them to hear without cheating. "That's our cue to skedaddle. No more interference from us. Let them talk. Spend time. Figure it out between themselves."

They fuffed out back to the sun, and Cale felt speechless as he forcibly pulled his attention away from the scene of Minya crushing Dale in her arms. Trying his best not to sneak a peek and pay attention. Artorian helped by tapping him on the shoulder. Bringing him to the present. "If it goes well, that's lovely. If it doesn't… then that's *their choice* to make. Now. I see you're having trouble. Let's talk about deities."

CHAPTER TWENTY-FOUR

More than one tap was required to keep Cale on task. He just really wanted to see how the initial events between Dale and Minya played out. Artorian wasn't having it. "Cale, they can sense your perspective. If you keep poking your nose in then you will be responsible for mucking it all up. What did you just say you would do in the meeting?"

Cale grumbled, begrudgingly removing his last tethers. "Fine. Fine. Also, Let's stick to 'Cal'. Cale was an amusing joke, but the welcome on it has worn out. Don't worry, I won't be forgetting that humanity lesson you punched in. What were we talking about? Right, deities."

The youth in front of him laced his fingers and leaned back in the oversized chair. "More supervising doesn't sound difficult. I have it on the nose that the difficulty of the concept has more to do with why such things or entities are *necessary* in the first place."

Cal scratched the top of his head. Why always so *direct* with the philosophy stick? Did he think these questions were easy? "I wasn't thinking about necessary until just now. Just that we had supervisors in my soul world, and that Eternium would benefit from a chain of command."

Artorian shook his head no. "I heard what you said, but you used the wrong words. What you *actually* just said was: I need a chain of janitorial staff to solve problems before they can get to me. That was never the query, or the part that was confusing. The question is why do they need to be termed, known, or classed as *deities*? That is *specific* language you're using. Why *that* concept?"

The dungeon made a face that convinced Artorian he was trying to process some difficulties. The lack of light in his eyes even told the youth he'd also rolled back his personal frames of reference to give himself more time to do so. When Cal came back, he did so with a plethora of three-dimensional visuals. Each showing events of past cycles they had gone through in soul world development. "Found it. Let me walk you through this."

The diagrams lined up in chronological order, and Artorian made a noise of concern when he could see it himself. Still, he let Cal get the matter off his chest. "In each iteration, and I do mean each single one, faith and religion of some kind popped up. I don't know how and I definitely don't know why. I just know it does. Here: iteration fifty. All worlds had shrines, and all shrines had their own little mini-divines. Grass, trees, flowers, bees. Each individual thing had something dedicated to it."

He rolled through the diagrams with a wave of his hand. "Iteration one hundred. Multiple big pantheons, each with divines that have lumped smaller concepts under specific ideals. Those ideals were then latched to stories. Those stories took on a life of their own, and the ideas perpetuated."

Making the same motion as before, Cal again rolled through diagrams. "Iteration one-fifty, monotheism. One divine for abyss everything."

A third, rougher wave of the hand forcibly scrolled the diagram shown to some at the end of the line. "Iteration four-thirty, specific individuals were uplifted and taken as more than what they were. Because of deeds committed and acts performed. Even if the tales are outlandish and wildly exaggerated, the same pattern from iteration one hundred happened. The people all passed, but the shrines and temples lived on. Now look at *this*."

Cal scrolled all the way back to the beginning. Iteration two. Artorian paled at the sight. "During the second run, Incarnates considered themselves the peak of being. Before we really had the system in place, they destroyed wantonly, and claimed superiority because they were so objectively stronger than their non-Incarnate counterparts. There was *rampant* desolation. Because they were effectively immortal, they ruled and reigned as tyrants. The power corrupted every last one; it all went to their heads."

Artorian said nothing as Cal shifted to iteration *one*. His tone bordered agitation now, and the youth understood why. "Then there's number one. That was *you lot*. Can you honestly tell me that went *well*?"

The Administrator sighed, kneading his temples. "I… see the problem. In other words, if you don't add it in, people *will* make up their own. Because the topic is so volatile and wildly problematic, you would rather that factor remain a control group. Rather than some other test bed. You picked deities as the word and function, specifically because that is one of the things you no longer want to see randomized. Even if it's not the best way things could be, it is better to install people you trust that can help janitor the impending mess than have another possibility for iteration two to come about."

Artorian pulled himself up from his slump, working on solutions. "We have access to the system of numbers, and we can change things to make sure that things don't get too out of hand. Such as, say, *someone cheats*. Or finds a way to break the game. Which, *given I exist*, is certain to happen."

Cal snorted, his unpleasant mood lifting. "Well, you're not wrong. Are we good on the *why*, now?"

Artorian conceded the point. He wanted more, of course,

though he could pattern the rest with what had been stated. "Onto the how. You mentioned a different track, or system for progression. That makes for... what. *Three*? I need to keep track of? Personal cultivation, Eternium, and deity. That first one is by far the most important, though there are complications."

Cal nodded, downing another gulp of strawberry goodness. "Dawn filled me in. She's on top of your well-being. I'm aware, and I know I can't stop the sudden energy conversions when you tick a rank. Since I promised that you would have the energy if you went through one. So while the others are doing their best to play nice with their cultivation, yours once again goose-bites me in the butt. Honestly, I should just connect Eternium gains to cultivation gains."

Artorian was up from his chair and on the table. "You mean to say you could have done that *from the start*? Cal! *You fool*! Why didn't you? Do you have any idea how much that would have helped!"

Cal's gears turned slow, but the Nixie Tube lit itself up in the end. "Oh. Yeah. Now that you... mentioned it. That *would* have helped, huh? I'll, uh... do that. I'll tell the others that's being implemented and pretend I meant to do that from the start. Yeah... That should add to the enthusiasm. Don't, uh... *don't tell anyone.*"

The youth leered daggers. "Make all three systems interconnect. Don't make us do triple work. You heard Henry's lamentations already. He's distraught and has convinced himself he'll never be able to unfield his Aura. It keeps just sloughing off of him. That is exactly the kind of thought pattern that *prevents* you from controlling your Aura properly. Don't do that to him. Make gains for one count as gains for the others. Even if we have eternity, it's not like time isn't a commodity."

Ideas burdened Cal. "Oh. That's a great idea! That solved my not-scared-by-deaths problem! I can just use the same solution as before, and institute time penalties if you die in Eternium!"

Cal quieted as the dagger-leer didn't let up. "Yes, yes,

making an effort for one counting for the others does sound good too."

That eased Artorian, who manifested his soul pillow in the chair before flopping back down. "Excellent. Now I guess I'll ask the question that you will like, and I will not. Tell me about *the numbers*."

Eeeee! Cal wiggled his arms close to his chest, giddy with a beaming smile. "Okay! So! Deities are going to function off of something called Divine Energy. Or 'DE' for short. I'm thinking DE can be traded for additional cultivation progress. Since I can already trade personal cultivation energy into currency for our fun little shop. I don't really need another direct transfer system. So you can use the game shop to make buildings, items, mobs, add blessings or titles, and the like. Actually, I should let deities have the ability to give one blessing for free. Incentive to join and all that."

The Administrator nodded. "How is it gained? You're only talking about spending."

Cal happily pulled up twelve diagrams. "Structures! I have long been puzzling over that same question. At first, I thought 'amount of people doing x for a deity,' but that got odd. Then I considered 'the amount of people in active worship' over a deity. That didn't fare any better. So while not exactly great, currently it's: 'If there is a structure plunked down that has directly to do with the deity' then you get DE points."

Artorian pointed at one of the floating diagrams. "Does that say '*per diem*'? Am I reading that right?"

Cal checked. "Spelling error. That should have said 'per day,' but it looks pretty so I'm leaving it."

They both shrugged, and got on with it. Cal made the DE-based information source larger. "If the structure ideas don't hold up, then I am going to add benefits to followers. Just having them, I mean. One follower adds twenty-five DE per day. Altars give fifty. Shrines give a hundred. Then there's temples, which I have divided up based on size and splendor. Honestly, in some of the prior iterations whole wars broke out over 'who had the better temple.' What a mess. That scuffle still had nothing over the world war in iteration seventeen, which started over a dumb disagreement of what *condiment* should go on toast first. People are strange."

Cal focused on the temple example. "Temples are going to be divided in order of rank. They can grant either two hundred and fifty, five hundred, or a thousand DE per day. I'm still tinkering with the details of what differentiates their qualities, but in simple terms, bigger is better. I'm thinking I'll give the structures special features of some sort as well. Guardians maybe. Don't know yet."

The youth listened, remaining patient as he absorbed the intelligence. "How many points to actually plunk a structure down?"

Cal quickly dismissed the relevant screens, but it was too late. Artorian had seen them. "Uh… not too much. Just a few million points."

Artorian choked on his water. He'd hoped he hadn't seen that right. No dice. "Crackers and toast, Cal. Millions of points?"

The dungeon moved his arms up in a 'what can I say?' motion. "I don't want deities to be overactive. I want them to be sparing with their actions. Doing things when it's really important. I have had my fill of the willy-nilly power-babies. Just throwing oomph around all the time is a no-go for Eternium. Now, I do plan on adding bonuses for structures you've added yourself. You, as an example, would have a special affinity for the beacons you've put up."

Artorian grit his jaw, then drew another sip of water when he evened out. "I'm going to deviate for a moment: We have maybe a hand's worth of deities. Are there going to be more? If so, how?"

Cal happily made a diagram reappear. "Certain people are going to get special quests. Based on their actions in prior iterations. While their souls can be *eh*, sizable changes have proven to get them back in gear. So, leaving my Soul Space and *going home* is going to reinvigorate the whole lot of them. Equally, a deity spot is something one normally only dreams of. So it gets the enthusiasm going. I don't fully know who all will succeed yet. But I expect a nice rounded pantheon of at least twenty-four individuals. Based on who finishes the questlines. More if needed. Though, I'll cap core pantheon members to around thirty. Now, *before you get mad.*"

The Administrator already didn't like where that weak excuse was leading. He set his cup on the table, but held to it with a firm squeeze. The dungeon went on. "Some individuals will not be good people. Specifically because I want a balance. There will be some morally upstanding deities, and there will be some morally questionable ones. I can't, I just *can't*, prevent people from acting on… less savory ideals. I have tried. Trust me, I have *tried*. It didn't end well for those iterations. I have to let people be people, and that includes the people who become the reasons that laws are made."

Artorian's displeasure remained palpable, but after some thought he was forced to concede the point. People like that would appear regardless. Nothing could always go well. Better to… have a place ready. He rubbed defeatedly at the bridge of his nose. "I can't say I like it. I can't. Yet I understand. I hope the inhabitants of Eternium can deal with it well enough. That is not exactly a problem I want to slap down with hard-to-get DE points."

Cal waved it away. "I know. I just didn't want it to be a surprise if an unsavory person suddenly sits in the second or third tier of our moots. It's not like I'm going to make divinity-gaining tasks easy."

Artorian could trust the dungeon on that. So that was a relief. "Alright. Well, back to the topic then. How do my beacons help me with points?"

The distraction from the distraction was welcomed. Back on topic! Cal pulled the relevant diagram to the table as the rest automatically moved away, as usual. "I'm thinking of classifying them as altars. Except that they have the teleportation function.

I do want other deities to be able to take over structures, so maybe you only gain the points from the ones that are active and keyed to you. Specifically for the beacons, because they can be costly: I'd say that their use takes a toll on the user."

Cal smirked a tiny smile. "The excess toll that doesn't go to paying for the portation costs becomes bonus DE if *you* own the beacon. We can make the beacons your special structure, as you are literally the only person to put them up. I'm aware you did it through cheating, but we are looking the other way on that. Since you're obviously not telling the other supervisors of our little *revelation hiccup* from earlier."

The youth inspected his nails rather thoroughly. "*Hmm?* What hiccup? I don't know what you're on about."

Cal nodded appreciatively, glad to have a fellow schemer on board. "Excellent! Any thoughts on your deity particulars?"

Keeping one knee over the other and steepling his fingers, the youth bounced his foot up and down. "Several. Per my followers or devotees. When they 'sign up,' since I don't know what else to call it, I want to institute that freebie you mentioned as a passive bonus. My blessing will be a constant, minor health regeneration. Just like I used to do with my starlight Aura. Also, I think I want to turn the earlier idea on its head."

Artorian was on a roll, and Cal enjoyed more ideas to play with. "If they're a person of mine, they pay *nothing* for beacon use. Since their being my follower by itself will grant me DE. Friends of theirs that aren't in the club will still need to cough up the toll."

Cal nodded, and Artorian continued. "When it comes to the DE itself... If it comes to pass that my beacons do become a structure that provides passive gain, I *don't* want it known that the beacons give it. I don't want to see it in a formula, I don't want to see it in a notification. I want to dissuade other supervisors from nabbing my beacons, because they put *no* effort into putting any of their own up. That includes deities, and people that are tied to said deities. For the moment, that's it. My theme will be sun-based. As *what else* is it going to be."

Cal had one of the diagrams recording. The information spoken in progress of being turned into Pylon code. "That'll work. I'll implement it when able. I think I'm going to tie a few of my own beacons into greater structures, but have it be a part of that building. So unless you own it, the deity in question will get the DE from the larger structure. Otherwise I think the beacon DE gain will be unique to *just* you. As was my plan. Any further questions?"

Artorian mulled it over. "When do I start?"

CHAPTER TWENTY-FIVE

Cal and Artorian stood in the Eternium version of Asgard. The youth grumbled to his friend. "You're *certain* that you want the deities to settle up here? Isn't this just a *touch* pretentious?"

Cal replied flatly while staring into the distance. "Do you know how many of you chose to live on a mountaintop, when given the chance? I'm just following the pattern here. Odin, and I don't believe it myself when giving him credit for this, made the *best* version of Asgard. Compared to every single other iteration. His shiny palace was just… *the* best thing that was ever up here. It was just a little empty, but if I get you all in here, it should be nice and lively!"

He motioned to the structure that screamed ostentatious splendor. Were *any* Asgard structures not made out of some elaborate expensive precious metal or adorned in Rune-reinforced aesthetic? Artorian looked around, and remembered it much the way it was when he visited in Zelia's fancy suit. Some alterations here and there. Clearly Cal-made. He wouldn't mention it. "Well… alright. There sure is room for us. I think I'll figure it out from here, Cal. You should get to your next personal meeting."

Cal stared at the youth with a checked-out, empty gaze, then remembered he had people to talk to. That had ever so slightly slipped his mind. "Right! Better to give Henry a pep talk. Toodles!" *Vwop*.

Artorian sighed, his arms pressing against his lumbar. He should decant his family... Yet, something about the reflection he saw in the gleaming, mirror-finished golden wall gave him pause. This... this wasn't right. It just wasn't. When he welcomed his family, he should do it with the face they knew. The face they recognized. Not some wet-behind-the-ears brat with cosmic power. He didn't want to wait, and forcibly attempted to alter his form.

That was a mistake. He passed out on the spot, collapsing in a heap next to the glittering stairs. His eyes opened in the bonfire space, and an excited Scilla was sitting on her haunches next to him, her nose a bare inch from his. "Eager to *change*? You know the rules. Resolve a regret."

Artorian groaned. Not again. Not so soon. Still, he had to know if she was being serious. "Will it restore my elder form, instead of keeping me trapped in this baby-faced body?"

Scilla rolled her eyes to think, considering it. Her blighted smile didn't set him at ease. Very much the opposite. "Oh, you *want* the wrinkled appearance? Well, that's nice to know. In *that case*, I'm saving it for *last*. A-nine if you're *good* and don't keep me waiting."

He groaned louder. "Scillaa~a~a~a, come oo~o~on. I want to get my family out of those Cores!"

Her monotone reply was as cold as Yuki's common speech. "That has *nothing* to do with me. My focus is you. *Only you*. You want your elder form? Okay. I consider that *motivation*. You being in that child form is your own doing. In case you weren't aware. You want to change your cosmetic appearance? Tackle the regret keeping you there. I'm ready. Are you?"

Artorian didn't want to do this right now. The last one had hurt so abyss much. He slapped his cheeks, knowing this kind of thinking got him nowhere. There was no point in delaying. It would come eventually, and it wasn't like his current circumstances made it inconvenient. He just didn't want to. Still, he needed to. He closed his eyes, and reminded himself of the goal. "All for them. It's *all* for them."

Artorian rolled his shoulders, resigning himself. "Well, I'm already on my ass. So I can't fall much further. I'm ready, Scilla. Hit me."

She smiled. "Sure thing, Merli. Hold tight to that shovel."

He didn't follow. "What shovel?"

A response was not forthcoming. His mind tumbled and twisted, falling from a brand-new sky until he slapped face-first down into the dirt. Hadn't *Dale* just gone through this? Was this a ha-ha from Scilla? Pushing himself up, he spat out Morovian bluegrass. Oh? Home again?

Wiping his face off, Merli got his bearings. He'd fallen asleep in the field. It had been maybe a day or two since he'd spat up the Immaculate Core. His legs had fully healed, though he couldn't remember how. Weren't they broken? After so much as a cursory glance, he found they were not. So... have a run? He felt like he should be running. Yeah, he'd go with the feeling.

Merli bolted through the field, and Artorian felt far more connected to this memory than the last. As if he experienced it directly once more. With the disconnect not nearly so strong, his actions felt like Merli's actions. Though he was aware that he took a back seat in decision making. The memory was playing, and he was an observer first.

Merli burst with joy at freely zipping around.

Air Essence rolled through his form, and he played with the zephyrs as he saw them. How strange. Artorian didn't remember any of this. He figured he would *remember* Essence use. That's not something you forget. Yet he didn't recall he'd done this, and lived through the motions. Merli and the natural idea of the air Essence were one. As he played, Artorian watched in fascination as the air-affinity channel *grew.*

"*What? Why?*" A theory blossomed before Artorian's eyes.

"*Essence* does not move to align with you. *You* move to align with Essence. Thus budding the affinities."

Merli said the words, but didn't himself hear them. That hadn't happened in the memory, so he remained oblivious. The wildling danced and leaped, ran and rolled through tall blue-grass. He tumbled down a large rock, and *thunked* into the side of something soft. Though his head struck something hard. A moment of darkness burdened him, but he woke to a large catlike tongue washing over his face with the tender care of wet sandpaper.

Regaining his senses, he found himself lying in a bundle of freshly born liger cubs. Originating from a ligress that had just given birth. Shouldn't he be very, very dead? Or nibbled on. You know, *eaten*? Apparently not, as the ligress unconditionally loved on him as if he was one of her own. Merli said nothing while being groomed, entirely stunned. Artorian, on the other hand, saw the rampant, extreme flood of what would one day be called oxytocin cycle through the ligress's system. She loved him like he was one of her own cubs. One moment. Cubs. Multiple? Didn't this species only have a sole offspring?

Artorian counted. No, that was a full-on litter. Why then did he remember there only being one? Was it perhaps just one that survived? Were there other cat rituals at play he had no clue about? There was too much he didn't know, and he needed to focus on the here and now. Use some of that Dwarven advice! Crackers, he missed his Dwarves.

Attempting to leave the nest made the ligress chomp him on the back of his robe, dragging his escape-happy rump back into the fold. Alright, no escape. Great. Artorian racked his brain. How in toast had he gotten out of this? Apparently he was smarter than he gave himself credit for when he saw it later in the evening. Merli snuck out during mommy ligress's naptime. Artorian hooted to himself. "Fantastic, freedom! Wait. Merli. Stop. What are you doing? No, boy. Stop!"

He slapped himself across the eyes as he watched his younger self be a troublemaker. Merli had gone back the next day, with slabs of meat. The ligress was in an uproar about her missing cub, but she calmed when it returned with a catch of food. Merli got his face aggressively licked clean, and was carried back to the nest by the back of the robe. The meat, however, was swiftly devoured by the mother.

She was less worried about that particular oddly furred cub, since she quickly understood it could already hunt and get food all on its own. His growth was a little fast, but this was certainly not a bad trait. She paid it no further mind as one of the cubs rolled over in the nest, flopping onto Merli. Tired for no discernible reason, the youth held the other cub tight, and took a nap without a care in the world as air corruption won out for the day.

"Crackers, I'm gaining that already? Drat." Memories flickered, and Artorian looked about at the scenery change. "Oh? What just happened?"

They had skipped a few days. Merli was in the field, playing. His father watched him, all of a sudden quickly bolting towards his son. Merli didn't understand why until the cub pounced him from behind. The youth had a good-natured laugh and rolled around with it, but his father clearly wasn't having any of that. "What are you doing, you brazen fool! That is a wild predator! It could have killed you!"

Merli disagreed, sounding defiant. "He's my friend. Family, even! We get along!"

The patriarch tore the cub off his son, tossing the creature far into the fields as it yowled. He was visibly unwilling to accept his youngest's words. "Are you blind to reality? That's it. I will not wait for the end of the week to come, you are being sent to the academy. Tomorrow! You have no grasp on what is a danger, and what is not. I will not have my air-headed child endanger himself like this."

Against his will, Merli was dragged indoors and confined to his room for the whole day. Thunder crackled in the distance as night fell. Rain was coming. Merli, of course, snuck out of said confined room like a skilled little weasel. The guards were none the wiser, and he was out in the fields during the hours of dark.

There were many reasons why one shouldn't be, but there he was. It took no time at all for the stalking cub to make himself known with a purring face bump to Merli's hip, and then his cheek. Merli's face was quickly covered in sloppy tongue thereafter, the liger cub cleaning him off because it deemed him dirty. It opinionatedly *mrowled* as it pushed its face into the youth's stomach, getting on its hind legs to grind cheeks into Merli's face again.

The boy sighed a soft exhale, hands scratching the cub's throat fur. "I missed you too. I…"

"*Merli.*" Thunder clapped, and lightning hit the plains as the rain fell. The patriarch stood in the distance, sword in hand. The youth paled and felt his heart clench. He tried getting in front of the cub, but the creature didn't understand what the threat was. It wasn't able to sense or smell his very displeased father. The patriarch had made sure of that. "Step away from the *monster.*"

Merli stammered. "Father, no. I can explain. Really. I can…!"

Shink.

How was his father always so *fast*? He hadn't moved, but his father was gone from where he'd stood, now behind him. His cub friend had been as well, and the sudden silence beneath the pitter patter of falling water made his heart heavy.

Merli turned, seeing the liger slain by his father's sword. His knees didn't have the time to fall to the ground. The patriarch clenched him by the shoulder, already dragging him home. Merli was promptly thrown in front of the council of elders, publicly berated for what he'd done, and the danger he'd put himself in, for a full hour.

When Merli didn't say he hadn't treated the cub as a friend, the elders unanimously decided it was best to send the youth away. They too, didn't believe that a monster and a mortal could be on friendly terms. Banished to his chambers to repeated mocking laughter that a monster could be his friend, Merli felt slighted. Their words chased him through the pavilion as he kept up his persistent statements that he wasn't lying! The elders refused to believe him, convinced the foolishness of the child outweighed his words.

Merli was moved to his chambers. Being once more confined to his room was as effective as it usually was. He escaped through a crawl space that led to a supply shed, catching a falling shovel that he knocked over while wiggling himself free.

Thunder clapped outside, and he squeezed the shovel in his grip from the sound. It struck him late that… he was going to need it. In Morovian custom, it was an honor to be buried beneath homestead trees. A tradition reserved for loved ones of great repute. Merli didn't think anyone of great repute existed in his family after today.

He stood in the rain shortly after, hunched over his dead, recently born friend. How cruel, and unfair the world was. How stark its views, and how sharp its reactions. The family social customs could *abyss* themselves.

Carrying the deceased cub on his back, Merli heaved it all the way to a homestead tree. He buried it there, in the rain and the cold. So nobody would see. So nobody would know. So nobody laughed at him for loving a creature that had adored him in turn. The heavy rain masked his tears. When he was done, he held the shovel tightly in hand.

This wasn't his fault. It *wasn't*…

Artorian grit his jaw, eyes closing in defeat as he spoke. "Yet, it *was* my fault. I was the one who frolicked and landed in that pile. I was the one who thoughtlessly brought meat back. I was the one who was there for that cub to get attached to. It was my fault it came. It was my fault he followed. It was my fault that he adored me, and came to an end on my father's blade."

Thunder clapped, and the rain masked Artorian's reaction as he stood next to Merli. His eyes also locked on the freshly tilled patch of dirt. "I'm sorry… my dearest friend. I wish… I wish I could make it up to you. With a life of happy wild hunting, and days of basking under the sun. I… I…"

Artorian felt a kernel of hope catch fire. "I have to go. Scilla. *Scilla, let me out.* I have to go! There's something I must do. Right now. *Right now*!"

Scilla smiled in the bonfire room, present and waiting as he woke back up to this stage of consciousness. "Hmm? *Why*? What do I have to let you go for?"

His eyes *burned* at her. "Not what, *who*!"

Scilla remained unmoved, and undaunted. "Who then, do I have to let you go for?"

Artorian drew a deep emotional breath, shouting the name. "*Decorum*!"

CHAPTER TWENTY-SIX

The Eternium realm of Asgard wasn't designed to handle normal cultivation improvements. So when Artorian forcibly hit A-rank two from resolving a regret, the dungeon wasn't happy. Eternium both as a dungeon Core and realm functioned based on **Order**, and numbers. Cultivation? Big no-no.

Eternium himself tossed Artorian out! Hurling him smack back into Cal's Soul Space where an immediate vacuum of energy plunged around his being. Eternium could partially say no for the moment, but the Soul Space could not. That space upheld Cal's deal, and gave Artorian all the Mana he needed.

A-rank two wasn't a cheap transition.

The second Artorian opened his eyes, he was up and scrambling. His rank increase was wholly unimportant compared to what he felt compelled to do. *Fuffing* to the sun room, and clawing at the floor once there, he hurried onwards. Trying to gain momentum and speed to bring him to the wall of memory Cores even a fraction of a moment faster. "Where is it?"

Information on the wall was devoured in instants. Where normally Artorian would have relished in waxing through waves of nostalgia, not today. Not right now. "There!"

Ripping the relevant Core from the wall, he cradled it tight to his chest and squeezed his eyes shut. Ideas struck him as if he were drowning. Too many, too fast, too copious. *Where?* Where did he need to be? Copious hunting ground. Easy sun. Foliage beyond count. The answer came with the sound of a mental finger snap, and his eyes shot open. "*Midgard.*" *Fuff*.

Eternium felt kicked in the shin when Artorian burst through their connections and shouldered his way back in. With one *bonus* item. The youth *fuffed* away before anyone could get a lock on him. Appearing on another continent entirely even though he hip-checked through several trees. Outright getting the positioning and velocity wrong would do that. Teleporting was precise business! You couldn't just pop from one moving place to another moving place, and expect all the variables to *conveniently* be the same.

Artorian didn't care about the hit his health bar had just taken. They were numbers. *Just numbers.* Accessing his divine energy point pool immediately, he slammed his hand onto the store button, yelling at the menu for it to move to the relevant sections since it was faster than manually scrolling. Honestly, he didn't know if that would work or not. Yelling at inanimate objects tended to yield no results. Now, yelling at something while infusing with a full-on Invocation? *That* got results. Even if it *miffed* the Eternium Core.

A liger cub body formed, lifeless, on the ground before him, and Artorian pressed the memory Core right to its forehead. Reforming his aura into resplendent starlight, he planned to… Wait, what was he doing? This was Eternium, and he had all the healer abilities! Skip the hard part, and go right to the source. His young voice shouted the words that swiftly sprung to mind. "[Origin Tree, Genesis Branch, True Nascence]!"

The memory Core shattered to dust in his hand, its energy infusing into the cub's body as the spellform worked its magic. That was fine. That was all fine as long as the cub was… *Badump*.

Yes! A heartbeat! *Success!* When Decorum groggily woke, he

was met by a not-as-sandpapery tongue smearing itself up along his face. The proper cat greeting, even if it didn't accomplish much. The cub *mrowled* loud, flopping over as it was too young to stand. His eyes hadn't even properly opened yet.

It didn't matter for long. The soothing waves of starlight comforted the uncertain cat, and while Decorum felt tired, he was held close in warm, welcoming hands that rubbed over his head. He was in a good place, and he was being cared for. It was safe to nap.

The cub conked out moments after, a busy Artorian hunting through the shop for easy milk-based nutrition. He had nowhere to put it for the moment, so just littered buckets of the stuff around him. "You're going to be well, my boy. I don't know if your old memories will filter in, or what they will be like for you. Though I'll be here. We'll go through those first motions together."

Artorian felt hesitant about a sudden thought that he may have just jinxed himself. Yet, when there is doubt, there is no doubt. He didn't like this strange crawling feeling, and considered an immediate contingency plan.

Wood Elf secrets he tended to keep to himself sprung to light, and the old man trapped in the body of youth skipped caution and sprung to action. Pressing their foreheads together, he shared those early memories of the Morovian cub. *Sans* patriarch execution. He didn't know if his freshly relived memories would help or hurt in addition to Decorum's original ones. As the memories weren't from the cub's perspective, but his.

The act seemed silly, and small. An *inch* of a soul, granted freely. Being mid-transfer, Artorian didn't notice the hint of Liminal energy that was added with the gifted memory.

Direct memory transfer was taxing. It also went entirely unappreciated by Eternium, who did the equivalent of bop him on the head to say 'no' the very second he was done. A bop was enough to drop him. Knocked out and down for the count, sleep took Artorian. Or it would have, had it not been for a meddlesome gatekeeper.

Artorian felt groggy as his consciousness collected itself in his bonfire space.

Scilla slowly clapped as he came to. She was pleased, announcing his success with calm joy. "Regret, resolved."

Pushing himself off the familiar floor as she spoke. He sat to glare at her, then collected himself and stood. Drawing a deep breath before looking himself over, he sighed at the sight of his child-like body. "*No change*. Abyss."

Artorian took a moment, then rubbed his brow and addressed Scilla. "Thanks. *I guess*. I don't feel as emotionally wrecked as I did last time."

Scilla nodded, her pink hair momentarily refusing to act along with gravity. "This memory you managed to immediately do something about, out in reality. Rather than curl up and suffer through it. Well, '*reality*.' You know what I meant. You resolved this one differently, but you accepted your part of it all the same. That's progress."

Artorian's words were flat. "Why am I *still* a child?"

The pink-haired girl copied his speech pattern. It was unsettling how eerily accurate she could just *copy him*. "*Ask. Your. Self*. I've said it before, but you are the reason for that form. That's not me, though I certainly don't want to help you side-step progress. So I won't be helping either. That aside, I think you need some actual sleep. I'd love to throw you into the third regret, but you're overburdened. Night!"

Artorian hated that he didn't have the chance to get a word in. Dreamless slumber was all he got. As usual, he lost track of time.

A wet sandpaper tongue in his face woke him. Oh, good! Decorum! Thank Cal. The youth sat up in a snap, shedding away the lichen and moss that had grown over him. Including a small army of fallen branches which went flying. Was he in a hole in the ground? No, some kind of nest had been built around him. A nest he had thoroughly trashed. "Oops."

Still, why a nest? Ligers didn't make branch nests. His face felt wet. He'd been licked a moment ago. In his wooze, Artorian's hand thunked against a rusted pail. Oh, one of his scattered milk buckets! He'd not really done anything with those, but the contents appeared to be missing. "I don't even need to guess that I was out longer than expected. That's just the norm. Alright. How long *this time?*"

He got up in time to find several pairs of eyes staring at him from both the foliage and tree line. He was addressed by one, and guessed that it approached based on the presence. Unfortunately, he couldn't make out any defining shapes just yet. "Well, look who woke up."

"Chandra?" Artorian looked around, but couldn't discern her human-based form even if he recognized the voice. Shifting modes of vision, he realized it was obvious why. The nature Mage's complicated dryad tree-form moved his way without any difficulty, regardless of the dense forest coils. His response was fittingly childish. "That is a marvelous shape!"

Chandra's voice replied with warmth. "That's strange to hear from the voice of a youth. Still, I'm glad you're well. Mr. *Immovable Object.*"

She reformed to the human shape he recognized as she shot her quip. Offering a hand to help him out of the hole in the ground that had previously served as a nest. "Now that you're awake. Mind telling me how you ended up crash-landed in one of my groves? Or shall I believe Decorum, as I am inclined to?"

"Decorum!" Artorian looked around in a frenzy, but didn't see his friend. He did, however, spot the dire bobcat responsible for the face lick. "Have you seen him? I brought him back, but in my rush I may have stumbled."

Chandra remained steady and calm. Her smile doing its best not to burst into being. The twitch on her lips made Artorian stop, and just look up at her. "You're trying too hard. What happened?"

The nature deity eased down to a knee. Settling at the youth's eye level. "Decorum wants you to know he loves you very much, and deeply apologizes that he was unable to help you wake. He knows you wanted nothing more than to watch him grow up, and spend the early days with him. He has instead prepared a memory Core for you. So you can catch up, and live the memories from his perspective. He hopes that will soothe your heart, and that you will find the time to visit him. He's uncertain if you want to see him the way he is now. Decorum is *not* the wildcat you may have hoped he was."

Artorian felt the words die in his throat. His jaw moved, but the sounds didn't survive their way out. Chandra just hugged him, and that helped him to speak. "I would like to see him. Even if it's not what I expected. Could we go immediately?"

Chandra beamed a motherly smile. "It is proper to announce one's arrival before a visit. I'll let him know to expect a party of two."

Artorian nodded, but had a thought. "Why are you being so overly polite?"

She smirked. "Did you forget, Administrator, that words and names have *power*?"

"Of course not, but I never named Decorum like I did the chosen. Or like Dawn named Caliph. I didn't. So I wasn't expecting a higher intelligence to come about. I just wanted him to live free." The youth clamped his grip. Eager to get going.

Chandra took him by the clammy hand. "Have you tree-stepped before?"

He sighed, squeezing the grip. "A long time ago, but I remember the feeling. Makes me think of some Wood Elves I'd like to see again."

Chandra beamed once more. "Where we are going, they call me Gaia. So you don't get confused at the naming. On that topic. Birch and Mahogany *are* there as well. A Hawthorn trio too. I'm sure they will all be overjoyed to see you, even if they're the offspring of the ones I'm told you knew."

Zwip!

They were moving through the root system immediately after. Artorian felt like he was back home in the Duskgrove. Holding onto Ember's hand as she ran through the woods, while he was just a flappy piece of cloth along for the ride. Or when Hawthorne pulled him through the roots, that last day before he left. When his feet felt solid ground, he released Chandra's grip and bent down. "Still as *wild* as I remember it. I don't feel sick. *This time*. That's a bonus."

"That is fortunate, sir. I would have taken it as most unkind had you sullied the floor." Artorian pushed up from his hands-on-knees position, and watched a highly groomed brown rabbit adjust its gloves. The tall-ear sported a silvered monocle, and was attired in a dual-tone vest tailored to his size.

Artorian didn't know what to do. "Chandra. Am I seeing things, or is that the most dapper hare I have ever laid my eyes on?"

The rabbit cleared his throat at the child. "Please, sir. I am a proud Leporidae Lagomorph. My name is Bentley. If you would be so kind as to hop along with me, I shall provide the relevant attire before your tea appointment with the master of the house. This way, please."

The look Artorian shot Chandra screamed 'what did you just drag me into?' The nature Mage only smiled, already following Bentley. Not wanting to be left behind in what turned out to be a mansion's foyer, just with all-natural trees functioning as support pillars for every corner rather than stone. Yes, this place was a mansion. A full on, multi-level, well-kept mansion in the middle of a forest. Grove? He wasn't sure. Big sprawl of thick greenery. The windows were crystalline amber or clear beeswax, and the light streaming through bathed the home in a warm orange glow. "This is a very fancy mansion!"

Bentley took a moment to pause and glance over his shoulder, his rigid posture never once broken. "Domus, good sir. The establishment is referred to as a domus."

Artorian felt out of his depth as Bentley hopped along. "We have arrived. Please step into the cubiculum and exchange your attire with the measures presented. A Leporidae of repute shall attend you once finished."

Cubiculum appeared to be a fancy word for what could just

as easily have been 'bedroom.' Chandra was escorted to her own, and seemed to have the drill down. The domus wasn't ostentatious, but it had a little I-don't-know-what. Rather, it felt like someone with a keen nose for art and organic architecture had spent years deciding the placement of every pillar and placard.

In his room, which was nice if small for what he was expecting, he picked up the prepared clothes. They reminded him of Zelia's fancy general-suit. It even had tassels! He might as well amuse his host; it was so deftly prepared, after all.

A good half hour later, and young Artorian checked himself in the mirror-finish slab of amber. "Spiffing! I look either like a tiny general, or a ridiculously dressed-up young'un for some play where we wave signs around and pretend to be trees."

Exiting the wooden door, he found a gray-haired rabbit waiting for him. Again, sporting a dual-tone vest and silvered monocle. He figured they must have had a tinkerer on staff. "Hello there. I'm Artorian. Nice to meet you."

The youth attempted to shake the rabbit's paw, but didn't receive the gesture in reply. His offer just hung there as the gray-fur replied. "Very good, sir. You are awaited in the atrium. My name is Royce, do feel free to call upon me if needed. This way, please."

Royce hopped along, and was an older rabbit based on the pace in hops. Unlike Bentley, there was a different method in which he carried his gait. "Well, it's nice to meet you all the same. Does your entire family work here, Royce?"

The butler-equivalent spoke without a pause in bounces. "Indeed, sir. I am the forty-fifth Royce to serve under my position in this family. It is a great honor to do so. Please do watch your step, young master. The stairs can be treacherous."

Artorian didn't see what the danger was about the steps. A mahogany had been grown in the shape of a spiral staircase, and it looked sturdier than many of the other stairs he'd seen in his life. "You'd need Dwarven or Gnomish creations to one-up this."

It didn't take long for them to arrive at a set of double doors. Which they... passed?

"We have arrived, sir. Please, after you." Royce pressed an outcropped piece of wood in the wall. Indenting it as he pushed a button. The double birch doors parted, and the flickering of a fireplace was the first thing Artorian saw on the opposite end of the atrium. Lavish couches rested to the left and right of the middle walkway. Each facing towards the oversized beeswax windows that overlooked a vast lake.

The actual walls were sprawling with artwork. Covered in paintings from what must be a truly eccentric artist. Artorian stepped in with delight and a touch of wonder, looking all around until he heard a *clap*. He knew that clap. Except that this time it *lacked* the C-ranked *oomph* behind it.

Mahogany, in all his sultanesque glory. Stood tall on the carpet, now blocking his line of sight to the fireplace. The regal nature of his voice was not lost, and Artorian's lips quivered into a smile as he was addressed with ancient terms. "It is *so good* to see you again, my *dearest* Starlight Spirit."

Artorian forgot he was old. He jump-hugged the ancient tree with a wail only a child could muster, the Wood Elf's name screeched without embarrassment. There was only one Mahogany, but *one* was better than none. He was thankful for the reunion. "You are well! Look at you! Tall and healthy!"

Mahogany laughed like a joyous sultan, and let the clingy starlight spirit down. He broadly motioned over to Birch, who daintily waved and spoke in a considerably softer tone. "Hello again, candle-sleeper."

Artorian screeched a second time, diving over the back of the couch to tackle Birch to the ground. Squeezed him half to death as the youth forgot he was *quite a bit* stronger than them. Especially in numbers land. "Birchy! Oh, you lovely splotch-barked beauty. I'm glad to see you again. I heard Hawthorne's saplings were around as well. It didn't register at first, but now I'm *so excited!*"

"Oh, I'm sure. Before that, I believe there is someone else

who is hopeful that you are happy to see him." Birch patted Artorian on the back, then from his prone position on the floor, motioned to the sole occupant of the other couch.

As Artorian got off his friend to help the tree man back up, he turned to see a person exemplifying the definition of stateliness. Was this *truly* who he thought it was? The human man was gaunt, sporting a trimmed, pointed white moustache that curled up slightly near the endpoints. A short tuft worth in beard, and a matching silvered monocle that all the staff appeared to wear adorned the rest of his face. His attire was the refined version of what Artorian currently wore.

Stately was the exact word for the style, and he didn't know how else to phrase it. Decorum's voice was hesitant, the pinnacle of politeness. "Hello… old friend. A delight to reacquaint with you. Thank you, for taking the time t—**hurk*!*"

Fancy speech was for people trying too hard. Artorian let his Aura explode, the manufactured light form of his old-self shaping to expand around him. Just like he had done during Halcyon's dancing lessons and acceptance hugs.

Decorum the stately was far larger than him as a youth, but nice and on par when the light form wrapped its arms around the man. Artorian wasn't letting him get a single, additional word in. "Decorum. *My dearest boy.* The memory of my oldest companion. You will never, *never*, be lacking in my affection for you. You are *prized* in my heart, and I would very much like to know *every last detail* of your story."

Decorum's walking cane dropped to the floor, his jaw quivering as tears marred his cheeks. Dropping his prized namesake, he squeezed tight around the light form, voice doing its best not to break as he discovered that he wasn't in the slightest unwanted by the person he hoped to receive recognition from the most. "It… It would be my greatest honor. *Father.*"

CHAPTER TWENTY-SEVEN

Eternium was ready this time. Artorian's light form shattered, and an amount equivalent to what it *would* have cost drained from his mana bar. The youth staggered, but Decorum had him well in hand as Artorian was reprimanded by the dungeon Core. "*Whoops.* I keep forgetting where I am. Don't want to get bonked again."

Artorian and Decorum settled on the couch, delving so deep into conversation that neither of them noticed Chandra's arrival. Her attire, a truly fantastic dress of leaf-shaped emeralds in its entirety, didn't glitter nearly as bright as the overbearing spark of happiness in the stately human's eyes. Mahogany and Birch cordially welcomed her with all the appropriate bows and mentions that a deity-class entity was entitled to. The sultan was downright reverent. *Someone* had a crush.

Though, it was the kind of affection one had for something grand and unattainable. The flicker of a moment as one experienced the sublime. Mahogany was of the earth, but every beat of his heart told him she *was* the earth. There was a wholeness to being in her presence. A connection of belonging and genuine welcome formed in him at each curve of Chandra's smile. To the Wood Elves, she was a fireplace's warmth in deep winter cold.

Chandra didn't mind not being greeted by the two distracted children, who talked while off in their own world. She was pleased as a spring sapling to spend time around the Wood Elves, even if they were classed as 'Advanced Treants' in Eternium. She was suddenly plenty busy when the Hawthorne trio burst through the wooden slats of the wall, as if they'd been in a race to get here.

Each perpetual Hawthorn child was distinct. They might have stemmed from the same root, but each had blossomed wildly different. They were stopped in their tracks by a look from Birch, and only then noticed the company. Sir Decorum was present! So was some odd shiny pipsqueak, and… Oh. *The* Gaia. *Right, best* behavior it was.

Their wildling forms shaped appropriate attire over themselves in a hurry, making it seem as if the little monsters classed as branch wraiths had been dressed all along. They swiftly zipped to Birch's side, pretending to behave. The little brats. They loved to just make a mess of things, but there was an order that was counterproductive to fun if opposed.

Sir Decorum glanced away from the conversation at hand mid-laugh. Registering there were more souls present than he'd accounted for. "Ah! Excellent. A moment, my dear friend. I must greet Lady Gaia with sincere propriety."

Artorian didn't know how to describe someone's very walk as stately. Not even when he watched the man-shaped beast effortlessly go through the motions. Honestly, Decorum, pick a second theme! The pause from Chandra being welcomed did provide opportunity for the troublemaking trio to slide up on the couch with Artorian. Having learned some of the old social conventions, they offered their branch-fingers to shake.

Close enough. Artorian wasted no time with a reply in kind, slapping his wrist to theirs for a mercenary's grip with a solid shake. "Well hello. Nice to meet you three. What do you go by? Please let it not be another rose-based name."

The trio snickered. They liked this one. Saying hello by poking snide commentary at an upper-echelon member of their social sphere? *Spicy.* "Nice to branch out and furl your acquaintance. We're the Hawthorn trio, but individually we go by Chaos, Entropy, and Discord. *For fun.*"

Artorian's pleasant attitude melted away to utter concern. Why did that sound so veeeery familiar, and why did he not like the creeping sensation that came with it? *Know what? Why not have some fun.* "Lovely names. It makes me think you might even believe *mine.*"

The trio's voices resounded as one. They hushed conspiratorial whispers between themselves, excited faces pushing closer. They loved a good secret! Especially ones nobody believed. When they were close, Artorian placed the back of his hand next to his mouth and hushed breathily. "My name is *Love.*"

Chaos, Entropy, and Discord couldn't believe their *luck.* The things they could *do* with that. Discord grinned his bark face from... well, he didn't have ears, but the equivalent of a big smirk plastered on his faceplate.

Artorian found the opportunity to nudge in a question. Might as well since he had them hooked. "Why, my boys, did you take *those* names?"

The trio snickered and sat up with him on the couch. But a sharp sound occurred on the other side of the room, some glass shattering near a stumbling Birch. He had accidentally dropped his water, no doubt due to his enamored gazing at Chandra. The four of them all snapped their gazes that way like tiny meerkats, heads turning in unison before they slunk right back into a clearly not-even-slightly-well-intentioned huddle.

Chandra squeezed the bridge of her nose at the notice of the troublesome trio having gained a fourth member. "Oh... *Eternium.* This is *going* to come back to bite me."

Eternium, if he could, would have *also* squeezed the bridge of his nose. He had enough problems with the original three and, given the track record of newly minted addition number four, this could only end terribly, and with lots of headache for him. No amount of being an all-powerful overdeity let Eternium skew his own rules.

This calamitous cadre, on the other hand, was going to be the source of eons of keister pain. Specifically because of what the original trio liked to do. Even he couldn't keep his attention on them all the time, and that's when the little monsters struck.

Chaos, Entropy, and Discord pulled their new friend 'Love' nice and snug into their circle. Chaos took the lead in conversation. The branch wraith's voice was smoother than the other two, his breath naturally minty. "We were assigned our names by someone who shouted at us. That or their voice was unnaturally loud. Don't actually know who, but they were just so perfect. We *had* to take them. It happened a good few years back. I think 'years' is right? We tend to skip out on math lessons."

Entropy poked him to get back on task. All three of them had the terrible habit of just veering off from what it was they were doing unless they had the checks and balances of the other two. Which was usually more 'additional fire and enthusiasm' for whatever crazy stunt they were on about. Rather than anything relating to 'balances.' They were fully in the camp of 'we can make this *better*,' when it came to any of their activities.

For Eternium, the Hawthorn trio's 'better' was always *worse*. It tended to be Entropy who pulled them back down to reality, and he performed that function now. By prodding his digits into Chaos's sides.

"Enty! That tickles! *Anyway*. So in the early days, we didn't really understand what was going on. There was always this… *thing*? Preventing us from playing. We had to use the *numbers*, it said. Use the numbers, it repeated. Well, *we don't want to*. Sometimes, on rare occasions. The thing that watches us, *stops*. When it does, that's when we play around the way we *want*! Our main gig is to circumvent and find ways around this *annoying* numbers system that we *don't* want to play with. Not when we have a far smoother and better-grown box of toys to pull from."

Chaos frowned, pausing mid-explanation. "Why did… I just so easily tell you that? That's more Discord's thing."

Artorian smirked. "Because Chaos, you *loved* telling me. I am so very pleased that you did. I'm on board. Consider me deeply interested in getting around Eternium's little numbers. Like you, I am very much bonded to my name. I seem to have some official business to get back to, but I would love to continue this talk again sometime."

He tapped the side of his childish nose with a wink. "When there's no *prying eyes*, or *eager ears*."

The trio grinned. Cadre power, achieved! With Decorum strolling back to their position, the Hawthorns screeched and scrambled as if Decorum was a big claw-and-fang monster that was coming to get them! Artorian enjoyed a good laugh, all smiles when Decorum sat back down gently. "It appears you've made friends already. Though I must warn you, they're a handful of problem children."

Artorian snorted. "You say to the problem *father*."

The stately man failed to repress the edge of his lips curling up in amusement when Chandra snorted. Needing to turn and look away to recover herself by pressing a hand over her mouth. Her shoulders lifted and dropped with tiny shakes, and Mahogany and Birch beamed at seeing Gaia be stricken by a bout of weak laughter.

Artorian took a proud sip from his water. "It's a frosty day in the Fringe before some bark spirit can one-up *me* on shenanigans."

He motioned at Mahogany and Birch. "If you don't know yet. Ask them. They easily have five years' worth of 'Artorian, no!' in upset fire-soul cadence to rattle on about. I was, and am, quite the *snoot*."

Winking with his cup raised towards his Phantomdusk friends, they faintly looked away in a mixture of embarrassment and impending horror. Recalling some stories as the memories resurfaced.

Setting his water down, Artorian turned to lay his attention back on Decorum. "Chandra told me of a memory stone you wished for me to experience? I'm not sure if I understand the origin of your well of guilt."

Decorum's jaws squeezed tight, and the gaunt lines on his face elongated. "May I speak from my heart?"

Artorian reached over and took his hand, squeezing supportively. "I would be *remiss* if you did anything but."

The stately man nodded, and produced the memory stone from his pocket. Artorian wondered why Decorum carried something that valuable on his person. Perhaps he'd just been expecting this question to be asked, but wasn't ready to address it himself without prompting.

Decorum took a breath, then spoke. "When I woke, I was aware of you for moments before something from the heavens struck you down, and then you were out cold in that crater. When I stumbled to get my nose close to yours, I knew you lived, but also that you were not *present*. I grew quickly those first few hours, fueled by a power not my own, but by thoughts that didn't belong to me. Spurred by a will... *no*. A *request*."

Decorum twitched, squeezing back on Sunny's grip. Artorian didn't mind, remaining supportively still. "Someone wanted me to run. *Run wild*. Run *free*. To hunt. To play. To have myself the *best* of days. I grew fast, and hungered. Around your form, strange containers of enticing smells found my nose, and my nose found buckets and buckets of what I now know to be varieties of milk."

Artorian slowly nodded, following so far as Decorum recounted his earliest memories. "I devoured the meals present, and then I felt torn as my ability to think grew before my eyes. Confused, and still hungry, I followed my senses and my needs. As you wanted, I went on the hunt. As you wanted, I basked in the warm sun. As you wanted, I ran across endless plains and fields of gold. Each time I did, I felt proud. Because

I thought that I would be doing *you* proud, if only you knew. Yet…"

The room stilled, and Chandra took the treants elsewhere to allow Decorum this precious time to lay his heart bare without interruption. When they were alone, the stately man was able to continue. "Yet it wasn't what *I* wanted. I visited you many times. Though as you were immovable, and too dense to affect or so much as budge. I could do naught but sit there and wonder if what I had done for you was… *enough*."

He needed a breath, and wasn't interrupted. "I knew from my advanced growth that my swift mind was something my claws didn't hold a candle to. I also felt it was present because you had instilled it. I knew that somehow, that tiny form that became ever smaller as I grew larger in comparison, remained responsible not only for bringing me into this world, but had provided all that milk. I realized only later that the place I had been brought was not just optimal for my growth, but perfect. That tiny form had brought me into being in some kind of a rush, at great cost to itself. To get me here. *Here*, in what for me is paradise."

Artorian smiled weakly with a frown, pulsing a squeezed grip on Decorum's paw as his features were growing whiskers. Humanization was a skill Decorum clearly had in spades, but it was never perfect. In Eternium, it was even rather costly unless you unlocked the title that made the second form free. It was a strange, tiny detail, and Artorian wondered how he knew.

A minor glance with a silent 'inspection' revealed that Decorum possessed a fat slew of titles, but the one he was thinking of just now was present as well. The whiskers were not due to a cost fluctuation then? A thought for later.

Decorum continued his tale apprehensively. "There came a day when I was so large, and so powerful, that I thought nothing on this land could oppose me. Yet, for all my strength, I could not budge you even a smidge. You remained immobile, and no force I could muster, no assistance I called, no force I attempted to have dealings with could either. I didn't know if what *you* wanted me to do was what I was *supposed* to do. I only knew that you desired it of me. So I did, until I could not. A day came where my mind overtook my physical nature by such an extreme margin that I could no longer consider myself a beast. Or something *primal*. I longed for the *beauty* in the world. I longed for a social structure of respect that had nothing to do with my strength."

Decorum glanced at the small youth that he'd called father. An odd concept to consider, but the stately one knew that something far more ancient resided behind those pain-filled eyes. They were looking at him with such care, actively listening to his burden. He didn't feel judged, rather it seemed that his creator just wished him to continue.

"When I broke from my path, the one that had weighed on my mind for so long, that was when I *actually* felt free, and the *guilt* I felt immediately afterwards sickened and burdened me. Everything responsible for the way I was. The thing I was, I had just abandoned to pursue goals of my own, unrelated entirely in concept and thematic structure. I learned art. I threw myself into painting when I was so much as a little humanized. I indulged in architecture and structural components. I adored planning for grand constructions that were grown over eons, rather than built in a few scant years." Artorian handed him some water, Decorum's beastly voice was starting to crack from dryness.

Decorum had a sip, downing the entire receptacle. "I came to know people. I learned of social conventions, and found them to be a sort of calling. There is pleasure in speaking properly. A delight in dressing well. It spoke to my soul, and with great regret I flung myself ever deeper into the lifestyle that made me truly feel whole. Except… for that tiny chunk of me, that could not relinquish the memory of a miniscule fallen form, stilled and unmoving in a hole in the ground."

He took a difficult breath. "So, to abate my guilt, I got my claws on a memory Core after long, grueling quests to attain one. I destroyed lives in pursuit of this goal. I was branded as a monster, and chased from the place I had come to cherish so much. They knew I was no mere man after that, but I could not bear the drain on my spirit."

Decorum swallowed, now talking with his hands as Artorian did. "Once I had it, I poured memories of my early years into it. So that when eventually, if you came back, whether I passed or not, you would know I tried to be a good son. Tried to be a good brother. Tried my absolute best. To do right by a tiny cub that I remember lying on, in a nest made from bluegrass. Even if that strange memory doesn't fit any place I have ever encountered."

Decorum shivered, now more animal than man. His clawed hand tried its best to hand over the Core. Artorian just pulled the liger into his arms, and made Decorum's feline face press into the crook of his neck. Even young, his arms reached around to rub the back of the big cat's head. For a moment, his voice wavered. His soul occupied the space of who he was as an old man, rather than a small youth. The depth of an elder speaking. "My dearest Decorum. I do not need a Core to be proud of you. I do not find you *guilty* of chasing the pursuits that stir your heart. I do not judge you *poorly* for what you have done with your life. I am only *elated* that you have filled your heart with events and memories of things that you love."

Artorian slipped the Core from the liger's grip, who now occupied the entire rest of the couch. Decorum's attire was straining to contain the muscle and added bulk of his breaking humanization. As Decorum watched, his father pressed the Core to his forehead to set the liger at ease. The once-again youth experienced a flicker behind his eyes, and Artorian, in the span of moments, experienced a century of life as a Liger Prime. At the end of it, when the Core was empty and no longer glimmered with content, Artorian spoke but a single word to describe the sights he had just seen.

"Beautiful."

CHAPTER TWENTY-EIGHT

Decorum's relief felt palpable when he returned to his senses as a fully humanized and stately individual over the course of a few minutes. Artorian was standing next to the clear beeswax window, gazing at the lake as the sun was coming up over the Midgard horizon. "I understand now why you called me *father*. I don't mind, my boy. I am whatever is needed to those who end up under my wing. Let's not pay too much attention to the fact that I'm currently *twelve*."

Artorian smirked and tapped the side of his nose with a wink. The motion helped Decorum break from his shell further. Though the man felt distraught over his ruined attire when he noticed the state it was in, and sighed. Putting the destroyed outfit out of mind, he joined the youth at the window. "I... thank you. Is something on your mind? You seem wistful, and distracted. As if you are elsewhere."

The youth nodded. "Astute observation. I am elsewhere. Currently I'm roughly in three places, and I can only actively do things in one at a time. Alas, the Long-form is still a fruitless endeavor. Even with a century of memories from the *best* liger in history, I've pulled myself back from that. Down to two… down to one."

Artorian inhaled deep, back fully in Eternium. "Always an experience. Moving one's consciousness between forms. The transfer is becoming less jarring, that's good. No, my friend. Currently my heart *races*. I know that you enjoy the finer things in life, but after those memories all I *want* to do is go on a *hunt*. I know how to move, how *you* moved. I know how to bite. How to claw. How to lunge and how to stalk. I feel the ripples of it move in my muscles, even if this form is wrong for the event."

Decorum's weak expression slowly blossomed into one of pleasant warmth. Artorian was going to give him all the time he wanted to get out of that shell, but for now he was dying for some quality time with his friend. Decorum knew it. Able to tell via animal instincts alone. Today, he was the father, and Artorian the cub that supposedly knew how to hunt. *Mhm*. He'd believe that when he saw it. Nobody became a top-grade hunter just because they'd watched a few scenes.

Artorian raised a brow at the sound of Decorum's hummed disbelief. "Oh really? Well let's go then. Where's the hunting ground? There must be something left that's a challenge for you."

The humanized liger dropped the pleasantries, his warmth slashed away by unwelcome thoughts as he forced out a sickening name. "*Mokono*. That blight-burned *boar*."

Steadying himself with a sharp intake of breath, the stately consul looked down to see a toothily-grinning child. "Tell me more. Also, does your human form also go by Decorum? Or did you attain more names?"

Decorum considered his memories from the depths of society. "I did… but I no longer wish it. I would take a new name, if I could ever return. I don't know what. As for that claw-clashed boar, it lives in a forest that borders the neutral, unclaimed fields of the Barren Lash. Nothing but Kudzu pretending to be filled with treasure as it tries to get you. Mokono is known as an *Area*

Boss, according to the screens that like to annoy my vision. However, he should have been killed long ago, and is now too high of a level to really belong in Midgard. I remain at the border of acceptable. Another 'level,' and I would get another prompt to 'move on,' and I have a terrible feeling that the next one will *not* give me the option to decline."

Artorian kept looking at the lake. "Do you wish to stay here? It sounds like you've exhausted the place, and you're ready to try another society dive. Somewhere they don't know you. Does moving on bother you? I can go take a look at the next area. If you want. As for a name… *Gomez.*"

Decorum considered the offer, and the name. "I can't ask that of you, and it would murder the mystery. Gomez? Feels… like a *bon vivant*. A heart that jumps with enthusiasm at each opportunity. A mind free of burden. Wrapped in pleasant, pleasing attire. A little *dark*, perhaps? Dark, but liberating. *I like it.*"

He spoke the last words with unbridled enthusiasm, his finger stabbing up into the air as he turned on his foot with a grand smile. "I shall be *Gomez*! I will indulge in my love for art! I shall take up fencing, and challenge life as a *gentleman*."

Artorian shot his pleased, vivacious friend a wink. "I like it. Are you up for a boar hunt, then? It might be a challenge, but however it is that experience works now, you could get started on a new life if you gain that additional level. Wipe an annoyance off your slate before packing it in."

Decorum tried to adjust his cufflinks, but his attire was too trashed for it to matter. His expression spoke volumes that he'd already considered moving on a few times. "It's a shame that I can't take my domus. Regardless, let us bask in the sun, and sink fang into… ah. No. Don't attack Mokono directly, the tar coming out of him isn't as flammable as it seems, but it definitely acts as an acid and will *peel* the health right off your bar. Still… how will you hunt? You are a youth. Not a beast."

Artorian smirked, and pushed up his sleeves. He held Decorum's hand, and *fuffed*, using Eternium's system so the already unhappy, grumpy Core wouldn't complain. Artorian didn't like it. The trip was seamless! It didn't feel like it cost him anything, and lacked the tactile, genuine feedback he felt when making the effect happen himself. It was *too easy*. This system method was... *convenient*. Too convenient. It had done everything for him, and all he'd done was add the will, tugging some mental levers to engage it. Eternium teleporting was so easy that not only did it feel like cheating, but it felt like *bad* cheating.

Ugh. Artorian squirmed a moment on arrival next to the Kudzu fields of hatred. You could tell that, if they could uproot, they would want nothing more than to hug you with the shadows created by the falling of a thousand swords. "You're right, I'm a youth. Though if you think having the wrong *body* is going to hold me back, then you too should hear of my Fringe days. I have an inkling of how I want to go about this. In truth, the system has just annoyed me. At the same time, I'm about to make it do some *work*."

Decorum rolled his shoulders. With a crack of flashfire, he burst from his ruined attire, dropping his humanization entirely to embody the truth of his being. Heavy air themes rumbled around him as his form grew outwards in mass. Expanding to a regal one-hundred-twenty-foot-long *beast* of a predator.

Artorian whistled, impressed.

Dismissing his status screen after having fiddled with it, hexagons of light flickered into place around his being. The light form shaped itself into a copy of Decorum's liger form, but not remotely with the same dimensions. Also, stalking was going to be difficult. The system had made his light form *bright*. So much for the sneaky options. Artorian performed a jump to store his youth-form in the center of the adapting frame, embodying the being of the big cat instead.

It would have been terribly awkward, and impossible to know what was right, had it not been for the gift of memories. He instinctively, and from a century of knowledge, knew how to be a liger. *Crackers*. He wished he could have this for the Long-form. "Well, this sure is convenient. Odd, but *convenient*."

Artorian performed the front paws out back-stretch. *Ooh, was it goo~o~od.* Oh yeah, that got *all* the spine spots. *Mmmm.* His jaws parted for a yawn, and he became aware of the seriously deadly arsenal of sharp things in his mouth. Now *that* was a set of *teeth*! Rolling his shoulders, he flop-rolled around a bit while the ten-times larger cat watched. The smirk on his whiskers was *cheeky*. Decorum was not remotely as stately in this form, and far more… well, cat-like in behavior as he enjoyed a grin. Watching the silly cub figure out where his legs were.

Decorum stopped grinning when the cub shot away as a line of light before his ears could pick the sound up. The line stopped on a hill, remorphing into a cat before blitzing off at an angle. The straight lines shot around him easily a hundred times. Always at sharp angles before coming to a standstill where it had started. "*Whoooo*! I'm *zippy*! Don't have the speed quite under control. I have to make sure I can see the endpoint of where I'm going to stop before taking another step. I get there far too quickly, against expectations. Going straight for too long is a big no-no, I *will* smash through the landscape. Chandra will *wring me* if I break her trees. Let's try this again."

The unamused, supposedly superior liger could barely keep up with the beam of light that formed patterns on the ground sheerly from how fast Artorian was going. He couldn't even follow where the beginning of the line was. His skilled predator-eyes only saw the line after it was there, at which point the cub was already elsewhere. Instinctively, Decorum started pawing and slapping at the lines. Like it was yarn to be caught.

Artorian stopped, looking behind him. "Did you just *bop* me?"

Decorum tried not to look guilty, eyes wide with his massive, house-sized paw hovering mere inches across a disappearing light line. "…No?"

Mhm. As if *that* was to be believed. "Sure. Alright. I've got the hang of basic movements. If I wasn't an A-ranker, I wouldn't have a hope in Cal of managing this zippy thing. Where's the boar? Let's go burden it. I think I can keep up with you. You seem big, but not that fast."

The massive liger took that playful comment as a personal challenge. Him, a Prime? Not that fast? Wind bustled around Decorum in response, ground exploding upwards as he took off by starting at Mach one. The sonic boom occurred, but neither of them were there to hear it as the Kudzu field was trimmed down to size at their passing. The plants didn't even register where all this insane damage was coming from. Whole sections of them were cleaved as if a scythe cut through the middle of their stalks, while others exploded into shiny particles as something bright passed through them.

When they cleared the weed field, Artorian's light line ever so slightly *bent*. Decorum had to slow down and veer off, because Artorian missed several steps in tandem. The light-liger crashed through four hills, a small glade, a very confused pack of bowled-over beavers who just lost their dam, and whatever was left of the riverbend. Which was now filling up with water, as the freshly formed hole in its place would form a nice new lake.

A dizzy light-liger staggered back to his feet while a family of beavers whacked him with sticks, flotsam, and bits of junk that had been their dam. He blinked as a branch swatted him in the face. It didn't do any damage, but rather just knocked a point of durability from the lightframe. Shaking his head, he watched the jumping beavers complain at him in an actual language. He didn't speak beaver. Should he see if there was a memory Core for *beaver*?

They screeched and scattered as a ten-times larger Liger showed up, followed by a cloud formation that had formed in his wake and done its best to catch up. Decorum's heavy, large voice growled through the words. "What happened?"

Artorian watched the beavers bounce away and dive into the start of the new lake as it began to rain, the clouds above them that Decorum had dragged in starting to do work. "*Tripped* over my own feet. I was doing well earlier too. Made a step too big and lost my balance. How far did I…? *Ooooooh. Ouch.* That is a big *carve* in the landscape. I guess the Kudzu is getting a new source of water soon. Oh well. Did I damage any trees?"

Decorum shook himself. "None that weren't already felled."

Artorian laid flat on the grass. "Oh good."

The sound of a dying Dwarven engine ground over the remaining hills, stirring him back up to his feet. Artorian's liger head looked, but could not pinpoint the sound. There were Dwarves here? That didn't seem right.

The awful rumbling only got louder, increasing in sharpness as the hill blocking their line of sight to the sound went up like an erupting volcano. Not for something erupting from below, but because they had found the boars. Rather, the boars had found them, and that hill had just been in the way. The shattered dirt rained back down, forming muddy patches with all the water coming from the sky. The hogs had arrived, and so had the system.

What interested Artorian the most was the freshly added pitch of a violin sliding into action. The sharp, quickly played notes stroking across the breadth of what was clearly their battlefield-to-be. The song was meant to get the heart going, and Decorum raced towards the oncoming horde to face the first wave. His first air-infused sideswipe cut through easily a dozen painted boars, mincing them like chopped salad.

Wanting some quick answers, Artorian shook his mane. The status screen pulled into view. The violin was boss event music. These boars hovered around level forty, and there was a wave of forty-fivers coming after. Then at the end of that line was a *seventy-two*? Wasn't that a thick discrepancy for Eternium's Midgard standard? That was *way* too high.

The cap for Midgard was supposed to be what? Around thirty or forty? Mr. Seventy-Two must have missed the memo. What level did that put Decorum at, now that he was looking? *Wo~ho~hooo*. *Seventy-four*. What a beast! Seventy-five must be a current hard cut-off point to get kicked out. Couldn't one just come back? Or was it still like iteration one, where the power-gain forced a one-way trip? What was the point of the rainbow bridges then?

Later. This needed to come later.

Steadying his footing, his jaw dropped as he tried thinking of a ranged attack that would work well. A nice, thick, straight *beam* was solid for enemies approaching on a flat plain. Nothing happened at first when he attempted to Invoke, hearing harsh static. Right, *right.* Use the abyss-cracked *system.* Going through the menu all the time was no good. Didn't he already get around this? All he had to do during the iteration one tests was yell out a Pylon spell… *Artorian, you fool!* It was always that simple. Uh… *what to call this.*

A quick thought crossed his mind. Could he just ask for ideas? Static was his initial answer. How about… "[Senate]."

The static faded, and Artorian partially found himself in the senate. The white marble amphitheater looked the way he remembered it. *Oooh.* He mentally rubbed his hands together. <[Forum connection to *Discord.*]>

Discord didn't understand what was going on when he was pulled into a private space. He only knew he *adored* what Love had just done, even if the communication went through a grainy filter. <Love! Buddy! What *is* this? You found a way to talk without being spied on by the watcher? You *beautiful sapling.* I can't wait to tell the other two about this!>

Artorian smirked. <Discord! I'm so glad that worked. Listen, this aside, I need a name for an attack. A line-based one, light or sun-themed.>

Discord was on the ball. <You want *random* ideas? You asked the right wraith! Let's see what I'm selling from under my bark coat. Solar flare, solar arc, glimmer stream, sparkle wave, lucent beam, radiant lance, and candesce.>

Love mentally clapped for one of the sources of trouble Incarnate. <Fantastic, I'll give them a try. You have fun playing with the forum connections! I'll come check in again when I'm on the spot and need some more ideas *wrangled.* Talk later!>

As Discord hastily ran off to *immediately* tell his friends, Artorian figured he'd dallied enough. The second wave was here. Decorum was slicing through them like they were hot cheese, and boy was that cat *agile* for his size. He wasn't even needed! Still, just sitting back was no fun. Not when he'd just been given all these lovely ideas. Let's get to *blasting!*

CHAPTER TWENTY-NINE

A clicking knock thunked on his forum space before Artorian could begin his stride. Oh? So that's what it sounded like when that happened in Eternium. He understood, rather than saw the pop-up message. [Forum request from Chaos.] Well that was nice, but now wasn't a good time, and he moved to reject.

When the connection was established regardless, it didn't take much guesswork to know who was responsible for *side-stepping* the system. *That little weasel*! <Love! *Buddy*! This forum thing is *fantastic*! Listen, real quick. I wanted to live up to my namesake and throw my own addition in. Discord blabbed without stopping to breathe. He's passed out on the floor now. Try Shining Ray! Oh, *moss*. The watcher's attention is coming. Gotta go!>

Click.

Artorian snickered. *Eh*, sure. Why not! Dropping his jaw, his claws dug into the muddy soil as his mana bar shrank, the Pylons drinking it away. "[Shining Ray]!"

He hadn't thought about why he'd opened his mouth. First, a hefty ball of energy gathered in his maw. From that condensed power, a *teensy*, narrow beam of light stabbed faster than he could see towards the horizon. Well, that wasn't very *flashy*… This line was barely a *sliver* thick! He was hoping for a big, tree-sized kaboom! With the ray ongoing, he dropped his head to move the beam parallel to the ground, then looked to his left in the hopes it would be more interesting over there.

The shining ray didn't seem so paltry when the teensy thing *divided* boars in its path, doubling the amount of friends they had! Even if there was only half of a friend left in the ray's wake. Crackers and toast! How much damage did this thing do to just cleave through the wave like that? He was happy his mouth stopped moving before Decorum came into view! It would have been horrible had the ray originated from elsewhere.

So much for an all-natural hunt. Then again, being bright and shiny in a landscape of wet and dark was essentially a euphemism for his life. There was never going to be any hiding.

Wondering how to stop the mana-hungry ray, the line fizzled out when he thought as much. Well, that was no fair. Couldn't activate the abilities with thought, but you could stop them that way? On second consideration, that was incredibly reasonable.

Snapping his jaws, he realized his cheeks felt sore. Li-Torian ground his teeth together. Head shaking around for proper bearings as he wondered what the floppy thing at the front of his face was. "Why ish my twongue nwumb."

The words slurred out, and the tongue in question hung aimlessly from the front of his mouth. Unable to react to his will as it *blepped*. Well, that's just not nice! Fine, another one then. *Not* from the mouth. Let's see, what does this do? "[Solar Flare]!"

Oh sweet Cal! Where did a *third* of his mana bar just go? He was glad to be solidly planted, because his form buckled under the pressure of the effect he'd just sent skywards. The rain stopped quickly. Well that wasn't so bad. Rising temperatures in the area surged from nippy all the way up to unpleasantly toasty. The mud under his feet hardened. "Uh oh."

Unpleasantly toasty turned into burnt toast, and the ground baked to brick as oppressive heat bore down on it. His form buckled more, honest-to-Cal cracks forming along the frame of his temporary construct. Why had he used something fire-related when Decorum had told him the boar they were up against was fire resistant? Well... fire resistant. Not fire immune. Ember was very clear on the difference.

Also slated as a very clear difference was the threat index that the boars considered between Decorum, and the shiny cub version. Their communicative horror sounds spoke volumes of the topic.

Decorum was big. Easy to notice. Slicing boars to ribbons with claws of pressured air that were longer in reach than antic-ipated. Decorum killed a good dozen of them with a swipe. That tiny bright one? That little sucker just wiped half of their second wave with a single ability, if not more. In addition, it had injured Mokono. Who survived only by being smart and burrowing underground.

The priority list for who should be fought shifted. This was why, when Artorian looked at the horde again, they were charging him! His form cracked some more. That told him it wasn't going to hold, meaning he would take actual damage from that point on.

How about... how about *no*? Sifting through the options as the squealing masses—who cried like broken engines—made quick work of the distance. He just picked one of the suggested abilities as the oppressive heat on the soon-to-be-desert increased. Life wasn't going to fare that well with the heat of the flare currently lying over them. The boars, even with their protections, were having trouble breathing. "Decorum! Get out of Dodge!"

Artorian had meant to say 'get out of the way,' but thought of the word 'dodge' last minute. Decorum glanced, and pogo-hopped into the air on tiny clouds he made below himself. Well, look at who was being a copycat now.

He didn't have time to be quippy. "[Sparkle Wave]!"

The violin hanging in the air changed its tune. Artorian's liger construct shattered when the ability went off, peppering the air to form fifteen-foot-high concentric rings of glitter that shot outwards in waves.

Artorian fell from the cavity in the liger that he'd been stored in, mind solidly home in his child shape now that he could not keep it extended anymore. He landed on his feet, then spun in place as the violin kicked up a tune that made him think of a transformation sequence. He wasn't some kind of magical girl, but the tune was just so abysally catchy. Given that he was mid spin, he stopped on a dime just to pose, hoping that last ability would actually be something useful...

When the boars charged through the outer ring of hanging glitter, the particles shimmered. The boars didn't care, and raged onwards! The shimmering particles—superheated from the flare effect still in play—snapped their metaphorical fingers and shot the posing youth some finger-arrows, revealing that, just like his pose, they were *sharp*.

Sharp, and immobile.

As a result, the rampaging horde cut themselves to shreds by battering through the stationary defense, suffering a swift end. The boars felt a thousand cuts as they barged into a field of dots they should have patiently dodged between. Each sparkly particle didn't do much damage individually, and the added fire damage was a laugh. But when you had more of them hanging in the air than could be reasonably counted over a year, perhaps it was best to proceed with caution and avoid the unmoving little flecks of sharpness. It wasn't like they were trying to do anything. They just hung there, being *fabulous*.

The charging wave died before a single boar got within an arm's length of Artorian. The innermost defensive circle barely expended, which was a pleasant sight. What was a touch unpleasant was the smell. Lots of meat cooked on the ground made Artorian pull a face. Were there descriptions to these attacks that he could look up? Surely there was something that didn't require him to default to random testing. Preferably an option that didn't need him to sit down in a workshop with twenty screens open to puzzle it out. He was *still* sour about that piece of magnetic pyrite.

On the plus side, no more enemies coming at him! On the downside, he was stuck in his own flare effect, and a shimmering field that didn't discriminate. He'd get cut just as easily if he moved through them. Be nice if they would just turn off.

He slapped his forehead, and the effects faded. The oppressive heat removed itself, and he could swear the sparkles performed a spin before winking, and winking out. Newfound bonus, no more mana drain! Newfound downside, his vanished reserves! The bar was so small that he got snappy. "Show me how much these abyss-cracked abilities cost!"

He stamped his foot, yelling at nobody as the ground under him crumpled a few inches. The land rumbled. It was easy to forget his stats were A-ranker sized, even if he didn't come up to an average person's shoulder. No prompt came up for his outburst, but Decorum did come down from his bouncy clouds. Artorian sighed. "I'm sorry, my friend. I'll try going hunting with you again when the form I take doesn't take such a shine."

Decorum didn't reply, his eyes focused as vertical slits. He crouched on impact with the ground, attention off in the distance. He surveyed a hill that had suspiciously survived the trampling.

Artorian turned to look, and noted the oddity. Now that didn't make sense. Those boars were big, and all the other hills had flattened. Then the hill stood up, and Mokono shook himself to clear his hide of wanton dirt. Had this clever brat dug under to protect himself from the flare, shimmers, and the ray? That cheeky waffle! With a strong exhale through the nose that erupted into a steam cloud, Mokono visibly taunted them.

Glancing at his dwindling reserves, Artorian figured he'd have to punch the thing. Great. Because that tended to turn out well. However, he noticed that Decorum was itching to attack. So why was he holding back? A few glances between the eye-locked region bosses, and he understood what both were waiting for.

A sign to start.

Decorum wanted this win. Mokono wanted this win. Artorian just smiled, and addressed his friend. Dropping the flag? He could do that for them. "Get 'em."

Decorum was gone in a flurry of wind! Gashing the landscape as he shot forwards. He roared, and the boar countered. Erupting with that terrible dead engine noise in reply. Artorian winced as their initial clash made impact. *Aiii...* not good. Decorum wasn't the only one hiding his reach, as the iron tusk of the boar reshaped mid-charge. Decorum's claw swipe grazed, and at best nicked, Mokono's hide.

The violin slowed its song, and Artorian snapped his vision around at the distraction. The music had been a cutesy background feature at first, but now it was irritating. "Alright, what *is* making that racket?"

The sight took him out of the fight when he located the source, cutting through the invisibility effect by cheating with his maximized perception. An Imp sat on a wide, ornate throne that hovered in the sky. Far too large for its tiny bum as the small demon playing tore up the musical instrument with such feverish skill that Artorian considered it a crime of passion.

"A *demon*?"

The golden violin's tune *screeched*, a wrong note hiccuping as the player's arm jerked, notes falling off as he ended his personal jam. Paganini was invisible. He knew he was invisible. Nothing less than a Sage quality perception, [Inspect], [Reveal], or [Locate] had even the slightest hope of giving him away. Now this *kid* was staring right at him. A kid had deduced his actual species at a glance, and looked royally *pissed*.

With a swift glance at his own status screen, Artorian raised a momentary brow. His mana bar was refilling all on its own? How... *convenient*. The reason *why* it recovered by itself would need to be puzzled out later. For now, there was a growing rage that demanded tending.

<CA~A~AL!>

CHAPTER THIRTY

Boom.

Artorian's launch turned the dry, cracked dirt into a full-on crater. Just the force of an A-rank two body alone was more than enough to severely damage and destroy Midgard-quality ground. The nearby lake received a new location for water to accumulate as the impact force shattered the underground, forming a vast, new aquifer.

The Imp screeched, his instrument and accompanying stick thrown into the air as his throne turned and zipped away. The instruments vanished into particles. Must have been a use of the [Instrument] ability.

While Decorum and Mokono hacked it out in the forest-turned-wasteland below, the demon hurriedly escaped for dear life as the angriest twelve-year-old in existence refused to let up. The very air around the boy *burned* out of being as the system constantly worked to convert his auric functions into Pylon applications.

Eternium's displeasure grew further as the Administrator-titled one failed to keep himself to the desired order. On the plus side, it meant this would be automated in the future. On the downside, this shouldn't have happened to begin with! Eternium had been stoic with Cal when it came to telling people that they *could not* use their cultivation abilities in his Soul Space. It was the system or bust! As a minor inconvenience, that information wasn't entirely correct. A person *could* use their natural cultivation abilities in Eternium, he just didn't like it. Thus he had asked Cal to tell them it couldn't be done, purely to dissuade them from even trying. Then there was *this* Imp-chasing pain in his Core.

Stay within the rules, you abyss-hating problem child! Eternium fussed as he automated ever more Auric options, shunting over far more work to the support crew. Yet, if he personally had to forcibly automate every last single cultivator function purely so it adhered to his system of **Order**, he would! He procedurally would! Blast this tier seven-twenty **Law** playing hooky. Had it been one tier lower—just *one* lower— Artorian would have been entirely unable to circumvent Eternium's rules. That meant there were *four* nails in his coffin now. *Uuuugh*.

Eternium considered asking Cal how Wood Elves—even though they were now something else—had not only gotten **Laws**, but particularly how they'd gotten *those* three. Please let it not have been that Cal was *bored*. He didn't get the chance as the core in question rushed in with his own questions.

<What. *What?* I'm here. What's going on? Why are you yell —*oooooh*. That's a demon.> Cal bit his metaphorical thumb. <How did *that* happen? I didn't make any demons. There shouldn't *be* any demons. You got them all, right Artorian? All of them? I went over those memories *easily* twelve times. You used that Mana storm, converted into a higher-function attack. One equivalent to a strike of roughly seventy-eight A-rankers, no less. Sternum punching all the existing A-rank demons back into oblivion. Including whatever grunts you missed the first time that ranked below them. What is a D-rank *Imp* doing in Eternium? I... *I will go figure this out.*>

Artorian was thankful that there was no need for a reply

when the connection clicked shut. All he would have done was bellow with seething rage. He was *livid*. Eternium's watchful gaze winked out to hurry off elsewhere. Artorian no longer felt the pressure, nor the bristling on the back of his neck. Weird how those sensations still happened even in a body that shouldn't reasonably be capable of it. No, that wasn't right. It happened, so it was clearly capable. Incarnate forms were so much *stranger* than A-rank bodies. He'd get used to it one day. A little more and he would have this Imp by the... "*Neck*! Got you!"

Paganini the small demon screeched, his tiny arms and legs wiggling on a potbellied frame. It chittered at him like some kind of deformed squirrel. Artorian didn't speak Abyssal. Or was it Demonic? Or maybe the language was called 'scree-scree,' based on the Imp's noises. Know what? He liked *scree-scree*.

The Imp squirmed, but had a hairball's hope to get free from the statistics clamping him tight. Breathing was currently off the table, and fright-based statuses populated on the demon's character screen. Which quickly became visible when the Administrator Invocation *ripped* the information out of him. Literally tearing the status screen out of the demon's being to have it available. Abyss just using [Inspect].

Fire burgeoned from his nostrils upon heavy exhale as Artorian scanned the sheet. He was *not* happy. A motion of the hand pulled up his store screen, and his voice commanded it directly. Several windows populated, each asking for something that the youth snapped his way through. "Administrator access. Deity options. Language Cores. Relevant language for touched creature. Select. Purchase. Confirm."

A Core appeared in Artorian's hand as points he currently couldn't care less about drained from a pool that didn't matter. The Core immediately pressed to his forehead, and he *knew*. The voice box in his Incarnate form twisted into an entirely different amalgam altogether as normal vocal cords just weren't up to snuff.

To speak scree-scree, there were sounds and intonations that a human mouth could simply never hope to achieve. The Imp's health bar bled away from suffocation damage until suddenly the grip loosened, allowing it a life-saving breath.

Horror and Terror status effects flicked into activity on the Imp's status sheet. As the youth suddenly spoke *impeccable* Fernalis. Or, as it was likely going to be named in the future: scree-scree. "You have a choice. You can silently follow me until you answer my questions. Or I can introduce you to my old compatriot, *Snap*."

The Imp nearly broke his arm from how swiftly it shot a single, stubby digit into the air. It was unable to lie, escape, or really do much else other than it was told with all the terrible status effects it was suffering from. Paganini thought to himself: Option one, please, dear Eternium. Option *one*.

The Imp deliberately chose not to speak, as the word 'silent' had been mentioned in the demand. Paganini needed zero explanation, nor further threat on what might occur if he didn't follow this order *to the letter*.

Artorian let go, and the Imp shivered on its throne. From basic inspection, it was the throne that could fly, when given direction from the one seated. The throne was also allowing the seated to remain under a very advanced set of illusory effects. Neat. The youth turned, and shot back towards Decorum at Mach two.

Concussive booms rocked the air, but the Imp couldn't pay attention to that as it clung to the plush seat for dear life. Mushed against the upholstery with squinty eyes as the transport chair followed the direction: 'Follow that one at all costs.' When the throne stopped, the Imp was certain its heartbeat had as well. It had never managed to push the throne to move at those speeds on his own.

Artorian commanded. "*Stay*."

The Imp couldn't reply, but did as ordered. Artorian would *not* be distracted further from quality Decorum time. Landing on the ground with a thud, the situation looked grim. His friend was losing, and Mokono was barely at half health. Artorian decided he had some residual anger that needed to be worked off, and would you look at that. A convenient *target*.

Inspecting Decorum, he read the name of the ability that allowed the massive liger to bump up his reach. "*Gale Claw?* Should have seen that coming. I've got air as an affinity channel, but it's not my strongest suit. No reason to experiment much here. Let's deconstruct that other one from earlier instead. Shining Ray? Let's see. If I think of it not as a claw extending from my hand, but rather as a construct that goes above and overlaps my hand on a categorically larger scale, *then* apply the energy in the shape of a claw, I *should* get an Eternium conversion for the bits the initial Pylons don't compensate for. Here we go, let's do this mid-stride. [Shining Claw]!"

The Pylons worked to combine the desired effects, learning a new ability in the process that an empty Pylon took upon itself to exemplify.

Boom.

Another new crater in the ground made it rain dirt and debris, the youth gone from his spot at Mach two. Mid-flight, he opened and closed his fingers to test the construct forming over them. The twelve-foot-long claws that hovered a good two or three feet away from his entire left arm copied the motion. *Excellent.*

Shining laser streaks cut through the air as Artorian attacked. The swift slice left residual lines of light behind as he yelled loud while mid-transit to get the Boss beast's attention. Mokono did turn his head, but only in time for five elongated claws to carve through its face and flank.

Mokono didn't have time to react. The attack had come and gone faster than it could respond to. To its great relief, Mokono's Ironhide ability had saved it from a majority of the piercing and slashing damage. The celestial element, on the other hand, had left some *nasty* wounds.

Artorian hadn't considered using a celestial infusion with hostile intent before. When he made a wide U-turn after a quick wingover, he was intrigued to find that the claws still functioned as intended. Deep gashes visibly scored the boss' flank; though rather than harm Mokono further, the added celestial damage merely *prevented* those wounds from mending, healing, or being otherwise affected in a way that would alter them. That lasting damage changed Mokono's base state, and his new Maximum Health took a sharp nosedive because of it.

That distraction was enough for Decorum to launch a follow up strike. Given the gashes Artorian's claw had made through the Ironhide protections, he had a clean target. Decorum's Gale Claw widened, the injured liger doing his best to strike the exact location of the prior claws. One of the pressured lines of air may have missed and sliced against the nullifying Ironhide, but the others *all* scored critical damage.

Mokono released a final, dying motor-screech, and burst into confetti particles as Decorum leveled up. Ascending above the maximum Midgard cap.

Slumping to his butt, Decorum formed into Gomez, taking on a humanlike guise as Artorian zipped back to him for immediate healing. The scars he'd attained from this fight could have been deathly dangerous, but the brother who had taken him out hunting was a very skilled healer. Odd how a single person could hold such varied positions. Still, that was how it worked with Artorian. He would be what was needed, regardless of that being a friend, a brother, or a father.

Laying a digit on the stately man, the youth spoke in a hurry. "[Full Restore]."

Artorian watched Gomez's health bar fill right back up. The scars, wounds, battle damage, and residual status effects all vaporizing to nothingness. Bleed statuses poofed, right along with bone fractures, muscle tears, fatigue, infections, a venom counter, and some disease called tetanus. Decorum sighed with relief. "Ah... that feels so much better."

Ding.

Artorian looked around, having heard the noise. He didn't see a new notification, but Gomez did, and moved his hand to point at it. "My friend, I have received an ultimatum notice. I can choose to immediately move on from Midgard, as I have so far refused to. Or I can become a part of the place permanently and take up the boss position Mokono had. I do not wish the latter, and this one has a timer. I have ten minutes."

Artorian nodded, understanding. "I think you'll be able to come back, somehow. I need to remember to look into it more deeply. Seeing as you're currently in a state of undress... let me give you a parting gift as congratulations for removing that iron-tusked pain, and to celebrate the start of your new life. Don't worry about where you pick to go next. I'll find you when I can. Let me just..."

Opening the shop again, the youth sifted through relevant sections until he found what he was looking for. "Modsognir-style suit. Sized to touched creature. Select. Purchase. Confirm."

A box materialized next to him. Artorian dismissed the system prompts, and picked the gift up, handing it over with a smile. "This is for you, my friend."

The dark, black vest and red undershirt alone were beauties. Gomez's eyes sparkled, and he slid on the entire outfit under a few minutes. The youth conjured a temporary mirror, and the broad-smiling stately man beamed. "*Cara mia.*"

As Gomez dressed, Artorian 'spoke' a fencing blade into being, weaving the energies while mumbling relevant Pylon names under his breath. He didn't know if they were right, but he supposed that was the joy of figuring things out. Using Mokono's tusk as a basis, the guise of a walking cane formed around the blade, doubling in function as a scabbard. Pleased with his work, he handed it over. "Best of luck in the next realm, my boy."

Gomez sucked in a breath. This was all happening so fast for him. Rising up to full height, he tested the walking cane, digging the butt end into the ground as he posed. "How do I look, Father?"

Artorian hovered into the air and adjusted the bowtie. "Like a thousand good souls packed into one. Ready to bring culture wherever he treads."

Gomez hugged the youth, the timer down to the last minute. "When you visit, my next domus shall be *grander* than the one I leave behind. So say I, Gomez of Decorum!"

Artorian smiled, and gave a gentle nod.

Gomez steadied himself, winking with accompanied salute. The timer blinked down into the ten second region. His cane twirled, spinning through the air as he used the end of it to press accept. Gomez blinked out of being, leaving behind Artorian, a wrecked landscape, a family of distraught beavers, and one very, *very pale* Imp.

CHAPTER THIRTY-ONE

In fluent scree-scree, Artorian addressed the Imp as part of the landscape behind him cracked, collapsing in on itself with quaking cacophony as underground caverns structurally failed. The Horror and Terror status marks couldn't be increased further, but the Imp would swear up and down that they had as the scary youth spoke. "Now. How many of you are there, and *where?*"

The Imp shakily rose that same stubby digit. Pointing up to the sky. Following the direction, Artorian thought he was going to catch fire when the creature motioned straight for the *moon*. The *new* moon here in Eternium. He had no idea what happened to the old one, the one in Cal's Soul Space which he liked the outside of so much. The inside… *Eh*. That was the kind of clinical discomfort he needed to learn how to stomach.

Holding that cold, unpleasant feeling, he channeled it into his words.

"*How. Many?*"

The Imp panicked, attempting to count on his fingers. Unfortunately, as good as he was at stringed instruments, he was a sore shot at math. Artorian started wondering how to go from here when Cal very loudly exploded in the Eternium version of the senate. <You w*hat*? This *whole* time?>

Glancing at the Imp, Artorian made his retort laconic. The Imp just wasn't going to have the answers he needed. From the sound of it, 'upper management' just might. "I'll deal with you later. You are free to go."

Verbally released, the throne shuddered as the Imp wanted it to be anywhere but here. The seat popped, porting out of Midgard and vanishing with the seated Imp entirely.

Artorian went right back to paying attention as Cal simmered with anger, vocally carrying on. <Why can't I...? Right. I'm in the Eternium Core. I think people can still hear me with these settings. Yeah. Could I please get all the supervisors to gather at the inner circle in *my* Soul Space? Preferably now. Occultatum, you *especially*.>

The connection cut, and Artorian slated the Eternium moon problem for later. Better yet, this was likely connected. Best to focus on more immediate issues. Would his body remain here if he shifted locations? *Probably*. He didn't want that family of angry beavers to whack him. Better to pay some compensation.

Opening his shop, he left some beaver-related goodies and treats behind, plus enough raw material for a whole new dam. After leaving them a small, apologetic note, Artorian zipped back off to the domus. He loved that Decorum had opted for the open-air addition smack in the middle of the structure. The central portion of the peristyle was the site of a decorative garden, adorned with gorgeous fountains. It let him cut right through the structure without harm, and zip into the room he'd been previously designated.

Bentley hopped along in a hurry, supremely displeased with this lack of manners as Artorian made his way inside. "Sir! It is uncouth to arrive and make oneself present without *proper* prior announcement. Sir! Do you hear me, young master?"

When the butler bunny reached the stilled form resting in bed, Artorian had long left it.

Waking in Cal's Soul Space, Artorian found his hunch was correct. He was not able to take that specific body with him. For just a moment, he enjoyed familiar comforts per the body of an elder. Though only for a moment as his form went *clap*, snapping back to that of a youth. "Crackers and toast!"

Rubbing his forehead in defeat, he dropped the matter and instantly teleported to the inner circle space at the top of Niflheim. Artorian arrived in the midst of a full-on *spat* between Occultatum and Cal. Snapping at one another, the argument was both loud and heated. Their arms flailed, hands speaking as wildly as their clashing words.

A very meek, odd-shaped orb floated nearby. Clearly trying to stay out of it.

Artorian recognized the consciousness as Eternium! Oh, this was going to be a *doozy*. He slid into his chair, but Dawn held her hand out towards him. He thought better of it, and hovered over to sit in her lap instead. She was quite pleased to hold him, and he wouldn't deny her that small comfort. Some people had not yet seen Artorian in this new child form, but they said nothing about his current appearance.

Actual problems were afoot.

Tatum was energized, and didn't hold back. "I told you, *millennia ago*, that *Barry* was going to be a problem. You ignored it until now, when he has figured out a way to influence the world without a body, complete sensory deprivation, and a zone around him that blocks Essence and Mana. Did you forget to block *Spirit* when you Incarnated? Now we have a whole *mess!*"

Cal angrily pointed at the orb representing Eternium. "I knew about the other S-rankers, but *not* that he was *harboring demons*. Nor that one of the S-rankers in question *is one*. I do not have to explain, to you of all people, why that is a problem. Why didn't you *tell me* about this?"

Eternium meekly hovered backwards, and Tatum stamped his foot on the soil, sending a tremor through the land. "We tried, Cal! We did! You wouldn't even take Barry seriously! This time, you're no A-ranker that can *afford* to push the problem to the next millennium. You have gone through the first step's life, and you are a *hair* away from the second step. I am in your *soul*, Cal. You *can't* hide this from me. One more hair and I will be all back to normal, and you will be forced to let all those S-rankers *out* or your *own promise* will crack you. Even if I still don't know the full details of the deal, because you have been *painfully vague* about the exactness of it all."

Cal conjured a flat rock just to throw it into the distance. "That's because I purposefully kept it vague! I don't want to talk about it because then you can prod me about it, and if you prod me about it, you'll change the patterns of how I *interpret* that vagueness! My current interpretation gives *me* all the wiggle room. I *like* wiggle room. There! Are you happy?"

Tatum buried his face into his hands and doubled over from imaginary headache pain. "*Ca~a~a~l.* No matter the interpretation, if you cross *your own rules* of the promise then it still counts as *breaking* the promise. You are going to need to let them all out of stasis, and let them live lives. The chains of chaos haven't shown a hint of weakening, you are stuck. We still *cannot* get out. You cannot wiggle-room this in the hopes that they will fade because you make the second step. The odds are not in your favor!"

"Never tell me the odds!" Cal snapped back, and a thousand screens dropped into full projection around them, arranged as a dome. "I know about *all* the odds, and now this one is listed too!"

The relevant screen was pulled, and he pointed at it. Upset. "This is the odds screen for the Barry-problem, and look. It's *fine*. It says…"

When Cal actually looked—really looked—his words died in his throat as his human face paled. "Oh sweet, merciful myself. That's… that's *bad*. That's *so* bad."

Tatum motioned exasperatedly, as if to say 'I told you so! Doofus!' then walked away just to collapse in his chair. His fingers pressed hard to his brow, as he didn't want to talk anymore.

Cal turned nice and pale. The dungeon steepled his hands and pressed digits to his lips. "Celestial Feces."

Chandra's hands were also steepled, her brow in a deep furrow. "Let me see if I understand this correctly. Eternium, the dungeon Core you picked up from the real world, is a Third-Step Incarnate that refused to 'go further.' I'm not pressing that right now. He has a Soul Space equivalent to yours, but a vastly differing **Law**, and outlook on how things should be done. Because **Order** is all-important to him, there had to be a balance in what he 'saved.' For lack of a better term."

She dropped her hands to the table, speaking calmly in her fully human guise. It was just easier. "Of those balancers, Eternium included: Several S-rankers. Demons. Hordes of creatures no reasonable individual would have ever picked up or associated with, and those *bark-cracked mosquitos*!"

Chandra was clearly miffed at their mention, but didn't halt her stride. "This hasn't been a problem. Until now, when lives and people were moved into Eternium to function under the 'system' Cal is implementing. Piggybacking on Eternium's **Law** for both convenience and structure. Unfortunately, because of that activity, and Cal's own Incarnate step. Entities in Eternium can *exit* stasis, or were made to exit stasis, and now roam free in Eternium. They're bound to the system, but they *exist*."

The dungeon was going to interrupt her, but Chandra doubled down on her sharp tone, cutting him right off. "*In addition*. Barry, the abyssal devourer and most royal of grievances, not only exists, but lives, and is *influencing* most if not all the demons somehow. Since someone forgot to seal off Spirit energy access. I was *so* confused about what that bar in my status screen meant. I can cycle between a measurement in Essence, and a measurement in Mana. Yet measurement in Spirit has always shown as zero, and I just didn't understand until now."

Artorian raised his young hand.

Chandra wanted to keep biting chunks out of their dungeon overlord, but huffed and threw him a ball. That ball was

Eternium, but Artorian grasped the point of what Chandra meant by it. He nodded thankfully. "Let me please deter the course of this event, just slightly. I currently don't understand the full extent of the problem, and am aware that demons in Eternium exist in or on the moon. Is Cal's moon safe? Memory Cores being in danger is not an aspect I even remotely wish to chance. One problem at a time please."

Minya raised her hand, and Artorian passed the orb. Her cheeks were full of color! Minya's voice had pep, and she seemed much happier about life in general. "I can confirm that Cal's moon is entirely unaffected. No demons. No damage. No changes save for the continual child improvements. Now that I am feeling a little better, and have a helper, we are working on improving the inside of the moon to be teenager-friendly with many hidden secrets to find. It's also where we're installing the classrooms and such. We want to allow the older children some space from the younger ones, if they need it. The deeper into the moon they go, the more arduous the challenge. If they can reach the center before a set age, they will be allowed to enter Eternium early. We'll have nothing left to teach them if they do."

That was good, and pleasant news. The gathering murmured appreciatively at that development. Odin raised his hand, and the ball passed. "I see not why we cannot simply defeat this Barry in single combat. Once destroyed, it will count as a life lived! He does not need to be brought back if he is such a concern. Ha! Send the goose after him! How mighty of a challenge can one who remains locked up for all eternity be?"

The silence that lay heavy over the inner circle didn't do Odin any good, nor did it sit well. "Surely you jest. This foe is not one that cannot be vanquished!"

Cal slid into his chair, and his hand waggled in the so-so motion. Odin gave him the orb, and the dungeon spoke. "I... I feel like I can address this. So long as it is *one* problem at a time. Barry. Right. So here's the problem with Barry. That title of his isn't for show. To defeat him the first time, we had to employ some truly devious, experimental, and oh-merciful-heavens-this-might-not work tactics. Infernal Essence cannons on an *Incarnate*? Had we not been right on the mark with his weakness fully exposed, we would never have gotten so lucky. Nor are we going to pull that off a second time."

Odin rolled his wrist for more. This still didn't sound like a problem, so Cal continued. "Barry is an Incarnate. A true Incarnate. Like Dawn and Tatum. So he doesn't just get the *body*, like the rest of you do. He gets *all* the bells and whistles as well. Our current Incarnates have already moved through layers a few times while in my Soul Space, and it gives me a horrible case of indigestion. Except in my soul instead of my stomach. Metaphorically, I mean… well, you get it."

Odin rolled his wrist more, and faster. Still not relevant! "Barry's **Law** is consumption, or the equivalent idea. He has a special method of attack where his 'soul,' the intelligent and sapient part of him, can leave the 'body' of the Incarnate behind, and attack using the prior. That which is attacked is consumed outright. Entirely. There's no defense. There's no blocking. Mitigation is a joke if you're in the area of effect he has spread himself to. He just eats you, and gets *all* your power. You need to be a true Incarnate to be a match, and if that is a battle that happens by jumping through layers, I am *not* going to feel great. Which is why I said what I did earlier."

Odin's wrist-roll stopped. That was less than thunderous news. He cleared his throat, feeling hesitant. "So… Even if we have the superbodies, if we ourselves are A-rankers, we essentially don't stand a chance. Not even with the system in Eternium? That's where he's stuck. Surely it *can* be done."

Tatum raised his hand, and Cal tossed him the ball. "You've got *no* chance, even with the system conversion. The difference between an Incarnate and a Mage is the same kind of difference as between a C-ranker and a Mage. You've got no hope of winning without some serious gimmicks. Except unless we can use the system for something *more*, there aren't any gimmicks that will work. Incarnates are a category of their own; we are something a normal person can't understand."

People didn't like that comment, so he clarified. "Remember that Dawn and I are *actually* immortal. Only if something harms or kills our souls do we kick it. Otherwise, we will be around forever. Barry also has that bonus, and unlike most all of you, he *never* needs to sleep in his Seed Core. We can't even contain him with the *best* methods we have currently applied. In addition, he was a student of Xenocide. You remember? The madman who was able to damage Incarnates directly, because his attacks destroyed or destabilized the concepts we have of ourselves. It would be foolish to ignore that he might know even an *inch* of that style."

Cal lifted his hand, and was tossed Eternium. "Tatum is right. Based on my first few checks, Barry is using a form of parasitic mind control to affect creatures in his immediate surroundings, and those spread his influences to others. It's like my totems? Except much better. I'm still surprised. Even given all the time he had to figure out how to do that. Especially while confined in Eternium, and limited as he is. I did not expect Barry to have such a *burning mind*. It's easy to forget he was a High Elf."

Aiden raised his paw, and caught the ball as it was tossed. "This sounds like something I cannot begin to help with. Can I remove myself from this problem? I will get in the way, and I have tasks elsewhere. It sounds like this 'Barry' is immobile, successfully confined, and using minions to do his bidding. That's as difficult to curtail as cutting off his access to things in his immediate vicinity."

Cal nodded, got the ball back, and dismissed Aiden. The Wolfman trudged to the teleportation beacon and winked out. Artorian jumped a little. A notification had popped up in his vision. He'd just been awarded a ton of points! He thought that only worked in Eternium? Must have been a bug. Dawn squeezed him, a silent question on her face. He gave her a quiet thumbs up, and adjusted his seating. They were trying not to talk without having the physical ball. Something new they were giving a whirl. Cleverly done, Chandra!

Artorian glanced over to Henry and Marie. It was so hard not to snicker. They were exhausted. Present, but completely wiped out of energy from the work they had to do. Now that so many hordes of people were active in Eternium, their tasks were endless.

Artorian put his hand up, caught the ball, and asked a question. "Why *now* all of a sudden?"

Cal caught the Core, and answered. "Deverash introduced a rogue element into the system I wasn't aware of. Not properly. It's a material called… that can't be right. Artorian, it says here you have a bag's worth of iridium? That's the material in question? Except it's not iridium. More like… Anything-ium. Oh, I love this stuff! If it wasn't currently causing me a headache. You didn't litter this anywhere, did you? Or give them out? It has allowed Barry to link from his confined space to the outside. If he gets too much of it, or more, this might get worse. I definitely don't want this to get worse. Particularly if this happens before I enter the second step, because then he can probably get out *early*. Which means we can't rely on Occultatum as a counter. With enough of that stuff he can probably form a body that can house a mind. *Eesh*. Dev. *Why*."

Artorian asked for the ball, and grumbled after catching to answer. "Why else? He was bored and thought of it as a good laugh. I… I may have *misplaced* a few pieces. Though I remember *where*. I suppose we can start here. Brianna. *Dagger?*"

Brianna hadn't said a word the entire meeting, but procured the blade in question. Her speech was curt. "*Dagger.*"

Everyone expected the sharp weapon to be hurled at Artorian's face, but she daintily placed it on the table and slid it over. The knife trembled, shaking in place as it bumped itself up to balance on the tip when Brianna removed her will from the dagger form. Bouncing an inch atop the table, it popped back into the shape of an Iridium Li. Well, that was *neat*.

Artorian teleported the pouch into his hand from where it

was currently stored, then upended the container, letting the full smattering of Li *click-clack-clatter* onto the inner circle table. He hoped they would remain nice and gathered together. It would have been great if nothing happened, but the previously-dagger-Li slid towards its brothers as if attracted by a magnet. They all shuddered, and combined together into a single coin-Li. *Interesting.* Artorian picked it up, but frowned. "Well... It looks small, but all the weight merged together. The density of this coin went up. Considerably."

He stared at it, sliding the Li back into the pouch as he thoughtfully affixed it on his waist. "I should... make sure to get the rest. So it isn't found by *wayward* hands. I'm going to just go ahead and do that. Please do fill me in with the plans that come up?"

Artorian received a round of nods, and gave Dawn the ball after a squeeze-hug. With goodbyes sorted, he teleported right off her lap to mitigate a problem he caused. He felt downright *crabby* about it.

Fuff.

CHAPTER THIRTY-TWO

Artorian pressed his hands to his hips. Svartalfheim had *clean* air. Not in the slightest how he remembered it. "Well... I guess *our* iteration wasn't... stellar. For *keeping*. No harm done. *I* hope."

The youth planned to comb the Cal versions of realms first, as they were abandoned and devoid of people. Currently, at least. He wanted to plunk his people back down... when he didn't look *twelve*. That was still eating him. It's fine. It's *fine*! He'd get to it. First Cal's realms, then Eternium's. Given the place was *empty*, no reason he couldn't go *fast*. This would be easier with a racing palanquin. Actually...

Artorian knocked on a forum door, uncertain if it still worked. <Dev, are you still alive and around?>

The youth didn't in the slightest understand the synthesized noises and pitches that he heard in reply. That... could be a language? <Uh... Dev? Was that you? I don't speak—>

Bwaauwp.

Moments later, an eight-sided die warped into existence next to him. Rather than reply in the forum space—the connection of which clicked shut—Dev used a physical voice. "Artorian! So good to see you! I'm so sorry about that. It's been so long since I've Gnomed the Gnome. I'm around! Just not as you knew me. I'm much happier in my new ways of being, after having split from the Gnomes that preferred being traditional crafters and tinkerers. I admit, I do miss the mad machines. Yet it doesn't call me as the Pylons do. Speaking of. You have broken quite a few of them! I have been quite pleased with discovering what causes those breaks, and how to prevent them."

The smiling face on the die altered to a frown. "Although, I am very upset that Tatum whispered use of the '*Majin*' Pylon to you. That one was not ready. Demon-based Pylons were supposed to remain experimental! It's like he wanted to *stir the pot* and bring attention to them. Not sure why. Not my problem. I just fix things."

Artorian raised a brow. "*Whispered?*"

The Deverash-die bobbed. "Oh yes, he does it *all the time*. A real headache. He knows he shouldn't because it makes Cal unhappy. As an example! When he can't go out in the field with Henry—who he does like even if they can't spend much time together—he cheekily uses some of his divine points to sneak a title into Henry's lineup. Such as the one that makes it ridiculously easy to use resurrection abilities on him. Usually, shortly before Henry takes a lethal effect. Cal has told him to stop because Henry can't be sure if he slotted the title in himself or not, as it *is* one of his favorites. Tatum does things like that all the time. Cal is even adding limits on what he can one day tell his followers. Tatum's cheekiness is legendary."

Artorian couldn't help but laugh; that was excellent! "Ha! I'm not even mad. That's amazing. Well, alright then. I'm here to recover that iridium you once gave me. We found out about the problems it has. Time to reel that in. Do you have a tracker of where I can find it all, and a racing palanquin so I can get there faster? I forgot to use a beacon to teleport with my last few jumps, and was reminded that it's *expensive*. Honestly, I got used to my Mana restoring in Eternium very quickly. It felt so natural, and it was out of mind right away. I never even questioned it!"

The die spun, showing a giggling face. "That's intentional! There are mental pushes present in Eternium to make you ignore certain things and notice others. Do be careful about those. Also, the Seed Core connection to Eternium is not optimal. You are at risk of not remembering things right away, and so long as you are in Eternium, you can easily forget things if they're fleeting. The **Order** in place doesn't want you to pay attention to the edges of the system, because you'll see how to break it. We are using the Pylons to balance it all out but, as you have discovered, system mechanics are actually extremely fragile. I even have the hordes of logs from all the errors you have caused by using cultivation skills in the system. Seriously, you broke a ton! Ripping the status sheet out of someone alone is going to require a century of work to patch."

Artorian wasn't sure if Dev was praising him, or upset at the additional work. Oddly enough, it seemed to be the former? "Well. Alright? I'm not sure how to feel about that, yet I will keep it in mind. Tracker and toy?"

"Oh, sure! One moment." Deverash *bwipped* out of existence for a moment. The sound played again as he returned. A soft pouch fell into Artorian's waiting hands, free for him to inspect. Digging around, he found it contained a compass and a cube.

Deverash spoke with scheming intonation. "Here you go! I've been hoping for that palanquin to get a test run. I loved what you did with the thrusters during our old bouts. Those have been added to all new models. I really wish we could do that again… Actually. Why not? I'll see what I can do, for fun! The compass in the pouch will point you to the closest unclaimed iridium in a realm. The cube will fold out into a racing palanquin if you click the button. Give it a go!"

Artorian felt a mite suspicious, but the button was pressed, and tossed a fair distance away. He didn't want to be near a Deverash-made self-expanding box. Not even at A-rank. To his delight and sharp whistle in response, the youth liked what he saw. "This thing doesn't remotely resemble a palanquin anymore! I do love how the thrusters keep it hovering and in place. Teach me how to operate this version!"

Deverash was glad to do so.

Two hours, a flattened forest, seven crashes, and one dirt-lunch later, Artorian got the hang of it. Shifting in the seat, the racing platform zipped over the landscape, boring itself forwards on Mana-thrusters that could swivel in any direction. "*Woo~hoo~hoo~hooo!*"

Deverash timed the circling laps Artorian made. He didn't understand why they were so *slow*, but remained supportive regardless. He yelled loud with adapted air Essence as the platform whooshed by. "Doing great, buddy!"

He checked this lap against the average on record. "That's seven times slower than the sluggiest Geometric Gnome. G.G.'s can't be faster by nature, when using *worse* versions of this palanquin. I will just add it to the records. This needs answers."

A dodecahedron popped into place next to Dev. "Boss. That platform you have active is kind of a drain on the accumulators. Are you sure you want it to keep chugging along the way it is? Racing platforms aren't meant to operate outside of Vanaheim."

Dev bobbed to the affirmative. "Let them drain. Look at these records and tell me what's wrong. I know about the regional design flaw. Bring this to R&D. This doesn't make sense. Let that platform drain as much as it has to. The more it gets used, the better. Here he comes again, best bwip out."

The dodecahedron *bwipped* out as instructed, along with the records Dev made. "All done! Do you think you're all set?"

Artorian wiped at his eyes. "I think so. Shame that I can't keep the wind out of my face without Essence shielding."

Dev had a great idea, and constructed a pair of darkened goggles. The pair was telekinetically tossed over when finished. "Here! Give these a try! I need to get back to work. Have fun with that compass!"

Artorian caught the aviator goggles, and affixed them to his face. Oh, this was going to be *much* better! "Thanks, buddy! Come be social sometime! I know I'm busy. Just pop in!"

They shared a Mana high five, and the eight-sided die *bwipped* out while the youth sped off at eight tenths of Mach one. Artorian achieved that speed after about ten seconds, starting from standstill. It required no expenditure on his end to operate the platform, and was all smiles as the landscape flew by in a borderline blur. He had to pull up on the levers to increase altitude, as getting tangled in trees always caused a crash, and never a great time.

This was fantastic! Could he make this better? Surely, he could make this better. His thoughts were drawn to the violin. *Eh.* Too slow. What had a bit more kick? Wait a moment, percussion? *Wubs!* In the back of his mind he could hear someone yell: 'Artorian, no!' His only reply being: "Artorian, yes!"

He hooted out the reply to nobody, as the cascade and repetition of bass drops formed a tune he remembered liking at the yellow line. It was the engine sound of some of the fatter palanquins at the time, thudding along as their Mana accumulators pulsed power to the rest of the craft. This made his deep, dirty wubs thrum as a very stable: *Dvup dvup dvup*.

Not a soul in sight, and not a person in harm's way. Artorian *punched* it. The sonic boom caused from breaking Mach one only broadened his smile. The compass which he had plastered to his dash shook wildly. Thrusters doing their best to keep his platform stabilized as he shot through valleys, sped over lakes, blazed through plains, and took sharp deadly turns around mountains in sideways drifts. He loved the *churn* of the speed he was making this thing go. Could it go faster? "Oh come on, we could go faster! We have places to *bee~ee~ee!*"

The mad youth laughed out loud as the compass spun around with a snap. He'd passed the entry point, too busy having a good time to see it. With a twist of the controls, he spun the platform around. Though kept going backwards even though the thrusters were trying their best to send him back the way he came. Odd how he came to a near standstill before darting off in his original direction. "*Aha*! There it is! A mine-shaft entry. Maybe I was going a little too fast to blindly burst through a mine at Mach one...? *Naaah*. Just slap on some *shielding*! That'd sort 'er. It's the Dwarven thing to do!"

Bright light-shields formed around the platform in an egg shape, the bottom of it failing to construct properly as the thrusters burned right through the shell. *Oops*. Little late to fix that now as he **fhwunked** into the darkness of the mine shaft. He was either going to have a spectacular crash, or come out the other end swinging. Either way, his smile didn't drop the smallest inch as the floor dropped out from under him. A large, vast cavern opened up as he took the plunge. *Abyss*! He still hated caverns!

Pumping more Mana to the shields, the floodlights flashed into activity, illuminating the area with far greater clarity. Much better! Now to find that iridium! He flicked the compass to steady it, and the metal needle shot to the left. Left it was! Pulling up hard on a control lever, the platform turned sharply. The shield took the brunt of the impact damage, but the bottom of the platform ground loud against both the rock wall and gravel floor. Sparks flew wildly with the ferocity of an active forge in the middle of smithing, but the platform remained functional and propelled itself forwards once more. This thing was meant to take some *dings*!

The compass began to spin uncontrollably after speeding a good distance down the twisting shaft, and Artorian pulled the control levers to slow him down. He hadn't gotten back up to sound-barrier breaking speeds down here, but that was fine. His wubs died out, and the platform hovered into the next cavern smooth as sailing on a calm sea. Oh, hey! He recognized this place somewhat. This looked similar to the Dwarven city he'd enjoyed meandering through the first time around.

No children playing around the fountain, but oh well. He parked the platform in the middle of the square and hopped off. It was a little dark, but when realizing they were dirty, he removed his goggles. A little starlight Aura took care of that in a pinch. He let the aviators hang around his neck, and tugged the compass free. "Let's see. Where to go…"

It took a few hours of trial and error, but Artorian found himself in front of a heavy wooden door. It *chinged* as a small copper bell rang out when the door parted. The ornate onyx desk caught his eye right away. Followed by heavy inspection equipment that was stacked wall to wall.

Following the compass further down this shop, Artorian made his way down carved onyx stairs, and right up to a surprisingly intact vault door. It definitely looked like it was meant to conduct Aether steam in order to get the massive slab of metal to move. None filled the tubes, and the mechanics of the system were dead and silent.

Likely had been for iterations.

How would he get in there? Oh. *Right*. A-rank two! Artorian grabbed the handles on the vault door, and just broke the whole thing right off the hinges with a horrific metallic screech. As if it were an inconvenient paperweight. "There we go!"

"Oh, *come* on." He frowned when he saw what was on the other end, and dropped the vault door with a deep *thunggg*. He stepped through the entryway to take in the sheer scale of the hidden operation. "*Deverash Neverdash the Dashingly Dapper*! You cheeky snoot! If you *ever* told me you only made a handful of this stuff, then you lied to me!"

Artorian honestly wasn't certain if Dev had ever actually said that, but he badly wanted to feel that it had been implied. Specifically due to the presence of the small *army* of Dwarven-shaped golems he was currently counting. *All* of them were constructed from iridium, and *all* of them had a memory Core implanted in their chests. "*Fa~a~antastic*. Cal must not have checked this place; any *one* of these could serve as a fully functional body."

Pulling the original Li out of his pocket, he sighed and held it up. His Aura bloomed, and he laid out his will across the entirety of the vault forge. "*Gather!*"

Solid metal Dwarves liquified, iridium sloughing off their current forms in waves. What had taken uncountable years to construct was undone in but moments. Over the course of a few minutes, the entire facility was drained of iridium.

The ground below Artorian buckled loudly. Unpleasant creaking rocked the facility as normal metal under the youth's feet indented where he stood. The ground suffered from easily a dozen tons of weight being gathered in that one spot, as all the goopy material gathered in the coin Artorian held up and increased its density. Well, almost. There was always an outlier.

Personally checking in on the remaining golem that didn't form into goop, he sighed, and kneaded his brow. He recognized the shape, and his heart sank. Tussle the Dwarf, in the exact shape the youth remembered him from the first iteration, stood tall, and firm. While his chest puffed out, his face was twisted in an expression of false strength. Like he'd been trying to stay strong and proud as the initial conversion happened to him.

"Oh, my boy... I'm so sorry. You had a family. I... *I* did this to you. With my foolish little gift." He placed his hand to the Core on the golem's chest, and squeezed his eyes shut. Tussle was still in there. "Abyss, Cal... your automated processes missed more than just a hidden army."

"Well, *crackers*. Now what to do?" He sighed and broke the golem to safely retrieve the Core. Once Tussle's minor influence was free, the last iridium golem liquified. Flowing into the coin as all the ones before it.

Artorian didn't want to be here anymore after that, and left the forge vault, now devoid of its great work. He sighed deeper, and silently returned to his platform since the needle had stilled entirely. He'd recovered everything here.

Once his hand was laid on the platform, he pulled the still hovering contraption over to a beacon, and **fuffed**.

Both Artorian and the platform appeared in his large foyer

within the sun. His solar archive. Leaving the racer be for now, he walked up to his wall and slotted Tussle's Core in where Decorum had been. After a solemn moment, he updated the nameplate.

He'd make this right. He would, but he needed to go to Alfheim. No! Alfheim could *wait*. It could wait the *five minutes* it would take for him to do right by Tussle. He tapped Tussle's Core and opened Cal's old system files. As if he was going to edit the object and check for inconsistencies. Just as he would fix a broken item.

Rather than doing so, he scrolled through tabs and directories, searching for Tussle's family tree. Wasn't this alphabetical? Oh, there it was. Selecting the correct tab for what he needed, he saw the direct lineage links in chart format.

Tussle had been the last of his Dwarven line. Artorian couldn't let that bite him deeper right now. Selecting the link of Tussle's loved one, Artorian opened *her* family tree instead. The lineage *itself* wasn't important, but rather that this particular menu allowed him to… *meddle*. "Let's just… do something we *shouldn't*."

He of course did anyway, and pulled up the Core information of Tussle's sweetheart. Starting from the point of where her existence began, to the end. According to the activity log, this soul was currently a shop assistant in Midgard, in a human form. That wasn't important, he just needed the personality version from iteration one.

It took *more* than five minutes, but he accessed the relevant memories. Artorian then pulled that iteration into a fresh memory Core, which he just outright bought from the shop. Before filling them in, he altered the memories so they would *end* the same day that Tussle had disappeared from her life. Based on some glances… it hadn't gone great for her after his mysterious disappearance.

Affixing the memories, he nodded. *Success*. Saving the Core, he slotted the memory stone next to Tussle on the wall. It didn't matter that he needed to make a fresh indent with his shaped

Aura. "There we go. A little awkward on my end. But that will be a family made whole, when they both decant. The place might be different, but the love will be the same. I owe them both that much."

Nodding with confidence as the feeling of regret faded; he hung his goggles on one of the racer's levers, and ditched the platform, *fuffing* to Alfheim.

He needed a change of scenery.

CHAPTER THIRTY-THREE

Alfheim didn't look as Artorian remembered it. There were buildings *everywhere*! He was in the middle of some kind of capital city. Except there seemed to be nothing *but* city. He'd seen something in Cal's notes that Alfheim was supposed to be more about plants and down-to-earth methods. Yet there was nothing rural about this place; it was *all* urban. He hovered upwards, easing high into the air. His frown deepened at the view. The landscape, mountains included, consisted of build-ings, buildings, and *more* buildings.

"What in Cal…?" Taking off at the usual sonic-burst speed, he zipped across Alfheim to look around. Confused about why both the compass wasn't reacting, and why the dang building sprawl didn't stop! How had these people even grown their food? There couldn't possibly have been so many Elves. Abyss! What had he *missed* the last iteration? This was nuts. At least he recognized all the black and gold flags representing Halcyon, but he was convinced she wasn't on this realm.

He stopped on the mountain he'd visited during iteration one. The thing had been hollowed out, and was all housing. What makes you need to hollow out a *mountain*? He checked the compass, but there still wasn't a *dent* on the needle's movement. He was sure he'd given what's-his-face a piece of iridium. Right? Or had it *just* been the bluebell? It *should* be here.

It wasn't.

A full day of searching and he came up empty, still none the wiser about the need for an endless city. He hadn't even found clues in the homes and living spaces themselves. Sure, there was some junk remaining here and there, but overall none really held information concerning the population boom that must have caused this.

The vacancies were *scary*. All this space. Empty. *Why?* Had something happened with the populace? Or maybe it had been the conditions? He just knocked on the dungeon's forum space. <Cal. Have a minute? I'm stuck.>

Cal's voice spoke in a garble, but then pulled away from Eternium to occupy his own soul again, clearing up the signal. <I'm here. What's the wrench in the plan?>

Artorian just motioned at the housing, sending the image. <What and why? It's massive! I can scarcely find farmland, if there is any. Why so much living space? There's nothing but. Also no iridium, but this is just jarring. What happened here?>

Cal glanced at the information, and understood why this must look odd. <Ah! So. In my prior iteration, before I stopped using Alfheim altogether because the landscape was done. I never took the buildings down. I ran a test to see how many souls I could actually fit on a single realm. Turns out, a good few billion according to the simulations. Though… *sardine packed*. Don't worry, I didn't duplicate people or split them like Bob. Many test dummies were used.>

The dungeon complained for a moment. <Midgard surprisingly has the worst of it, with capacity for *barely* half a billion. It wasn't great, but I don't see that as a problem. If for some reason more souls got shoved in, there's an incentive for them to move to the other realms! Which means more active people for me to giggle and quip at with snarky goodness.>

The Administrator rubbed his forehead, releasing a heavy

exhale. <Alright. Well… thanks, Cal. Sorry for interrupting. There's no iridium here, so I'm just going to move on. Not sure why there isn't any, but there's little I can do.>

The connection clicked shut, and the youth moseyed over to a beacon. Once there, he sat down, taking a moment to look at the sky. "Iridium doesn't just vanish. So let's see. It could have gone with a person to the next realm over, or it could have gone with a person into the Eternium version if they held onto it. Did I forget to check Midgard? I should. Just in case."

Pushing himself up, he *fuffed* to Midgard. It didn't take more than a few minutes of looking at an immobile compass to figure out this place didn't have what he was looking for. That crossed the first three off the list. Might as well take a trip home.

He *fuffed* to Jotunheim.

"Took you long enough." Zelia was waiting for him at the beacon platform next to his mountain residence. Tower? Castle? Since when was it a giant, reinforced *castle*? Thing was massive! "Dreamer…? Is that *actually* you?"

Artorian turned on his heel, and shot the full humanlike spider a broad smile. "Zelia! So good to see you. Yes, it's me. I'm aware of the… *packaging*."

Zelia eased to a knee and offered a hug, which was gleefully accepted. "I am glad you are well, my Dreamer. We have been 'keeping the peace' in your absence. Though I believe that if we were to count lifetimes in eons of awakeness, all your chosen have vastly outstripped you in age. Even Vol. He's fond of life here, so long as it's hunting in the jungles. Likely the only one that you might remember as who he was. That boy has a one-beast mind."

Artorian nodded appreciatively. "I heard you became the Soul Space secretary. Good on you! It's been going marvelous with you at the helm."

The spider considered the job to be arduous, but a little positivity on her performance was never a bad thing. "I make it go well, with a lot of 'or else' in the mix. Speaking of work, here you go. All the iridium we've found in Jotunheim over the iterations. It's surprisingly little, though we are all very fond of the crab-killing chunk. Even if it's just a deformed metal rock."

Artorian took the offered cloth package and merged the chunks with his coin. Checking his compass after, he found it inert. "Looks like that really was all of it. I expected some Alfheimers to come by and drop theirs here. No dice?"

She shook her head, barely moving a line of fabric in her kimono. Her hands twirled her tiny parasol as she replied smoothly. "If they did, it wasn't through here. I've kept *exquisite* track over everything the chosen have considered problems over the ages. There have been so many that it took up all your old warehouses."

He squeezed his chest, having a second gander at the castle. "Probably were attacked a few times as well."

She smirked, and nodded. It was nice to have a person with *actual insight* around for a change. "Indeed. Halcyon ran it as Daimyo. Though with the end of this last iteration, she is taking a long, and very well-deserved rest. It was taxing for her to rule, and she is glad to be free of the burden. I understand there will be no further people for us at this point? A shame, really. I would have liked more company. We even got that copy of your old academy installed below. It took us a few whole *iterations* to get done, but what is time when you have nothing but? Spare a moment to see it?"

Artorian gladly took her by the hand, and Zelia folded slipspace around them. It was seamless! Like she'd gotten even better at teleportation. Should he really be surprised? Probably not. He wouldn't mind a few iterations of time just getting to practice and refine abilities either. That sounded splendid. Exiting slipspace, his eyes stabilized upon the sight of Mayev's Spire. "Well... will you look at that. *Magnificent.*"

Checking his entry point, Artorian stood on a ceiling-spun walkway made from webbing. Looking down, he could see that the hexes around the spire were back as well. Some even copied the structures that had been there when Dawn and Gran'mama were in charge. Still, it was the *zoning layout* that caught the eye. He always had loved the way they'd carved the land up. Also, Turtle islands! *Yes*! "You're right, a true shame we don't have people…"

Zelia raised a brow, and Artorian filled her in on what his sudden pause was about. "We… *might* have some… people unaccounted for, who need a place to be. Could you, by chance, finish this region, or replicate what the original Fringe looked like? Here, in the Beneath? Now that the gravity problem is controllable, I have… thoughts."

The spider secretary inspected her nails, pretending to be none the wiser of the request. Too bad, really; she had become much more skilled at social convention, but that smirk on her lips gave her away. She procured documents via teleportation, the same way he did. "Oh… you mean perhaps, as outlined in blueprints like *these*?"

Snatching the document from her dainty fingers, his toothy smile told her that the Dreamer was ecstatic. She had discovered his Midgard attempts! Back in iteration one when Henry had told him about the little bonus corner of the Midgard realm.

Honestly, she was in charge of all the mail and checking the beacons. He had put one smack near his little project. Had he thought she *wouldn't* find it? That landscape was measured, copied, and transcribed onto the blueprint. With a little bit of work, they could easily reform some things in the Jotunheim below to get it all in place. "Yes. Yes, this will do perfectly. Zelia, you beauty!"

Her smirk was prideful, hands pressed on her butt as she wiggled from side to side, ever so pleased. The compliments made her happy, as only words from a Dreamer could. "Good. Now that there's no people, we can continue construction. It will take us a while, but again, what's time? Come back when Halcyon is awake. She will be glad to see you. For now she sorely needs rest, and I don't want to wake her. Not even for this. Yuki is on Asgard, and Vol doesn't need a check-up."

She sharply nudged her nose over to the teleportation beacon next to them. "Now shoo. You have work to do. Oh, and you will likely find some goodies on the Eternium version of Alfheim. Though my spiderlings say it's in an odd place. Look for a statue of someone called... Yiba-Su-Wong? Bluebell sigil on the flag. That's all I've got."

She opened her arms for a goodbye hug, and once again received a tight squeeze. She patiently waited for him to step onto the beacon, and waved daintily as he *fuffed* out. Slipspace folded next to her after the Dreamer had left, and Halcyon stepped from the opening. She looked exhausted, and had a splitting headache. "Am I too late?"

Zelia nodded, and Halcyon groaned, held by the spider as the tall human woman had her back patted supportively. Cy was wobbling terribly, barely able to keep upright. "You need to rest. He'll be back. You don't want him to see you like this. He will get distracted and want to heal you, but you're only going to get better with sleep. He does not need to know just yet that the *staying awake too long* problem affects more than just Dreamers. You took care of the last iteration while I slept. I take care of this one. Back to bed with you."

Halcyon grumbled, but felt the sharp pains in her Core return. She needed sleep, and quickly. Nodding while disgruntled, she held the side of her head. Zelia watched her walk back through the borrowed slipspace rift before seamlessly closing it behind Cy.

Zelia squeezed her brows and frowned, her voice clicking. There had been a great number of problems she was still catching up on, and that was just one of them. Still, there was a time and a place to handle things, and considering the latest news from her spiderlings... This was not a good time for yet *another distraction* to occupy their Dreamer.

He needed to stay on task and keep focused, and that wasn't going to happen if new problems kept being tossed at his head the way badly drawn scripts ended up crumpled in the wastebasket.

Best to give some good news, and show things were automated at home. "Good luck, my Dreamer. You're going to have one *demon* of a headache soon."

CHAPTER THIRTY-FOUR

Artorian skipped a few realms and started on Asgard. Leaving Yuki waiting—now that he knew that Zelia had known he was *faffing about*—was a terrible idea. Much like the prior, the lady of winter awaited him as well. "Dreamer. You attend. *Good.* Come."

No greeting? No hug as hello? Well, it *was* Yuki. Hadn't he made progress? Why the cold shoulder? Or perhaps this was the *warm* shoulder, if he recalled the faces of nervous A-rankers lined up in the mead hall. Yes, probably. Her skin was the snowy hue he remembered it as, but her clothes were far more elaborate and intricate. She was easily wearing multiple layers of patterned fabric, but his favorite was that the top one had *fluffy bits*!

On closer inspection… "Yuki… are you… A-rank *eight*?"

He could *feel* her smirk, even if the frost princess didn't give him a verbal reply until she had turned a corner. When he could *see* her smirk, his eyes narrowed at the coy retort. "Nine, my Dreamer. A-rank *nine*."

His face scrunched, hands rising palms-up in a questioning motion that asked '*how*' with incredulous muster. She indulged him after studying that contorted face of his. Payment enough, for her story needs.

Yuki glided smoothly onwards, delighting in the moment as she spoke. "The chosen grow and cultivate not when we are able, but when the Great Spirit allows it. He has flip-flopped on the decision several times. Sometimes it's as much as we want. Other iterations there were limitations. Lately it has been an outright no. Now, the grapevine sends word that we can continue to grow if we 'play the game,' so to speak. Through the Great Spirit's precious little system."

Artorian verbalized his question, because that wasn't answering his concern. "A-rank *nine*? I'm at two! Crackers, Yuki. You shot right past me! Do you know how *little* time I spent in the B-ranks? You would know more than me at this point, on one of the topics I'm best at! I just feel…"

If he had a hat, he would grip onto both sides and pull it the whole way down his face. His groaning expression was food to the chosen, and she continued to delight in the details as she agreed with him, just to hammer her icicle deeper. "I *do* know more. Why, my Dreamer? Do you need proof? Go ahead. Ask your questions. I know how much you love them."

His eyes narrowed at the challenge. "Oh, *really*?"

She slowly nodded, secure in her knowledge as she pushed open a vast golden door. The watery scents fumed as hot vapor, and the youth's attention was cast inwards. Dawn's voice greeted them, and suddenly this entire conversation felt like a setup meant to distract him.

"There you are! Took you long enough. Meeting has been over for ages. What's with the fo—*oh. Yuki~i~i.* Did you have to prod him? The confusion is oozing from his face. I can even tell *without* all the wrinkles. Come. In with you. You've needed a bath since well before that meeting and I couldn't just drag you off then. It has that unpleasant 'new form' odor. So I'm dragging you off now. You're dirty and you smell."

Artorian was affronted. He didn't sm—a momentary alteration of his senses, and he didn't even dare make the customary sharp inhale that told his surroundings he'd realized he was wrong. "Fine! Though, you're both going to tell me how Yuki blitzed past me in cultivation, and I am vehemently taking her up on her little *dare*."

Dawn crossed her arms, wearing little more than a loose toga meant for the Asgard thermae. Granted, as luxurious as the Asgardian baths were, the quality of the simple-looking toga Dawn rocked dwarfed it by a few thousand platinum. She still loved looking fancy. Good ol' Dawn! Her voice was filled with pep and a sneaky smirk. "Oh? Well, expect to get trounced, youngster! That's Caliph's godmother you're trying to get the better of. She holds information like you hold wild theories."

Tossing her hair, Dawn hovered away after pushing up on her toes. S-rankers didn't care about gravity. This still felt like a setup to Artorian, and the edge of the cliff had not yet been reached. This was akin to the Fringe kids herding him onto the river-hill, before a very wet fall. It felt like it was such, even if he didn't have the details of this scheme all put together. "I am supposed to be hard at work gathering iridium!"

Dawn's voice rang from afar. "Far ahead of you. It's in the vault! Now quit stalling and get in here before I drag you Phantomdusk style!"

Yuki caught herself, holding back a chortled snort from the haste and speed the youth suddenly discovered in spades. His strides were short, tiny legs zipping him over the reflective flooring as he made a beeline-rush to the very baths he'd... *caught*... Odin in.

He was expecting the playful trip from Dawn, and dramatically stumbled over the outstretched foot hiding behind the opened doors. With matching flair, he exclaimed his mock surprise. "*Oh no~o!*"

Splash!

With a mighty wave of hot, steamy water, the baths rocked and gained waves as the liquid tried to balance out all the extra density and force it had just been smashed by. A tiny satchel hurled from the raging waters, and a smirking Dawn caught it.

Taking the single Iridium Li coin out of the bag, she admired it for a moment. "Nice to see you have an *affection* for my gifts of old."

Yuki strode past her and controlled the situation with a flick of her wrist. The waves swirling in the chamber halted mid-motion. To Artorian's soaked surprise, not one droplet of it froze. It all just… *stopped*. Like a painting he could walk through.

He didn't get the chance as it all came crashing down on him. The soaked youth shimmied up the provided stairs, soppily escaping the baths. Artorian trudged right up to the two women who were trying to contain their heaving giggle fit. "Alright. *You got me*. I can't figure this one out. Where is the setup? You essentially ambushed me in the middle of work. I have several realms to see, followed by the Eternium versions. I have a special appointment in Alfheim. So why the… *this*?"

He motioned his arms around, but received a fresh towel to wear rather than an immediate answer. Yuki was smiling at him. Why was that so incredibly unsettling? Her voice was even… lukewarm? "For no reason other than we are pleased to see you again. All work and no play… well. Even for me, it does only harm. So we planned the interruption. One we painstakingly did our best to get by Zelia, who was dead set on avoiding giving you additional distractions. We did not agree."

Dawn was clearly a main culprit of this plan, as she smirked wide and picked up the thread. "This was, granted, easier to do given her absence during the last iteration. In our view, you returned only to throw yourself into work. We didn't like that, so have cut your tasks short. I gathered any iridium that may have been in Eternium, and the remaining iridium from all the realms we figured you would check last. I didn't expect to get them *exactly* right. Maybe you're becoming predictable!"

The youth mumble-grumbled, taking his current robes off just to dump them in Yuki's waiting hand. Wading back into the waters, Dawn snickered as she could measure the temperature increase by a full degree, just because he was in it. Silently *fussing*.

She spoke further. "The gathered material is in the Asgard vault, which is where I'll be taking this *sizable* chunk. There is far more here than meets the eye. Honestly, I'm surprised you were able to carry it. How did that pouch not tear? That's the real mystery."

Artorian's mind was spinning. The *pouch*! She was right. It shouldn't have been able to… No. This was a distraction! She was… *gone*. "Crackers. Pulled the wool right over my eyes."

He sighed, sunk into the water, and just made bubbles while scrubbing himself off with a provided rag. He mumbled out a sour question, since Yuki was sitting nearby being all happy with herself. "What's the difference between the A and B-ranks?"

Without missing so much as a beat, Yuki replied. If she had done that because she expected it… He didn't want to think about it. Being accused of becoming predictable only made him blow bubbles more aggressively. "The A-ranks are a much easier explanation point. A-ranked Mana is solid, rather than fluid. Where B-ranked Mana is a fluid that must be willed and shaped into temporary solids before being retrieved, A-ranked Mana is a solid that must be willed and unshaped for proper mobility and energy transfer."

He blinked, completely having forgotten he was washing. "It does *what* now?"

Yuki flicked open her fan, covering the movements of her lips. "*Hmm*? You didn't notice? **Tsk tsk**, my Dreamer."

The sour expression was right back on his face. He was being toyed with, and treated like a child! "Is this all *just* because of how I look?"

The fan did not move. "Would you expect otherwise, from *your* chosen? Can *you* resist the once in a lifetime opportunity for the quip?"

His sour leer dropped to the hot water, suddenly very interested in the foamy bubbles moving over the surface. His reply was one of dejected defeat. "…*No*."

Had there been a tiny rock to kick, he would have half-heartedly punted it a few inches away. "*Fine*… Madame currently a *cool* A-rank nine. What's so different about A-rank solid Mana? I haven't had noticeable problems."

Yuki nodded. That was also expected. "I was told that this information was mentioned to you in passing, but in the A-ranks—especially the upper echelons—the identity and idea of your manifestations becomes paramount. Launching techniques without an in-depth grasp of what it's supposed to do becomes detrimental. You can outright *brick* your body and abilities if you don't give this denser Mana the proper input. I'm sure it *loves* your Invocations. Yet to an ordinary cultivator, including someone with ice-carved skills such as myself, A-rank Mana is *entirely unusable* without the proper context. I will admit, I also despised the compressions. Including feeling like I was being packed into the size of an ice cube when making the stronger connection. Dawn was there for me as well. She was there for all of us."

Artorian needed a second, but believed he'd caught up. "From that… can I safely take it that almost all the chosen are at or near your current ranking?"

Yuki sounded abyss-blasted chipper. *Mhm*!

Artorian slapped his forehead. "Of *course* they are… I'm surprised I didn't notice. Then again, I had to really stare at you for a while before the inkling dawned on me."

Since he was going to touch his face again for a sigh anyway, he just scrubbed it with the rag. For a moment he considered loudly yelling under the water, but didn't feel like it the second after he had this passing thought. "Here I was convinced the identity thing was S-rank territory."

The frost princess nodded again. "Oh, it most certainly is. The A-ranks are merely preparation for the complete dive. If you cannot climb the A-ranks due to a gap in your ability to control yourself on a more cerebral level, you have no business Incarnating. It was wonderful *fun* to prod at Zelia when she first made the leap. She was bricked for a *week*. Couldn't move a single muscle. We drew art on her because she was so statuesque."

Yuki snickered again, and something about the tiny laugh just made Artorian's heart feel warm. It was nice to see her just play around and express pleasantries. That seemed out of reach, based on his prior memories. It was awful to miss such massive swaths of time.

Alas, that's the boat he sat in. Sighing, he created an orb of Mana. Just to really dig in and look at it. "Right, well I'm sure she gave you all a *goosening* of a time when she figured it out. Though I really *don't* see a difference. It feels the same, acts the same, responds the same. It feels more dense? That might be the extent of it."

Yuki sat nearby, dipping her feet into the hot water. Artorian had expected some kind of reaction, but again there was none. Wasn't she freezing all the time? He should be glad for it, he supposed. Better a hot bath than an icy one.

Yuki answered. "For you, that may feel like the extent of it. The tier of your **Law** plays a great role here. For us gentle souls below tier thirty, these small changes you feel are vast and daunting. Your tier, given the heights of where it rests, has always pressured such a hidden burden in density upon you, that an extra category is meager snowfall while you are in the lower ranks. Now, as you continue ranking up, the pressure you experience in your Mana—that density you feel—*will* grow."

The youth held his chin, observing the Mana ball that he turned into shape after shape. It was mimicking Dev's forms. Artorian was starting to gain a fondness for these dice shapes. Maybe he could do something with it in the future? It reminded him of Rota, the Dwarf who loved his dice and blew up some Gnomes with them. What a pleasant fellow he was.

Artorian got back on topic. "So, because currently I'm A-rank two, the feel of my Mana isn't so different yet. As the main hurdle is something I passed long ago. The concept is flipped from the B-ranks, but given that the main hurdle is building the identity of your actions and will from the ground up is something I do each time, it's not a difficulty on my end. I expect that people who are used to aimlessly throwing fireballs around without a care in the world will suddenly find themselves… What did you call it?"

"*Bricked*," Yuki delightfully informed him, her feet kicking at the water slightly. "Due to the concept of the A-rank version being the bricks, and the B-ranked version the mortar. The compression that occurs leaves many people feeling stuck, if they survive it when the process completes. Still, it can be the case that when they do, they are unable to move ever again. Action without thought is folly. This is the lesson of A-rank zero."

CHAPTER THIRTY-FIVE

Clang.

Cal's Soul Space shattered like a mirror. The event came sudden, unannounced, and as a total surprise to everyone. Soul Space residents were suddenly mired in a landscape of sharp lines, which indiscriminately sliced through existence like indestructible piano wire.

Artorian registered the impact late, even when his face suddenly attempted to smash through the ceiling. Which didn't hurt as much as he expected it should. It wasn't the jarring and sudden journey up that had been the problem. It was the world around him which had suddenly decided to spring like an excited kitten, only to haplessly fall off the table's edge from a miscalculated jump.

As far as Artorian was concerned, he hadn't moved an inch from the baths! Landing was the dangerous part, as the severed space represented by mirror-fracturing piano wire directly crossed his downwards trajectory. He was going to hit it!

Or not? He could have remembered to engage his ability to fly, but Dawn had already caught him mid-fall. He could swear that sometimes it felt like there was barely a difference between being a mortal, and being a Mage. Maybe he was getting used to it?

An indent of his face marred the metal ceiling, which he briefly saw before being whisked to safety. He coughed out a paltry mouthful of water after he was set down, wiping his mouth clean with the back of his hand.

Wasting no time to search for answers, he stepped right into the senate. <What just happened?>

Dani answered frantically. <I don't know! Cal is unconscious, the connections to most of the other Cores aren't working, and I'm seeing nothing but red appear on all the charts in the workroom. Half of the total Eternium population just outright *died* and were sent back to their memory stones.>

Tatum's mote appeared, joined swiftly by Marie, Chandra, and Dawn. The rest of the supervisors were oddly absent. Wouldn't this be something important to show up to? Their world just fractured around them!

Occultatum filled in, sharing Dani's haste. <Cal is alive. Some of the seams are already starting to mend, though it will take time. I do not expect that he will be able to fully wake until all these cuts are mended. Do not touch them! Nothing at all can protect you from the damage they will cause. They are *literal tears* in Cal's Soul Space. Dawn, we need to go to the workroom and help. *Right now.*>

Dawn and Tatum immediately vanished from the senate, along with Dani. Off to the mysterious 'workroom,' no doubt. Marie felt queasy, and it showed clear and plain in her voice. <That wasn't as informative as I would have hoped. Anybody have *any* idea what caused this?>

Chandra's mote zipped to her side, helping to steady the sickened Mage. Her voice tried to be soothing. <Unfortunately, yes. I've perhaps been spending too much time around Ramset. Oh, sorry. Tatum. I was thinking about it the entire time, and based on what we've talked about before, the options are slim.>

Artorian hurried to the other side of Marie's mote, assisting in the steadying. He didn't need to ask Chandra to continue, she just did. <Cal's Soul Space can't be harmed from the inside. Not *really*. Not with the deals in place. So the damage must come from the real world, on the *outside*. Cal's main, real Core, is hidden deep underground. Tucked away somewhere nice and safe. So for the real Core to take an amount of damage that would crack the space we are in to this extent, some kind of extinction-level event must have damaged the earth itself. I don't know. Some giant rock from space maybe? We won't know for certain until Cal wakes, and even then it might remain a mystery.>

Marie stopped wobbling, and bobbed her mote to nod. Chandra kept speaking. <Let's count our clovers that we survived. Tatum and I were out with Odin when it happened. The space shattered in his location, and those wires cut right through him. He was immediately severed into chunks and shoved back into his Silverwood Core.>

Marie rolled her mote's shoulders so her helpers would let go, filling in with her own perspective. <The same happened to Henry and Aiden. They were finally going to try to have a sit-down talk, but I imagine this didn't help things. They both Cored immediately. I tried to get a backup body from the shop, but nothing happened without Cal. I heard only static. I'm going to check on him physically, in the tree. I think he's fine, but that forced resting time has probably triggered.>

Her mote vanished, leaving Chandra and Artorian behind in the senate. After a moment of contemplation, Chandra piped up. <You're not normally this quiet for this long, Administrator. I expected a barrage of questions.>

The celestine mote shrugged. <I was having a surprisingly *nice* day. I wish I could say I was surprised? In the middle of work, I get tackled with good news. My iridium issue was handled for me. Terribly nice of them. Then I get treated to a lovely herbal bath, and *wouldn't* you know it… I start thinking 'well, this sure is a nice change of pace.' And as I consider really settling in and maybe delving into a playful scheme or two, *the world breaks*.>

Chandra snorted at the shining mote's sigh. She didn't mean to, but it came out regardless. <Yes, well. I think so long as we don't touch the wire weirdness, we will be fine. I'm going to check on all the middle realms. As you're the only one left here, do you mind taking the upper ones?>

A voice they hadn't expected cut in. In a huff of smoke, Brianna's mote unveiled itself from invisibility. She could hide herself in the senate as well? Well, that was... *inconvenient.* <You're not the only ones left, and I shall take your lack of notice as a sincere *compliment.* I shall check on the lower realms, though I must admit that I am not certain what we would be looking for. Survivors? Why do we care? They will all be canted into their relevant Cores. Even if the entire populace in Cal's Soul Space perishes, what is the harm? Cal will recover, and they will be put back after.>

Chandra's retort was far more snide. <So there is, of course, *nothing* preventing Cal from healing. Or doing any further harm while he's unconscious. Right?>

That thought hadn't quite crossed Brianna's mind, and her self-righteous tone was dropped in favor of a more reflective one. <I... understand what you mean. No, you are correct. I do *not* know that with certainty. This also answers my query on what to look for. Threats? An assassin's bread and butter. I shall check the realms I mentioned.>

Brianna's mote vanished in the smoke it came from, and Artorian's brightness pulsed in confusion. <You know. I have no idea what to make of her now. I think I'll start over from scratch. Brianna may have the same name, but she seems to be someone... new. I am judging her as the person I knew her as. That does not appear to be who just spoke to us. Although, Chandra? I can feel you scowling from here.>

Chandra huffed, hard and strong. <If she wasn't already an Elf, I would call her one.>

Artorian had to admit he didn't understand. <I'm sorry, this is off topic. What do you mean?>

The green mote dimmed. Right, not everyone hung around

Tatum all day every day. <Elf as a *word* came by due to some rather specific circumstances. Dawn told Ramset as a joke, but apparently Elf is an acronym derived from: 'Especially Long Funeral.' Dawn laughed it off like it was a joke, of course, but it didn't sit well with Rammi.>

Artorian's celestine light thunked to the ground, indenting the floor. <You *jest.*>

Chandra shook her head. <I am not. It gets even better. Dwarves? Same deal! In the earliest of ages, they were known as: 'Deep Whiskey Activists, Regretfully Found.'>

The celestine mote rolled across the ground laughing. <Ha! Haha! I believe it! I bet deep whiskey is what they had when they lived in the depths.>

Agreeable nodding was Chandra's only reply on the topic. <It was. I'm going to go ahead and check the realms. With Brianna checking the lower ones, that leaves just Asgard and Hel for you. Think you can handle that?>

Artorian rose from the ground and bobbed to the positive. <Should be fine. I'm going to make sure the iridium is in my pocket. I don't know if the Asgard vault was damaged, but I don't want anyone or anything to get possession of the stuff until it can be properly neutralized. Asgard is tame at the moment, and Hel is likely quiet.>

Chandra gave the hum-pulse equivalent of a thumbs up. <Just be wary of Wagner.>

Artorian formed the question mark above his head, with his own mote serving as the dot. <Wagner? Who is that?>

Chandra snorted again from amusement.

<The goose. That's what we call him. He never went to Eternium. Couldn't convince the infernal thing to wobble through the portal. As a Hydra-goose variant, he has many noisy heads. He likes to use them to honk out what we call 'flight of the quackeries.' It's a loud calling card. You'll hear him coming before you see him. Good thing, too. *Incarnate ranked butt-biter.*> With that sour mention, Chandra vanished from the senate.

The goose. *Again?* Artorian followed suit, eyes opening to the sight of the wrecked baths. Now that he wasn't dazed, he could see the awful cracks and tears in space. It was like the building had smashed at speed into a cliffside. *Twice.*

Yuki carefully prodded him. "My Dreamer? Are you well? The fire Dreamer woke from the thought trance earlier, and vanished as Zelia does."

He nodded, though frowned as his eyes took in further details. "Yuki, are you *missing* an arm?"

She calmly dipped her head to reply. "One of those splintered cords passed against my left side, and my arm instantly obliterated upon touch. I have frozen the wound, and will be fine. Are you well? Are you injured? We have many questions."

Artorian slid from her grasp, and checked himself. Not difficult to do since a towel-wrap counted as his only clothing. "Looks like Dawn spared me from damage. I'm tip-top, save for the face that feels like it should be sore. Though, *'we'?*"

He glanced at Yuki again, this time with effort. The look of her gaze was not her own, and through the deep connections they held he discovered the truth. He could feel an awake Halcyon and concerned Zelia present in a forum space that Yuki remained connected to. He approved of the idea. Multiple minds sharing the senses of one? Clever! He liked it. "Ah, I understand. Hello, dears. I'm well. I perhaps… need some clothing, and to fetch the iridium. I'm not leaving it here."

Yuki smiled, but now Artorian realized that it was distinctly *not* Yuki speaking. It was Zelia doing the talking! Well, well. That brought up the question of just who might have been talking to him before. Or were they rubbing off on one another? He'd been wondering what was off with Yuki! "Of course, my Dreamer. A yellow ginkgo leaf robe will be provided."

Yuki blinked, and a cold veneer crawled over her features, setting deep into her expression. "The iridium? Very well. *Come.*"

Ha! He knew it! There she was! On his feet without a

second to waste, he hurried after Yuki as she formed ice on the path below her. She was skating through the cracked, twisted, and broken halls. How novel! He'd been running along, but now that he had seen her do it… he *needed* to try.

It was just some water Essence, given shape as blades. Additional water Essence was released beneath the blades to allow for smoother sliding, and 'let go.' Ordinarily, that would have been called wasteful in a technique. Given it was Mana-powered however, the water Essence retethered into the chilly Aura that hung around her. The frozen energy returning to her with ease.

Well, then! Jumping onto the ice road she was forming anyway, he copied her technique. He eased smooth and clean into the ice tube, then immediately slipped, skidded onto his fallen face, and slid the entire pathway to the vault down in that fashion. He fumbled around, but kept slipping, entirely unable to get up without wrecking the road, which he currently didn't want to do.

Yuki tried not to smile when she stopped at the vault doors, and watched her Dreamer slide in face-first. He wasn't at all amused, and that made it all the better. "We have arrived."

"You don't say?" The tiny undertone of chagrin seeped through his words, but he pushed up properly to stand now that he wasn't at risk of wrecking the entire half-tube. Making that trip wearing *only* a towel had been less than stellar. That meant this was, of course, the exact moment a spiderling popped out of slipspace with a package.

Pop.

Artorian sighed. "Like *clockwork*."

The spiderling was ecstatic, and looked entirely human. If it wasn't for his face dehumanizing from how giddy he was, the spiderling would have sold the ruse perfectly. Six eyes gave it away, though. "Thank you, my boy. Mind helping me get this on?"

Kiii! He'd never heard a spiderling 'squee' before. That was new. *Kind* of adorable? Once clad properly in the yellow

ginkgo robe, he noted that it was far softer than the original version he recalled. Ah! Spider-silk quality. Yes, that would do it. The spiderling folded out of his vicinity before he could properly thank him, but given the humanization had almost completely undone, perhaps it was for the best. Did he have fans?

Yuki had opened the massive, nine-door barred set of interlocked rooms in the meanwhile. Rather elaborate? Then again, it was supposed to be a vault, and Asgard should be realm nine? No, it was eight. Guesswork for the number of doors on his end. He dropped it. Not important.

Yuki's voice rang from inside the vault, and Artorian hurried in. "My Dreamer? I have encountered a problem."

Artorian saw said problem right away. *Eeesh*. Nine doors didn't matter when they were all busted to the abyss. Good call on not leaving the cheat-metal behind. The intricate embossing he passed on the way in was artfully exotic. Asgardian culture at its finest, with matching imagery of mead halls over the ages. He saw what the specific issue was when Yuki failed to budge the Li from its pedestal. Right. Dawn had brought it down here. She could carry the thing, Yuki could not. "Allow me."

Stepping back, Yuki gave her Dreamer the room as Artorian walked up self-made light-brick steps. He wasn't currently tall enough to reach the pedestal. Picking the Li up, he tried to smile and show off! He got as far as a half-smile before the light frames beneath his feet shattered from the ridiculous added weight.

Yuki enjoyed another quip. "That's twice you've been on your cheek today, my Dreamer. Perhaps another bath would do you well? Since you *insist* on using your face to clean the floor."

Artorian responded flatly. "Ha. Ha."

Grumbling as he got to his feet, he just kept the metal Li in hand. His scowl faded when he noticed Yuki's quiet, worried expression as her eyes remained on a visible tear in the world. She had a question in mind, but didn't want to voice it.

Artorian could guess what it might be, and just started

answering the unspoken query. "In short, Cal, our Great Spirit, probably got hit with a rock. The place we're in has shattered, and is healing. Slowly. The supervisors are going around to see if anything might stop or hamper that process down. My vote is to remove causes, if found. I have the sneaking suspicion I'm going to find problems on Eternium, but as I can't seem to shift into it, it must be cut off, connection wise. I'll find out why when I can. Marie will likely beat me to it, but my guess says it's a Silverwood issue. In short, we're fine. Don't touch the wiring. Heal up."

He somberly regarded Yuki's wound, and grit his jaw. "I currently don't know how to fix your arm."

Yuki shrugged like it was no big deal, sated with the answers. "It's but an arm. If one were to attempt to make a joke that I am disarmed, the jest would be but on the surface level. Observe. I gained this idea from a story I gathered."

From her wounded shoulder, three Ice-mimicries of her arm burst out. She moved them with all the difficulties of a normal limb. They even combined into one, her dexterity fluid as water as she articulated her fingers. "See? No harm. I shall take to seeking these threats on Asgard. I do not wish you to see it further in this state. Leave. I will tell you when you may resume your bath."

Artorian frowned. "Are you sure?"

The snow lady merely blinked at him, adamant. "*Shoo*."

The youth surrendered, raised his hands in defeat, and *fuffed* out.

CHAPTER THIRTY-SIX

Hel was just as *drab* as ever. Gray here. Gray there. Gray everywhere. Tatum, would it have hurt to add a color scheme? Young Artorian kicked the ground, sending a wave of soot flying at Mach speeds. *Oops.* Looked like Svartalfheim was going to experience a little dark fallout. It'll be *fi~i~ine.*

Pressing a hand to his hips, he knuckle-tumbled the Li and had a cursory check around. Odd. Where were all the skeletons? Last he knew they were all h— *"Sweet Cal!"*

He jumped from shock. A massive steam Elemental deer had just soundlessly popped in from nowhere. Like it had slid between the layers of existence and stepped out without effort to shove its curious nose into his face. He turned, but there was a second doe, also with its nose in his face. Where did these deer come from? On second thought, a little obvious, wasn't it? Incarnate-ranked creatures could do the layers thing. *Great.* At least he wasn't getting squished purely by gravity. A nice boon.

Since the deer were being dears, he did nothing and stood there, letting his face and outfit be nuzzled, nudged, and sniffed. Well, they seemed docile enough, and the spider ginkgo *did* smell nice.

The deer weren't skeletons anymore. Instead, they looked like truly souped-up versions of the original creature. When the third doe showed up with a fawn in tow, he could see that affinities were passed down through the lineage. How interesting. The initial two deer possessed serious water affinities, and that showed clear and obvious in their Incarnate forms.

He considered that these Incarnate Beasts 'wore their power on their sleeve,' as if to tell anything that might see them just how dangerous they were to hunt. Like some kind of fish that glowed because it was poisonous.

He wanted to pet one.

Before doing so, he thought about it twice. He was an A-ranker in an Incarnate form. These were Incarnate creatures, in Incarnate forms. Would the tier of his **Law** be enough to offset the difference in power? Were the deer even *tied* to a **Law**? How did this work for creatures at their level?

His questions went unanswered. All the deer scattered by folding themselves into a different layer. In the span of a heartbeat, they were all gone. What could scare off S-rankers? He closed his eyes, and inhaled sharply.

He knew. He just *knew*.

Honk?

"Makes a loud song before approaching my about-to-be-*bruised* butt." Exhaling his remaining breath, he winced and looked over his shoulder. *Sure enough.* The all-gray multi-headed cobra-chicken horror was curiously staring him down. That only lasted a moment before recognition kicked in. *Abyss.* Not only did the goose remember him, but it remembered that it didn't *like* him. "Well, it was nice seeing you, there's clearly nothing wrong here so I'm just gonna go and—"

fffffFFFFFFF

The goose was on him like white on rice, and Wagner loudly honked with all its heads. It chased Artorian at break-neck speeds as they both took off, sending waves of soot out behind them as they passed. It didn't seem to matter how wide Wagner's wings spread, the air wasn't slowing it down even a little while Artorian *booked it*. "Teleport, teleport, *teleport*! Come *on*. Why can't I *teleport*?"

Artorian wildly dodged an incoming bite. Skidding sideways to avoid a nasty bite that would have taken his entire torso off. He hoped the soot-cloud his slide kicked up would deter the beast.

Honk!

It hadn't.

"I require *immediate* fuffening!" Artorian didn't even know who he was yelling to. Nobody was listening as he zig-zagged through soot dunes to avoid neck-extending goose bites. Brown flames sputtered from the mouth of one while arcs of electrified ice seared the landscape near him from another. A third was expelling copious pockets of oil, and those quickly caught fire. Igniting from the heatless brown flames. Oddly enough, the oil burned green. Those details really weren't his problem right now. Running onwards for dear life as he tried again and again to engage his ability to fuff. This was a terrible time for this to not work! Was the *goose* doing this to him? Not fair!

Hadn't he put a teleportation platform onto Hel? Yes! He had! Just the *one*. Where was it? Oh, how he *missed* dilation abilities. He could have easily... *Hang on*.

Who is *that*?

Artorian's dead run turned from escape for dear life to an enraged charge. *That* was a demon. The slaughter-class infernal dropped to a knee from its arrival in Hel. It was having an incredibly difficult time just *existing* here.

How had it gotten to Hel? It shouldn't have... Oh. *Well*. There was the teleportation pad! Active, too. Best to shut that down before annoyances occurred. Since the goose was hot on his tail, he lobbed a celestial ball at the demon's head mid-run.

The discordant flash-bang went off right in the demon's face as he got to his feet, becoming aware of the approaching creature that was honking discordantly. The infernal newcomer surprised the goose, who now had *two* unwelcome unpleasantries to deal with. "What in the name of the Saccharine Abyss is that awful malady?"

Artorian could hear it speak in its guttural tongue. He hadn't expected knowledge of scree-scree to come in handy so soon. The demon thing had no idea what he was up against. Excellent. Oh, that was a Mage! *Possessed* by a demon. The Abyssalite just happened to be in charge at the moment.

The slaughter-class didn't know what to make of the scene of a twelve-year-old being chased by a house-sized, multi-headed freak of nature. Except perhaps, to *not* be in its way.

Akravid the demon tried to turn and run a different way, but found himself unable. His feet had been locked in light-bricks! How in the abyss were they so heavy that even he, when merged and in control of a *Mage*, could not budge? The explanation that followed didn't help one bit. "Yuki, you beautiful sculpture of a woman! It *is* solid! Haha!"

Artorian ran right past the rooted Akravid, who had a mere moment to complain a single syllable before Wagner tore him into misty chunks. "Observation. Incarnate creatures tear Mages to tiny giblets. Noted!"

He jumped onto the teleportation platform, the impact forcing waves of soot to roll away from his location. He victoriously punched both his arms into the air. "Ha! Success! See you later, you… *Why am I not going fuff?*"

Snap.

One blink later, and Artorian was standing like a fool in his bonfire room, his arms still raised like some kind of victor. He had been shunted back to his Core in the Silverwood Tree. "*Abyss*! He got me! That horrible little… *my iridium*! Oh, *no*."

On Hel, Wagner wasn't feeling too great.

That first bite? No problem. That skippy little annoyance? Stomachache. Something incredibly heavy had been swallowed, and the weight was unpleasant. Wagner stood, shook his feathers, and steadied. Then Wagner had a thought and flapped. Iridium began coating the outside of Wagner's body, and a far more mechanical and shrill sound rumbled from his many throats. He wanted to sing his beautiful song, and the iridium responded to that desire. In order to make the goose sing better, it merely needed a greater range of options. To give a greater range of options, it just needed to bond with the creature. So it *did*.

When Wagner craned his many mechanical metal necks, all were coated in shiny, dense, Incarnate-ranked iridium. Wagner *liked* this feeling. It made him feel unique, and the reflection coming off his own feathers was pleasing. To anyone else, the goose appeared as some kind of house-sized golem. Monstrous and terrible. To Wagner, it was simply time to honk beautiful music! Loud enough to keep unwelcome guests away from its home.

The world was his lawn, and nobody was allowed on it!

When another demon entered through the hijacked beacon, it lived for about point two moments before death ensued. Wagner wasn't having any of their *quack*, and had found out where the nuisances were coming from. Wagner thus decided to camp in this position. There would be *no* trespassers.

In Artorian's bonfire space, the youth grumbled in lament and rubbed his forehead. "Lost the iridium, didn't find out what a demon was doing on Hel. Didn't find out why I couldn't teleport. It was going so well! Can I just go back to having a nice *bath*?"

Scilla appeared with her chin pressed to her fist, her pink irises locked on his slumped form. "You sound rather... *motivated*... to get back and get working."

Artorian whined. "Clearly! Though that was my only body in Cal's Soul Space. He's unconscious and I'm a useless orb now. I cannot return until Cal wakes up and forms me another one. Even worse, I've still got *no* access to Eternium, and now I can't even go check on Marie."

Argh.

Scilla nodded to agree with him, like it was the truest thing ever said. "Sounds like you're in a pickle. Would be a *shame* if I knew how to get you back into the Soul Space."

The youth's eyes sharpened to those of a veteran warrior that had just been slighted. "Young lady, don't you *toy* with me."

Scilla grinned, and winked at him. "I would *never*. I do actually have something in mind. But…"

Artorian's sharpened gaze dropped, his forehead returning to the palms of his hands with a flop. "But you want me to face a *regret*."

Scilla grinned wider. "Ding! We have a winner. You're stuck anyway. Right? Motivation to go back? Well, here comes Scilla from Chasuble, with her basket full of laundry. I have *one* clean piece, ready for wear. If you don't give me a hard time, I also won't remind you that you had Zelia's yellow robe for maybe ten minutes before you *lost* it."

She pressed her cheeks against her knuckles, smushing the puff as she smirked.

"Wagner *ate* me!" He motioned to the wall, as if that damnable goose was hiding right on the other side. "I will just… have to be honest with Zelia."

Scilla snapped her fingers. "Dang. Was hoping you'd try to hide it to give me an easy one. Oh well. *So*. Ready?"

Artorian grumbled. "Don't have much of a choice, do I? Fine! Let's get through the third one. Where is this one at?"

Scilla's phantom digit appeared at her lips, rather than move her arm naturally. She was pensive a moment, but found the location. "Skyspear library."

The youth was confused. "Skyspear library? I don't have any regrets at the *library*."

The smile he was getting back from his warden of the liminal was unsettling. "Really? Well then, this one will be quick. See you in a bit!"

As usual, Artorian was not afforded a chance to respond. Unlike the last few times, he knew it was coming. Scilla had inherited his love for dramatic flair.

CHAPTER THIRTY-SEVEN

Scratch.

Merli lazily looked at the wooden desk he sat at in the Skys-pear library. He was practicing calligraphy. Rather, that's what he *should* have been practicing. Instead, he was carving an 'M' into the table. He drew a breath, and the misty wetness of the waterfall graced his nose. The refreshing intake came accompanied with the fresh sting of mountain air, crisp and sharp.

That had been why he liked *this* desk. It had the best breeze, and something about that made it the most important place to be. He didn't know why, just that it was. Artorian watched Merli, leaning next to the window in a body that was mostly see-through. He could play passenger if he wanted to, but he too wanted to take in the view right now. How nice this place had been. Things would have been so different, had he remained.

Actually. Why *hadn't* he remained? He slapped his forehead. Now he *knew* what the regret was. This was the day he'd been kicked out. This was the day he *flunked*. Based on Merli's build and appearance, he was around... What? Twenty-two? He'd filled out nicely, and was no longer some emaciated youth. The

Academy had taken good care of him, and he had… squandered it. Yes. He'd *squandered* it.

Cataphron appeared in the doorway, and Artorian thought his eyebrows would crack the ceiling. So *young*! Yet already so *sour*. Cata had been his superior as a student, but he'd never paid the head student a copper's worth of attention. Abyss, he barely paid attention in classes.

That flighty nature, at least, was no longer a mystery. Merli's weak air affinity was flowing strong. "Slacking *again*, I see. You were supposed to have those scrolls complete before the sun set. You haven't gotten through… what? Five sets of repetition. Your vowels are *sloppy*."

Artorian played passenger, and Merli turned to shoot Cata the widest smile. "I have it down. No need to get antsy. They're all acceptable, and they will pass. As usual. Why do the extra work?"

Cata squinted, sucking air between his teeth. "Because Skyspear is a place for those who *excel*. Not for those who do the minimum and then laze around with their head in the clouds. I'm going to take you to the lecture, since it was expected you would forget to show up on your *own*. Get moving. I'm not going to get snapped at by an instructor for your tardiness. Unlike you, I put *effort* into what I do."

Merli moved his palms to the air, and Cataphron sneered at the lack of ink stains. He turned on his sandals and beat it to the door, where he awaited with crossed arms. Not much changed between his young and old states, it seemed.

Masters Sho-lin, Fen-que, and Diomedes were waiting for him. Odd, wasn't this supposed to be a lecture? Artorian just gritted his teeth, forced to watch this again. He didn't like being in this *test* the first time. He didn't like it any more the second time either, even if he knew what was about to happen.

This was the moment. This was when he'd gotten the worst headache of his early life. The masters were about to *grill* him. Merli asked a question. "Is this a private lecture?"

A response was calmly provided by Sho-lin. "Of a sorts, student. Please, take a seat."

Sho-lin was a pleasant and portly master. He enjoyed drinking fine wines while reading his many books. He enjoyed drinking twice as much when reading them aloud to a class. Given he gave daily lectures, that ended up being quite a bit.

Fen-que was less amused. A tall and lanky fellow in stark comparison, Master Fen-que merely huffed out a *Fuu*! then flourished his robe in order to sit. He remained rigid in his pose, arms making sweeping motions to make himself look wise and important. Unfortunately, Merli already knew it was all hubris. Fen-que was a man who valued appearance over knowledge.

Master Diomedes, on the other hand, was a warrior of muscle who looked like he'd just crawled out of a mud pit and hadn't given a single thought to cleaning off. His robes were stained and matted with thick layers of brown earth. The mud caked his robes, and he didn't care. Instead, he smiled from ear to ear, clearly glad to be here. For him, this was just going to be *fun*.

Artorian groaned internally. This was going to be a *long* evening. When Merli sat, Sho-lin began. Sitting directly in front of him, he warmly mused. "I have a *question*."

Merli was confident, but Artorian just buried his face deeper into his hands. This was such a trap, and Merli didn't have the life experience to know better. In hindsight, it was this exact event that had helped turn him into the sharp-nosed miser he was today. Without this long talk that would last until the sun came up, he would never have had his perspective so thoroughly *broken*.

For hours, they asked Merli the simplest of questions that ended in contradictions. Then they asked him to explain the contradictions, which only made him dig himself into a *deeper* hole. By midnight, Artorian just wanted to go home. Merli had his head in his hands, holding his temples as he struggled with questions. Wrestling with the lack of answers while he fought for ways to get out of the mire he'd dug himself in.

When the sun crested over the horizon in the morning, Merli was in tears. "Look, I don't know. I just *don't know*!"

The three masters were undisturbed by the amount of time that had passed. They merely nodded, but Diomedes giggled. "Finally, you say something that is true!"

Merli was glad for the affirmation, but did Diomedes have to be so abyss-darned *jovial* about it? The man was nearly laughing!

Sho-lin took over again. "Well, if you have found that you don't know, what is there that you do know? Can anything you see be trusted? Anything you hear, or smell, or taste? Can you be certain that what you experience is the same experience everyone else has? Or is it merely the experience you are *able* to have? Do you see more colors than a butterfly? Do you pick up scent sharper than a crag wolf? Is your sight that of a thunderhawk?"

Merli wiped his face off with his sleeve. "Well. *No.* But I don't have any of those things. I am *not* any of those things. How could I possibly *know* what they know? I know I exist. That I'm sitting here and talking. That I'm sitting on a rock. I have no idea what you're asking me. I don't know what you want me to answer. We have been doing this all night and I still don't grasp any of this. This is *nothing* like the classes, even when I *did* pay attention."

Fen-que huffed. "*Fuu…* finally! A good question. It pains me that you don't understand the purpose of this conversation. Why you are asked a thousand questions, nor why you have failed to correctly answer a single one. You have written verses from the wall of virtue for years, and yet none of it has stuck! Fellow masters, I waste my time here. I rescind my welcome of this student. Decide yourselves. I am finished."

Fen-que got up, and unceremoniously left, walking in sharp, yet sweeping motions.

Sho-lin looked up at a standing Diomedes. "I thought that last question showed progress. What do you think?"

Diomedes smiled broad, crossing his arms as the stretch on

his face widened. He was clearly having a good time. "I think that another question or two and he'll stand at the edge, if not over the edge. Though, given the answers of the evening, what he can learn at the Skyspear is clearly at its limit. Ask him the question, and we will see."

Sho-lin nodded. "Young Merli. We accepted you due to the sizable influence your family had, including the welcomed addition to our coffers. We were warned you were a rambunctious one, and that has proven to be true. Yet over the entire duration you have been here, you have shown but a feather of enthusiasm for what we do here, when the others could be said to be whole birds. Sure, you study and pass the tests. Yet we see the longing in your eyes anytime you look off the mountainside."

Merli said nothing, and listened. "You are cursed with a gift, young student. That curse is that you can learn information like the rest of us breathe. You organize it in your head at the speed I drink wine, and you dismiss the finer details of the rest just as swiftly. Completely, once you have decided you are done with a topic. This ego has no place on the mountain, and most relinquish it in their third or fourth year. You have been here much longer, yet you are aloof. Acting as a leaf on the wind, rather than a rock on the ground. So tell me. What will you do when you are faced with a problem that you cannot easily grasp or answer?"

Merli frowned. That seemed obvious. "Seek the solution?"

Diomedes closed his eyes, and shook his head. "What must one do if there is no solution?"

Merli just scratched the back of his head. "That can't be right. There's always a solution."

Both remaining masters shared a solemn shake of the head. It didn't look good. Sho-lin spoke. "It seems he does not grasp it. Let me try one last time."

Diomedes nodded, and Sho-lin returned to Merli. "There are problems for which there are simply no solutions. One day, you will recognize this. In those events, what is it one should seek?"

Merli didn't get it. That much was clear. He pressed his cheek to his fist, and racked his brain for an answer. Nothing he had said before had gotten him anywhere, so he crossed another answer from the list. There was no right answer to the question. There didn't seem to be a right answer to *any* of these questions. "What is the point of these questions if they *have. No. Answers?*"

The frustration showed on the youth's face. No longer choosing to play passenger, Artorian sighed, and lowered himself to a knee next to Merli. He was resigned to watching carefully. "Alright. Here we go. Say it."

The masters said nothing, patiently waiting for the last answer they would accept from the youth. There was no right answer. So what was he supposed to look for to get anywhere? Trapped in the moment of thought, Merli reached so deep and clawed so far that, for a moment, his mind was the only place that existed. Nothing about the real world mattered. His body was irrelevant. Conditions were irrelevant. He was wholly outside of himself, by diving deeper than he'd had before. Just to dig, and dig, and dig for *some* kind of answer that would satisfy them.

Yet he found none, and the light started to drop from his eyes. "If there was no answer to the question… then, was it even… the *right* question?"

Artorian went slack jawed. "You must be joking. It happened *here*?"

Rather than watch Merli have the epiphany, he watched the boy's center. The youth had aligned himself with an idea, and that idea found both solace and a foothold in his soul. Merli's gaze was empty as he looked at the two masters, uncertain of his answer. Sho-lin appeared to have given up, but what Diomedes saw was clearly to his liking.

It was then that Artorian saw the light in his mud-caked master's eyes. That was *refined Essence*. Diomedes was—much like him at this very moment—*inspecting* Merli's center. They were both watching the moment of the formation of a minor

Essence channel. The youth gave his answer, and as he did, the affinity channel *blossomed* with celestial.

Diomedes's smile fell immediately. That was *not* what he'd hoped for at all. The muscled man turned on his foot, and nonchalantly waved a hand over the shoulder. "That's a failure in my eyes. I stand with Fen-que. I rescind my welcome of this student. I am finished."

Wait. Wait, wait, wait, wa~a~ait. Artorian snapped his vision between the dismissive master and Merli. The latter now gaped wide-eyed at the sky as the epiphanies hit him one after the other.

Merli's head spun while Artorian fumed. It… it had *never* been about the answers? This awful, *awful* test. This toying with him, grinding him into a puddle of anxiety, and peeling him apart to get at an answer, was in the hopes he would develop an *infernal* Essence channel?

A bewildered Artorian returned his eyes to the scene at hand, where Sho-lin spoke. "Well, that is unfortunate. That makes for a majority vote. Still, before we are forced to evict you as a failed student… Could you please tell me again? Even if the other masters rebuke you, I find myself intrigued with your response."

Merli blinked, and repeated himself. "It's not about… finding the right *answer*. What you have been teaching is about finding the right *question*. The answer can't come if the problem faced is approached incorrectly, or in a manner that won't help. If the answer cannot be attained to the question as made in its current form, then what is wrong is *not* the unattainable answer, but the *question itself*."

Sho-lin sighed, so celestially proud. "How I wish you would have said these words *moments* sooner. That is one of the best answers I can hope for. Can you answer the earlier one as well, now that you understand? What exactly is it that you know?"

Artorian copied Merli's words as they were said. In the exact pitch and tone. "Nothing, Master. I know *nothing*."

Sho-lin beamed, still awfully proud. "Congratulations,

young Merli. You may be relieved of your student position after today, but with *that* answer, I find that you are a *graduate* of this Academy. Even if it can never be publicly stated. Such a discovery is made by all who find the path. With such a discovery, I will see fit that you are well equipped before you are sent on your way. Stay strong, young student. You have a bright future ahead."

CHAPTER THIRTY-EIGHT

Artorian opened his eyes in his bonfire space. Scilla was there of course, deeply inspecting him for the slightest detail. The now twenty-two-year-old academy student sat in the location the twelve-year-old previously occupied. He remained quiet. Mulling over recent discoveries. When he spoke, Scilla just nodded. "It was *never* my fault. It was a *setup*."

Scilla smirked, stretching with ease. "*Mmmm*! Look at me, being right. Wasn't that just such a doozy? All these years you've beaten yourself up that you could never please those walking contradictions. **Tsk, tsk**. Do you still feel like they abandoned you, exiled you, or threw you away? Was it really your actions that made you get kicked out of that tall rock you liked lounging around on so much?"

Artorian's response was older. The voice of a resolute twenty-something youth speaking. "No. No, it was not. That series of events was premeditated, and my involvement was never something that mattered. Only the result. A result that Diomedes did *not* get. I remember Cataphron speaking of him. That something was odd. That things *changed*. Now that I know he was a cultivator even in those days, I believe it with firmness.

The Skyspear didn't rebuke me. It was *tainted*; and I was in the way."

He heard the snap of fingers, and felt his power increase to A-rank three. He blinked, observing his own hands. "I don't understand. Just like that? But… that was so *minor*? I didn't do anything."

Scilla shook her head, even though it was her shadow that moved, rather than her. The girl herself didn't move a muscle, and that felt eerie. "The regret went away. One less thing that tethers you to the old world. One less thing that can hold you back. One less worry lingering that could poke you at an inopportune time. One less full plate on the table for a blight to eat."

Artorian said nothing. She was right. His mind instead wandered to what had been going on before the memory trip. "How long has it been since I sank into the regret? Not another hundred years, I hope?"

He was half-joking about the time, but Scilla answered him deadpan. "Seventeen seconds."

She… she was also joking. Right? He'd been gone for *hours* in the memory. His frown made her smirk. "Seventeen seconds, and not a blip longer. Remember, I am the one that controls how long it takes. I change those times according to my needs, and currently my needs are for you to move your butt. Unless you'd rather jump into number four right *now*."

Artorian knew he shouldn't ask, but if it had merely been seventeen seconds… a little foreknowledge would do no harm. "When and where is it?"

Scilla observed her nails, and turned them bright pink. "Phoenix Kingdom. You know *when*."

The young adult winced hard. "No. *Hard* no. That is definitely *not* something I can live through right now."

The pink monster shrugged. "Suit yourself. It's next. It's ready. Just waiting on you. The rest of them are as well. Maybe some motivation will help? Or fear? It will likely serve the same purpose, as you're going to ask regardless. Perhaps it will give you courage to know a few in *advance*. Ready?"

That was a clever trap, but he saw right through it. "If you mean ready for the memory, that's still a no. Ready for the primer? Yes."

Scilla clicked her tongue. *Tsk.* "I'll tell you the next *four* locations, since you're being a sour lemon. You're smart enough to figure out the rest. Phoenix Kingdom. The Wilds. Socorro. The Fringe. Don't those sound like a great time?"

Artorian went pale. "You're *horrible.* I despise this. Yet I already have the feeling that I'll be thanking you when they're done."

Scilla agreed with him there. "Not even for the rank, either. Now. I believe I have a *promise* to fulfill. You know how we feel about *promises*, don't we, Merli?"

The young adult scowled back, but said nothing. The pink horror instead fulfilled her part of the bargain. "You *do* actually have another body in the Soul Space. Though, it's not a convenient one."

Artorian rolled his wrist for her to get on with it. She fell back into her telltale smirk, and giggled. "The Long, mark three! They may have fished the remains of that second attempt out of that tree. Though our dearest Great Spirit made a third one, and shoved it into storage when distracted by something else. It's keyed to you, so I can feel it even if you do not. It's still there, lying in storage. Doing absolutely nothing after Cal finished the Incarnate version of your favorite flag."

He squinted his eyes at her. "Are you going to give me fecal matter if I try to move to it?"

Scilla pressed a finger to her lips, but winked and vanished into the ceiling. "No. I'm done. Good luck in version three! From what I overheard, it's even more complicated than the first two. Though lucky you! You are going to have such a *long* time to figure it out."

Artorian gritted his teeth. There was no point in quipping back. Her eyes were closed and she was 'gone.' As much as she could be. Cheeky *brat*. He rubbed at his face, and closed his eyes to look for the available body. Given it was best to take lessons from important parts of history, what was the right question here? Not 'where is the body' but rather 'how do I find the body.' That one he could do.

Funneling Mana into his **Law**, he tried something different and directed the flow towards himself. He needed to see his own connections, rather than someone else's. His bonfire room exploded with lines, patterns, and pieces of people. Chunks of memories played, organized themselves, and neatly folded together in orderly rows. Well, well. Looked like he could locate Scilla. Now that was interesting.

According to this odd mishap of a map he was looking at, she was wherever he was. Though that was perhaps because he was in the Silverwood Core. Next he saw strong, direct lines to all his chosen. A glance in their direction let him get a general feeling for what they were up to. Well, that was neat!

Zelia was yelling at someone. Halcyon was asleep, and Yuki was... Was Yuki destroying scores of Beasts coming out of a lake with ice bolts? *Hmm.* Seemed like it. Best *not* to interrupt then. His attention moved to his family, and the bright lines turned blurry gray. Those all connected to memory Cores. That was *definitely* going to be one of the regrets. He had already dallied far too long with decanting them, and finding reasons to wait longer didn't sit well. "One day, my sweets. One day."

Odd. One of his chosen lines was also blurry gray. "Oh. Looks like Vol was stored. Wonder how that happened."

Just thinking of the question must have satisfied some condition, as Artorian became privy to the last five seconds of Vol's life. The hungry boy had charged at a fracture made of thin wiring, and... yup. It *shattered him* when he bit into it. Classic Voltekka.

Closing that visual, he followed more of the bright lines. Dawn! Oh, well, hello. Where might *this* be? How interesting. He'd never known this pleasant little location to exist before. Cal's private, special workroom was in Hel's core? Tatum seemed to be there as well. He supposed it explained why Hel was so insanely oversized. It overshadowed Jotunheim, and that realm wasn't even round. He could sneak in on them… but a faint ethereal glint caught his attention.

In Cal's workroom, one of the warehouses had… *Aha*! The Long! *Found you*! Artorian rubbed his hands together, and focused purely on that connection as the rest of them fell away. He wondered for a moment how to get there, but changed his question to a statement. From 'how do I get there' to 'I'm going there.' Will to action! His consciousness shot from his Silverwood Core straight to the longest of noodles.

Stirring in the small confines of the warehouse, which was really just a carved-out rectangle in solid… What was this stuff? He thought of the words 'corrupted concrete' but didn't know what that meant. It didn't matter. There didn't appear to be a door, just an open space that led to an unlit hallway. So now it was just a matter of figuring out where his face was.

Puzzling that out was as strange as one might expect. All his movement was Long-like, rather than human-like. The limbs… helped? Sure. In a kind of whine-while-agreeing way. *Aha! Found the face*. Now what?

He laid in the storage room for a while, just trying to get used to the feeling. Unfortunately, it just wasn't clicking for him. He may have done this before, but it was like he was a human-sized thing operating a body that was otherworldly in size difference alone.

Artorian was approaching this incorrectly. He was trying to fit his existing self into a form that wasn't an appropriate fit, then expecting that form to smoothly function as intended anyway. That was the bottom-up method. He sucked at the bottom-up method. What was he *doing*? He was the big ideas first guy! So. *Big ideas*!

Did the Long need to be the entity that was larger? What about flipping the script? Artorian had a grand thought, and bloomed out his Presence. With Cal unconscious, perhaps he could take over some of the space, rather than just reform his Aura? *Yes*! *Success*!

His Presence filled the entirety of the workroom, and now it was the Long that was tiny! Ha! This was just like what he'd done while stuck in The Between. Except as a rectangle instead of a sphere. *Eh*. Potayto potahto. Still, the experience was *liberating*. Akin to finally taking off a confining suit.

After a breath of relief, he collapsed himself around the form of the dragon. He didn't know how long he spent painstakingly re-molding himself so he and the form were a custom-tailored fit. It was important to get this right, since this was his *only* body. He couldn't afford to play it fast and loose with his backup chance. If he lost the Long as well, he *really* would be stuck until Cal was back. Unacceptable! He may not like it, but he was going to flawlessly meld with the dragon's frame. Cost be abyssed!

By the time he could flex his claws, he could also roll his shoulders, and feel the sensation of pressure to his scales just as clearly as if a leaf was pressing onto his skin. The Mana-form body had been too solid, rigid, and stale with its senses. The Incarnate version, on the other hand, was *fantastic* for haptic feedback. He no longer felt like he needed to completely rely on water pressure just to gain a sensation of what was where.

With his Presence cleanly molded to the Long's shape, he could even make proper facial motions after a few tries. The Incarnate form added new muscles according to his mobility needs. He loved it. So much more responsive and reactionary! 'More complicated' must have meant 'more adaptive.'

Sending a shake from his neck all the way to the very tip of his tail, he was pleased with the progress. "That's full dexterity. Feels nice and natural."

His voice didn't boom when he spoke. He only realized after that it hadn't. So this form didn't wreck that for him either? Such convenience! A little deep and gravely, but not bad for his first attempt at speech. He wouldn't break the environment just by talking. Big plus.

He tested his **Law** connections, and found that he would have no issues teleporting. Great! Now why had it been blocked off beforehand? He wasn't certain, but he had a gut feeling that infernal goose had prevented it somehow.

Could he hover? A quick test said yes. As a bonus, due to his Presence controlling the hover, he didn't bash into the ceiling or fly several miles up into the sky like last time. Honestly, did they think flailing around in this thing and being a flag was *fun*? It wasn't! Being stuck in a body that disagreed with you was *anything* but a good time. *Hmmm.* He was likely not the only person that felt that way. Perhaps once back in Eternium, he could make some of these quests to do something about it? Yes. That sounded nice.

Arrive with poor eyesight? Have a quest to set it to the average instead. Don't like something about your body? A quest to customize it sounded fair. Just like he'd just done with the Long form. An excellent series of ideas! Let people be who they want to be. All for it. In the event there ever *were* new people. Maybe skip the quest entirely and let people change how they begin? He'd put that on the backburner for when he could do something about it.

First. Taking stock.

Artorian couldn't reach his chin with his physical hand, so he formed an extra light-construct arm near his neck to scritch at it instead. "What's my to-do list? Let's see. I'm not getting the iridium back from Wagner. I'm just not. Visiting Hel at all is a one-way ticket to nowhere. Crossing that off. Realm checks are going to be fruitless for me. While I'm this big, I can't fit in person-sized places. With my tenuous grasp on dragonflight, I'm just going to accidentally bump into a wire tear and get shattered. No good, plus others are on it."

He performed a silent barrel roll in slow motion, and continued musing. "What about this Barry fellow? Is he actually stuck in Eternium, or was he in the Soul Space? I'm having severe trouble recalling. My Silverwood Core connection must be hampered. Actually, that *needs* to go on the list; my connection has to be solid. I need to check myself before the event where I wreck myself."

He added it to his temporary to-do list. "Barry himself was an Incarnate. So that's outside of my scope. Was he the one blamed with being responsible for demons? No, that was Eternium. Barry was... doing something with them. Talking? Influencing? *Something*. Either way, demons are back, and that's a big no-no. Demons I can do something about, so that goes on the list. I need to find out how they are getting into the Soul Space, since they were certainly stuck in Eternium. Plus how they managed to use my beacon network."

A thought struck Artorian. "Those are probably *directly* connected. Yes. It's such an obvious link. So what to do... do I just go play *exterminator*? A little dangerous in a brand-new body that I'm not in the slightest accustomed to. Still, it should probably go on the list. That's *my* vendetta."

Adding it to the list, he figured it best to start with safety measures. Let's check if forum connections functioned. <Zelia. Can you hear me at all?>

Her voice was as surprised as it was elated. <My Dreamer! You live! We were so worried when your Presence winked out all of a sudden. I have not been able to get a spiderling to Hel in order to check on you. The connection cuts as soon as they arrive, and I have deemed it too dangerous to continue. Are you well?>

Warmth returned on their connection. <I'm well, my dear. Events did not go according to plan, so I'm going to handle priority issues for a while. I'm glad the link works, though it feels more personal. Like some of the assistance is missing. It doesn't even feel like a forum space, more of a peer-to-peer only thing. Oh, silly me. That's exactly what it is. Took me a moment. I really need to check on my Core, that isn't good.>

Shaking himself from the distraction, he addressed his needs directly. <Zelia, I think I need slipspace lessons. My body is currently far larger than I am used to. I've obtained a Long-form, and I'm not getting out of my current predicament the casual way. If I fuff out, I have no idea if I'm going to teleport right into a wire tear. If I recall, you were able to

deeply understand your exit point, where I have sort of been... *eyeballing* it.>

Zelia's reply took a little long, but she grumbled when the answer came. <I attempted to personally shift to you, but the pressure in the place you are is weird. It's not like the surface of Hel at all. We will have to talk through this method, and I do not appear able to send images. The short of it is yes, I am very aware of my exit points. Though if I have to explain it rather than show it, this is going to take a very long time.>

Artorian resigned himself, but remained stalwart. <Then I will *make* the time. Teach me.>

Zelia was happy to oblige.

CHAPTER THIRTY-NINE

Zwip.

<*I li~i~ive!*> Artorian's outcry cheered loud and proud when he appeared in the sky above Niflheim. The Long-form uncoiled from itself, having fumbled together into the equivalent of a ball of yarn. He extracted himself from the tangle, clouds of fog pouring from his back as he stretched with regained freedom. <*Ahhh*. Yes. Sweet success.>

Zelia cleared her throat in their connection. <Are you *done,* Dreamer?>

The dragon coughed at the sudden embarrassment, steadying himself with a throat-clearing grunt. Like he was trying to play it off. <*Ghmm?* Oh. Yes, of course! I'm just having a good *stretch.*>

Mhm. Her tone was flat. Amused, but flat. <Now that you have succeeded, does it make more sense? Proper teleportation is an experience that has to be felt before it can truly be understood in full.>

Artorian coiled through the sky. Straightening himself out while cloud-swimming along. <Absolutely! The wavelength of

the Mana used really *does* need a specific tune. Had I not been in the know of certain musical practices, this would have been entirely beyond me. Slipspace is fantastic! It provides a much smoother transition than what I was using. All it took was some *expensive* adjustments. *Ah well*. I'd rather expend a rank of my Mana than my life. Previously when I fuffed, I just kept the destination in mind. Then funneled relevant Mana through my **Law**, which piggybacked the **Teleportation Law**, to accomplish the effect.>

Zelia was appreciative, but she had more questions. <Lovely. Now I know that your success just now *didn't* piggyback. I would have been able to tell otherwise. What did you do?>

Artorian wiggled his tail. So quaint! <I didn't! I applied your suggestion directly to my **Law**, rather than send it down the grapevine. I suppose I always thought that higher **Laws** might perform the functions of lower ones, but I'd not tested it so *directly*. Performing the action was easy, but the *cost*. Sweet honey-covered crackers. *The cost*. Given the choice, I would rather become skilled and use your **Law**. **Love** may make it easy, but the expenditure is daylight robbery! On the plus side, I made it! I'm going to try to not do that again without significant practice. I scarcely have a grasp on your '*seeing the mirror*' trick.>

Zelia sighed with relief. <Well, I'm glad my lessons were understandable enough for you to grasp the basics, my Dreamer. To be honest, I am quite taxed after dealing with you for so long. Your breadth in ability to question is… *unique*. I would like to rest now.>

Artorian understood, feeling apologetic as he knew how he could get when chasing after a theorem. <Terribly sorry, my dear. I can be a bit much. Not being right next to you unfortunately didn't help, but thank you so much for helping me through this. Please don't let me take more of your time. Have a lovely rest. Give Cy a hug for me.>

After confirmation that she would do so, Zelia closed the conversation. Exhausted. Good Great Spirit, her Dreamer could *ta~a~alk*. Not wanting to use her voice again for at least a year, she flopped face-first into a pile of pillows next to Halcyon. When one of her spiderlings rudely came to prompt her, her only reply was a dejected groan. It was not time to get back up yet.

Not after that *slog*.

Artorian felt a little bad. He'd needed lecture after lecture to get this far. Teleportation was complicated! Still, the hurdle was jumped. Time for the next problem. Where the heck was *his* Core?

Turned out, his Core was easy to find. Shifting from hovering, he flew right towards it in a serpentine pattern before he realized he'd made a grievous mistake. Compounding this newfound fun, he was intercepted before he arrived at the Silverwood Tree.

Marie jumped in the way of the wailing noodle that beelined it towards her charge. The Queen's halberd and regal armor shone bright, the effects of both fully active as she planned to rebuke the creature like some common monster. Which is exactly what she saw Artorian as before the wailing turned into words. "Marie! Good to see you! Catch me!"

Rather than hack the falling creature in twain, Marie blinked under the helmet when her senses registered the call. It was the understanding bit that held up the queue. She hiccupped in disbelief. "*Administrator?*"

"*Catch me~e~e*, I don't know how to *sto~o~op*." Artorian flailed his dragon arms, but it was to no avail. Flight and hover were vastly different animals. While hovering was manageable, flight interacted with the Runescripting on his bones. Those sneaky buggers functioned all on their own! Unfortunately, that meant he didn't know how to properly control them.

Marie caught him alright.

Funneling Mana to her **Law** of **Glory**, she dropped her halberd and swept her arms out to the sides. Her feet set against the air as if planted on the sturdiest of stone, and a powerful radiance spread from her form. It looked similar to when his

Aura expanded to make a light construct of himself. The larger form he used to hug the tall ones.

Marie instead grew considerably larger *herself*. French horns blared to orchestral life in the background as the boat-sized Queen caught him without moving a hair. He bashed right into her armored chest, half-crumpling into a noodly pile. Thank Cal for sturdy plating! *Oof*! "Got you!"

"Administrator! Why are you a… *this*?" Squeezing him by the face, she pushed him away so she could inspect him properly through her helmet. The strength of the push caused the rest of his body to fly outwards. Making it clear just how poor his flight control was. "Do… do you maybe need something to hold on to?"

Artorian sighed, mumbling with muted tones while his cheeks were held. "*Yeah…* Just don't call me a *flag…*"

Marie snorted out a laugh, extending a hand to the ground. Her halberd stirred, shooting skyward from where it had landed. The weapon cut swaths through the air as it spun, whirling right up into her waiting grasp. She turned it upside down, holding the halberd right above the sharp and pointy bit to allow Artorian a handhold on what was ordinarily the bottom of the pole. Sure enough, the Long mark three looked like a wavy flag. One fantastic at complaining. "I'm going to figure this out. I will! In the meanwhile, I will just have to learn to deal with all that *infernal giggling*!"

Pffbrlt. Marie pressed a hand to her helmet. It did nothing to help stifle the continued snorts and spouts of giggling. This was just *so funny* to her. She tried to speak through her amusement. "First you show up as a twelve-year-old. Now you're in this noodle form again. Honestly, I should have this sight painted, and then *embroidered* as my Queendom's heraldry."

"*Don't you dare.*" Artorian glared at her with his puffed-up, leery dragon face. However, since he was holding onto the halberd with both his arms while also being somewhat coiled around for proper grip, he couldn't *really* stop her. Not without *letting go*. Artorian couldn't even alter his Aura or Presence! If he did, it would destabilize the form he was inhabiting. So Artorian had to just *hang in there* and bear with it while Marie suffered another giggle fit.

Ha~aha~aaah. "Oh, that was good. Well. Since you're here. Come meet the Wisps. I'm guessing you're here for your Core? I'm handling it. Chandra has been feeding me instructions, and she's coming herself when able. There's a few nasty tears through the tree, but nothing we can't heal or salvage save for the tar streaks around Eternium. The Wisps have been our saving grace. Without them, we would have lost Odin. *Hang tight.* I'm going down."

When Marie said 'going down,' Artorian had expected a gradual decline. He had not expected her to turn her flight off entirely and piledrive to the ground below at terminal velocity. She landed with a solid *thunk*, the ground wavering as she made it look seamless. The crumpling wet noodle that piled up next to her wasn't so graceful, but it did allow Artorian to repress his own flight capacities. The Runescripting ceased their rambunctiousness, and he sighed weakly in relief. "Well, at least I won't jettison off into the sky just to tenderize the ground a few times. That wasn't fun."

When Artorian slowly opened his eyes, a field of flying dots littered his vision. Was he seeing spots? Hundreds of flying colored orbs were congregating before him, though they all appeared to make way as a single purple one raced at full blast towards his face. Grace the Wisp slammed into his forehead hard enough to tackle his somewhat risen face right back to the grass. So much for not tenderizing the ground. "*Towian!*"

Towian? Was that a toddler version of his name? Shouldn't Grace be significantly older by now? Or did Wisp aging function in a method that was unknown to him? Likely the latter. Still, he'd treat her all the same. "Sweetheart! Hello, my dear. I've missed you too. Are these all your friends? Can I meet them?"

Grace bounced off his face like a rubber ball that made its own momentum. She spun in place as she hit the ground and did a twirl. In front of his eyes, Artorian watched with glee and wonder as the purple ball of energy sparkled, spinning into a pre-dressed human body. Specifically, a three to five-year-old in a *suspiciously familiar* dress robe. Looked like Zelia had been *advertising*.

Her voice was giddy, filled with excited, boundless energy. "*Ta-daah!*"

"Wonderful! I would clap, but my arms are too short. I would make a spare arm, but found that it causes a few setbacks. Look at these wiggly claws!" He flailed his arms around, and it looked as ridiculous as it sounded. They were far too small for the body, and the Wisps in attendance snickered. He *ignored* the hapless laughter erupting from Marie, who needed to hold her stomach as she bent over and heaved. It wasn't *that* funny…

Grace put her hand into the air, and the reactions stopped as if a copper just fell on the floor. *Oof.* Now that was *some* influence. "Towian should just tuwn? It's not hawd. We can all do it. Then youw awms will be nowmal!"

He had to admit he was a little out of sorts. Did they mean undergoing the humanization effect the chosen went through? He didn't think that was an option for him. On second consideration, *why* had he thought that? Weren't Spirit bodies specifically useful *because* they were so malleable? "That's a wonderful idea! Yet, I may need a hand getting started. Marie over there is laughing too hard for me to ask her anything. Would you or any of your friends have insight?"

Grace bit her finger and thought about it. Her mother wasn't around, otherwise she would have just deferred to her. Given Dani wasn't, Grace pointed at a particularly blue Wisp. Noticing he had been prompted, Invictus hovered closer. His humanized form morphed from it smooth and clean, hands immediately adjusting his sleeveless brocade vest.

A word hadn't fallen from his lips and Artorian had already thrown him into the box of 'silver-tongued advisors who whisper into the ears of Kings.' The Wisp-turned-man just had that air about him. That tiny smile on the edge of his lips, the suave and steady gait of playful confidence. Invictus rocked a square jaw that could sell flowers before they'd even been planted. His eyes glinted with tiny schemes.

"Salutations, friend of Grace. I am called Invictus; *please* feel free to just call me Vi for convenience. I would be delighted to present a step-by-step process for you. May I be allowed?" Invictus pressed a hand to his chest, performing a light court-quality bow.

This little sneak! Vi was placing the impetus of the action squarely back in his hands, to make it seem as if the ideas that arrived from this discourse were his own, no doubt. What kind of dungeon would need such a silver tongue to keep it on task? Actually… this might be the *perfect* time to find out. A smirk formed on Artorian's face. Schemer versus schemer? Well, let the *games* begin!

The following two hours turned all of Marie's giggles into excruciating winces. If she wasn't forced to stay, she would have taken *any* excuse to escape from this *slimeball* of a fight. The Administrator and Wisp were speaking to one another as if they were Dukes attending a court ball. Resorting purely to wit and clever wordplay to try to get the best of the other, while ever making it seem as if the spoken word was neither insult, nor rapier-jab to the kidney.

To Marie, who was sickened by the honeyed attempts of countless advisors and chancellors over the ages to get her to do one thing or another—that may not always be in her favor, but definitely to theirs—this exchange was *torture*. She likened it to listening to two high-on-their-horse Nobles use procedure and unspoken rules to really stick it to the other while somehow remaining both cordial and informative.

In this instance, Invictus played the role of the court chancellor, appointed by the crown. He considered himself better and superior due to practiced skill and innate talent while his rump rested squarely on a plush pedestal of status. Artorian, on the other hand, played the part of the fresh-faced Noble, arriving to jam several wrenches into otherwise well-oiled spokes. The longer it went on, the more Marie wanted to just sink back into her throne back at home and cover more of her face with her palm.

"I just need to tune them out."

CHAPTER FORTY

After checking out for a while to just not hear it anymore, Marie gathered herself to look back up. Where did the noodle creature go? Something that big didn't just *disappear*. Her mood altered from wrenched and taxed to confused and concerned. He hadn't shot off into the sky like the stories recounted, had he? A cursory glance upwards found nothing, but an in-depth look at a gathering of nearby people explained why her eyes had glossed over the matter.

All the Wisps had taken their human forms, and gathered up in a loose circle based on the hue of their attire. In the center, a very much human Artorian and frazzled Invictus were *still* going at it. Perhaps it was time to pay attention, and she tuned her senses to listen in.

The mention of 'courts' had been right on the money. The Wisps divided themselves as such, and within their own schema of color held a rather specific hierarchy. This was the topic Marie became privy to. Which by itself came as a surprise as she'd never gotten so much as a *detail* on Wisp society out of any of them. Yet Invictus was so out of sorts that he was just about *yelling* them at the man. The pleased little smirk plastered on a young Artorian's lips told her volumes of the story.

Marie hushed to herself. "Administrator... what did you do?"

She also noted that he physically appeared to be around two decades in age, but was quickly distracted by the frustration pouring out of Invictus as Artorian was purposefully getting something wrong to rile him up. "So you're in the family of *fish*, then. Well, alright. I'll make sure to write it down properly."

"No, no, *no*. Not *fish*. Fae. Wisps belong to the family of *Fae*." Invictus's vest had come a few buttons undone, and his slicked hair had dried up, gaining the contrast of tumbleweed. Where the square-jawed smooth talker normally had no issues getting people to curve along the bends of his river, this absolute madman before him was making him pull the remnants of his short beard out.

The Wisps around the dueling duo were delighting in the abyss Vi was being put through. A little *catharsis*, as they indulged in the slime speaker being fed some medicine too bitter to swallow. Artorian nodded sagely, clearly pretending to understand even if he'd spent the last few minutes just dropping verbal hammers. He wasn't even *trying* to smoothen jabs over anymore, and that made it all the more enjoyable for the gathering. "Of course, of course. The Fae family, of which you are a blue affiliate of the water tribe."

The pink Wisps, recognizable by the color of their attire, collectively snickered. As that was so *obviously* wrong. Or it was to them, even though their own smiles and lack of Matron was distracting them from remembering they *shouldn't* be talking about this. It was just too juicy of an enjoyment to pass up. They secretly had bets on when Vi was going to pull his hair out.

Not if! Only when.

Vi boiled over. "No! I am a celestial affinity Wisp, and my *coloration* happens to be blue. Our colors don't necessarily reflect our standing. That *only* reflects our affinity links. It has nothing to do with our familial ties. That's all just for helping to discern where we fit per our *function*."

Artorian's sagely nodding continued, stabbing an extra wrench in the spokes. "Of course, my good sir. Blue matches blue, so it must be the water dungeons you are suited to."

Solid rhyming, and yet the pink Wisps silently squeezed their eyes shut and looked down, shoulders bouncing as they worked to keep the sound in. Nope! That was them again! Invictus turned red, and threw his proverbial hat to the ground. "I am a celestial affinity Wisp! I match celestial affinity dungeons, because of the specific psychological quirks I cancel out. A single affinity, to match a *single* affinity."

Vi *fumed*, and like a dam pressured by too much water, his patience broke. The Wisp freely gushing secrets. "Celestial dungeons, those *stuck up*, self-important pale yellow and gold Cores. Like to irradiate an area with their power, littering it with goods to just lure people in and make them quarrel over the territory. They ignore doing *any* building, doing *any* work, or putting *any* effort into anything aside from lounging on their cozy little thrones, letting everything and everyone else do the work for them. Like a fat Lord in a fat fief. *I*, as a matching Wisp, guide and convince my dungeon to work *with* the other Essence types, because I can convince him they're *useful*."

The blue Wisp was on a roll. "As example! When I asked my dungeon what it was up to, it just mumbled 'something' back at me. When I prodded if that meant it was actually doing 'anything,' it smirked and had one of its favorite creatures perform a lazy stretch, claiming that it did 'everything' around here. I spent years prodding at that prideful, homeless brat to actually make its dungeon. Then just to toy with me, it filled it with *goats*!"

Invictus the Frazzled needed a breath, breaking right back into the topic as he was so far past keeping the proper decorum. This needed to be hurled off his chest. He needed to slam this person and *prove* once and for all that he knew better. "Water-based dungeons have blue Cores, and while they have the full ability to build their own dungeons, they are flighty and prone to distraction. Pink Wisps bond to these blue Cores, specifically *because* they are naturally blessed with the ability to reduce mind altering effects. A pink Wisp can keep a blue Core on task like no other, and that type of combination is a nigh guarantee, as other Wisps will decline *on principle*. It was originally believed that water dungeons went with the flow, but ever since Cal, that theory has been thoroughly drowned."

Pink Wisps were nodding along as the information was provided. Invictus wasn't done; he wasn't going to let this Dragon-turned-man get even an off-hand *quip* in! Not until he was *finished*. "Purple Wisps bond to lapis Cores. Lapis Cores are air affinity dungeons, who, unlike blue Cores, are *not* able to build their own dungeons. They can only occupy and spread to preset or pre-built areas. Thus they rely on purple Wisps, who specialize in using ambient Essence to *reshape areas*."

"In this bonding, it is the Wisp that makes the dungeon, and the dungeon Core that plays backup. Air dungeons are quick to give up and need encouragement, since moving air all the time is tiring. Purple Wisps are natural encouragers, helping their dungeon to keep it up and keep going. They are catalysts, happy to tell their dungeon that they're proud while giving positive reinforcement. Air dungeons are unsure of themselves, and purple Wisps point them to the finish line. Sneaking in little actions they want their dungeon to do via sweet suggestions."

He pointed up at the Silverwood Tree. "As an example, we have a Core here called Mu. Mu didn't do so well when he first got here. He lived Wisp-less for a good majority of his pre-Soul Space days in a bag—and later a treasure chest—because he just couldn't make progress. Once he was here, surrounded by supportive Wisps, he has made the most amazing dire turkey-based dungeon we've ever seen."

Approval from Grace followed, that explanation correct as Vi marched on. "Then you have the complete opposite dynamic with fire affinity dungeons. Green Wisps bond to red Cores. Those Cores, for all their significant power, are *lazy*. They hate doing work more than a celestial dungeon does, which is why green Wisps are so compatible. Fire affinity Wisps are natural *taskmasters*. They know how and where to prod their dungeon to get it moving and make it *do* some *work*. A fire dungeon will happily rage all day and play around without a second thought, but rarely do anything with substantial value. Fire dungeons delight in turning up the heat against adventurers, and will forget entirely that they rely on these same adventurers to grow. Green Wisps know how to handle these uncouth little children, and innately know the difference between when to spank them and when to thank them."

The green Wisps smiled wryly, secretly pleased at the mention. "Orange Wisps bond to green dungeons. As earth affinity Cores are uncanny *perfectionists*, they will find one, *tiny*, specific thing they want to work on and plow forward solely in that vein. They are horribly forgetful of any project they are not currently working on, and suffer from tunnel vision that can't be dwarfed. Orange Wisps are *fantastic* at soothing, and can make their dungeon pay attention to *quantity*, rather than *quality*. An earth dungeon will work on *one* thing, *forever*, if you let it. Earth dungeons will make the single most majestic entryway while the rest of their dungeon falls apart, if orange Wisps didn't help them be more attentive."

The orange Wisps shoved a thumbs up in Vi's direction. That was on the nose. "Silver Wisps bond with opal-black dungeons, as those hungry Cores brim with infernal. An infernal dungeon surprisingly isn't a glutton for matter, as much as it is a glutton for material. *Informational* material. Given the option, an infernal dungeon wouldn't leave a library until every last scrap of know-how had been consumed. They thrive by gaining knowledge, and will endlessly break down anything and everything to keep on learning. To a fault! As they will never put anything *back*. Silver Wisps force the dungeon to replace what has been lost and destroyed, because otherwise there would only be an ever more sizable *hole* in the ground."

Silver Wisps agreed in unison. Again, a correct portrayal

concerning the kind of headache they had to deal with. "Infernal dungeons are so hungry for new things that they tend to border on the ravenous and monstrous, and it is only by the grace of Silver Wisps that they are—for lack of a better term—humanized. Infernal Wisps instill fairness, cleverness, and the importance of social connectivity. Just to stop an infernal dungeon from eating anything that walked through its doors in the most unfair manner. Because unfair dungeons just get hunted down. With an infernal Wisp, they gain the crucial trait of patience. Teaching the dungeon about timing and how important it is to not reveal one's hand too early."

Artorian had remained silent for now, but gently motioned in the direction of a salmon colored one in their midst.

Vi sharply inhaled. "Pure affinities of a single type are the most direct and plain examples that can be easily correlated to the dungeon in question that is best for them to bond with. It is also the case that dungeons with *multiple* affinities function best with a Wisp that also has *multiple* matching traits. *Talia the Fourth* comes from a long line of Wisps, who all mix the earth and water affinities. Pink and orange mixes visually to produce her lovely *salmon* hue."

Artorian thought he followed. "She then matches best to a dungeon with both the relevant water and earth affinities?"

Talia the Fourth laced her fingers, and calmly gave a single nod. That had been the way of things in her family line. Her clothing altered temporarily to a soft teal, before her salmon-colored dress regained its original luster.

Invictus took the display as an opportunity for yet another stick to smack the miser with. "Wisps communicate not in a spoken language, but in an emotional display of colors, feelings, and imagery. Our coloration always restores itself to our affinity, even if a bond with a dungeon can change that base color permanently."

He smirked in his assumed superiority. "*Several times*, if the circumstances are correct. If a dungeon somehow manages to gain new affinities—rare, though it does happen—the linked

Wisp will gain the benefits of such a discovery, and rise in power as well. The more affinities established, the higher in the courts such a Wisp sits. It is therefore improper and impolite to speak to a Wisp with more affinities without their prior assent."

The Administrator was starting to understand the political landscape. "Intriguing. Though I did see everyone defer to Grace earlier. From what I could tell, she's young, and of single alignment. Yet you all fell in line regardless."

Invictus was going to loudly speak of the topic, but he stilled without another word when Talia the Fourth stood. The hierarchy at play, no doubt.

Her voice was brusque, and full of push. "It has been an enjoyable routine of comedy to watch you work, master Administrator. No need to quirk your brow at me, the Matron has spoken of you in discussion. Before more is said, I must ask with sincerity that you do not further divulge what you have heard. These are court secrets that our frazzled blue has let slip."

Artorian paused, and shot Invictus a questioning look. Marie, off in the distance, pretended that she could hear nothing. Vi gave a reply under his breath. "The socially accepted response is to stand, and lightly bow as I did when first greeting you."

Understanding the necessary convention, the Administrator stood and proceeded to do so. His clothing was nothing fancy, as simple robes were all he could make by himself. He'd needed to do *something* with all that extra dragon-mane fluff.

Still, the act was sufficient for Talia the Fourth, who gently closed her eyes to make an approving head motion. She spoke slowly when Artorian sat, the brusqueness gone entirely from her voice. "Above the courts sits Dani, our Matron. As an all-affinity Wisp, her location in the hierarchy goes unquestioned. While she may stick to her current purple coloration, it is merely for the comfort of her dungeon. Grace, her dearest, may be of a single affinity, but that in no way means we do not respect the family line. It is that same family line that keeps her in the psychological stance she chooses to portray."

Artorian frowned deeply, trying to follow. Talia understood the difficulty, and continued her explanation. "Cal, the dungeon we reside in, carries a burden that one Wisp cannot fully contend with. While Grace may not be his direct Wisp, she functions as a member of his family line. In that family line, it is incredibly beneficial for Cal to have a daughter who is young. Her giddy, childlike laughter sets him at ease."

She made a welcoming hand sign. "This lessens his heavy burdens. While she could have chosen to grow up, in order to best assist with her function in the family line, she remains as such. We are all aware of the situation we find ourselves in, and do not find this choice uncouth. In the age of old, this behavior would have been crass, as the supported motion would be for her to find her own dungeon. Those who know of the original court rules turn a blind eye, as that isn't properly possible here."

Talia motioned at the vast Silverwood Tree above them. "While Cores do grow, they cannot flourish. Not *here*. All but a few rest in slumber eternal, waiting to be released so they may properly awaken and grow in a place where there is an over-abundance of their particular Essence combination. This is the function of the dungeon Core, after all. To balance the world where it has excess Essence. To curate that which would other-wise overflow, and wreak havoc."

Illuminating!

Artorian didn't make his customary 'go on' hand motion. He felt that, in this instance, it would be rude. Talia appreciated the restraint as she explained a tidbit of Wisp culture, as it was more dangerous for Artorian not to know at this point. "In our social convention, while it is allowable to speak of another Wisp, it is not allowable to speak *for* them. Thus why I rested Invictus, and now speak myself. If a Wisp of higher court status wishes to speak, the rest must fall silent. This is the way."

The Administrator stood again, performing the appropriate bow for the situation. It was sufficient, and Talia sat. Grace shot forwards since the others were done, her arms stretched out wide towards him. He had learned what she wanted him to learn, and it was time for him to go before her mother showed up. "You have awms now! Up!"

Stifling his own laugh even as the smile slapping his face couldn't be stopped, Artorian dropped to a knee in order to hug the sweet Wispling, picking her up to carry her like any other five-year-old that needed to be held for a while. He released a deep exhale, vision returning to stare up at the vast silver-leafed tree. "Right. Well then. That was incredibly insightful. I suppose it would be best if I go ahead and get to *work*."

Grace squeezed her arms around his neck. It seemed he was going to have a *tag-along*. Marie walked within twenty paces of them. Though not a single *inch* closer. More mystery hierarchy? She cleared her throat, and pointed at a specific branch a mile or two up. "Henry's over in that cluster. Mind if we start there? On the way up there, you can tell me how you figured out humanization in… what? *Two hours*? It's farther than it looks."

With a nod, and additional bow to excuse himself from the Wisps, both the Mages shifted their flight into activity, bursting from the ground like fireworks. Artorian released a liberated *Whe~e~ee*!

It was good to be in a *comfortable* body again.

CHAPTER FORTY-ONE

Grace's smile spread wide as they zipped between massive branches. Her screeches erupted proud and loud as Artorian practiced his flight skills by taking some peculiarly *sharp* turns. He needed to make sure that the Dragon-bone Runescripting was *properly* repressed. It seemed to be, but that wasn't good enough.

Marie shouted after them as she followed from behind. Irritated, since rather than a straight journey to Henry as she'd wanted, this had been an exercise in *detours*. "Will you *stop* playing around!"

Artorian considered it for a moment, then whispered the question to a clinging Grace. "Should we slow down?"

The Wisp shook her head 'no' with resolute vigor, instead sharply pointing upwards with an antagonizing arch of her brows. Onwards! Well. Grace had spoken. The Administrator glanced over his shoulder, replying to the Queen. "Sorry, Marie~e~e! Gotta go *fa~a~ast!*"

Marie's helmet fluted like a fully charged pressure cooker, her armor glowing hot and red as a cracking boom expanded from the Administrator's vacated position. That cheeky brat had taken off at Mach five! Between *Silverwood branches*! When she caught him, she was going to tear him a new one! "Artoria~a~an!"

Boom.

Avoiding even the largest of branches was a true test of Mage dexterity and response time. Especially when going at these breakneck speeds. Grace didn't in the slightest mind the rollercoaster ride, shrieking to go faster.

Artorian agreed wholeheartedly with a '*Ha!*' as his face dodged a lesser branch. He wanted to speed up some more, but a powerful grip squeezed around his ankle before he could turn and up the ante. Marie's grasp threw him off-course entirely. He sped up, but only enough for him to slam flat against his back along the underside of a bigger branch. Mach five or not, the Silverwood Tree didn't even dent. *Ooofooo*!

"I. Said. Stop. Playing. *Around*." Marie's armored digits drummed loudly on the metal of her bicep once she came to a standstill, her hover a menacing one. Her armor was still sizzling, and Artorian shook his head to get the daze out.

"*Fhoo*. Well, I'd say I can fly well enough. How are you holding up, Grace?"

The humanized Wisp had also smacked her face against a minor branch while mid-swing, but no amount of leaves between her teeth was stopping that boundless enthusiasm. "*More!*"

"Young lady, that is *quite* enough!" Grace's mirth dropped to a cold shiver. Her human form vanished with a *pop* as the purple ball quickly hid inside the chest pocket of Artorian's robe.

Dani was here.

Her voice matched Marie's in its upset cadence, but Artorian pulled his robe shut just a little bit more, clearly pretending he hadn't the foggiest where Grace might be hiding. No matter how much the bump in the cloth covering his heart shivered.

He shot Marie an innocent smile. "See, Marie? Dani agrees with me, and even considers you a young lady. It was fi~i~ine."

Thunk.

"*Ow!*"

Both of the Administrator's hands moved to the bruise on the top of his head. Dani had reprimanded and smacked him with some solid Mana. Even though she was in her orb form, he could feel the judging glare. Though the furious red color may have had something to do with it.

Dani wasn't happy. "Not a *peep* out of you. You steal a body out of Cal's warehouse, change it without permission, and then wriggle the most secret of information out of a talkative Wisp? Invictus isn't going to get *half* the beatdown you're about to get!"

Artorian's jaw clamped shut, and not by his own volition. He mumbled something, but even that was stifled in front of the two rather... *displeased* ladies. His straightened finger, present to make a point, curled in weakly, then fell away entirely as Grace peeked from the inside of his robe.

Dani was cross with *her* as well. "*Come. Here.*"

Grace looked up at Artorian, but he was all out of options to protect and defend her at this point. The purple Wisp sighed weakly, bobbing in a half-hearted wave over to Mom. Her head hung when she pulled up next to the currently furious red mommy Wisp. "Good. Marie? I'll take it from here. I'm not letting you suffer antics from our Administrator any longer. Please take my little one to Henry so she can repair that connection... a task she should have been working on *this entire time*."

Grace turned a queasier shade of purple, and silently bobbed over to rest in Marie's upturned palm. Her armor wasn't red hot anymore. That was a... *plus?* Artorian mentally winced at the thought. *He* was still in the fire as Dani snapped at him. "*You*. With me. *Now*."

The Administrator wasn't about to fight with the Wisp Matron. After a slight wave to Grace, he couldn't suppress feeling Marie glare at him from behind her helmet. Her free hand sharply extended to point in Dani's direction.

He didn't need to be told twice! "I'm going, *I'm going!*"

Dani took off, and he swiftly followed. Their journey was one spent without words, and perhaps that was for the best as Artorian watched Dani shift between a variety of colors that showcased her personal emotional states shift through fields and varieties of 'upset.' He supposed he *had* just gotten a hold of rather valuable information. He doubted that giving Grace a laugh was a sufficient reason for this much anger.

Dani led him straight to his own Core, where another Wisp was waiting impatiently for them. Wait. *He* had a Wisp? He wasn't a dungeon!

It was a *green* Wisp. *Oh no.* Not *another* mind trying to keep him on point. Why did this keep happening? He had Zelia! Before that… ah. Gran'mama, Jiivra, Yvessa… Right, this seemed to be a bit of a *trend.* It might ever so slightly be helpful when he had someone to prod him to do specific work. Though green Wisps bonded with… what was it, Fire Cores? Red Cores were lazy… he wasn't *lazy*! A moment of consideration later, and he was already thinking about being buried neck-deep in a room full of pillows. Where *nobody* could bother him. Okay… a *little* lazy. Just a little!

Dani stabilized when she hovered next to the waiting Wisp, who performed the Wisp version of their court bow. Visually, the act was little more than a bob in mid-air, but it had *nuances* to it. There was also something oddly familiar about the green dot. He couldn't put his finger on it until the Wisp spoke. Well, *abyss*, he knew *that* voice. Dani addressed her, checking up on current progress. "Yvessa, how does it look?"

Hearing it confirmed stirred Artorian. Maybe this was all a set of curious, accidental circumstances? "*Uhm.* This isn't the Yvessa I know, right? She should be safe on my wall."

The green Wisp altered her pending response, as a salt-boulder-sized chip needed to be removed from her shoulder. Her color flared, voice booming. "You *insufferable codger*! You kept me on a *wall* for celestial-knows-how-long. Were you trying to get away from me? Do you have any idea how *angry I was* at learning you've been keeping the entire Fringe village tidy and snug on a *wall*? I woke up inside of a room I couldn't in the slightest recognize, and suffered a *week* of headaches as I was explained all I had missed. Push comes to shove, and the culprit responsible is the same nosy Elder I used to *swaddle*. Because he just couldn't wait to poke at more of his corruption. I found out a week ago that you were a Mage, and yet: *surprise, surprise.* No amount of support staff keeping you on track seems to work. What a *shock.*"

Artorian forced a smile, eagerly looking around for an escape route. Given his Core was *right there*, and that a Wisp version of Yvessa was hovering dangerously close right above it. Best to just… let her at it. "Then I get asked very *kindly* if I would be up for helping to handle a *slightly out of control* Administrator, as I had prior experience. The only downside was that the body I would need to inhabit wasn't a *human* one."

A harmless-looking wooden spoon appeared next to the green Wisp. "A *small* price to pay to do *this* to you."

The spoon *whapped* down on the celestine colored Core. It was the pearly center of an unfurling silver flower on one of the many, many lesser branches. When the wooden implement struck, Artorian's entire world *shook*. The world itself didn't budge; but the transfer of information between his current body, and the Core he was actually in, experienced *serious turbulence*. His flight winked out on the spot, and he scrambled to grab the side of the wide branch as he fell, hauling himself up while existence *spun*.

Wisp-Yvessa leered at him. "Paying attention *now*?"

It took several minutes for Artorian to be willing to have anything less than a clinging death-grip on the branch below him. That was how long it took for the vertigo shocks of even that *tiny* impact to go away. Crackers. That was one *abyss* of a weakness. "M'here… I'm here. Please don't do that again. That was… *awful*. So awful."

Yvessa threatened to bap the Core again, and Artorian reflexively went right back to clinging to the branch below him. His face scrunched in expectation of being struck by nausea.

The vertigo didn't come, and he opened an eye to peek before looking up at the Wisp duo. Dani hummed bright pink *satisfaction*. That *devious* little… he felt a sizable chunk of empathy for Cal. Wisps were *cheeky*!

"Alright. *Alright*! I lose. What's the deal?" He groaned out the words, forehead pressing to the pleasantly cool temperature of the branch.

Yvessa made the spoon go away. Had he heard right? If she'd barely been a Wisp for a short length of time, how was she so good at… Wisp*ing*? How did you describe being a Wisp and being good at what a Wisp does? *No idea*. Didn't currently matter. Yvessa huffed. "That's better. In short, you need supervision. So I'm going to tag along and stick to your shoulder. We're going to check and repair every single Core on the tree, and only *after* do you get to go *galivant*."

Artorian silently replied with a thumbs up. He wasn't fighting this either. "You got it. How do we get started?"

Dani bobbed at Yvessa, again with defining nuances that told the observer it was a motion of appreciation. One that included an 'I leave it in your capable hands.' Yvessa proudly returned to her natural coloration, hovering above the celestine Core. "You can start by getting up and touching your own Core so we can get your current mind aligned. Then we can start mending the connection."

Getting up and pressing his hand to the orb, clarity rushed to Artorian's faculties. Connecting his mind to his body served as a breath of fresh air for his weariness. Like he'd just woken up from a week-long nap. His thoughts filtered in easily, and the difficulty in remembering ceased. A sharp pitch in his ears also subsided, and he noticed only because it was now missing. He appreciated the relief regardless. "That is *much* better. I'd prefer it to stay like this, rather than feel some kind of *splintering*. How do I help prevent this from happening again?"

Yvessa was glad she didn't need to get the whip out right away. Or spoon in her case. "It was explained to me that, in this world, something *tore*. The tears are physical, and destroy or shatter what they touch. Some of those tears happened in this tree, or moved through it. We are tasked with finding these tears, and filling them back up. Someone named 'Cal' is healing the tears from this area first, even if he doesn't seem to be aware of it, which is a topic I just don't understand. Then again, I don't need to. See that big cut in the branch where you were lying? Add Essence to it."

Artorian looked to the spot. Now that he was specifically looking for it, he did notice a wire-thin cut that went rather deep. Kneeling down next to the wound, he hummed to himself. How best to heal a tree? Well, maybe just 'adding Essence in' was the way to go where this was concerned. Normal botany was out of its depth when it came to Silverwood Trees.

Keeping his hand pressed to the wound, he invoked his Mana, directing it to restore harm, as that seemed more effective than just pouring some on. It appeared shortly after that it hadn't mattered much. Mana was small cheese compared to Spirit, which appeared to be what was required.

The natural density of his Mana allowed for the conversion to happen apace. His Tower tier easily allowed him to release a quality of Essence that didn't need to condense or gather further for a trade to occur.

His Mana just globbed, filling the space as the wound closed up while Yvessa hovered nearby. With the Wisp's careful attention, the wound closed. Gently melding new wood with the original as the energy altered to form Silverwood matter at her direction.

Clearing even that small cut made a pleasant warmth cross Artorian's shoulders as the connection to his celestine Core came that much easier. Yes. *This* was important. Standing, he half turned with hands pressed on his hips, and Yvessa was pleased the old codger still retained his work ethic as he spoke. Youthful body or not. "Where is the next one?"

CHAPTER FORTY-TWO

Exactly how much time was spent mending the scars was an uncertainty, though the guess would have to be measured in months. Artorian just knew he'd needed to stop and cultivate like the old times, *twice*. Cultivating had offered a nice break from an activity that had otherwise turned out to be monotonous.

Surely *this* wasn't what Scilla had needed him to hurry for? Since all he could do was play Mana battery for a process only a Wisp could handle, Artorian spent a large amount of time seated in meditative self-reflection, letting his Essence fill the damage while his taskmaster worked to apply the healing.

The taxing process was less dull when surprise visitors dropped by to check in on them and their progress. Unfortunately. He learned that during such events he needed to keep working. He couldn't stray too far from a wound currently being tended once his Mana transfer started. Such was the way of things. So Yvessa did the talking.

Marie and Henry had come by, delivering good news that Aiden's Core was close to safely reconnecting. Artorian had asked Henry how he'd gotten a body, and Marie cut in that he'd copied the cheat Artorian had used himself. A Beast body that was compatible, reformed into a convenient human one.

Good to know that worked for more than just him. Even if it made the Administrator *suspicious*. Artorian was locking down his entire Presence and Aura capacities just to *keep* this human form. Henry *didn't* have those skills, yet was visibly having far less difficulty than him to attain the same result. Definitely *suspicious*. Artorian was sad that he hadn't the chance to ask before they left.

Chandra had also come to say hello, but more because Yvessa and Artorian had run into a snag with a particularly confusing wound. The piece of Silverwood was infected, rather than missing wire-cut chunks. Chandra had directed them to excise and cut the damaged parts away, and to burn them after. The downside of cutting away the afflicted patches was that those sections would have to be replaced entirely. A price they'd have to pay, as the tarry bits would otherwise spread. Given it was only Yvessa that could modify the Silverwood, that did provide Artorian some cultivation time.

The source of the tar was found late, but didn't come as a surprise. Artorian and Yvessa scratched their heads, wondering how to handle the current Core with all the grayish-black lines spreading out from it.

To the great misery of them all, the Core the tar was spreading from was *Eternium*. Yvessa verbalized her distaste. "That's a *lot* of tar. The entire *branch* is afflicted. I'm not even sure what to do here. This wasn't in the instructions. Do we just cut the *entire branch* off? What do we do about the Core?"

Artorian shrugged. "Why not just *pluck* it? Stick it somewhere else. Not like it can stay where it is."

Yvessa waffled on the suggestion. "I don't know... That seems dangerous. Maybe we could... hey. *No. Don't pull the—*"

Pop!

The green Wisp shrieked while inhaling, the sound one of absolute panic. When nothing further happened, she hovered away without a word and plunked down on a non-tarry branch just to yell into the bark. To *cope*.

Artorian hovered mid-air, Eternium's Core kept in hand like it was just some apple. Odd how a triple S-ranked entity just… *neatly* fit in his palm. This thing could have easily wiped him out of existence outside the Soul Space, but here… even Eternium was limited to remaining one rank below Cal's current level. Odd how it was so quiet. Should he shake it like a snow globe? *May~ybe* not. There were people in there that he cared about. Such as Decorum. Best to treat the Core with care, even if Eternium strongly disagreed with the way he did things inside of that realm. He spoke to it, unsure if the core could hear him at all. "Everything's going to be alright."

When Yvessa returned, he showed her that Eternium was just fine. "All's well. I've got the Core. Let's just slice the whole branch off and… What's that *zipping* noise?"

The Administrator looked around, trying to get a fix on the sharp whistle that was clearly getting closer. Oh, it was a Wisp! The charging orange glow clearly meant to smash him right in the face, but Artorian snatched him before impact. "*Gotcha!*"

The orange Wisp fought against the Mage's fingers, released only after the mad bouncing ceased. Artorian was never intending on keeping the lad trapped, but once free it was *moody*. "You let my dungeon go this *instant!*"

Artorian blinked, and glanced at the green Core in his hand. Orange Wisp, green diamond Core. Eternium had started out as an earth affinity dungeon? Well, *no wonder* he was a perfectionist with tunnel vision! That was exactly the down-side Invictus had spoken of. That made it nice and clear why he wanted the game system to fall in line so much, even without considering the **Order Law** at play. "Sure. Where would you like me to put him? I won't put him back in the tar."

The fighting spirit of the orange Wisp petered out. The plucker wasn't here to cause him a grievance? That would be a first, and the moody voice calmed without losing any of its haste. "Erm… let me just find a spot."

"What's your name?" Artorian directed his question to the distracted Wisp, thinking it was polite to ask. Calling him *mandarin* came to mind, but that was just to be a snoot.

The orange Wisp turned to face him, not seeing a good location in the vicinity. "I've had a few. It's hard to tell, but I'm older than Eternium is. Call me Oberon. Please do not stand on courtship social convention with me. I am tired of the displays, and quite sick of them. Yes, I know courtship means what it does. Still *no*, if you don't mind. Could I ask you for *your* name?"

Artorian smiled, and took a breath to answer. He didn't. There was a *glint* to Oberon's orange sheen. A *suspicious* one. He'd already had his fill with Henry, and there was no celestial way he wasn't discovering the details of this one!

Rather than verbalize a response, Artorian channeled Mana to his **Law**, desiring to perceive what Fae trickery was at play. While he expected shenaniganry, he hadn't expected the sheer *depth* of the network he was currently looking at. "Well... I would say you can ask. Though, based on what I'm looking at, the particular phrasing of your question implies that if I tell you my name, I am quite literally giving it to you. It will no longer be mine. That's quite a *sneaky* trick of you, Oberon. I do not grant you my name, but I will let you know what it is. My name is Artorian, and I would say it is nice to meet you if not for this *guile* you just slapped me with."

Oberon's grinning smile was toothy. Even if he didn't have any teeth. "Oh, I *like* you. Tricks like this are what keep my dungeon on his toes. Eternium is clever now, but in the beginning he loved to just ignore me and what I said in favor of working on his projects. He learned different, becoming very wary of the wording involved in any interaction with me. It snapped him from his trances, and made him wise to both my wiles, and that we should be working on a broader range of projects. It's also what got him so good at contracts and land oaths. Always pay attention to the *fine print*. Spoken or otherwise."

Artorian quietly listened, but tilted his head as another light-blue dot was rushing to their current location. "Friend of yours?"

Oberon sighed softly. Looked like this was all the time he was going to get before needing to get back to work. "That would be Niall. Celestial aquamarine Wisp. He's a good sort for all his work in chasing after... well. *Me*. Much like a certain dungeon, I also tend to focus on topics rather deeply. Niall is my support Wisp for making sure I don't dig myself into a hole I can't get out of. Niall *can* be scatterbrained, so if I'm not paying attention to my surroundings and him, then I am inviting disaster upon my house. Not that he does anything bad, but he gets distracted like I get focused. Nice balance."

The Administrator understood that kind of circus act, glancing over his shoulder to silently look at a waiting Yvessa. She was already tapping a spoon onto open air, as if she pretended there was a hand there. He could just about *feel* the impact. Best get back to work. "Right, well I'm going to help cut this branch off and get to restoring. Maybe if it heals back the way it was, and we get lucky, we can plunk the Core right back where it belongs. How about that?"

Oberon liked that idea. Especially because that would be convenient. "I'm all for it. Let Niall and I help to make sure the restoration goes well. It will be easier with three Wisps, rather than *one*. Though she seems... *scarily* capable. Why does she make me fear for my life?"

Artorian snickered. "That would be the natural response, my new friend. Do be wary of that spoon. It's *dangerlicious*."

Thunk.

"*Ow*."

Yvessa's spoon dangerously threatened another strike. "Distracting yourself from work by *making friends*? I'm getting the distinct feeling he's another *ploying plotter*. Oberon, was it? Are you going to hover there *all pretty*, or will you get your hovering light over here and help?"

The orange Wisp stilled. A momentary flush of pink

crossing his edges as he turned to address Niall. "Did you hear that? She called me pretty."

The aquamarine Wisp said nothing in reply, and casually hovered a foot backwards. *Thunk*! Oberon vibrated like an oversized bell. His flight pattern anything but straight as he wavered in an uncertain line until Niall caught him. "*Ow*! Niall! You're supposed to protect me from danger!"

The sigh from the celestial affinity Core came with depth. "I've explained this before, Obi. Large, deadly threat? Absolutely. Yet another angry and upset lady that is chasing you with a kitchen implement for something you did all by yourself? *No*."

Oberon was mockingly affronted, clearly playing. "You are a Wisp Champion! You protect me from everything!"

Niall let the orange Wisp go, his response matching his agreeing nod. "Including yourself. She's going to hit you again."

The spoon whizzed down and missed. Oberon had spun out of the way, moving with perfect flight in a pattern only a Wisp could. Observing the event made Artorian smile. That kind of sharp-angled precision flying had been so swift that the after-glow of an open orange triangle slowly faded from his eyes. Now *that* was a perfect flight!

His smile also faded when the spoon turned his direction. "Hey now, I'm just waiting on the verdict! Don't look at me with that murderous cook gaze like I just nicked the last block of cheese from your pantry. Are we cutting the whole branch or what?"

Yvessa stared him down like a mouse that *had* in fact taken the last block of cheese. It was Niall that helped make the decision, since Oberon was ready for full evasive maneuvers, and he recognized that the green Wisp was, in some odd fashion, young. "The infection spread far too deep. This entire branch needs to go. We will need more Mages than just yours, Yvessa. Though if he's all we have, then so be it. The Core in his hand is what Oberon was all up in arms for. Given there's no threat to Eternium, we can begin right away. I know where to cut the branch, and no other Cores live further down the path. It is safe to excise. Please move back a moment. I am making the cut."

As the others moved away, aquamarine light solidified around Niall. The oblong forms shaped into long blades of matching-color grass, visibly sharpening as the edges took on an intimidating golden glow. The sound of whips moved through the air, taking the span of less than an eighth of a second to make all the precision incisions. Without so much as a croak or a crack, the tarry branch began to fall. A sound emanated from Oberon akin to the snap of fingers, and flame surrounded the falling branch. "That should be clean ash by the time it hits the ground. Nothing like a little fertilizer."

Oberon tried to look like he'd done all the heavy lifting, but the other three were staring down, rather than at him. Well, that was no good! It was just a burning branch, nothing inter-esting to see there. Looking down himself, his expression moved to match the frown of the other three. The branch was no longer burning. Stranger still, it wasn't *falling*. It just hovered awkwardly in mid-air. Yvessa chimed in, uncertain. "Is that supposed to happen?"

The branch crumpled in on itself. This time, the expected croaking, crunching, and cracking sounds very much did accompany the display. The condensing pops and tarry splotches continued to collapse into a single space, until a shiny black orb was all that remained.

Oberon and Niall answered in unison. "No."

"Ah. Then this does not bode well."

CHAPTER FORTY-THREE

The orb didn't stay an orb, and the onlookers were speechless as further changes occurred. From the tarry substance, a muscled arm cadaverously tore itself free. Using the sphere itself as a floor to push up and away from, more and more of a quasi-human shaped body erupted free from the diminishing source.

A pit formed in Artorian's stomach. A painfully familiar one as the creature wrested itself out of the tar. When it had, the orb was no more. Matter consumed in the forming of this... thing. It spoke like a *gutter*, and then Artorian *knew*. "Sumptuous suffrage! Extricated at last!"

Artorian swallowed, his hand weakly motioning for the Wisps to run. He spoke hesitantly, trying to find solace in what were proving to be poorly rooted facts. "This isn't right. You *died*. You should be dead. I watched you break into a thousand chunks from the inside out. Banished back to the *abyss*."

The stretching being deformed. Breaking its own neck to twist its vision all the way around, even if it was just its head turning. "*Curious*. You know of me? Pleasing that the tales of Torture Savant *Ghreziz* still live!"

Ghreziz popped as the majority of his body moved while

the head remained immobile. He grinned maliciously wide, even if some expected solidity was lacking as he checked himself over. "What a *peculiar* form. No matter. The tar will provide me mastery soon. Though it appears I was not entombed for long enough. *No matter.*"

The greater demon squeezed his claw shut, and a wave of brisk infernal power resonated across his forming knuckles. It easily spiked into the A-ranks, even without a Mage serving as host body. Ghreziz considered this minor setback, then realized a body was conveniently available. Right before him! As an added bonus, he pointed at the Core in Artorian's hand. "What a fate it must be to be both fortuitous and lucky. I emerge, and come to face a mind that both knows me and *brings* me what I seek! Without so much as me needing to ask."

The demon's eyes formed glossy as onyx, and with his vision came confusion. Ghreziz kept his claw outstretched, as if awaiting the gift of an offering. Up until this moment, he had thought the Mage a servant, and the Core merely a delivery. The Mage's words hadn't properly clicked, save that it had recognized him for what he was. A demon of the deep abyss. A savant. Forming the ability to see, the uncanny likeness to an undesirable *misery* was all that stained the abyssalite's thoughts. "Wretched foulness! You must be the son of that long-bearded fool responsible for my last vanquishing."

This seemed like an excellent spot where they should run for it. Artorian had the thought, turned just as swiftly, and managed a single step before he realized something *else* was wrong. Yvessa's invisible face was wrenched apologetically, and his eyes followed the tether of Mana she was holding. She had already begun the process of mending the branch, and his Mana was *locked* to it. He wasn't going anywhere over thirty paces. *Abyss.* No wonder they hadn't run. Just like him, Yvessa was entirely *unable* to flee.

The lethargy of their responses, as they spent precious seconds realizing their additional problems, provided Ghreziz the moments he needed to parse memories back together. He wasn't all here *yet*, but he would be. Barry's plan, after all, was foolproof. "Yesss. I remember now. You have his *nose*. That blasphemous *sympathy Mage*. I was going to welcome you with my offerings, but instead I believe I'll crush you as an insect. If merely to *slake* my thirst for vengeance."

A fight was pending, and even though it was four versus one, Artorian did not like his odds. The last time, he'd had *options*. A Mana storm, frame of reference dilation, Presence control, Auric effects... all of those were currently *canned*. He was bleeding Mana, rooted to Yvessa's vicinity, and was *certainly* going to need to protect her. Oberon and Niall were wildcards, but he felt the sudden weight of the Core in his hand. Reminded that this also happened to be exactly what his old enemy was after. He didn't quite have a grasp on Barry before, but given the company he kept... Artorian decided he was going to rip him asunder.

If he survived *today*.

Pocketing Eternium inside his robe where Grace had hidden, his worried eyes glanced over to the other two Wisps. His voice the barest of whispers, even though he was certain they all could hear him. "Please tell me you can *fight*."

Ghreziz chuckled, and an orange light became responsible for pulling Artorian's robe by the neckline, tugging him out of the way of an infernally laced fist that whooshed through the space his face had been. So fast! Ghreziz was of a higher rank than him? He couldn't win here!

Aquamarine grass blades whipped through the air, blocking the second blow as Oberon again pulled Artorian out of the way of what would have been a nasty snatch. The orange ball fumed, red on the edges. "Pay attention! You are distracted! Stop focusing so hard on what's eating you!"

Oberon's priority was for the *thing* not to get its claws on his dungeon, so pulling this Mage out of the way was the best he could do while Niall stepped up to the plate. Wisp *Champion* wasn't just some fancy title, as aquamarine crystal blades sprung into existence, slashing at the tarry fiend with calculated abandon. "Obi, *go!*"

Artorian's eyes cleared when he caught up to the reality of the situation. An *embarrassing* display for him. He was so caught up thinking about what he couldn't do that he hadn't paid attention to all the things he still *could* do. Ember's change of axiom came to mind.

Lesson one: If you can't, *try anyway*.

Channeling Mana to his feet, the Mage darted to the underside of the branch. His feet stuck to it without difficulty as the Core he had just stuffed into his inner pocket was palmed. Pushing it against Oberon mid-movement with some sleight of hand. Artorian wordlessly mouthed 'Go!' at the Wisp. His stride continued unbroken as he came up the branch from the other end, a technique he thought he'd never use springing to life in his hand.

From the Elves of the wood, he had learned utility techniques that had fallen to the wayside. However, those techniques were *refined*, not reliant on Cal's currently non-functioning Pylon system. He didn't need to test it, he could feel the lack of connection and hear the loud static as easily as he could breathe. Purple Heartwood's 'Instant Bo' came to mind.

With a brush of his fingers across the Silverwood bark, the technique allowed him to grasp a piece while moving. Rearing up as his arm rose, a Silverwood staff successfully formed out of the branch, the business edge of which swiftly descended upon the top of Ghreziz's unwitting head.

Thunk!

The staff *held!* Smashing into the bark from Marie chasing him, and not leaving a *dent*, had become useful. The Silverwood was *sturdier* than he. Ghreziz didn't appreciate the finer details of the technique. Instead he broke his own neck, twisting his head to face the miscreant while temporarily locked down by Niall's crystal grass.

A gout of infernal fire roasted across Artorian's form, yet when the blackened flames faded, only a bark-quality skin coated the young warrior. From underneath the impromptu helmet, defiant radiant eyes shone. "Baobab. *Fire immunity*."

Taking a breath in the tiny moment that Ghreziz was bewildered that his flames for some reason hadn't melted the nuisance from the inside out. He also gained enough control over himself to outright rip free of the grass whips, shattering Niall's technique and forcing him to reform it.

Though even Niall knew that at this point they were just *stalling* for time. Ghreziz may have been tricked, but Niall knew with certainty that an invisible Oberon was speeding off like a child with an ill-gotten prize. The demon's attention was kept on them, and it needed to stay that way. Unfortunately, that meant Ghreziz's rage was kept squarely on the annihilation of them both. "You lack your father's skills, *whelp*! At least he knew to come at me without direct engagement. I am a *Torture Savant*! You think *melee* is my weakness?"

The breath Artorian took erupted with another strike of the bo. The Mage warrior spun it in his hands, stepping back to increase the stick's momentum as it aimed squarely for Ghreziz's ribs. The demon wasn't so careless, blocking it with his arm. Concern wasn't even a consideration for the creature of the abyss, and his grinning smirk spoke that truth in volumes. Until Artorian's technique went off. Or rather, *Mahogany's*.

Channeling the sonic voice technique that old Sultan loved to use with his claps, Artorian spun the ability into the whirling stick. Striking with reverberations that hammered the point of impact repeatedly! A hundred strikes occurred while he performed the work of one. His voice may have been silent, but Ghreziz's bicep sounded like it had been struck a multitude of times in far less than a second. For the first time in this bout, the greater demon *staggered*.

The guttural reply was expectedly unappreciative. "You *dare*! I will possess you and show you pain a thousand-fold for this insult you level upon me. Striking a savant with a *stick*?"

Niall attacked again, but Ghreziz had already understood the pattern, grasping the whipping grass out of midair just to crush it in his palm. Half a spin later, and he roundhouse kicked the Wisp far out of sight. Leaving only a bleeding aquamarine light trail behind. "One *less* nuisance."

So much for the wild cards. Artorian couldn't stay here. This arena was terribly dangerous, and he called out to his old friend in the hope he'd get some good news. "Yvessa! How much longer until it's done?"

Good news was not forthcoming. Yvessa's tone was somber, and her reply dark. "Until it's *done*."

Until it was *done*? Mending some of the larger cuts had easily taken weeks. Here they needed to replace an entire *branch*. He was hard location-locked. *Crackers.* Should he abandon his human guise to gain access to his Aura and Presence toys? It was tempting… but he would revert to the noodle form, and he could control that thing about as well as he could eat actual noodles with chopsticks made from oil. *No dice.*

Something about the youth getting bad news made Ghreziz experience a pleasant shiver. Out of sheer curiosity, he jumped away. To the demon's delight, it was quickly obvious that his quarry *failed* to follow. "Well, isn't that just a *treat.*"

This was a great turn of events for the demon. Not only was this suddenly looking like an easy win, but he could *play* with this toy before he eventually *broke it*, and made it scream like the rest. The youth was so out of sorts that it was even putting on a dumb little dance for him! What were those *ridiculous* move-ments? All the wood-armored child was doing was make some leaves flutter about himself. Ha!

Ghreziz stopped laughing when Silverwood leaves tore through his legs and torso at *Mach eight*. The booming noise didn't throw him off as much as the actual *damage* he took did. His exoshell didn't just crack, like that stick might have if it had hit even a little harder. No, his exoshell suffered straight up *cuts* through it. Those leaves were *sharp*, and of a far more potent density than he was. Was it something about the silver? That was just a *myth*. Though, that dumb little stick hadn't broken against his arm like it should have.

Tsk.

Artorian was pleased as punch to see Cherry's 'petal dance' tear outright holes through the demon. Ghreziz healed his wounds on the spot, some of the tar expending. Well, *toast*. So much for that short-lived victory. The demon sent back an infernal assault of his own.

Artorian attempted to block the incoming cloud of darkness, but even spinning the staff didn't prevent some from getting through and eating away his armor… and *robe*.

Instead of the psychological damage he'd hoped for, Artorian instead watched Ghreziz point, and *laugh*. Ha ha. *Very funny*. The demon must have thought it hilarious to strip him. Quite literally. Artorian just narrowed his eyes, and extended his hand in concentration. "Rosewood… this one's for you. *Flash tailoring*!"

Ghreziz's mirth died as he dumbfoundedly watched the child condense his Mana and expend it by pulling a fully functional robe straight out from the gathered power. Slipping it on, Artorian quick-tied the belt. He rolled his shoulders as if that had been no big deal while speaking in a mocking voice. "*Oh nooo*, embarrassment attacks. My greatest weakness. It's like I've never been around children before that haven't done far worse. I thought you were supposed to be a big-shot demon? Three-year-olds have caused me more grief than you. In their *sleep*."

Pissed and fuming, Ghreziz did not see the trap before him as he roared and charged. He would have gotten a delicious, clean hit in. Yet the robed youth plucked a mystery string that had appeared in mid-air. More lockdown techniques? Paltry! Ghreziz launched himself right through, having no idea that he'd just dashed right through a field of Hawthorne trap lines. When one of the lines broke, the rest whipped around. Unlike Niall's grass blades, Artorian's had the Mana density to do some actual damage. Not that Ghreziz seemed to notice or care that he'd lost *both* legs.

Needing to dart out of the way of the strike as the demon got cut up by wires, Artorian blocked his vision and path to

Yvessa. Now that his foe was *annoyingly* close, he was running out of tools here. The demon had figured out Niall's grass after… What? Two, three tries? He needed to keep his arsenal fresh, or Ghreziz was just going to get a cheap shot in on him. What did he still have? Cotton's 'fluff expansion'? Well, that was *no good* here! There weren't any pillows to… *Oho.* About that.

Much like earlier, wounds and damage were more of an inconvenience for Ghreziz. More of his tar siphoned away, and his exoshell was starting to look *brittle* rather than *goopy*. "Disgusting. You fight too well for a *whelp*. It's a shame that I've decided to consume you rather than possess you. You're not worth the effort. I'm just going to sunder you limb from limb, and send boxes of your remains to that idiotic fluff-lover. Or wherever he's *buried*."

Artorian narrowed his eyes. "Don't. Mock. The pillow."

Those exact words stung a little hard for Ghreziz. They were said with the same pitch. The same tone… His frown deepened, claw rising to an accusatory point. "You…"

Ghreziz's sudden pause was a blessing in disguise. Materializing his Soul Item on the spot, Artorian coated the plushy weapon with his Mana right away to give it extra oomph. As last time, the twelve by twelve crackled with a deep hum. One that emanated a high-pitched *wuuuu*.

Quickly trying to build momentum, he swung the pillow around by a corner as if it were a nunchuck, making further sharp noises himself while whizzing the plush weapon around and bringing it down upon Ghreziz.

To his horrified dismay, Ghreziz *caught it*. The sickening bastard had been *hiding* his power, and his pillow accomplished fluff-nothing. The coating even fizzled out entirely in the demon's lacerating infernal grip. "You're not the *son* of that Mage. You *are* that Mage. Scratch my prior commitment! You've discovered a method to become young again? A *true* immortal body? Oh… I am *definitely* going to possess you."

His voice oozed with greed. "Until the end of time."

CHAPTER FORTY-FOUR

Ghreziz inhaled deep as his form shifted to a more beastly one. His features popped once more from within, allowing bat-like wings to stretch and twist from his back. Quills and spines rippled over his exoshell, and his teeth shone like onyx shards as he craned his neck in an elaborate side to side lull of pleasure. "Nnn. How sweet the sugary taste of your despair is."

Tightening his claw, Artorian screamed in pain as his Soul Item popped like an overfull balloon. It forced the youth to suck in a heavy breath far too quickly, aches reeling across his spine. He got the energy back, but the backlash of having your Soul Item damaged *hurt*! Ghreziz just smiled wider. "Ah! My first scream. How I have longed for such *succulent music*."

Wincing deep, the Mage shuffled through his mind for options. He *needed* help. With a quick feeling check for his reserves alone, he could tell that it looked dire. B-rank five levels of Mana? *Crackers*. He threw a quick jab at the demon's face, but Ghreziz caught him by the wrist with all the difficulty of controlling a toddler's tantrum. "Oh, how cute! You think your little fist is going to harm me, when even your stick had trouble?

You dropped it, you know. Did you even realize both your hands are empty? *No?*"

Struggling against the significantly higher-ranked grip, Artorian was confused that the tier difference wasn't being as helpful as it should be. He winced hard, but his strained face only brought the demon bliss. "What's wrong? I can tell you're higher ranked than you used to be, and that your available Mana is even higher than it was the last time I saw you. Yet you're having *so. Much. Trouble!*"

The demon pursed his lips, and for a moment Artorian feared the ugly thing was going to kiss him. Now *that* would be an awful fate. Ghreziz just savored the victory, his guttural voice sweet, yet crass. "Can't figure it out? Look down."

Artorian frowned. Look *down*? Not having many better options unless he wanted to risk pulling an actual destructive Essence technique out, and risk damaging the tree, he glanced. His struggle stopped cold. "*Oh…*"

Ghreziz nodded, glad to point out the obvious so his prey would give off more of that delightful panic. "Oh, *indeed*! Look at that lovely Mana-shaped branch. I considered punting that little green ball that's clearly so important. Yet in your haste to defend it, you scarcely noticed that killing it would have given you a fighting chance. That green little monster has been siphoning Mana from you at a pace that even *I* find impressive. All in order to… get this. Make a *branch!*"

Artorian winced deeply, but cracked the faint edge of a smile on his lips. Ghreziz may have pointed it out, but he saw what the demon *didn't*. "I suppose we can go ahead and call her a branch manager!"

Ghreziz smirked. "That would have been amusing, my old foe. Sadly, I'm aware you're stalling. Did you think it was you I was laughing at when I destroyed your attire? I noticed what I seek didn't fall from your pocket. Do you truly believe I didn't notice one of those light balls escape for dear life? That squire-blue one *also* didn't return. My punting may be perfect, but that was insufficient for it to be knocked out of the fight. I merely wished to induce *pain*."

His expression widened. Gaining teeth when the gnawing understanding dawned on his captive's face. Yes. He had indeed used Artorian as a plaything. The clear difference in fighting style between now and then was obvious. This version had limitations, where the person going after them in the Ziggurat had nothing but options and bright ideas. Speaking of. "What's wrong, pillow boy? Out of *options*?"

Artorian just smiled, and wriggled his wrist. Still stuck? Still stuck. *Good*. Ghreziz may have been talking, but he hadn't been paying that much attention. Artorian was in other conversations, though his falling facial expression did denote things weren't going so well on their end either. When he'd first started the chat, he'd known right away something was awry.

Immediately after the arboreal joke, he'd thrown open a connection with his chosen, though only one managed to connect. <Zelia. I need help!>

Ooof.

Artorian felt the gut punch as Zelia received it. <Busy! We're all under attack by tar creatures, and, by the sun, they are *strong*. We could use some help ourselves! They are in every realm, fighting every supervisor and chosen. The fire and void Dreamers have their hands full, and are currently fighting just *one* tar creature equal to their rank in the middle of empty space. Or something. I can't follow. They pop in and out worse than you do!>

Another punch to Zelia's ribs made him grit his teeth, forcing a gnawed facial expression to wrench over his features. <Dreamer, I can't talk! I'm losing and must focus. These things caught us at a terrible time, and their power only seems to increase as fighting goes on. I have no idea where they are getting this type of strength from, and damaging them is so *webbing* difficult! There is fighting everywhere except on Hel. I need to go!>

The connection winked out in time for Artorian to notice he'd been called pillow boy. Hel was vacant? *Good.* His eyes locked with Yvessa's exhausted light, the Wisp form of his ancient friend bobbing above the very end of the branch. She gave him the first piece of good news that had come this entire fight. Her voice may have been tired, but it held the fire he relished and knew. "*Done.*"

Yvessa hadn't been idle. The only way she was going to manage to get out of this fight and stop the brawl from happening here, was if the bout could be elsewhere to begin with. That wasn't happening so long as the fighter of their duo was Mana tethered. The only way to end the tether, was if all the Essence it would take for the branch to reform had been invested. Not finished! *Invested.* She was responsible for turning it into Silverwood matter, but she could do that anytime, so long as the energy was present and available. It was easier if Artorian funneled the energy in slowly, but she'd make do. On finishing this endpoint, that part of the task was *finished.*

The tether ceased, and Artorian was released. "Pillow boy? Well, if you're going to flirt with me, then allow me to indulge you in the *ziggurat zoom!*"

Ghreziz had ignored the green ball's comment. What did it matter if she was done? The victim in his hand was weak and drained all the same. "What might that be? Another version of the *derby dance* you performed last time?"

Artorian shot a wink at Yvessa, and set his plan in motion. "Of a sort. You never did see what happened after you checked out of the party. So I doubt you'd know *this* was a thing."

Fuff.

The teleportation trip to Hel may have taken only a moment, but Ghreziz *screamed* the entire way. Those lessons from Zelia were worth their weight in *gold.* The thing about tele-portation was that it didn't happen instantaneously, so much as the wavelength of the trick allowed you to go… *elsewhere.* In that elsewhere, the properties of that place reigned supreme. Certain places, such as the one described as slipspace, were more of a smooth, single, condensed point that was, in a way, everywhere at once.

Using that place to teleport was one of utter convenience, in addition to how pleasantly gentle and swift the ride was. If Artorian had to describe these somewheres, he likened it to… well, *layers*. S-ranked cultivators moved between these layers freely. Or at least, he was convinced this involved the layers. Whether the layers were the old idea of 'heavens,' or something else entirely, wasn't that important yet.

What *was* important was that the teleportation **Law** essentially allowed you to *skirt the edges* of those layers. Not breaching through, but more of an effort in skating upon their icy surfaces. When you did so, you came into contact with that place's… *properties*.

Slipspace? No side effects. Clean, easy, near-instant *vwipping*. Was that a word? *Eh*, it was now. Didn't feel like anything. Fuff space? That was like being hugged by a thousand blankets. Abyss space? Felt like your soul was being torn out through your rear. Celestial space? Felt like you just woke from a nap, wildly invigorated.

It was that last one he'd skirted with this particular trip, and since touch was all that was required to *haul* Ghreziz along for the ride, what amounted to a pleasant, restorative journey for him was a keelhauling for his travel buddy. To the demon, the trip was akin to being dragged along a cheese grater as the overbearing affinity of the place caused rampant havoc to the infernal creature's well-being.

Ghreziz was a smoking wreck when the remnants of his tar-bleeding body slopped onto Hel's surface. Artorian just got to his feet and savored the triumph with a good stretch. Now that he wasn't on Niflheim anymore, he didn't need to limit himself to things he was terrible at. As he raised a palm, a radiant solar fireball sprung to life above it. "Round *two*."

A lime green line shot through his tiny sun. Much like his

pillow, it too popped like an overinflated balloon. The Mana returned to his hand, but his attention shot towards what should have been a mostly defeated writhing demon puddle. Which was instead pulsing with lime-green light from within, looking stronger than before as Ghreziz got up. "*Ahh.* Gifts from the Patron, *delivered at last.* Praise to the devourer! May his hunger find *slaking.*"

Well, crackers. Artorian was toast. He'd gambled on the teleportation trip to do most of the heavy lifting, since his reserves weren't looking too good. He really needed some *abyss-blasted* help. He formed a hat using Rosewood's technique, just to throw it upon the sooty ground. "Are you *kidding* me? Do you know how difficult it was to pull that off? Then you just… *get up.* Like it was *nothing!*"

Ghreziz bellowed with laughter befitting an amused sewer, watching the youth repeatedly stomp his foot on the hat. His foe was flustered! Luck was on the demon's side as Barry's gifts coursed through new-formed veins. It felt abysmally good. His mirth only grew, and sharpened teeth revealed themselves as he heard the ridiculous idea currently spouting from Artorian. "Are *all* demons like this? I am going to summon some of my *own* just to kick your ass!"

"*Bwahahaha!*" Ghreziz needed to hold his stomach. What a twist! What an absurd notion. Both that any demon would be willing to take up arms against him, and that the youth could pull such a feat off in the first place. "Ha! *You*? Summon one of *my* kind? Do you even know *how*?"

Artorian dismissed the hat, as it was thoroughly covered in soot. His heavy footfalls had even caused earthquake-quality thrums to vibrate throughout the landscape. The world didn't really shake, but the impacts were obnoxious and obvious. "I will figure it out. Just to *spite* you! It *can't* be that hard. I may not be a necromancer, but if those C-ranked boys can pull it off, I certainly can as well. I will just… throw my hands in the air and call loudly! They'll come!"

That was so dumb, Ghreziz simply couldn't help himself. He doubled over as his arms and torso doubled in muscle mass. He looked like a strongman who had always skipped leg day. He was laughing so loud, the soot around his feet was forced away with every emanation. Ghreziz was in a crater a mere half minute later, just enjoying the idiocy of it all as he watched the youth enter the silliest poses.

Consternation and constipation crossed his foe's face. Artorian was just trying so hard to do something he hadn't the slightest clue how to commence, and that tickled the demon pink. "Don't you laugh at me! I will figure this out!"

Artorian's tone was serious, but his actions only turned ever more dramatic. The antics amused the demon greatly, as suffering and grunts freely fell from his beaten foe. Free entertainment! The best thing to have when it came to killing eternity. "Not like *that*, you whinging fool. Like this."

Ghreziz stretched his hand out before him, and grinned with delight when the youth stopped to pay attention. As if Artorian could discern the dark, deep nuances that this technique required. The Mage stopped on a copper, his dramatic exposure having bought him some time. As a minor bonus, he had a front row seat to the mechanics of demon summoning. The guttural voice spoke proud, fully expecting the youth to be unable to follow. "Summoning is like *fishing*. You bait a lure, attach a wire, and toss… The quality of your bait will determine what you can catch. The tastier the treat, the bigger the fish that comes to have a peek. You want an Incarnate demon? Better offer Incarnate energy. You want the Dragon of the Darkness Flame? Better have tasty Mana!"

Artorian did not like that Ghreziz knew about Dragons. Hopefully he was referring to a different creature entirely? Surely what Bob had made for him didn't exist beforehand. Surely.

Thin, lime green and tarry onyx lines descended from Ghreziz's clawed fingers. Rather than dig into the soot, they vanished mid-way down to the ground. The truth did not remain hidden from Artorian. Those fishing wires went to the Between! From there, they followed a process similar to teleportation. The infernal Essence bait brushed against the border realm of the infernal wavelength, and just like that, five lesser demons were pulled *free* from the Abyss. *Crackers*.

Four C-ranked and one B-ranked demon formed from the droplets that fell from Ghreziz's claws. Their bodies broke and popped upon manifestation, and only the B-ranker rose to weakly stand upon the soot. The C-rankers all died as the pressure of Hel had enough of an effect on them to quash them outright. Hadn't that been fixed? No matter. Artorian was glad for the boon right now. Even one extra demon to contend with was a nightmare. *He* was the one that needed backup!

With a howling screech, four demons perished. Death by gravity.

Fortunately for them, they were unable to return to the abyss. Cal's Soul Space was a one-way trip while the chains were on, and the four demons were stored in memory Cores. That those memory Cores began to pulse an *ominous* green was likely unimportant.

"*That's it?*" Artorian sounded a little disappointed. He'd figured the process of summoning to be one of vast complications. Yet it was just… that easy? Throw some Mana at another layer and hope something bites? "That's all it takes to summon something? It can't be that easy. What else did you do? You didn't even *try* to skew your Mana's intent."

Ghreziz raised a brow, and the surviving B-ranked demon dropped to a knee next to him when realizing just who it was that had called upon a lesser. The savant spoke with amusement. "*Easy?* More entertainment in the form of some joke I'm too powerful to understand? The act of drawing from beyond is *art.* You can't just throw a line in and expect something will bite. Easy? Ha! *Prove it.*"

The lesser demon was used as a seat, and Ghreziz lounged, indulging in the oppression of another. He laced his infernally empowered claws as they danced with ignoble green light, and watched the show with relish. Everyone failed the first time, and he couldn't wait to see the pillow Mage *abyss this up*.

He observed a youthful Artorian push his amateur sleeves up. "*Fine!*"

Artorian had bought the time he'd needed. The ground had responded to his earlier stomping, and a ripple returned from far away. Just a little longer. He just needed to *stall* a little longer. Since he had a play to perform, there was no reason he couldn't go ahead and milk this for all it was worth. Extending his hand, he formed the tethers easily enough. Fishing wasn't his strong suit, but he'd seen an example. That was enough.

How did Mana go to the Between? He considered it, and much like every other time he tried something like this, he just formed the identity to match the intent. His lines faded at the midpoint, already in the Between. This part wasn't that hard. He'd been there, after all. Even connecting to the wavelength he was looking for wasn't a challenge. He skirted the layers with teleportation often enough, even if at times with all the skill of cheek-sliding across Yuki's ramp. Mage necromancy could function with as little as the first tier **Law**, so what would happen if he used *his*? What does **Love** call when it is in need?

The concentration required sapped him of more Mana than the attempt did, and his eyes fluttered shut. The nearby demon was just waiting to savor the moment he screwed this up anyway. Artorian didn't know how to communicate with another layer, but given his experience with senate and forum use, he just gave it a try, and spoke to the layer. <Help. I need *help.*>

In response, the layer *demanded* his experiences, and he felt the tug twang his line. Pulling his Mana tether until it was *taut*. Perhaps he should have chosen a different place, but this one... this one just seemed *apt*. He let flow the requested thoughts freely, but the pull drew more than he expected.

The layer took memories in reverse, starting with the fresh, and going back in history. The layer learned of his fight with the demon that was toying with him. Tasks as an Administrator.

Meeting his chosen. Entering the Soul Space. Pleasantly teaching Dale to walk in the Phantom Academy. Becoming a Mage. The search for family. His bed in the Fringe, basking in the sun.

He didn't realize tears rolled down his cheeks when the demanding pull ended. He only felt his eyes snap open, gasping in shock as an unseen force clasped wrists with him. Ghreziz eagerly awaited the visuals of the backlash. Tears had been a good start. No, tears had been a *great* start. If only he had something to snack on. Some roasted poultry would be excellent.

When he felt the youth succeed, his amusement bled away like all his blood had been *ripped* from him. Ghreziz was on his feet, readying a charge to halt whatever incoming blasphemy this miscreant had summoned. This wasn't a *demon*. This wasn't a demon at all.

This was *worse*.

Hraaaa! Roaring as he exploded forwards, soot backblasted for miles behind him from the sheer power with which Ghreziz propelled himself. His claw formed a fist, and he threw it straight at Artorian's jaw.

The blow didn't connect. A single, shining digit stopped Ghreziz's advance *cold*. May the curses of the abyss fall forever more from his mouth. The pillow-damned had summoned a ruinous *celestial*.

Artorian dropped to a knee, heaving as his Mana vanished. He was sitting at a very *uncomfortable* B-rank zero. Almost all out. *Almost*. Burnout hid right around the corner, and he could feel it creeping in with every deeply drawn breath.

He coughed out a greeting. Hoping whatever had come to help was also friendly towards him, rather than merely hateful towards his enemies. When Artorian looked up, the golden-eyed, smiling youth gazed lovingly back down at him. His expression was full of care and kindness. The affection freely given as his single finger stopped his opposite outright. "H— *cough* Hello. Might I ask for your name?"

The celestial pushed Ghreziz away like he was a toothpick

caught in a maelstrom. Ghreziz's energies were fully canceled out by the overbearing celestial affinity he'd just been *flicked* by. The celestial's voice sounded as one expected a Heavenly might. Ecclesiastic, and reverberating with chorus. "Of course, friend of my friend. My name, the one you might be familiar with, was *Adam*."

CHAPTER FORTY-FIVE

The celestial eased his other hand upward, and the weight and fatigue dropped from Artorian's shoulders. Mages could experience fatigue? Apparently so, because all of his just went away like a freshly dropped salt pack. "I know of your plight, mentor of Dale. Escape freely. My stay may be fleeting, but I shall *make you* the time."

Adam whispered something else to Artorian, and a brightness illuminated in both their eyes. With the celestial's whisper, a clue clicked into place, causing a vast mystery of what had been disconnected pieces to assemble itself.

Like finding the exact corner piece of an assembly puzzle, and being able to connect all the edges. Artorian looked at the smiling, supportive celestial a moment longer. Then, he replied with a sharp and curt nod. He understood.

The spare B-ranked demon charged at Adam, but a luminous golden sword burst into being within the celestial's grip and skewered the abyss summoned via his own charge. Unlike normal, this demon did not go back to the abyss, nor a memory Core.

He had been *purged*.

Artorian drew breath, steadying himself as Ghreziz readied. Answers were still unfolding in his mind. He'd been looking at the problem entirely wrong! As he often did. He didn't need to lock his Presence off in order to use his current body. He just thought he needed to, because it was the first thing that had worked. Henry clearly didn't do it this way. While in Niflheim, his Long form had been an incredible detriment, but here? Here it was the answer.

Mana starved and close to burnout, Artorian slapped his hands together and exclaimed a word as it came to mind. It may have been a nonsensical one, but it just felt so appropriate for the situation. A cloud of glittery fog burst from his current form as he yelled. "*Alakazam!*"

Boof!

Ghreziz was confused. He just had several of his brand-new bones broken, via a *flick*. He had seen the young Mage succeed at a summoning on the first try, and had now also seen that same youth explode into a *three-hundred-foot-long noodly monster*. What?

Feathered wings widened from Adam's back, and his sword hummed with power. That sight was what drew the demon's current attention, the empowered savant quickly on his feet as his own ruinous weapon was called forth. The lime green and onyx axe formed in his hand. Its sharp, serrated edges dripping with infernal poisons.

He spat on the ground, deciding to ignore the dawdling noodle that suddenly hurled itself sideways through the air. It seemed so unintentional? Though at the same time, the strange self-toss offered the Long thing an escape. Ghreziz had different concerns. Those of the celestial kind as the two affinity-opposed warriors circled one another. "I'm surprised one of your kind would deem themselves *so unworthy* as to bow to this realm's attention!"

Adam didn't give the demon the satisfaction of a rise, his calm demeanor pleasantly shining forth. "The request was made. Offering given. Memories provided. Heartfelt sympathies in the right place. I saw that man, and saw his life. I saw my place within it, and knew it was right that in *this moment*, I be *here*. Let none say that **Love** cannot cross all boundaries, for her cries were crystal, and her actions pure. I have but one question for you, *infernal*."

Ghreziz didn't like this, his second axe forming quickly in his offhand. It looked just as imposing and deadly as the first. The guttural spew rolled forth over his tongue. "What is that, *lightling*?"

Adam smiled, his voice amused. "How many *options* do you have, when all you have is *one*?"

Ghreziz didn't like the answer either as their weapons crossed in a chaotic display of discordant fireworks. He spat out the answer, hating that he knew this ancient little riddle. "The same as your chances of defeating me, celestial. *None*."

Hel became a battleground, matching the events occurring just about everywhere else as Artorian snaked his way to the exit. He was out of his depth here, and needed to just get far enough away! The Runescripting on his bones was the boon here! They allowed him to fly with a fraction of the ordinary expenses. He didn't even feel a drain on his admittedly burnout-ready Mana, and flew as fast as the Runes let him in search of his beacon. That his control over his flight was laughable didn't matter at this moment. He needed to get *off* this rock!

Honk?

"*Son of a celestial!* Not *you* too!" Artorian was miffed. He'd meant to get the goose's attention, but that had been in order to direct it at Ghreziz! Not him! Now he was running away from this feathery monstrosity for a third time! "Crackers and abyss-burned toast! Could *anything* go well today?"

The honking was more metallic than he remembered; a detail so trifling that he barely paid attention. That was, until the Metal-God-Goose decided to remind him it was a blasted *Incarnate*, and could just fold out of existence right next to him, anytime. He noticed it was covered in iridium right then and there.

"Welp, no mystery where that entire chunk of metal went!" Which was *pre~e~etty* obvious now that it was chasing him to bite him in the butt! To make matters just a teensy bit worse, there was now a whole lot more *butt* to go around! "Forget crackers and toast! I am upgrading to *biscuits*!"

Why biscuits was an exclamation of greater value, he didn't know. Again, that was something for the backburner as he pulled his own tail out of the way of the amalgamation between a Gnomish and Dwarven love project. The dang thing was even bigger! What, had it been *too small* the last time? Didn't *impress* the missus?

The chaotic clatter behind him increased in intensity at an unwelcome, faster rate than he was managing to flee from the death-goose. At the minimum, he was able to discern where the beacon was and did his best to beeline right to it. *Beeline*? Now there was a thought! If he could compress this oversized snake down to a manageable human form, surely a bee wasn't out of the ballpark either? Maybe that tiny, the goose would lose track of him!

He dismissed the thought entirely when one of the mecha-goose's many heads replaced the empty air in his path with a goopy square block of acid ooze. Weren't those the things limited to living inside of Jorm's stomach? Oh, speaking of. He should visit that big snake sweetums. Maybe he'd find some kinship now that he too was a noodle. Noodles unite!

Ow!

Artorian pulled himself up to skid over the surface of the ooze. Regardless of how slippery it was, it was unfortunately just as caustic, searing some scales right off his hide as he Yuki-technique skated across with the help of some traded-in ice Mana. It burned for him to use it, but what options did he really have? Then again, in the Long form he had the liberty of Aura and Presence use.

A pinkish voice replied to him, originating from his own thoughts. "Why don't we actually go ahead and use that, Artorian? That would be, I don't know... *clever* to do!"

"Scilla?" He'd thought the response to his own query, but the bit about being clever sounded like a distinctly different voice in his head. Sure enough, the pink-iris warden was out and about. Awake in the bonfire space that he currently did not have the clarity of mind to visit. There was escaping to do! "Is *this* what you wanted me to hurry for? I still don't know!"

Scilla whined in his bonfire space, but he heard it loud and clear all the same. "Boy! I wanted you to get a move on with your projects, you have far too much to do. You forget half of the things you're going to do, and stop paying attention after you have made a little headway in your current one. You make all these lists but you don't stick to them. It's infuriating! Why isn't your family decanted?"

Artorian dodged a gout of flame, snapping back in a rush. "This is a *terrible time* for that conversation, Scilla! Kind of bolting for my life here!"

Scilla wrinkled her nose. "You're always running for your life, or something equally as pressing! So, *no*! Now is as good a time as any. Why not just become stronger so these things don't affect you the way they are? You could just *defeat* the goose, instead of holding onto the end of your own tail and hoping you go faster if you just pull it hard enough."

Artorian couldn't do this right now. "I am *not* going to Phoenix Kingdom in this state! I know what's there, and I refuse! That is a heartache I don't want to live through again. No!"

Scilla didn't let up. "Fine! This was incredible motivation, and you again forgot that I can control just how long you're away for. If you did them all. Right now. That goose would be child's play. You could Incarnate. You could! If you just tackled all of the regrets. You could get out of this without needing anyone else's help!"

Artorian still just couldn't bring himself to do it. "No!"

"Fine! Be *stubborn*." Scilla slammed the door in his face, and his connection to the conversation severed. Scilla retreated back to the ceiling. She couldn't force him to make the jump, she could only be there when he stepped through the door. Even trickery only took her so far. The participant needed to be *willing*.

Honk!

Artorian squeezed his Presence inward, the Dragon body humanizing just quickly enough to avoid several metal goose beaks from snapping him to pieces. He landed on a soot hill and tumbled, using the Dwarven earth-talon technique to gain additional footing. Propelling himself forwards so he could run out of range for the next few seconds.

Okay! So Scilla was just a *tiny* bit right, and he had some lists that needed wrapping up. A few hundred years of technique practice also wouldn't go misplaced, but he didn't exactly have the time for that either now did he? Decant his village? With demons about? Ha! *Abyss no*! He'd find a moment. A perfect moment where he could do exactly that.

For now, it was dealing with Cal and his *accidents*. Not to mention that at the end of this road, he'd have to find a method to deal with the true culprit of this annoying infernal invasion.

Barry.

He ran fast, but the goose was always faster. It had an anytime teleport, without needing the entirety of its body to come through at once. Some of the heads erupted out of nowhere to bite and snap at him independently, and he was playing hopscotch and bunny-hopping soot hills just so he wouldn't suffer the same goosy fate as before.

To his credit and good fortune, the attack patterns were predictable as could be. He even had several seconds of warning and heads up from whatever patch of space the goose was going to burst free from, since a visual cue occurred before a head sprang forth.

He hadn't understood at first, but when you got attacked by the same method over and over, you started to see how it worked. What he had forgotten was just how massive Hel was. Just running wasn't going to cut it. He needed something faster.

Something that didn't drain his mana. A Nixie Tube flickered above his head. "Deverash, you devilish die!"

Using any more Mana was dangerous, but what choice did he have? Extending a hand, he gritted his teeth and cried out as he ate the cost of an item teleportation. The racing platform warped in with a pop.

His speed balanced out with the platform's stillness, momentum equalizing him to a swift heel-dug standstill while the goose tumbled over him from above. It tripped over a soot hill more than it did his stilled form, but the mechanical marvel's messy fall was enough for a pained Artorian to bite through the agony. He rumble-revved the palanquin into activity as he rolled into the control seat.

Thrusters flared to life, and Artorian barely got the goggles over his eyes before jamming the *Oomph* lever forwards. The thrusters roared! Soot burst off the ground, forming vast clouds behind him as he sped off with a sonic boom. Breaking the sound barrier right away as he forced the platform to go as fast as it could, as quickly as it could. Abyss the threats! There was nothing to bash or crash into while on Hel, nothing but soot hills and cracked landscapes all around. He had a need, a need for *speed*!

Breaking Mach three after half a minute, he glanced over his shoulder to notice that fire-spewing mechanical menace was *hot* on his exhaust trail. A pain struck his stomach, and he sucked in a breath as his hand snapped to the wound. He only had to glance down to finally see what burnout actually did to a Mage. It was *literal*. Both his legs had *burned out* from within, nothing more than hollow husks that looked like logs in a fire. Well, it wasn't like he'd done a good job walking with them regardless!

The damage spread to his midriff, where the burnout stabilized. He had enough Mana to retain healthy control of everything above the waist, but not a drop of Mana more for anything else. Biscuits! He had tried *so hard* not to damage this body! Gritting his teeth, he forced the damage out of his mind, needing to sharply veer left when he noticed the needle on the compass flick to the right.

That blasted goose had learned! There had been no visual cue for the incoming attack, but the compass to track rogue iridium was still perfectly functional. Needle to the right? Threat to the right! He looped in a circle to avoid blasts of fire, cones of acid, and lines of electricity before resuming the beelined path towards the beacon. So much for trying to turn into a bee! "Survive, old man! Just *survive!*"

Honk!

The mechoose bleared at him. Miffed that this nest-intruder was still not dead. Artorian didn't care, and just needed to get off this rock. "Complain all you want, you feathery mongrel! You won't get me this time!"

Artorian punched it to Mach seven. He finally heard something break inside of the platform from the turbulence he was putting it through, the controls were shaking in his hands! A flash of light blipped in the distance. *His beacon*!

Tatum stood upon the platform, frantically looking around for something, or *someone*. The Incarnate spotted Artorian from the soot cloud his racer kicked up, thrusters burning bright and on the verge of joining the old man in burnout. Though, the angry sounds of his not-very-cooperative-chosen may have had something to do with it as well.

Tatum planted his feet, and outstretched an open hand to the side as if to catch an incoming projectile. Artorian understood. He just had to touch him, and they'd be abyss-free.

All he had to do was *grab. That. Hand*!

CHAPTER FORTY-SIX

Roaring over a particularly tall soot hill that made the racer veer up and over, the teleportation beacon cleanly entered his sights on the way down. A straight shot. He was *so close*. "Biscuits! Finally!"

Racing right to the escape point in as direct a line as he could, Artorian was at risk of failing a few dodges when one of the side-thrusters spectacularly exploded. For a powerful Incarnate, the goose was surprisingly easy to circumvent. His entire driving method had adopted several patterns specifically for avoiding all of the attacks his assailant had within its arsenal. It was surprising how good you got at dodging when you really couldn't afford to haplessly throw your life away.

Tatum impatiently waited, and Artorian could swear the man was yelling 'Come on!' at him. Well, he was trying! With a hop, skip, and a jump that stalled another set of thrusters, he banked the palanquin hard to the right and stretched out his hand while nine open goose bills converged on his location. Tatum shifted his foot upon the beacon, and smirked as his wrist tightly clasped with Artorian's, easily accommodating the speed of the burning racer. "A new hand touches the beacon. Ha!"

The mechanical heads bore down on him, maws wide open and eager to finally gobble up the prize. Tatum squeezed Artorian tight and folded into nothingness, dragging both him and the platform right into the void as the goose snapped its iridium beaks shut on empty space.

Denied!

Artorian was happy as could be when he came out the other end, falling face-first to the floor of the living room in his archives as the palanquin sputtered and fell to the floor with a thruster cough, its power supply fried. He was heaving while lying cheek-down on the floor of his solar foyer. Oh, how he'd missed this place.

Dawn's voice chirped. "Are you going to kiss the floor because you're so happy to see it again, or are you going to wash and save those for me?"

Tatum snickered, helping the Administrator up since it was clear he was entirely unable to stand on his own. Not with those legs the way they were. "See? I told you that if I just kept paying attention to the beacons, he'd show up eventually. Ta-da. Tatum twelve, Dawn eight!"

Mhm. Dawn slid from her seat, decked in full armor as she rose from the dining table to take over supporting her Sunny. "We'll fix that number next time there's a demon breakout. It's your turn for the dishes. I'm taking this one to the baths. He clearly needs it."

Artorian didn't fight the assistance. He was glad for the company. Glad for the help. Glad to be away from Ghreziz and Wagner the Relentless. A little dull… but relentless! "Thank you, Dawn. It's good to see you again. Nice armor."

She nodded quietly, taking his filthy soot-smeared robe off just to hold it by the tips of her fingers in disgust. "How is this…? Never mind. This isn't salvageable."

Flames licked his self-made robe, conflagrating the entire thing in seconds. It didn't matter. It had held up well when it needed to. Bundling in an oversized towel while in the baths, he was far too busy wading neck-deep in a nice large vat of hot water to mind the robe. It was high time to indulge in a break, and the second half of the Asgard baths as he sat on the vat stairs. "*Aaahh…* sweet relief."

Artorian had questions.

As usual, they would have to wait until later. He needed a break, and to somehow mend his legs. "Dawny. How does one repair burnout damage? I didn't expect the effect to be… Well. I understand why it's called *burnout*."

Dawn's heavy plate thunked onto a storage spot on the nearby shelf, changing her attire out to something more comfortable that she could bathe in. "That's but one of the possible burnout symptoms. It can be much worse. Be glad you didn't shatter like spun glass—that's what happens to the lower **Law** tiers when they overdo it. I'm also fairly convinced that you'd have outright cracked to pieces if that wasn't a Spirit body you were in. It held up against the damage far better than an A-ranked one would have. You best thank Cal later. Now sit back and don't ask me questions. I can mend the damage, it's just going to take me a while. Relax."

Artorian gave a quiet thumbs up, and sunk into the water just to blow a few frothy bubbles. He felt crabby. "Not even one q—"

Bop.

"Ow."

"No. Not even one question." Dawn was short with him, and his bubble blowing intensified. Dawn had just begun with healing when Tatum dragged himself in. He didn't even bother disrobing, and walked straight to a free vat to dramatically fall face-first into it. He was just done with the world, and too tired to care about social convention. Artorian looked at the other tub, gently chancing a question anyway. "You alright there, buddy?"

Tatum heard him just fine. Water or no. A line of bubbles garbled from the bottom of the vat, but unlike Dawn who smiled and snickered at the response, Artorian had no idea what was said. He glanced at her, and she softly shrugged. "He spoke a line of egregious expletives. We didn't have a good time handling that S-ranked demon, though we managed to defeat and Core him. If you wanted to know how bad that brawl got, *I* needed armor for it. Also… don't go to Vanaheim for a while. It's not pretty. Don't be surprised if all you hear from Dev for the next few years is nothing but screeches and crying. We broke that realm to ugly pieces trying to bring Yasura down."

Artorian quietly nodded, and reached out a hand. She held it pleasantly, giving it a squeeze as he felt hot lines of Spirit energy stab into his digits and course through his veins. He tried to tug away from the sudden pain, but Dawn didn't let go. "I told you to relax. Healing burnout is possible, not *pleasant*. Be glad you have a Spirit body and that I've had to put my own back together non-stop since the earliest days of our Soul Space jaunt. Outside of Cal, it would have taken me a century, here I can accomplish it in a day. He's not going to be happy about the Essence expenditure we've drained from his Soul Space, but it was for the best. Now lay back, much like that time I was surprised I could heal you in the Phantomdusk. This is going to burn."

Artorian did as told, but felt no noticeable difference. "Okay… anytime? I suppose?"

He peeked at Dawn, but she was stumped on something. "Is this a humanized body, with something else as the base? You can't be a three-hundred-foot-long noodle thing. I'm sensing this wrong."

His finger swiftly shot to the air. "No, that's correct! I nicked this body, since my original one got… goosed. I have a spare in Eternium, but that's no good since I can't get to it. Henry figured out a way to make this look easy, but I'm expending my Presence in order to stay like this."

Dawn ground her teeth together in contemplation. "Would be easier to just ask him, but the senate is down. Nothing but static."

Artorian considered it, but recalled something odd. Hadn't he successfully talked to Zelia? Out of raw curiosity, he tried knocking on Henry's forum door. The burning in his legs spread up his spine half an inch from using Mana, and he hissed in pain with his eyes shut. "*Ow!*"

Dawn didn't feel a need to chide him. It just meant mending was going to take that much longer. "What did you think *that* was going to accomplish, burnout boy?"

Artorian winced, but a smile slowly spread across his pained features as he spoke through the discomfort. "No… *static*."

Tatum was upright so fast that he caused a wave to roil and turn over inside his vat. "Did you just say *no* static?"

Getting a weak thumbs up as a response, Tatum closed his eyes and checked out. Dawn and Artorian shared a look, but had to shrug since they had no hope of following wherever it was Tatum was going. Dawn had a clue, but her attention was entirely on mending Sunny's burnout. Which she couldn't currently proceed on since the base form was… a problem.

When Occultatum vanished from the baths, his voided out Presence created a vacuum that the water happily filled in order to settle. A **vwop** popped in the air a few seconds later. Given the girly screams that accompanied Marie's surprised yelp, they could both discern that Tatum had both found and fetched the Royal duo. Artorian didn't know Henry's pitch could go that high. They'd prod him about that later, and snickered as his voice retained the pitch during his outburst. "How did you *do* that!"

Laughter erupted from the baths. Both Dawn and Artorian could feel the gazes of the Royals turn regardless of there being walls in the way. Artorian smiled, finally relaxing a little as he leaned back against the vat's wooden wall. "I needed that. Some lively stupidity…"

Dawn nodded. "We all needed that."

Tatum started laughing at something Henry had just told him, and his stomping could easily be overheard as it trekked towards their direction. "That's it? You're kidding. That's all you did, and it worked?"

Henry followed the best he could, and his eyes lit up at the sight of the baths. He caught his reflection in one of the mirrors. Oh, wow, he was *dirty*. Something had liberally dragged him through the mud. Possibly some rock. Artorian's money was on a mountain that now had a Henry-shaped hole in it. Hehehe.

Henry was still speaking to Tatum, but his attention turned to the Administrator mid-sentence. "Yes, really. Artorian, did you *not* use the title?"

Artorian's head was turned to look up at the filthy King, but he had to blink as an initial answer, not following the thread of conversation. "What *title*?"

Henry tried to pull up his status screen, but winced from the sheer raw static. "Looks like I can't show you. I unfortunately don't know how to assign it to you. Marie told me we got this body to work the way it did because you found out that Spirit body creatures could be humanized. So she assigned me the title that makes it not cost anything, and something about it being counted as a secondary base form? I didn't follow that part, but I can go back and forth between human and creature at will. I won't do it here, though, no room."

A Nixie Tube flared to life above Artorian's head. The title Decorum had! That's right! His hopeful eyes snapped to Tatum, but the Incarnate was already one step ahead of him. "I didn't imagine circumventing Cal's system on the regular would come in handy like this. There we go, and select, and paste, and *finish*!"

A light flickered around Artorian. An instant soothing coursed down his spine as he happily melted into a puddle, the pain fading while his Presence unlocked. Dawn's Spirit didn't burn as bad as he thought it might as the nerves in his spirit frame slowly healed. "*Ohh… thank you.*"

Tatum proudly smirked a toothy smile, though he was getting demanding glares from the others. Marie was at his side in moments, her accusing digits digging into his chest. "How exactly are *you* able to access the system while it's static for the rest of us?"

Tatum merely winked in response. "Same way I always do it. Pylon-direct. Bypass the will of the system entirely. The Pylons light up all the same if you give them a little zap in the right order, and Eternium and I have had plenty of chats on **Order**."

Dawn squeezed her eyes suspiciously and turned her head to face the boasting Incarnate. "Didn't we break most of Vanaheim, including Pylons?"

He nodded in a hurry. "We did! Though the record for breaking the most in one go is still held by Sir Burnout over there. We have backups in other realms. Vanaheim is just the main hub that we are going to have to fully replace. That's going to take… a few millennia."

CHAPTER FORTY-SEVEN

Thinking about how long this project was going to take made Tatum sigh and hang his head. An act which got Marie off his case while Dawn resumed mending. Now that the human form of Artorian was a base form, it could be treated like one. They all found a place to sit, and decompressed in silence as they all lounged, exhausted.

Tatum left again for a while, returning with a moody Chandra who was still cleaning tar from her thorns. "There's a secret hideout in the sun and *nobody* told me?"

She flashed a dangerous green spine at Tatum, but his hands were already up. "We all have private, personal little spaces. This one is Artorian's. It's called The Archives in the beacon system. You remember? The gray one you couldn't access when you tried to see where all you could go?"

The spine went away. Chandra tiredly took a seat at the edge of the baths, wading her feet in for comfort. "Can anyone explain to me what the *abyss* has been happening? Cal getting hurt was one thing, but a demon outbreak? Someone pinch me and tell me it's not real."

Tatum sat down next to her, and while many didn't turn their heads to look, their ears were very much paying attention. Tatum sighed and spoke. "Barry. It's all *Barry*. I didn't have much time to dig around, but here's what I've found. Barry, the S-ranked or double S-ranked cultivator from the old world we all know as the Devourer, is stuck in a Core in Eternium's version of the moon. When Cal Incarnated, he gained access to free-floating Spirit energy, since that's what Cal was forced to upgrade to. While I can't be certain of what cracked the Soul Space, the demons are all Barry's doing. I'm not going to blame Eternium for bringing them along. His **Law** required it, and we all know how *that* can get."

A few grumbled nods did the rounds, which told Tatum essentially everyone present was paying attention. It didn't change his explanation. "Whatever tasks or requirements we may have had before? Forget them. They no longer matter. While we can't be sure all the demons are under his influence, it's safe to guess most of them likely are. So just like the old times, if you see a demon, smite on sight."

Tatum counted on his fingers, mentioning what was on his mind. "Until Eternium can be reconnected, and we can go in to look, we're stuck in Cal's Soul Space. Based on what I can sense, we have slapped down all but *one* demon. It's the one on Hel, though based on what I can tell from a feeling, he is fighting something that is thoroughly matching him. I cannot pinpoint or recognize the energy signature, but it's got Artorian's fingerprints all over it. Administrator, mind explaining that one?"

Artorian gave a pleasant thumbs up. "That demon's name is Ghreziz. A-ranked annoyance. I beat him down before in the old world, cheating with a Mana storm that I funneled into a costly attack. I was certain I offed him, but I guess demons can be resummoned from the Abyss. He pulled a few demons in right before my eyes, so I taunted him and played him into letting me do the same. Except I didn't draw from the abyss after seeing him do it. I pulled from the celestial affinity layer. Heaven? Plane? I really need help with terms here. Some fellow named Adam showed up, and while I don't know the lad, I felt in my heart that I could trust him. I'm surprised he's still around, based on what he said about his time being fleeting. I thought he might have winked out."

Tatum closed his eyes for a quick check. "I can confirm your Adam is still there, wiping the sooty floor with Ghreziz at the moment. My chosen, as impossible to guide or control as he is, is on the way as well. Wagner doesn't take kindly to anything other than himself being on Hel. Some wildlife is fine, but people? *Ooof*, he hates people. I don't actually believe the entity you summoned is able to leave? The chaos chains around Cal's real body force a one-way journey until they fade."

Chandra stretched, lying back. "I am not going to complain about one more ally actually able to give our primary enemies a what-for. Now what do we do about the demons?"

Tatum nodded, and got back to counting fingers. "When Eternium is reattached to the Silverwood Tree, the demon influences will once again start seeping out. Each demon we defeat will likely go to a memory Core, and unless we get all of them there is a chance for one to get free and envelop Eternium. If that happens, it will have control over that Core and will be able to let Barry out in a heartbeat. Or at least, that's what I think their plan is. As additional bad news, with Cal being out cold, Barry will have the easiest of times defeating us. Everything is food and power for him, and Cal is full of it."

Chandra rolled her wrist. "How do we *win*?"

Henry raised his hand; he'd been having a decent idea. The proverbial ball had been passed to him, so he spoke. "Wouldn't that just be to go into Eternium and squish all the demons? While some of us remain outside and keep tabs on the Core for protection? We also need to rebuild several realms, and we aren't doing *fantastic* on manpower, in terms of people who can do effective work. On that note. Could I go ahead and make a request?"

Marie moved her hands in an 'I don't see why not' motion, so Henry continued. "Artorian. This is going to sound harsh, but please know I do not mean this with malicious intent. Please *don't* help with the Soul Space reconstruction."

Artorian wasn't the only one curious, and he slowly turned in the vat to lean on his arms, interested in the explanation. "Henry, would you mind telling me why? I'm not upset at the request, I'm just… not *following*."

Marie squeezed her brow. "Henry. Take a bath, you smell. Let me explain this for you before it turns into another court catastrophe like with the Marquis."

Henry said nothing to the contrary, moseying over to the rack to start putting his armor up. It didn't seamlessly hold together with Cal out of the picture, and he wasn't in the slightest against a nice bath. He also hoped nobody would ask for the story of the Marquis. That the most voracious flirting he'd ever been subject to.

Queen Marie pressed the flats of her palms together, and got right to it. "You make messes. Not bad messes. Just *inconvenient* ones. You missed a lot of meetings, but the short of it is this: Your chosen are *amazing* at realm management. You turn wind-chimes into… *artwork*, when they were supposed to be useful for training. While we call you the Administrator, you've had neither the chance to really show your skill at it, nor have we a great number of recorded examples where your style of managing causes a realm to flourish. You get bored with nitty-gritty tasks like land-building, and you have an extreme penchant to go and *alleviate* that boredom. Keeping you on task is so rough, we had a group vote to let Dani decant someone from your old family to help keep you focused, knowing full well that might upset you."

Her hands dropped towards him. "You, on the other hand, excel when it comes to people, and sneaking your way into complicated social situations, regardless of how labyrinthine the rules are. I admit I checked out when you were playing court jester with the Wisps. Yet you got them to blab to you about heart-kept secrets in less than *three* hours! On a topic that would have taken me... I don't know. Two millennia? With accidentally getting lucky and overhearing it?"

Artorian deflated, sinking back down into the water. "I... well. Yes. I'm sorry. I didn't do a very good job being a realm supervisor. In hindsight, I sort of just... let it handle itself, and that caused some issues my chosen had to jump for in my stead. You're right that I didn't do so well, though I also only got *one* iteration of chance at it. As for being an Administrator..."

He sighed heavily, rubbing at his face.

Marie filled the void, and spoke for him. "When it comes to how we feel we were handled: It's not great. You were the only one able to use the senate for a while, even though it was somewhat our own fault we were rebuked from it in the first place. We were not checked up on frequently enough. While some people are great with working in isolation, I am certainly not one of them. There is a specific kind of administrative skill you excel at, but it wasn't the kind that worked well with us."

Artorian kept quiet as he was getting slapped. Marie wasn't wrong with her assessment. "You thrive in situations where a civilization is in full swing, and you can plod around and stick your nose in. So, in the Soul Space, you're not a great fit. You are most certainly a massive boon for Cal when he gets stuck somewhere and needs an idea. Here and now, however, you're going to get bored. There's nothing left to fight, save for one demon that's already losing, and is going to get ganged up on by us after we've had a breather."

Tatum motioned for a moment. "Actually, it just died. Brianna got it after Adam distracted it and got struck on purpose. Adam got Cored, but it was very much on purpose, it seems. Ghreziz just got assassinated. I'll go fetch her."

Marie motioned to Tatum to make her point, but Artorian was already holding a hand up. "I'm sorry, my friends. For how it has gone. I will give up my Administrator position per the soul realm immediately. It's obvious I was no good at it. Honestly, I think the Soul Space would be better off if that position simply didn't exist. We all flourished when we could speak freely in the meetings. Or at least I felt so. While my particular brand of oversight was limited due to… well. I'm a bit of an *absentee*. Not a great feeling to reflect on."

Artorian had expected some kind of pull, didn't feel anything when giving up the position. He wasn't sure if Cal not being around failed to make it official, or if it had been revoked from him beforehand. Without a status screen to check, there was nothing he could do to be certain. Either way, his admittance of failure put his friends at ease. Dawn even rubbed the top of the youngster's head. "What was that for?"

Dawn took his hand, and resumed mending. He could tell when the burning prickles started up again. "I told them it wasn't going to be a problem. Marie has been a little worried you would try to cling to the position like Brianna did, long ago. You have a terrible habit of taking tasks upon yourself that you can't truly handle. Don't be too disheartened? You are an excellent Administrator, but only in a setting where that is possible. I heard stories of what you did to the Academy on Cal's old dungeon. I giggled for *days*. That was you at your best, with bright-eyed students in tow seeking tales of wonder. Snooty instructors that needed to be knocked down a peg, and more. I think Henry's mention was actually harsh, even if Maric explained it."

Henry scrubbed himself with a rag in the baths, his lips forming a thin, apologetic line. Clearing his throat, he amended his statement. "It… Well, yes. With us, we did a lot better when you were in stasis for several iterations. Though I think because the first iteration left such a sour taste in my mouth, it stuck with me. You're not a bad manager, Artorian. I just don't remember it fondly. As a person, I like you very much. If we could continue being friends, I would be very happy."

Marie nodded in agreement, and Chandra followed, though she had different things to say. "Personally, I don't match their grievances. I understand needing some… time. The first itera-tion was rough for me, yet you came when you were able and swiftly moved to get things done. I think you did good, given what you had. Which was an admittedly harsh situation. If you wanted to stay and help with the soul realm, I would not be opposed. Though I understand why Henry and Marie think you could flex your particular set of skills in Eternium. Especially when we put the lost people back. Also… the other reason that hasn't been mentioned."

Artorian raised a brow. He tried looking to Tatum, but the man was gone. "Did Tatum leave already? I wanted a—"

Vwop.

"Oh. Never mind. Hello, Brianna."

"You wanted to *what*, Artorian? I half-listened in from afar." Tatum stretched after bringing in the assassin Queen, who sat down in an available seat. Remaining cordially quiet. Chandra poked Tatum in the ribs when he sat down next to her. "I… What? Oh, you want *me* to tell him?"

Brianna just smirked, and decided to be helpful. "Allow me. Could we have a show of hands as to who actually enjoys Cal's number system and living in Eternium?"

Artorian quasi-raised his hand, but his heart wasn't really in it. Nobody else budged an inch. He blinked at everyone, his head snapping to make sure he wasn't the only one that moved. "I… I can't be the only one that doesn't mind?"

Brianna shook her head, explaining given the group didn't seem to want to talk. "I won't speak for others, but I *despise* being in Eternium with a passion. I do it because I have to. The other Royals do it because they have subjects and must practice for the real thing. I believe this has come up before, but even with Cal mentioning that normal cultivation gains will be tied to game progress, I want nothing to do with it. I of course will when I have to, but let us never mistake that for genuine inter-est. You, on the other hand, possess a boon in Eternium the rest of us simply do not. A boon only Tatum partially matches, though not remotely with your level of freedom."

Artorian was even more confused, craving some elucidation. "Are you… going to leave me in the dark?"

Tatum didn't really want to say it, so Brianna kept hold of the ball.

"*You* can cheat. *We* can't. You have the blessing of Anima."

ABOUT DENNIS VANDERKERKEN

Hello all! I'm Dennis, but I go by a myriad of other nicknames. If you know one, feel free to use it! I probably like them more. I'm from Belgium, and have lived in the USA since 2001. English is my 4th language, so I'm making due, and apologize for the inevitable language-flub. I still call fans ceiling-windmills. The more shrewd among you may have noticed some strange sayings that may or may not have been silly attempts at direct translations! Thank you all for bearing with me.

I started writing in the The Divine Dungeon series due to a series of fortunate circumstances. I continue writing because I wanted to give hungry readers more to sink their teeth into, and help them 'get away' for a while. If you have any questions, or would like to chat, I live on Dakota's Eternium discord. Feel free to come say hi anytime! Life is a little better with a good book.

Connect with Dennis:
Discord.gg/MountaindalePress
Patreon.com/FloofWorks

ABOUT DAKOTA KROUT

Author of the best-selling Divine Dungeon and Completionist Chronicles series, Dakota has been a top 10 bestseller on Audible, a top 15 bestseller on Amazon, and his first book, Dungeon Born, was chosen as one of Audible's top 5 fantasy picks in 2017.

He draws on his experience in the military to create vast terrains and intricate systems, and his history in programming and information technology helps him bring a logical aspect to both his writing and his company while giving him a unique perspective for future challenges.

"Publishing my stories has been an incredible blessing thus far, and I hope to keep you entertained for years to come!" -Dakota

Connect with Dakota:
MountaindalePress.com
Patreon.com/DakotaKrout
Facebook.com/TheDivineDungeon
Twitter.com/DakotaKrout
Discord.gg/Mountaindalepress

ABOUT MOUNTAINDALE PRESS

Dakota and Danielle Krout, a husband and wife team, strive to create as well as publish excellent fantasy and science fiction novels. Self-publishing *The Divine Dungeon: Dungeon Born* in 2016 transformed their careers from Dakota's military and programming background and Danielle's Ph.D. in pharmacology to President and CEO, respectively, of a small press. Their goal is to share their success with other authors and provide captivating fiction to readers with the purpose of solidifying Mountaindale Press as the place 'Where Fantasy Transforms Reality.'

Connect with Mountaindale Press:
MountaindalePress.com
Facebook.com/MountaindalePress
Twitter.com/_Mountaindale
Instagram.com/MountaindalePress

MOUNTAINDALE PRESS TITLES

GameLit and LitRPG

The Completionist Chronicles,
Cooking with Disaster,
The Divine Dungeon,
Full Murderhobo, and
Damsels of Distress by Dakota Krout

Ether Collapse and
Ether Flows by Ryan DeBruyn

The Lone Wanderer by Kyriakos Georgiades

Unbound by Nicoli Gonnella

Lion's Lineage by Rohan Hublikar and Dakota Krout

Wolfman Warlock by James Hunter and Dakota Krout

Axe Druid,
Mephisto's Magic Online,
High Table Hijinks, and Brindollan Affairs by Christopher
Johns

Dragon Core Chronicles by Lars Machmüller

Pixel Dust and
Necrotic Apocalypse by D. Petrie

Viceroy's Pride and
Tower of Somnus by Cale Plamann

Henchman by Carl Stubblefield

The Undying Immortal System by Greg Tolley

Artorian's Archives by Dennis Vanderkerken and Dakota Krout

Incursion by Dennis Vanderkerken

APPENDIX

Abyss – A place you don't want to be, and a very common curse word.

Adam – A celestial elemental from Dale's original party as a cleric. Now he serves as an embodiment of the celestial plane.

Adventurers' Guild – A group from every non-hostile race that actively seeks treasure and cultivates to become stronger. They act as a mercenary group for Kingdoms that come under attack from monsters and other non-kingdom forces.

Affinity – A person's affinity denotes what element they need to cultivate Essence from. If they have multiple affinities, they need to cultivate all of those elements at the same time.

Affinity Channel – The pathway along the meridians that Essence flows through. Having multiple major affinities will open more pathways, allowing more Essence to flow into a person's center at one time.

Affinity Channel Type – Clogged, Ripped, Closed, Minor, Major, and Perfect. Perfect doesn't often occur naturally:

- Clogged – Draws in no essence, because the channel is blocked with corruption.
- Ripped – Draws in an unknown amount of essence, but in a method that is unpredictable and lethal.

- Closed – Draws in no essence, because the channel is either unopened, or forcibly closed.
- Minor – Draws in very little essence.
- Major – Draws in a sizable amount of essence.
- Perfect – Draws in a significant amount of essence. This affinity channel type cannot occur naturally. It is very dangerous to strive for, as the path to this type leads to ripped channels.

Aiden Silverfang – The new leader of the Northmen, this Barbarian turned Wolfman holds deep grudges easily. He is one of the many supervisors of Midgard.

Alhambra – A cleric that lives in Chasuble. Kept down for the majority of his career, he remains a good man with a good heart. His priorities for the people allot him a second chance, one derived from an old man's schemery.

Amber – The Mage in charge of the portal-making group near the dungeon. She is in the upper A-rankings, which allows her to tap vast amounts of Mana.

Artorian – The main character of the series. If you weren't expecting shenanigans, grab some popcorn. It only gets more intense from here on. He's a little flighty, deeply interested, and a miser of mischief. He is referred to by the Wood Elves as Starlight Spirit. In Cal's Soul Space, he takes the position of head administrator, and supervisor of Jotunheim.

Assassin – A stealthy killer who tries to make kills without being detected by his victim.

Assimilator – A cross between a jellyfish and a Wisp, the Assimilator can float around and collect vast amounts of Essence. It releases this Essence as powerful elemental bursts. A pseudo-Mage, if you will.

Astrea – The Nightmare. Infernal Professor at the Phantom Academy. She is a daughter of the Fringe, and one of Artorian's grandchildren. Even as an Infernal Cultivator, she finds herself in the most unlikely of company. Including her best friend, Jiivra.

Aura – The flows of Essence generated by living creatures which surround them and hold their pattern.

Barry the Devourer – A powerful S-ranked High Elf with the ability to turn all matter within a certain range into pure Essence and absorb it. Like his appetite, his desire for power is ever growing and seems to have no sign of stopping in Cal's soul space.

Basher – An evolved rabbit that attacks by head-butting enemies. Each has a small horn on its head that it can use to "bash" enemies.

Baobab – A wood elf with innate fire resistance. Strong-willed, this woman can handle the heat.

Bard – A lucrative profession deriving profit from other people's misery. Some make coin through song or instrument, but all of them love a good story. Particularly inconvenient ones. This includes Kinnan, Pollard, and Jillian.

Beast Core – A small gem that contains the Essence of Beasts. Also used to strip new cultivators of their corruption:

- Flawed – An extremely weak crystallization of Essence that barely allows a Beast to cultivate, comparable to low F-rank.
- Weak – A weak crystallization of Essence that allows a Beast to cultivate, comparable to an upper F-rank.

- Standard – A crystallization of Essence that allows a Beast to cultivate well, comparable to the D-rankings.
- Strong – A crystallization of Essence that allows a Beast to cultivate very well, comparable to the lower C-rankings.
- Beastly – A crystallization of Essence that allows a Beast to cultivate exceedingly well, comparable to the upper C-rankings.
- Immaculate – An amalgamation of crystallized Essence and Mana that allows a Beast to cultivate exceedingly well. Any Beast in the B-rankings or A-rankings will have this Core.
- Luminous – A Core of pure spiritual Essence that is indestructible by normal means. A Beast with this core will be in at least the S-rankings, up to SSS-rank.
- Radiant – A Core of Heavenly or Godly energies. A Beast with this Core is able to adjust reality on a whim.

Blanket – The best sugar glider. Blanket defends. Blanket protects.

Blight – A big bad. Also known as a Caligene, this entity can take many forms. Widespread and far-reaching, this thing has been around for over a millennia, and enjoys scheming to play the long game.

Birch – A friendly set of wood elves, of the Birch-tree Variant. They're friendly and well meaning, even if limited in what they can do. They like scented candles, particularly vanilla. They now spend their days with Mahogany, preparing to raise the next generation of Wood Elves.

Blooming Spirit – The Wood Elven equivalent of Aura. See Aura.

Bob – Cal's original goblin shaman. Remade to the best of his species. Bob becomes a Mage bound to the Death Law. Due to the myriad of tasks Cal set before him, several copies were made of Bob to complete them. Several then became several thousand. Bob is both a coding reference, and a small nod to the fantastic 'Bobiverse' series.

Boro – A trader in exotics, this man allied himself with the raider faction. He assists in swindling deals, and robbing villages blind after flooding them with gold that they will not keep.

Brianna – Having begun as princess of the dark elves, she is now both queen and supervisor of Niflheim. She is known by many names, such as the Hidden Blade, the Empress of Niflheim, and the Pinnacle. She has spies everywhere, and you never know what she's planning until she's already done steps one through six. Be wary of the Lady of Mists.

Cal – The heart of the Dungeon, Cal was a human murdered by necromancers. After being forced into a soul gem, his identity was stripped as time passed. Now accompanied by Dani, he works to become stronger without attracting too much attention to himself. Oops, too late.

Cataphron – One of the Skyspear headmasters. Uses the Imperius body technique of the Iron-Shelled Mastodont Kings.

Cats, dungeon – There are several types:

- Snowball – A Boss Mob, Snowball uses steam Essence to fuel his devastating attacks.
- Cloud Cat – A Mob that glides along the air, attacking from positions of stealth.

- Coiled Cat – A heavy Cat that uses metal Essence. It has a reinforced skeleton and can launch itself forward at high speeds.
- Flesh Cat – This Cat uses flesh Essence to tear apart tissue from a short distance. The abilities of this Cat only work on flesh and veins and will not affect bone or harder materials.
- Wither Cat – A Cat full of infernal Essence, the Wither Cat can induce a restriction of Essence flow with its attacks. Cutting off the flow of Essence or Mana will quickly leave the victim in a helpless state. The process is *quite* painful.

Celestial – The Essence of Heaven, the embodiment of life and *considered* the ultimate good.

Center – The very center of a person's soul. This is the area Essence accumulates (in creatures that do not have a Core) before it binds to the Life Force.

Chandra – A ranked mage who is a masterful cook. She has prior history with Ramset (Occultatum), and runs the 'pleasure house' restaurant establishments. She has an affinity for all things plants and nature, finding comfort within the green, more-so than with people. In Cal's world, she is stationed as one of the many supervisors on Midgard, and is responsible for all the basic flora and fauna in the soul space.

Chants – Affect a choir-cleric's growth, and overall fighting ability. A Choir war host in action matches the chant of every other. Each voice added to the whole increases the power and ability of each person whose voice is involved, through celestial and aural sympathy. Church officials get very upset when interrupted by half-naked men.

Chasuble – The name of both a particular type of scarf worn loosely around the neck, and the name of a major church-controlled city. Chasuble scarves are marked to show the rank of the person wearing them.

Church – 'The' Church, to be specific. Also known as the Ecclesiarchy, is one of the few stable major powers active in the world. It has several branches, each operating under different specifications:

- The Choir – The Face of the church, they carry to torch and spread the call far and wide. Operates as exploratory force and functions on heart and mind campaigns. The Choir's special function is to use harmonizing sound to buff and empower every member included in the group-effect.
- Paladin Order – The Fast-Attack branch, these mounted warriors function as cavalry would. The mounted creatures in question vary greatly, and most members employ a high-ranked beast for these purposes.
- Phalanx Sentinels – The Siege or Hold branch, the Sentinels are a heavy-armor branch that specialize entirely on securing locations. They are well known to be notoriously slow, and just as notoriously impossible to uproot from a position.
- Inquisitors – The Information gathering branch. This branch remains secretive.

Church Ranks – There are multiple Ecclesiarchy ranks, stacking in importance mostly based on cultivation progress.

- Initiate – A fresh entry to the church faction, the lowest rank. Generally given to someone still in training.

- Scribe – An initiate who failed to become a D-ranked cultivator, but was trusted enough by the faction to remain.
- Acolyte – Achieved by becoming a D-ranked cultivator. The second lowest rank in the church faction.
- Battle Leader – A trusted acolyte who shows promise in the fields of leadership and battle.
- Head Cleric – A high D-ranking cultivator, or a person who has been a Battle Leader long enough for their achievements to grant them their personal unit. Head Clerics are trusted to go on missions, excursions, and expeditions that differ based on the specific church faction.
- Keeper – Ranked equal to a Head Cleric. People who specifically keep administrative records, and interpret ancient texts. Keepers famously do not get along, and hold bitter rivalries due to said interpretations of the scriptures. Keepers tend to be Head Clerics who failed to enter the C-ranks.
- Arbiter – Achieved upon becoming a C-rank cultivator. An Arbiter is a settler of disputes of all kinds, whose authority is overshadowed only by those of higher rank. Otherwise, their say is final.
- Friar – A B-ranked cultivator in the church faction. Friars are glorified problem solvers.
- Father – An A-ranked Cultivator in the church faction. A Father may be of a high rank, but has fallen out of favor with the upper echelons of church command.
- Vicar – An A-ranked Cultivator in the church faction. The de-facto rulers, movers, and shakers of the church faction.
- Saint – An S-ranked Cultivator in the church faction. They do as they please.

Choppy – The prime woodcutter in the Salt Village. A very good lad.

Chi spiral – A person's Chi spiral is a vast amount of intricately knotted Essence. The more complex and complete the pattern woven into it, the more Essence it can hold and the finer the Essence would be refined.

Cleric – A cultivator of celestial Essence, a cleric tends to be support for a group, rarely fighting directly. Their main purpose in the lower rankings is to heal and comfort others.

Compound Essence – Essence that has formed together in complex ways. If two or more Essences come together to form something else, it is called a compound Essence. Or Higher Essence.

Corruption – Corruption is the remnant of the matter that pure Essence was formed into. It taints Essence but allows beings to absorb it through open affinity channels. This taint has been argued about for centuries; is it the source of life or a nasty side effect?

Craig – A powerful C-ranked monk, Craig has dedicated his life to finding the secrets of Essence and passing on knowledge.

C'towl – A mixture between cat and owl. Usually considered an apex predator due to the intermingling of attributes and sheer hunting prowess.

Currency values:

- Copper – One hundred copper coins are worth a silver coin.
- Silver – One hundred silver coins are worth a gold coin.

- Gold – One hundred gold coins are worth a platinum coin.
- Platinum – The highest coin currency in the Human Kingdoms.

Cultivate – Cultivating is the process of refining Essence by removing corruption then cycling the purified Essence into the center of the soul.

Cultivation technique – A name for the specific method in which cultivators draw in and refine the energies of the Heavens and Earth.

Cultivator – A cultivator is a silly person who thinks messing with forces they don't understand will somehow make life better for them.

Dale – Probably not important.

Dani – The most important. Wisp to Cal, and the sole reason the entire Soul Space is still standing. Many mental notebooks have "don't cross Dani" underlined no less than nineteen times. Surely there's a reason for that.

Daughter of Wrath – A ranking female servant to the Ziggurat, that showed promise and was given troops to lead.

Dawn – The name taken by Ember as her S-ranked incarnation. A full perspective change from her original self, new options and a new life have opened before her. While the way of being Ember espoused still exists within her, room for the new is now possible. Even though she is stuck in an A-ranked body for now, there's no way she's letting that stop her. Dawn is the supervisor of the fiery realm Muspelheim.

Decorum – A Morovia Liger who, through some meddling, has gained new life as the snazzy and mysterious Gomez. His rebirth gave him the opportunity to be the ultimate apex predator, but after a life of hunting and being hunted on Midgard he is pulled to move onto a greater stage. A true gentleman, or well, gentletiger.

Deverash Editor Neverdash the Dashingly Dapper – Also called Dev, or Dev Editor. A gnome that retained his intelligence, and may have quite the impact on adventures to come.

Duskgrove Castle – A location within the Phantomdusk Forest. It is the primary hideout for the Hakan's group of raiders.

D. Kota – An initiate in the choir, who has grand aspirations of becoming a scholar; and does. His works span the great ages. Known for all time.

Distortion Cat – An upper C-ranked Beast that can bend light and create artificial darkness. In its home territory, it is attacked and bound by tentacle-like parasites that form a symbiotic relationship with it.

Dimitri – Also goes by Dimi-Tree, due to his size. A mix between a dwarf and a giant, this brash and brazen mountain loves to dabble. Doing a little bit of everything, he has a reputation that there's nothing he can't fix.

Dreamt Ones – Creatures made of Liminal Energy, having manifested through dreams:

- Caliph – Dawn's dreamt one. Manifested as a Djinn and baby. Deemed relevant for reasons pertaining to the blocks in her continued growth.
- Scilla – Artorian's dreamt one. Manifested as a mixture of the small child he met in Chasuble and

the bane of the Phantomdusk Forest. She withholds Artorian's Liminal Energy from him, at least, until he can work through his many, many regrets.

- Items – Cal's specific difficulty resulted in objects and challenges rather than creatures, as his Liminal Energy deemed that he needed to learn the lesson of how to rely on others, rather than perform all tasks himself.

Dregs – A dungeon Core that has limited intelligence. It was installed into Cal's dungeon to control floors 1-4 so Cal could focus on other things.

Dungeon Born – Being dungeon born means that the dungeon did not create the creature but gave it life. This gives the creature the ability to function autonomously without fear that the dungeon will be able to take direct control of its mind.

Dungeon Cores – Curators of wild Essence.

- Gold/Pale Yellow – Celestial affinity dungeons who tend to be a tad on the lazy side. These dungeons are notorious for ignoring their work and simply kicking back and letting others bring the Essence to them.
- Blue – Water affinity dungeons tend to be the type that go with the flow. Since Cal's existence this theory has been debunked.
- Lapis – Air affinity dungeons are unable to build their own dungeons. They rely on their wisps to build the dungeon and often are the type to give up projects quickly from being discouraged.
- Red – Fire affinity dungeons are lazy. Unlike celestial dungeons, they would rather play in their sandbox of toys. Raging and destroying as they please, rather than build or keep their dungeon squared away.

- Green – Earth affinity dungeons are perfectionists. They focus on sheer quality and often ignore quantity without a wisp keeping them on track. These dungeons exemplify how the term "tunnel-vision" came to be.
- Opal-Black – Infernal affinity dungeons are gluttons for knowledge. They lust for more information constantly, even to the point of destroying all who enter their dungeon in favor of new tidbits of data.

Dungeon Wisps – Beings made to balance out dungeons in the world. A very secretive group led by an all-affinity wisp. Each base color corresponds with an effect to match their dungeon:

- Blue – Celestial affinity wisps whose ability is to convince their dungeon that they are useful, and should use other Essence types beyond celestial.
- Pink – Water affinity wisps who are best known for reducing mind altering effects, and are incredibly skilled at keeping these dungeons on task.
- Purple – Air affinity wisps. These wisps must shape the world around them for their dungeon, as air affinity dungeons cannot do so. They provide the homes for the air affinity dungeons and constantly encourage the Cores like cheerleaders.
- Green – Fire affinity wisps are excellent taskmasters who keep their childish dungeons from breaking all of their toys, and assure they continue to improve and build out their dungeons.
- Orange – Earth affinity wisps are naturally soothing. They help alleviate the tunnel vision which earth affinity dungeons suffer from, and encourage their dungeon to value quantity as well as quality.
- Silver – Infernal affinity wisps remind their dungeons that patience is a virtue, and make sure

their knowledge hungry dungeons do not destroy everything that enters their doors.

Don Modsognir – Goes by Big Mo. Leader of the Modsognir clan. Responsible for trading and caravan operations. Known to be a troublemaker, he has an impeccable link of loyalty to his family. He enjoys finery, nice suits, and better company. He's got the heart of a king, and the trouble-making penchant of a feisty five-year-old.

Dwarves – Stocky humanoids that like to work with stone, metal, and alcohol. Good miners.

Dwarven Traditions – Complicated unspoken rules that exist purely to protect the core dwarven heritage and ways of life. Specifically used against anyone deemed a non-dwarf or outsider, to sustain a public image that is of benefit to all clans as a whole.

Eucalyptus – A Wood Elf skilled in defensive and protective Essence techniques.

Ember – Secondary Main Character - A burnt-out Ancient Elf from well over a millennia ago. She's lived too long, and most of it has been in one War or another. She finds a new spark, but until then suffers from extreme weariness, depression, and wear. Her sense of humor lies buried deep within, dry as a cork. Ember enjoys speaking laconically, getting to the point, and getting fired up. She will burn eternal to see her tasks complete. No matter the cost, and no matter the effort. She becomes Dawn upon graduating to the S-ranks.

Egil Nolsen – Known to the world as 'Xenocide,' he is a Madness cultivator. Ranked SSS. He is but a moment of good fortune away from entering the Heavenly ranks, and is responsible for a majority of the world's problems, in one way or another.

Electrum – The metal used as Chasuble's currency. These coins are collectively known as 'divines' due to the very minor essence effect on them that keeps them clean. Their worth and value differs greatly from the established monetary system many other cities use, specifically to undercut them.

Elves – A race of willowy humanoids with pointy ears. There are five main types:

- High Elves – The largest nation of Elvenkind, they spend most of their time as merchants, artists, or thinkers. Rich beyond any need to actually work, their King is an S-ranked expert, and their cities shine with light and wealth. They like to think of themselves as 'above' other Elves, thus 'High' Elves.
- Wood Elves – Wood Elves live more simply than High Elves, but have greater connection to the earth and the elements. They are ruled by a counsel of S-ranked elders and rarely leave their woods. Though seen less often, they have great power. They grow and collect food and animal products for themselves and other Elven nations.
- Wild Elves – Wild Elves are the outcasts of their societies. Basically feral, they scorn society, civilization, and the rules of others. They have the worst reputation of any of the races of Elves, practicing dark arts and infernal summoning. They have no homeland, living only where they can get away with their dark deeds.
- Dark Elves – The Drow are known as Dark Elves. No one knows where they live, only where they can go to get in contact with them. Dark Elves also have a dark

reputation as Assassins and mercenaries for the other races. The worst of their lot are 'Moon Elves,' the best-known Assassins of any race. These are the Elves that Dale made a deal with for land and protection.

- Sea Elves – The Sea Elves live on boats their entire lives. They facilitate trade between all the races of Elves and man, trying not to take sides in conflicts. They work for themselves and are considered rather mysterious.

Essence – Essence is the fundamental energy of the universe, the pure power of heavens and earth that is used by the basic elements to become all forms of matter. The six major types are named: Fire, Water, Earth, Air, Celestial, Infernal.

Essence Cycling – A trick to move energy around, to enhance the ability of an organ.

Eternium – A dungeon core who can hold all of Cal's soul space, aligned to the **Law** of **Order**.

Faux High Elf – A person who has the appearance of a High Elf, but is not actually one. It is a 'Fake' Elf, who takes the position in name only. A mockery and status-display rolled into one.

Father Richard – An A-ranked Cleric that has made his living hunting demons and heretics. Tends to play fast and loose with rules and money.

Fighter – A generic archetype of a being that uses melee weapons to fight.

Fringe – The Fringe region is located in the western region of Pangea. It has been scrapped from maps and scraped from history, by order of the Ecclesiarchy.

Gathering Webway – A web of Essence created around one's center. For the purpose of gathering and retaining Essence. This was the first method concerning Essence refining techniques. It should never be sticky.

Gilded Blade – A weapon, status title, occupation, and profession all in one. A Gilded Blade is a weapon of the raider faction. They are brutally efficient at a single thing, and terrible at everything else.

Gomei – Brianna's right hand and general. He despises humanity with extreme contempt. For no reason other than that they deprived him of his favorite condiment. Wars will start over this. Again.

Grace – Offspring of Cal and Dani. Adorable sm0ll wisp. All the energy of Dad. All the smarts of Mom. Was a wisp's color important again? Grace's color is purple~

Gran'mama – Ephira Mayev Stonequeen is Grand Matron of all the centralized Dwarven clans. She goes by Matron, or Gran'mama. While not a royal, she tends to be treated like one due to the vast respect she holds. She also keeps the great majority of land contracts. Beware of the dreaded chancla.

Hadurin Fellstone – Supposed Head Healer of the motley Fringe expedition crew.

Hadurin Fellhammer – Grand-Inquisitor Fellhammer. Executor of the Inquisition, Lord of the Azure Jade mountain, and slayer of a thousand traitors. While not fully of the dwarven race, he is short, portly, jovial to a fault, and as sly as a certain old man. I hear him with a thick Scottish or Irish voice.

Halcyon – The second of Artorian's chosen, granted the Blessing of Aurum. An uplifted Orca Matron, Halcyon shrunk into her shell as her sapience grew. Shy demeanor aside, a natural leader lurks within. Halcyon has multiple forms just like Zelia, such as fully human, fully Orca, and a hybridized state of flux.

Hakan – A gilded blade, she is the main antagonist of AA1. Her personality is as unpleasant as her fashion sense. She's snide, cuts to the chase, and speaks abrasively without much poise or respect to anyone else.

Hans – A cheeky assassin that has been with Dale since he began cultivating. He was a thief in his youth but changed lifestyles after his street guild was wiped out. He is deadly with a knife and is Dale's best friend. Now Rose's husband.

Hawthorns – A set of Wood Elves that has taken it upon themselves to guard and patrol the edges of the forest. They are generally abrasive, as the threats they come home with aren't taken seriously enough. Or abundantly happy to see you, with matching Southern cadence and happy reed-chewing style. Rules are actually guidelines. Make no mistake. In any other setting, Hawthorne would be a dastardly set of troublemakers.

Henry – Previously the prince-turned-king of the Lion Kingdom, he is now one of the several supervisors of Midgard. Henry is childhood friends with Aiden Silverfang.

Hulk – Odin's greatest nemesis, best squirrel friend to Yuki.

Incantation – Essentially a spell, an incantation is created from words and gestures. It releases all of the power of an enchantment in a single burst.

Infected – A person or creature that has been infected with a rage-inducing mushroom growth. These people have no control of their bodies and attack any non-infected on sight.

Infernal – The Essence of death and demonic beings, *considered* to be always evil.

Inscription – A *permanent* pattern made of Essence that creates an effect on the universe. Try not to get the pattern wrong as it could have… unintended consequences. This is another name for an incomplete or unknown Rune.

Irene – A Keeper in the Choir. There is more to her than meets the eye, and is far more powerful than she initially appears to be. Do not argue with her about scripture. This world-weary Keeper plays with subterfuge like children play outside. Though when able, she speaks with her fists. Her rage meter is tiny, and fills with a swiftness.

Jiivra – A Battle Leader in the Choir, she aspires to be a Paladin. She has the potential to become truly great, if only given the opportunity. Young, and full of splendor. She's hasty, sticks to order, dislikes surprises, and answers to them with well-measured responses.

Jin – The child of Tarrean and Irene, a Keeper in the Fringe.

Karakum – Only two things are certain: Death, and Taxes. Karakum is both. This fire-dungeon turned scorpion gained new life just as Zelia did. He's snippy, and can be a bit much to handle, but after becoming Dawn's chosen, he does what is required of him by the Lady of Flame. Karakum is based on Zorro.

Lapis – A mineral-mining town in the vicinity of the Salt Flats. They refine the color Lapis into varying shades of Blue, and are a prime exporter. Lapis is located in the Fringe.

Liminal – Also called Liminal Energy, or the energy of thought. It is the intermediary between Mana and Spirit. Liminal

Energy is both sentient and sapient. It develops a mind of its own when the Mage reaches a certain point of progress. This energy can manifest itself in a variety of ways, but is difficult to control after it gains sapience. Sapient Liminal Energy frequently manifests as issues the Mage needs to tackle. Whether that be items, people, or challenges.

Maccreus Tarrean – Head Cleric of a Choir expeditionary force. His pride is his most distinguishing feature, next to that ostentatious affront known as his armor. Short and portly for non-dwarven reasons, this blundering, ego-driven voice blusters through life like a drunk through a tavern. Elbows first. His ability to craft schemes is as sharp as a dull, smooth rock. His Charisma unfortunately doesn't notice and charges on anyway.

Mahogany – Chosen leaders of the Phantomdusk Wood Elves. As a congregation of Sultans, they care deeply for their people. Forced to make difficult decisions on behalf of the people as a whole, they function with the full permission of the S-ranked council. Which is less active than they'd like it to be. A good soul, they speak with deep voices. Together with Birch they seek to rebuild Wood Elf society within Eternium.

Mages' Guild – A secretive sub-sect of the Adventurers' Guild only Mage-level cultivators are allowed to join.

Mana – A higher stage of Essence only able to be cultivated by those who have broken into at least the B-rankings and found the true name of something in the universe.

Mana Signature – A name for a signature that can be neither forged nor replicated, and is used in binding oaths.

Marie – Previously the princess-turned-queen of the Phoenix Kingdom. She is now one of the many supervisors of Midgard, establishing the human presence in Cal's soul space. A Mage of **Glory** and not afraid to use her trumpets to harken it.

Marud – Choir second-in-command Battle Leader, of the second expeditionary force to the Fringe.

Meridians – Meridians are energy channels that transport life energy (Chi/Essence) throughout the body.

Memory Core – Also known as a Memory Stone, depending on the base materials used in their production. Pressing the stone to your forehead lets a person store or gain the knowledge contained within. As if you'd gone through the events yourself. Generally never sold.

Minya – Ex-leader of the Cult of Cal. After entering Cal's Soul Space, she now presides over the research and development on the Moon with Bob. All she wants is peace and quiet. Maybe a small store.

Mob – A shortened version of "dungeon monster."

Morovia – A world region located in the south-eastern section of the central Pangea band.

Necromancer – An Infernal Essence cultivator who can raise and control the dead and demons. A title for a cultivator who specializes in re-animating that which has died.

Nefellum – Head Cleric of the second expedition force into the Fringe.

Noble rankings:

- King/Queen – Ruler of their country. (Addressed as 'Your Majesty')

- Crown Prince/Princess – Next in line to the throne, has the same political power as a Grand Duke. (Addressed as 'Your Royal Highness')
- Prince/Princess – Child of the King/Queen, has the same political power as a Duke. (Addressed as 'Your Highness')
- Grand Duke/Grand Duchess – Ruler of a grand duchy and is senior to a Duke. (Addressed as 'Your Grace')
- Duke/Duchess – Is senior to a Marquis or Marchioness. (Addressed as 'Your Grace')
- Marquis/Marchioness – Controls a section of land in a kingdom outside of the heartland. Is senior to an Earl and has at least three Earls in their domain. (Addressed as 'Honorable')
- Earl/Countess – Is senior to a Baron. Each Earl has three Barons under their power. (Addressed as 'My Lord/Lady')
- Viscount/Viscountess – Thought of as the lieutenants of the Earl in their region. Is senior to a Baron, if by just a small margin. (Addressed as 'My Lord/Lady')
- Baron/Baroness – Senior to knights, they control a minimum of ten knights and therefore their land. (Addressed as 'My Lord/Lady')
- Baronets – A member of the lowest hereditary titled order, with the status of a commoner. (Addressed as 'Sir')
- Knight/Dame – Sub rulers of plots of land and peasants. (Addressed as 'Sir')
- Esquire – A young nobleman who, in training for knighthood, acts as an attendant to a knight. (Addressed as 'Sir')
- Gentleman/Lady – Those of high birth or rank, good social standing and wealth, and who did not need to work for a living.

Oak – A set of Wood Elves that embody the purest spirit of flamboyance. Rules might exist, but Oak won't care to listen.

Oberon – Eternium's clever, cunning, orange wisp. Constantly finding new ways to con his dungeon to keep him on his metaphorical toes. Let's see how many times this wisp's name gets underlined by the end.

Occultatum – Previously known as the Master, he now resides on Hel as its supervisor. Cal supposedly stationed him due to the high Mana density, but in reality, it's to deal with those abyss-blasted swans and geese.

Odin – Elemental of Air and supervisor of Asgard. His ego is almost the size of the Valkyries stationed outside his baths; though, a certain frosty individual manages to keep him in line.

Olgier – A trader from Rutsel, whose greed greatly exceeds his guile.

Olive – A Wood Elf who is very down to earth. A little greasy, he likes to dig holes and hidden pathways.

Oversized Infernal Corvid – Really big raven with the Infernal channel. D-ranked creature. Intelligent. Moody.

Pattern – A pattern is the intricate design that makes everything in the universe. An inanimate object has a far less complex pattern that a living being.

Phantomdusk Forest – A world region that borders The Fringe. It is comprised of vast, continent-sprawled greenery that covers multiple biomes. Any forest region connecting to this main mass is considered part of the whole, if entering it has a high mortality rate.

Presence – In terms of Aura, this refers to the combined components that Aura encompasses. Ordinarily a Mage-only ability. Presence refers to the unity of Auras and them acting as one.

Ra – Lunella's first daughter, who causes an amount of trouble equal to the amount of breaths she takes. *Cough*, much like a certain grandfather.

Raile – A massive, granite-covered Boss Basher that attacks by ramming and attempting to squish its opponents.

Ranger – Typically an adventurer archetype that is able to attack from long range, usually with a bow.

Ranking System – The ranking system is a way to classify how powerful a creature has become through fighting and cultivation.

- G – At the lowest ranking is mostly non-organic matter such as rocks and ash. Mid-G contains small plants such as moss and mushrooms while the upper ranks form most of the other flora in the world.
- F – The F-ranks are where beings are becoming actually sentient, able to gather their own food and make short-term plans. The mid-F ranks are where most humans reach before adulthood without cultivating. This is known as the fishy or "failure" rank.
- E – The E-rank is known as the "echo" rank and is used to prepare a body for intense cultivation.
- D – This is the rank where a cultivator starts to become actually dangerous. A D-ranked individual can usually fight off ten F-ranked beings without issue. They are characterized by a "fractal" in their Chi spiral.

- C – The highest-ranked Essence cultivators, those in the C-rank usually have opened all of their meridians. A C-ranked cultivator can usually fight off ten D-ranked and one hundred F-ranked beings without being overwhelmed.
- B – This is the first rank of Mana cultivators, known as Mages. They convert Essence into Mana through a nuanced refining process and release it through a true name of the universe.
- A – Usually several hundred years are needed to attain this rank, known as High-Mage or High-Magous. They are the most powerful rank of Mages.
- S – Very mysterious Spiritual Essence cultivators. Not much is known about the requirements for this rank or those above it.
- SS – Pronounced 'Double S.' Not much is known about the requirements for this rank or those above it.
- SSS – Pronounced 'Triple S.' Not much is known about the requirements for this rank or those above it.
- Heavenly – Not much is known about the requirements for this rank or those above it.
- Godly – Not much is known about the requirements for this rank or those above it.

Refining – A name for the method of separating Essences of differing purities.

Rune – A *permanent* pattern made of Essence that creates an effect on the universe. Try not to get the pattern wrong as it could have… unintended consequences. This is another name for a completed Inscription.

Rose – Chaos cultivator and wife of Hans. She spent most of her life with her Aunt Chandra before making her way to

Mountaindale and meeting her friends. She will happily slay a man with her speech or with her arrows. They decide.

Rosewood – Wood Elves with an unbreakable passion for fashion, and making clothes.

Rota – A sturdy and strapping Dwarf whose jokes latched him with the nickname "Otter," he once tried to scribe Runes onto a set of gambling dice. Beware of the explosions around this wily lad.

Royal Advisor – A big bad. Direct hand to the Mistress, the Queen and Regent in charge of the Ziggurat. Lover of the Cobra Chicken, and Swans.

Salt Village – The main location of Artorian's Archives One, where the majority of the story takes place. It is located in the Fringe, and is a day's journey from the Lapis Village.

Salt Flats – A location in the Fringe. The Salt Village operates by scraping salt from the Salt Flats, a place where the material is plentiful. It is their main export.

Scar – Known as 'The Scar.' A location in that Fringe that includes the Salt Flats as one of its tendrils. It is rumored to be a kind of slumbering dungeon.

Scilla – A small girl that lives in Chasuble. She is afflicted by an effect that caused her irises to permanently turn pink.

Sequoia – Wood Elves that will not be forgotten, even without them speaking.

Shamira – Scilla's mother. She is a resident of Chasuble, and not particularly happy about the conditions there.

Sproutling – A title for a child in the Fringe who has not yet been assigned a name, and thus is not considered an adult. Until a certain key event, this includes the famous five: Lunella, Grimaldus, Tychus, Wuxius, and Astrea.

Skyspear Academy – An Academy present on the world's tallest mountain.

Socorro – A desert in the central-band, eastern portion of Pangea. It used to be a place for something important. Now there is only sand, and ruin.

Soul Item – A construct made in a Soul Space that specializes the Mage to a certain set of ideas and concepts, allowing for advancement into the A-ranks and beyond.

Soul Space – A realm accessible by cultivators that exists outside of the self. Vastly important for Mages to keep increasing in rank. Soul Spaces are morphous in size, and tend to hold a Mage's 'Soul Item.'

Soul Space [Cal] – Cal's Soul Space is being designed to hold an entire world. Divided by several landmasses and unique locations:

- Midgard – The human, wolfman, and plant-people realm in Cal's soul space. This skyland supports anything in the G- to D-ranks, and is where a majority of individuals are decanted. Run by Marie, Henry, Chandra, and Aiden.
- Alfheim – The realm for the majority of Elves in Cal's Soul Space. This skyland supports anything in the C-ranks. Is built around having pill cultivation. Alfheim has no supervisor.
- Svartalfheim – The realm of the Dwarves in Cal's Soul Space. This skyland supports anything in the

ranks. Is built on Aether cultivation. Svartalfheim has no supervisor.

- Vanaheim – The realm of the Gnomes in Cal's Soul Space. This skyland supports anything in the low B-ranks. Vanaheim is home to all the pylons that run Cal's bracket spells, and a land of many wondrous inventions. Beneath its shiny exterior, a civil war takes place. Deverash is Vanaheim's supervisor.
- Jotunheim – The realm of massive Beasts and gigantic Jotun in Cal's Soul Space. Home to many wonderful chosen and a door named Ellis, this skyland supports anything in the mid B-ranks. Artorian is the supervisor of Jotunheim.
- Niflheim – The realm of Mists and home of the Dark Elves in Cal's Soul Space. This skyland is set almost completely on its side, and supports anything in the upper B-ranks. Niflheim is run by Brianna.
- Muspelheim – The realm of fire, sand, and goblins in Cal's Soul Space. This skyland has many separate layers, from the floating triremes in the sky, to the paradise beneath the surface, and supports anything in the upper B-ranks. Many different races have found a home in Muspelheim; including Lamia, goblins, C'towl, Lizards, and a giant serpent named Jorm. This realm is overseen by Dawn.
- Asgard – The realm of elementals, heroes, and small party accidents. This skyland supports anything A-ranked; from minimum to apex. (As well as Odin's ego, if just barely.) This realm was having a swarm problem, but after some… suggestions, those were taken care of. Odin is the supervisor of this realm.
- Hel – The realm of all things S-ranked in Cal's Soul Space. This is the only spherical realm in Cal's world, and is made of all the corrupted ash from things dead and dying. Home to Gibble, the bone gazelle. Hel is supervised by Occultatum.

- Sun – Giant ball of interlocking rings and runes meant to provide light to all in Cal's Soul Space… Before the administrator caused it to explode. Home to Artorian's Archives.
- Moon – The place where most of the research and development takes place in Cal's Soul Space. The Moon's topside is a large area for the children to grow and enjoy themselves. Beneath the surface, however, is the Rotunda of Holding, and a large laboratory where Minya and the Bobs work.

Soul Stone – A *highly* refined Beast Core that is capable of containing a human soul.

Surtur – Dawn's first chosen. A Lamia. She was granted a weapon made by Dawn, and uses it to lead her tribe to ever greater heights of prosperity. Even if her tribe keeps incorporating more and more races.

Switch – A village Elder of the Salt Village in the Fringe region. She croaks rather than speaks. Though that's only if she speaks. Usually she complains. Loudly, and in plenty. If forced to interact with Switch, consider stuffing one's ears with beeswax.

Tank – An adventurer archetype that is built to defend his team from the worst of the attacks that come their way. Heavily armored and usually carrying a large shield, these powerful people are needed if a group plans on surviving more than one attack.

Tibbins – An Acolyte in the Choir. He has a deep passion for all things culinary, and possesses a truly unique expression. He means well, but there's something about his poor luck that keeps getting him in someone's firing line. Sweet, loves to cook, and loyal to a fault. Tibbins is just in the wrong place at the wrong time. His voice tends to tremble when he is uncertain.

Tom – Former exiled Northman. Friend of Dale, and a general smashing success with his hammer: 'Thud.'

Vizier Amon – A big bad. Direct hand to the Mistress, the Queen and Regent in charge of the Ziggurat. Things will get better before they get worse. Unless maybe one can pull the strings of a few favors. Sang with serpentine tongue. His time as grand vizier was short, becoming more nope than rope.

Vol – A chosen one of Artorian who prefers his beastly Teslasaur form. He may not be the sharpest tool in the shed, but certainly has the speed and chompers of an apex predator.

Wuxius – Son of the Fringe and one of Artorian's five grandchildren.

Wagner – Hel's premier goose of spite, gifted with the best pipes known to Eternium. Beware your ankles in his presence, they are prime targets for his rage-filled bites.

Yuki – A lady of snow and ice. Artorian's third chosen, gifted with an unaccepted blessing. Her cold countenance and sleety demeanor reflect her current perspective of the world.

Yvessa – An Elven name that means: 'To bloom out of great drought.' She is a Choir Cleric going up the ranks, and holds incredible promise. A girl of destiny. A demon-lord with a spoon. A caretaker who gains wisdom beyond her years from the kind of abyss she has to deal with. Her voice gains energy as she ages, as does her spirit.

Zelia – First chosen of Artorian, gifted with the Blessing of Argent. She is the mind of the Fringe Teleportation core, given life anew. A passionate artist, secretary, and seamstress. She is the sole peak of her spider family. Zelia is able to tap into her Dreamer's abilities and memories, and uses her Teleportation gifts with uncanny skill and efficiency. She grows to deeply care for her Dreamer beyond the constraints of what being a chosen forces, and has decided for herself to stick around. Zelia has multiple forms, including fully human, fully spider, drider (half and half), and a state of flux.

Ziggurat – Both the name of a region, and a large building central to it. Ziggurat is the current raider stronghold where all their activities are coordinated from. The hierarchies here are simple and bloody, but the true purpose of the place is to serve as a staging area for necromancer needs.

www.ingramcontent.com/pod-product-compliance
Lightning Source LLC
Chambersburg PA
CBHW030758260626
47169CB00001B/105